Those Empty Eyes

Charlie Donlea is the critically acclaimed, *USA Today*, Indiebound and #1 internationally bestselling author of *Summit Lake, The Girl Who Was Taken, Don't Believe It, Some Choose Darkness, The Suicide House* and *Twenty Years Later*. Published in nearly 30 countries and translated into more than a dozen languages, Donlea has been praised for his 'soaring pace, teasing plot' (BookPage) and talent for writing an ending that 'makes your jaw drop' (*The New York Times Book Review*). He was born and raised in Chicago, where he continues to live with his wife and two children. Visit him online at CharlieDonlea.com.

Also by Charlie Donlea

Twenty Years Later
Those Empty Eyes

CHARLIE DONLEA

THOSE EMPTY EYES

First published in the USA in 2023 by Kensington Publishing Corp.

This edition published in the United Kingdom in 2023 by

Canelo
Unit 9, 5th Floor
Cargo Works, 1-2 Hatfields
London SE1 9PG
United Kingdom

A CIP catalogue record for this book is available from the British Library.

Print ISBN 978 1 80436 466 6
Ebook ISBN 978 1 80436 467 3

Look for more great books at www.canelo.co

Printed and bound in Great Britain by Clays Ltd, Elcograf S.p.A.

Follow the evidence wherever it leads, and question everything.

—Neil deGrasse Tyson

McIntosh, Virginia

January 15, 2013

Sin was a mystery.

Some believed their sins went unnoticed and could be committed without consequence. Others repented in the conviction that an omnipotent God witnessed all discretions and forgave unconditionally. The shooter, dressed in boots and a long, sweeping trench coat, believed something else—that the most egregious sins should always be noticed and never forgiven, and that those who commit them should be punished.

The shooter climbed the stairs silently while the family slept. At the top of the staircase, the figure approached the bedroom and used the barrel of the shotgun to push open the door of the master suite. The hinges creaked and disrupted the otherwise quiet home. The door came to a rest with just enough space to pass through the door frame. The shooter slipped inside and walked to the foot of the bed. The soft breathing of the woman could be heard between animalistic snores from the man lying next to her. The shooter lifted the shotgun and secured it—tight to the shoulder, right cheek against the cold metal—so that the barrel pointed at the snoring man. A finger settled over the trigger, paused momentarily, and then twitched, unleashing a deafening blast. The sleeping man's flesh exploded as buckshot tore into his chest. Disoriented, his wife sat up quickly. In her confusion, she never saw the shooter standing at the foot of the bed or the barrel of the shotgun rotating toward her. A second blast sent the woman's torso ricocheting off the headboard.

Reaching into the pocket of the trench coat, the shooter removed three photos and dropped them onto the bed. As the ringing of the gunshots dissipated, floorboards creaked outside the bedroom. Quickly, the shooter cracked the barrel of the shotgun open, allowing the spent shells to sail into the air. With hands protected by latex gloves, the shooter retrieved two live shells from the second trench coat pocket, inserted them into the smoking chamber, and snapped the barrel closed before aiming toward the bedroom door. An eternity passed until the hinges whined again as the door opened fully to reveal a young boy standing in the door frame.

Raymond Quinlan was thirteen years old, a troubling age for the shooter—old enough to be a viable witness, but young enough to make the next decision challenging. As Raymond struggled to understand the scene before him, the shooter allowed no time for the boy to orientate himself. The barrel of the shotgun was trained at the boy's chest, and a third deafening blast filled the home.

As the concussion ricocheted off the bedroom walls, melancholy began to settle in but was quickly brushed aside. There would be time for despondence when the mission was over. A job that moments earlier had been complete was now only three-quarters finished. The shooter walked quickly from the bedroom. Raymond lay in the hallway, an expanding pool of blood seeping across the hardwood. A quick glance back into the bedroom allowed the spent shells to stand out against the carpet where they'd landed. But they were not a worry. Nor was the gun itself. In fact, the plan had been to lay the weapon at the foot of the bed when the night was over, but Raymond had spoiled everything. Stepping over his body, the shooter hurried down the hall to the far bedroom. There was another family member in the house that now demanded attention.

Reaching the end of the hallway, the shooter used the barrel of the shotgun to push open the bedroom door. This time, however, the door did not budge. It was latched shut. Twisting the handle and finding the door locked, the shooter lifted a knee and aimed a boot heel at the doorknob. The wood splintered but did not give. A second effort burst the door open and sprung the top hinge from the frame so that the door hung crooked from the jamb. Entering the room, the shooter saw that the bed was empty but the covers were tussled. Placing a palm to the sheets, the bed was warm from where someone had been sleeping just moments earlier. As the shooter turned from the bed, attention fell to the closet. The wicker door was closed. Walking over, the shooter used the barrel of the shotgun to tap on the door.

When no answer came, the shooter turned the handle and slowly pushed the door open. But the closet, like the bed, was empty. It was then that the cold chill of night drifted across the back of the shooter's calves, below the hem of the trench coat. Across the room, the window curtains twirled as they filled with the night air that passed over the sill. After rushing across the room, the shooter ripped the curtains to the side and pushed the window fully open. The screen lay on the walkway below, broken free from the frame when the final family member had escaped through the window.

It was a problem. A serious error created by careless miscalculation, but not the only one the shooter committed that night.

PART I

The Final Witness

"If it bleeds, it leads."

—Garrett Lancaster

Fall 2013

CHAPTER 1

District Courthouse
Thursday, September 26, 2013
3:05 p.m.

Garrett Lancaster walked to the courtroom podium as television cameras recorded his every move and millions watched the live coverage. The defamation trial of Alexandra Quinlan versus the state of Virginia had captured the attention of the nation. Ever since the night the Quinlan family was slaughtered and the seventeen-year-old daughter was arrested for the murders, the country had been fascinated with Alexandra Quinlan. First, when she was accused of the crime and labeled a sadistic killer. And later, after she was exonerated when evidence surfaced that proved her innocence. And especially now, when Alexandra had turned around and sued the state of Virginia, claiming that the McIntosh Police Department and the Alleghany district attorney's office had not only botched the investigation into her family's murder, but ruined her life in the process.

Because of the media attention the Quinlan murders had received, Alexandra's defamation case had been fast-tracked. Predicted to last two weeks, the trial was right on schedule. For the first few days—Monday through Thursday morning—the jurors had listened to testimony from a careful list of witnesses Garrett Lancaster had called in strategic order. Now, Garrett had Thursday afternoon and all of Friday to finish presenting his case. He planned to fill those hours with testimony from just two individuals, his final witnesses. If things went according to plan, the state's defense attorneys would sit silently for the final two days of the prosecution's case. They wouldn't dare go after the testimony they heard today, and wouldn't so much as *think* of cross-examining his witness tomorrow.

Garrett knew the untenable position he was about to put the state's defense team in. He knew this because Garrett was usually the attorney doing the defending. It was only through a bizarre set of circumstances that he found himself in the unusual position of being the prosecuting attorney representing Alexandra Quinlan in her defamation suit against the state of Virginia. The managing partner at one of the biggest defense firms on the East Coast, Garrett was a defense attorney by trade, and therefore in the unique position of knowing his opponents inside and out.

Garrett had designed his strategy carefully. Despite the temptation to allow the jury to hear testimony from his two star witnesses earlier in the week, at the start of the trial when juries were easy to impress, he instead saved their testimony for now—Thursday afternoon and Friday morning. The plan was to wrap things up the following morning before lunch and then persuade the judge to adjourn for the weekend. Garrett wanted the testimonies from his final two witnesses—as well as their faces and tears and cracking voices—to be fresh on the jury members' minds as they headed into the weekend. He wanted the testimony to linger for two long days before the jury reconvened Monday morning to listen to the attorneys for the state of Virginia mount their full, unfettered defense against Alexandra's claims that the McIntosh Police Department was incompetent and that the Alleghany district attorney's office was corrupt.

"Your honor," Garret said after reaching the podium. Dressed smartly in a crisp navy suit and yellow tie, he carefully arranged his notes in no hurry, putting forth a sense of composure and confidence. He knew a television audience of millions was tuned in and he did not shy away from the attention. In his midfifties and handsome, Garrett knew how to use his presence to work a jury and was no amateur when it came to high-profile cases. "The prosecution calls Donna Koppel."

The first officer to arrive at the Quinlan home on the night of January 15, Donna Koppel was the first into the house, the first up the stairs, and the first to witness the carnage in the master bedroom. The four other police officers who had responded to shots fired at 421 Montgomery Lane had already taken the stand. Garrett had expertly used the officers' testimonies to lay out for the jury exactly what was found the night the officers entered the Quinlan home. Their testimonies were identical—they'd each described the bloodshed of a family slaughtered in the middle of the night. They'd each testified about finding a young girl, identified as Alexandra Quinlan, sitting on the floor of her parents' bedroom holding the shotgun that had been used to kill her parents and brother. Garrett hadn't attempted to sugarcoat or soften the officers' recollection of the scene. In fact, he made sure each offered painstakingly detailed accounts of that evening—from arriving at the scene, to climbing the stairs, to stepping over Raymond Quinlan's body in order to gain access to the master bedroom, where Dennis and Helen Quinlan lay dead in their bed.

It was part of Garrett's strategy. Initiating each officer's testimony and eliciting it in step-by-step detail had essentially diffused the defense's cross-examination. Nothing more could be ascertained from the witnesses. Garrett had not refuted any of the officers' testimonies about what they had seen and found when they entered the Quinlan home. Instead, Garrett took the officers' recollection as gospel and confirmed that each officer's testimony matched perfectly with that of the others—a gruesome night that had shocked each of them to their core, and a disturbing crime scene that had gone on to astonish the nation.

Earlier in the week, Garrett had called forensic specialists to the stand who testified that the gun used to kill the

Quinlan family was a Stoeger Coach side by side 12-gauge break action shotgun belonging to Mr. Quinlan. In court on Tuesday morning, Garrett had dramatically presented the shotgun to the jury. Many jury members, when Garrett asked, admitted that outside of television they'd never seen a gun before. Garrett knew from jury selection that eight of them had no experience with guns, and that four were registered gun owners. Holding the weapon that had been used to kill three people, and allowing the jurors to see it up close, was startling. But this, too, was part of Garrett's plan. He did it so that when he brought the gun out again tomorrow morning when he questioned his final witness, it would seem less lethal and more ordinary. The gun would not cast Alexandra Quinlan as a deranged teenaged killer, but as the clever young woman she was.

But that bit of showmanship was for tomorrow. Today, he stood at the podium and listened to Donna Koppel's heels click as she walked up the courtroom's center aisle to whispers from her fellow officers in the gallery. The entire McIntosh police force considered the testimony Donna was about to give a betrayal. Things had gotten so bad leading up to the trial that Officer Koppel had taken a leave of absence from the McIntosh Police Department. The leave was scheduled to last for as long as the trial went on, but Garrett suspected the chances were slim that she would ever return to the McIntosh police force.

Donna pushed through the wooden partition and walked past Garrett. He noticed the quick sideways glance she gave him on the way. If looks could kill, he'd have fallen dead on the floor. Instead, from Donna's brief eye contact he read her predominant thought: *I hope to hell you know what you're doing.*

Donna sat in the witness box.

"Please raise your right hand, ma'am," the judge said from the bench to her left.

Donna did as instructed.

"Do you swear to tell the truth, the whole truth, and nothing but the truth, so help you God?"

"I do."

"Counselor," the judge said, nodding to Garrett.

Garrett took a moment as he stood behind the podium to turn a few pages in his notebook. The stall was not to impress the jury with his command of the courtroom this time. It was for Donna, to give her an opportunity to gather herself with a few extra breaths. When Garrett saw that she was steady, he found his place in his notebook and looked to the witness stand.

"Ms. Koppel," Garrett said. "Can you please state for the court your role inside the McIntosh Police Department?"

"I'm a police officer."

"How long have you been employed by the department?"

"Eighteen years."

"And you've served as an officer the entire time?"

"Yes."

"Are you *currently* working as a police officer?"

"I'm on leave, presently."

"Why is that?"

Donna swallowed. "My testimony this afternoon is not... popular inside the McIntosh police force."

"It's not popular, but it will not be dishonest in any way, am I correct?"

"You're correct."

"Why do you think your testimony will be unpopular?"

Donna hesitated and took a brief glance into the gallery and at her fellow officers.

"Because it goes against the narrative."

"What narrative is that?"

"The one set forth by the McIntosh Police Department about what happened on the night of January fifteenth, both at the Quinlan home and then later at police headquarters."

"Okay," Garrett said. "But since no one here is trying to win a popularity contest, only seeking justice for the errors made that night, I believe your testimony is vital even if it's not respected by your colleagues. Do you agree?"

"Objection," the state's attorney said.

"Sustained," the judge said.

Garrett nodded at the judge and looked back to Donna.

"Before we begin, can you let the court know how you and I are related?"

"We're married."

Garrett walked from behind the podium and approached the witness stand.

"Hi," he said when he was next to her.

Donna smiled and the jury members let out quiet laughs.

"Hi," Donna said.

"On January fifteenth of this year, were you on duty working the overnight shift?"

"Yes."

"Did you receive a call that night?"

"Yes. I was on my routine patrol route when I received a call for shots fired at a residence."

"What did you do?"

"I immediately responded. I was just a few blocks away."

"Were you the first officer on the scene?"

"I was."

"Can you take us through that night, Officer Koppel? From the moment you first arrived at the scene, and describe what you did and what you observed?"

Donna took a deep breath, and Garrett felt her nerves. No matter how many times they rehearsed this at home, there was no way to re-create the stress of sitting on the witness stand and talking to a packed courthouse with twelve jurors hanging on your every word and television cameras rolling.

Come on, baby. Garrett encouraged his wife with a subtle nod. *You've got this.*

Donna pulled her cruiser to the curb and aimed the vehicle's spotlight at the front of the house, illuminating the two-story home against the otherwise dark neighborhood. She was responding to a 911 call of shots fired at 421 Montgomery Lane and was the first officer on the scene. Well past midnight, there were no lights glowing from inside the house and other than the few neighbors loitering outside the scene was quiet.

A man walked up to the squad car as Donna was climbing out. She held him at bay with an outstretched arm and a hand on her gun. The man stopped his advance and held his hands up.

"I live next door," he said. "I'm the one who called nine-one-one."

Donna kept her attention simultaneously on the house, the man in front of her, and the growing crowd of neighbors slowly gathering around her.

"What happened?" she asked.

"I was watching television when I heard a loud bang. I muted the TV and then heard another, so I opened my back door and stepped onto my deck. A few seconds later, I heard a third bang. Only this time I was outside and recognized it immediately as a gunshot. Shotgun, probably a twelve-gauge. I'm a hunter so I know that sound."

Donna pointed at the house where her spotlight was directed. "You're sure the shots came from that house?"

"Sure as shit, ma'am. 'Scuse my language."

"Inside the house?"

"Yes, ma'am."

Keeping her eyes on the front door, Donna grabbed the radio clipped to her shoulder. "This is Officer Koppel at the scene for calls of shots fired at four twenty-one Montgomery."

"Go ahead, Officer."

"I have a witness who confirms shots fired from inside the home. Requesting backup as I assess the house."

"Roger that. On the way, three minutes out."

"I've got plenty of guns, ma'am," the helpful neighbor offered. "Just say the word and I'll give you all the backup you need."

"Stay put," she told him as she headed toward the house.

Her shadow grew longer as she strode through her car's spotlight, until the black image climbed the front of the house and stood over her like a phantom. She removed her flashlight from her belt and shined it through the front windows, but curtains blocked her view. When she reached the front porch, she banged her flashlight against the door.

"Police! Open the door."

When there was no answer, she looked behind her to see the group of neighbors watching from the street. Thankfully, another cruiser's lights blinked in the distance as reinforcements arrived. A minute later she was standing on the front porch with two other officers. A third had gone around back to check things out, and now his voice crackled over the radio.

"Quiet back here. No lights. No signs of life."

Since Donna was the first to arrive, the scene was hers to command. She reached for the handle of the front door and was surprised to find it unlocked, the door clicking open as soon as she twisted the knob. She looked at her fellow officers, who nodded their heads. With weapons drawn, they entered the house.

CHAPTER 2

District Courthouse
Thursday, September 26, 2013
3:30 p.m.

Garrett walked back to the podium and set his hands calmly on the sides of the lectern. He consulted his notes.

"At that moment, Officer Koppel, as you entered the home, what was your state of mind? What were you thinking?"

Donna paused a moment. "I was nervous."

"You had a witness who lived next door to the Quinlans tell you that he distinctly heard gunshots emanating from inside the Quinlan home. Nervousness would be a fair emotion for anyone to feel. But what else did you and your fellow officers feel?"

"Objection," Bill Bradley said, the government's lead attorney in the case of Alexandra Quinlan versus the state of Virginia. "Officer Koppel can't offer her opinion on how the other officers felt that night."

"Sustained," the judge said.

"Besides being nervous," Garrett continued, "what else did *you* feel?"

"A lot of adrenaline."

"So you were nervous and filled with adrenaline. In your opinion, the other officers felt the same way."

"Objection," Bill Bradley said.

"I'm asking Officer Koppel about her mindset when entering the house, not her fellow officers'."

"Overruled," the judge said. "Go ahead."

"So you were nervous, and you were filled with adrenaline, and you felt that your fellow officers were experiencing the same emotions?"

"Yes."

"Had you ever before, in your eighteen years on the McIntosh police force, responded to shots fired or to a call involving an active shooter?"

"No."

"Had any of the other officers with you that night ever responded to such a call?"

"No."

"So entering the home with a suspicion that there was an active shooter inside was a new experience for you?"

"Yes."

"Other than department training on such an event, you had no practical experience?"

"No."

"Is it reasonable to say, Officer Koppel, that handling a stressful, dangerous, and unique situation with which you had no previous experience opened the door to the possibility that things could be handled poorly?"

Donna paused, then swallowed hard. "Yes."

"Nervous and filled with adrenaline, is it possible that the four officers who found themselves in a situation they had never before been part of could have misinterpreted the scene inside the Quinlan home?"

"Yes."

"Knowing what you know today, would you have handled that night differently?"

Tears welled in Donna's eyes as she answered. "Yes."

"Can you tell the court what you found when you entered the Quinlan home on the night of January fifteenth?"

Donna took a deep breath to settle her nerves, blinked away the tears, and told the courtroom what she, and her fellow officers, discovered inside the home.

"Hello?" Donna yelled as she walked into the house, her pistol trained in front of her. "Police. Is anyone home?"

It was approaching one in the morning, the house was dark, and the last thing she wanted was to surprise a gun-owning homeowner in the middle of the night should this be one colossal misunderstanding. She and her colleagues made as much noise as possible from the foyer.

"Police!" she said again. "Is anyone home?"

"Police officers are in your home!" another officer yelled. "Is anyone here?"

The house responded with eerie silence. They split up, each clicking on lights as they moved through the first floor. Nothing was out of place and there were no signs of forced entry. Donna clicked on the foyer light. The upstairs hallway was protected by a spindled railing that overlooked the open-ceilinged foyer. She started a slow climb up the stairs, her gun out in front of her. As she neared the landing of the second story she was able to see the far end of the hallway through the spindled railing. One of the bedroom doors was badly damaged and hanging from the frame.

"Up here!" she yelled to the other officers, who gathered quickly with guns drawn and raced up the stairs to join her.

"Bedroom at the end of the hall. Door looks like it's been broken down," she said, still crouching on the stairs and unable to see the master bedroom to the right of the landing.

"I'll lead," she said. "You cover."

The officers behind her nodded and they all started a slow creep, one by one, up the steps. As soon as Donna crested the landing, the carnage outside the master bedroom came into view. A young boy lay on the floor. The pool of blood around him and the chest wound immediately told the story. The neighbor had, indeed, heard gunshots.

"Holy shit," Donna said, gasping as her chest tightened.

The officers quickly scaled the remaining stairs and crouched into shooter stances as they aimed their guns at the open door of the master suite. Donna had a sudden feeling that the shooter was still inside the house. She grabbed the radio off her shoulder.

"Requesting backup and EMT at four twenty-one Montgomery Lane. At least one gunshot victim inside the house."

"Roger that," squawked a voice from the radio. "Backup is on the way. Dispatching EMT and ambulance."

Donna pointed to the master bedroom. She tried not to look at the young boy on the ground, instead concentrating her focus on the bedroom and what might be waiting inside. As she got closer, she heard a noise and held up her hand for the officers behind her to stop. She listened until she confirmed what she thought she'd heard—crying. It was coming from the master bedroom. She moved closer and the sobbing grew louder. It sounded childlike. With her back against the wall, she yelled, "Police! You need to put your hands in the air. Do you understand?"

More crying came but no verbal response. With adrenaline flooding her system, Donna eased the pressure she was applying on the trigger of her firearm, knowing that it wouldn't take much to discharge. She stepped over the dead boy and into the bedroom. She took a shooter's crouch as she aimed her gun inside the room. What she saw confused her. A teenaged girl sat on the floor with her back pressed against the foot of the bed, her nightshirt stained red with blood, and a 12-gauge shotgun lying across her lap. Behind the girl, the bodies of two adults lay in bed, the sheets covered with blood. Freckled spatter coated the wall behind them.

Donna tried to understand the scene. The bodies. The girl. The gun.

"Put your hands in the air!" Donna told the girl, pointing her weapon at the suspect. The girl continued to cry but followed the order by lifting her arms.

While Donna kept her gun trained on the girl, another officer raced in and grabbed the shotgun off the girl's lap. The third officer pushed the girl face-first to the floor and secured her hands behind her back. The fourth officer cleared the room and confirmed that no one else was present.

Donna slowly approached the sobbing girl, nodding at the officer to give her some space. Besides being first on the scene, Donna was the only female present and it seemed natural that she be the one who spoke to the girl. She helped the girl back into a sitting position, and in the process got a closer look at the blood that covered her nightshirt.

"My parents are dead," the girl said.

"Did you shoot them?"

"My brother, too."

"Did you shoot them?" Donna asked again.

The girl's eyes were wide as she looked at Donna. "They're all dead."

"What's your name?"

The girl's cries softened.

"Alexandra Quinlan."

CHAPTER 3

"What was your first impression upon entering Mr. and Mrs. Quinlan's bedroom?" Garrett asked, still standing at the podium.

"I saw three victims and a suspect with a gun."

"How would you describe the atmosphere inside that room?"

"Tense. Our weapons were drawn and I was on edge. My first impression was that Alexandra had shot her parents and brother, and that she was a danger to herself and my team."

"And so you disarmed her?"

"Yes. We followed department protocol for disarming an active shooter."

"And then you placed Alexandra in handcuffs?"

"Yes."

"During those initial moments when you entered the master bedroom—when you stepped over Raymond Quinlan's body and saw Dennis and Helen Quinlan dead in their bed, the sheets stained red, blood spatter covering the wall behind them, and a teenaged girl sitting on the floor with a shotgun across her lap—would you describe those moments as confusing?"

"Yes."

"Officer Diaz," Garrett said, flipping a page on his note pad, "who was the second on the scene, also described the scene as 'terrifying'. Would you agree with that notion, as well?"

"Yes, we were all scared."

"Objection," Bill Bradley said. "Again, Officer Koppel cannot offer testimony about how her fellow officers were feeling."

"Sustained."

"Your Honor, I understand that Officer Koppel can't speak for her fellow officers, but their testimony is already on the record. Each of them described feelings of confusion, horror, sadness, and a sense of being overwhelmed by what they found inside the Quinlans' home. I'm asking if Officer Koppel felt those same things."

"The objection was sustained, Mr. Lancaster," the judge said. "Move on."

Garrett took a moment before he nodded and readdressed Donna.

"Officer Koppel, in the moments after entering the Quinlans' bedroom you felt some powerful emotions. Was confusion among them?"

"Yes."

"Horror and shock?"

"Yes."

"Sadness?"

"Yes."

"A sense that the scene was overwhelming?"

Tears welled in Donna's eyes. "Yes."

"With all those emotions coursing through you at once, was it possible that seeing a teenaged girl sitting at the foot of her parents' bed—parents who had clearly been shot—was it possible that you could have mistaken the scene for something it was not?"

"Yes. We obviously did."

"With your emotions so high and wild, you assumed Alexandra Quinlan had killed her family. Is that correct?"

"That was my assumption, yes."

"Did you ever while you were at the Quinlan residence consider that there was another explanation for what you found?"

"Not while I was at the crime scene, no."

"Did you speak with any of your fellow officers about other possibilities that might explain what you found inside the Quinlan home?"

Donna shook her head. "Not while I was at the scene, no."

"But there was a moment, Officer Koppel, wasn't there, when it dawned on you that your interpretation of the crime scene was inaccurate?"

"Yes. When we got back to headquarters and I was watching Alexandra's interview, I began to suspect that we had gotten things wrong."

"What was the time frame from when you entered the scene and experienced all those overwhelming emotions, to when this epiphany finally came to you? This realization that you might have gotten things wrong?"

"It was probably two hours later."

Garrett checked his notes. "You responded to shots fired at the Quinlan home at twelve forty-six a.m. You called for backup and EMTs at twelve fifty-eight, after entering the home. Detective Alvarez started his interrogation of Alexandra Quinlan at three-twenty in the morning. So almost *three* hours had passed from the time you responded to the call until the time you watched Alexandra being interviewed. Do I have the timeline correct?"

"Yes."

"So after you entered the Quinlans' bedroom, it took you three hours to process images and emotions few officers ever experience in their careers. It took three hours to allow those overwhelming emotions to dissipate. Three hours to allow reason and logic to attach themselves to the confusing crime scene and allow common sense to sort things out. Do I have that timeline correct?"

Donna nodded and wiped away tears. "Yes."

Garrett paused for effect. He stood without speaking long enough for the silence to make the jury uncomfortable. To make them alert and hyperfocused.

"When those emotions settled, Officer Koppel, and reason and logic came to you, what was it that you noticed?"

Donna cleared her throat. "I watched Alexandra being questioned in the interview room and assessed that she was no longer in shock, as she clearly had been when we found her at the scene. It was then that I saw a girl who was lost and confused about what she was being accused of."

"You noticed after three hours—a time period sufficient for Alexandra to process what had happened—that she finally understood she was being accused of killing her family. And when that understanding dawned on her, what in Alexandra's demeanor changed?"

"She was no longer in a trance. It looked to me like she finally understood that she was being interrogated, and she looked scared and lost and like she needed help."

"So a *seventeen*-year-old girl who was the sole survivor on the night her family was killed needed help from the adults around her. Is that what you thought?"

"Yes."

Garrett walked from behind the podium to the front of the jury box.

"The idea that a young girl in that situation would need adults to protect her seems like common sense, doesn't it?"

"Objection. Argumentative."

"Sustained."

"It seems like the first thing adults *should* do is protect this girl who just lost her mother, and her father, and her brother. But instead of help, what Alexandra Quinlan got were responding officers who misread the scene and jumped to conclusions, didn't she?"

"Objection! Argumentative."

25

"Sustained."

"Instead of help, what Alexandra Quinlan got was an aggressive detective who, during an illegal interrogation of a minor at three-thirty in the morning, accused her of killing her family. Instead of help, what Alexandra Quinlan got for surviving that night was a two-month stay at a juvenile detention center. Instead of help, what Alexandra Quinlan got was to be dragged in handcuffs from her home while a news crew recorded every detail and broadcasted it to the world. Instead of help, what Alexandra Quinlan got were weeks and weeks of headlines accusing her of killing her family—because we all know that in the news media, if it bleeds, it leads. We also know that the twenty-four-hour news cycle is quick to cast judgment, but slow to repent. So what Alexandra Quinlan *got* was a lifetime's worth of branding and slander to overcome. What Alexandra Quinlan *got* was the terrible nickname of 'Empty Eyes,' given to her by an overzealous reporter and repeated by every news organization in Virginia, and many around the country. All because a young girl had the audacity to look lost and confused in the moments immediately following her entire family being killed. What Alexandra Quinlan got was the exact opposite of what a civilized society and an ethical, impartial justice system should have given her."

"Objection!" Bill Bradley was on his feet and angry. "Your Honor, Mr. Lancaster is giving a closing argument when he should be questioning a witness."

"Mr. Lancaster," the judge said, "you're testing my patience. Do you have a question for Officer Koppel?"

"I do."

Garrett's voice softened as he looked from the jury members back to Donna.

"Alexandra's family was killed on the night of January fifteenth. Alexandra survived. Officer Koppel, do you agree that the misconduct of the McIntosh Police Department that night, and in the weeks to follow, will negatively affect Alexandra for the rest of her life?"

"Objection!"

Garrett watched as Donna began to cry. It nearly ruined him to exploit his wife's role in this situation.

"Withdrawn, Your Honor. I have no more questions."

"Mr. Bradley?" the judge said. "Your witness."

Bill Bradley simply closed his eyes and shook his head at the judge. He didn't dare make an attempt at cross-examination. Not while the jury was so clearly emotional.

"Officer Koppel," the judge said, "you may step down."

The courtroom was silent as Donna left the stand and walked down the center aisle. This time, Garrett noticed, she did not make eye contact as she passed him, and there were no whispers from the officers in the gallery.

"Mr. Lancaster, do you have further witnesses?" the judge asked.

"Just one, Your Honor. Our last. Alexandra Quinlan."

The judge looked at his watch. It was after 4:00 p.m.

"Considering the late hour, and assuming that Miss Quinlan's testimony will surely take up a substantial amount of time, we will adjourn until tomorrow at nine a.m."

The judge banged his gavel. The jury box emptied and the gallery filled with cloistered whispers as the spectators and reporters discussed what they had witnessed that day. The defense attorneys packed up and left. Garrett gathered his notes from the podium and sat at the prosecution's table. He took a few deep breaths, knowing that he had just one more day to make this right.

CHAPTER 4

McIntosh, Virginia
Thursday, September 26, 2013
6:08 p.m.

Donna and Garrett sat on the back patio of their home and listened to the evening cacophony of chirping birds and buzzing locusts from the wooded lot that abutted the back of their property. Neither had spoken since they left the courthouse earlier in the afternoon. Emotions were high and nerves frayed, but so far their strategy had worked to perfection. Donna's time on the stand had taken them to the end of Thursday. Alexandra's testimony would start Friday morning, and if things went according to plan the judge would adjourn for the weekend when Garrett rested his case, leaving the jurors to mull Donna's and Alexandra's testimony all weekend. The problem, Garrett realized now as he sat in silence with his wife, was that their words would stick with him as well.

Ice clinked against the glass tumbler when he swirled the bourbon in front of him. He took a sip and allowed his mind to flash back to that night. To the cold night in January when this chapter of their lives started. He looked across the patio where Donna sat with her hand around the stem of a wineglass. Her eyes were closed and Garrett knew she was thinking of the same night.

The Channel 2 News van pulled up to the address on Montgomery Lane where the scanner they monitored had indicated there was an active shooter. The house was bathed in the spotlights from police cruisers parked out front. The news crew hurried out of the van to capture footage. The neighborhood was alive with red and blue lights pulsing from the tops of squad cars and an ambulance. A coroner's van had just backed into the driveway and the news crew had arrived in time to capture the medical examiner entering the home. With any luck, they'd soon have prime footage of at least one gurney rolling out the front door, a white sheet draped over its occupant.

The reporter tapped the microphone to confirm it was live and then positioned herself so that the brightly lit home was behind her, the morgue van over her shoulder.

"This is Tracy Carr reporting from the Brittany Oaks subdivision in McIntosh where police have responded to shots fired inside the house behind me. As you can see, the medical examiner has just arrived but at this time we have no word on how many casualties might be inside."

Off camera, the producer gathered a couple of willing neighbors who agreed to be interviewed.

"I'm joined now," the reporter said as a man entered the frame and stood next to her, "by a neighbor who heard the shots and called nine-one-one."

The reporter placed the microphone to the man's face.

"I'll tell y'all what I told the first officer when she got here. I was watching TV when I heard a loud bang. Couple seconds later, heard another. So I walked onto my back deck to see what was going on. That's when I heard the third one and, 'cause I was outside this time, I knew right away it was a gunshot. I'm a hunter and the noise registered immediately, 'cept nobody's hunting this time a night."

"The shots were coming from inside your neighbor's house?" Tracy asked.

"Yes, ma'am."

"That's when you called the police?"

"Yes. I was tempted to go over there with my own gun to see what was happening but the police arrived real quick. A whole bunch of 'em are in the house now."

"So you heard three gunshots?"

"Yes, ma'am."

The reporter turned to the camera and offered her audience a summary of what she knew. "Again, I'm at the Brittany Oaks subdivision in McIntosh, where police are currently inside a home where at least three shots were fired. The medical examiner is now on the scene and entered the home only minutes ago."

Just then, the front door opened and a female police officer led a teenaged girl out of the house, her hands cuffed behind her back and her shirt painted red with blood. Tracy Carr beelined to the end of the driveway with her cameraman close behind, arriving just as police escorted the girl into the street and toward one of the police cars.

"Officer, Tracy Carr with Channel Two News. Can you tell me what's happening?"

The female officer put her hand up to block the camera. "Please step back, ma'am."

Tracy reached the microphone as close as possible to the young girl's face. "Did you fire the gunshots that the neighbors heard?"

The girl looked up just then, and stared into the camera. Her eyes were vacant and black. "They're all dead," the girl said.

A second police officer hurried down the driveway to push the camera away, but the cameraman recovered in time to capture footage of the empty-eyed girl being placed in the back of the squad car. The female police officer ignored the reporter's barrage of questions as she hurried into the driver's seat, turned on the sirens, and drove off into the night.

The detective arrived an hour after Officer Koppel placed Alexandra Quinlan in the interrogation room. Donna watched now through the one-way mirrored window as the girl sat alone in the hard wooden chair. A detective approached Donna. She knew him, but not well.

"Officer Koppel?" the detective asked.

She nodded. "Hi. Donna Koppel."

"Romero Alvarez," the man said with a no-nonsense tone. "You were first on the scene?"

Donna nodded again. "Yes, I responded to shots fired."

"Give me a summary. I've only heard secondhand information so far. I've got my evidence techs at the house now, I'll head over after this."

"The house was quiet when I arrived. I waited for backup before we entered. I first knocked on the front door, no answer. We discovered that the front door was unlocked. Inside, we found three victims—two adults, the parents, shot in their bed. One male child shot in the hallway outside the parents' bedroom. It was, uh, the girl's younger brother." Donna lifted her chin toward the interrogation room. "The girl was sitting on the floor in front of her parents' bed."

"All three were dead?"

"Yes. A single gunshot wound to each of them. Chest shots. The girl had a twelve-gauge shotgun on her lap. We're running forensics now to make sure it was the gun used to kill the parents and the brother. We also took samples from the girl's hands to confirm residue matches the gun."

"Good work," the detective said. "Anything else before I talk to her?"

"Yeah, we called Child Protective Services but they said it'll be a while before they can get anybody out here. The girl's got no other family that we can find."

"Anything else?"

Donna paused a moment, not wanting to overstep. "We should assign her a juvenile officer advocate before you speak to her."

The detective glanced at his watch. "I'm going to feel her out first."

"She's still in shock so take it easy on her."

Detective Alvarez offered a condescending smirk. "She killed three people. The very last thing I'm going to do is handle her with kid gloves."

"I just meant—"

"The problem with this world, Officer Koppel, is that we are not in more shock after something like this happens. It's just become part of our culture. It's her own family today, her school tomorrow, a movie theater the next day. And we're supposed to have sympathy for her because she's in shock after mowing down her entire family? Give me a break, Officer. This is an interrogation room, not a safe space."

The detective stared at Donna, daring her to respond, before turning and heading into the interview room. Detective Alvarez sat across from the girl. Donna watched through the window.

The girl looked up at the detective.

"I'm Detective Alvarez."

The detective's voice was clear as it came through the speaker positioned above the window.

"I'm here to figure out what happened at your house."

"My parents are dead," the girl said, her eyes as empty now as when she was marched from the house and placed into the back of a police cruiser. "And my brother, too."

"Yeah, the police officers told me about it. But let's start with your name."

"Alexandra Quinlan."

"Okay, Alexandra. Again, my name's Detective Alvarez and I'm here to help you, okay? But only if you're honest with me. If you lie to me, well then, I can't help you. You understand?"

"Are you sure they're dead?" Alexandra asked. "I never really checked."

"Yes," the detective said. "They're dead. The two adults at the house, they were your parents?"

"Yes."

"And the boy was your brother?"

"Yes. Raymond."

"How old are you, Alexandra?"

"Eighteen. I mean, I'm going to be eighteen in a few days."

"Were you having an argument with your parents?"

She looked up at him. The first attempt at eye contact. She shook her head slowly. "No."

"So what happened last night?"

"Nothing. I just went to sleep after I finished my homework."

"Whose gun were you holding when the police arrived?"

"The gun?"

"Yes. You were holding a shotgun when the police came into your parents' room. Whose gun was it?"

"My dad's, I think."

"You think? Where did you get it from?"

"He normally kept it in the garage."

"So you got it from the garage?"

"No."

"Then where did you get the gun, Alexandra?"

"It was in the foyer."

The detective paused, and Donna saw that he was attempting to piece together what little he knew about the scene so far.

"The gun was in the foyer of your home?"

"Yes."

"Did you hide it there?"

"Did I do what?"

"Did you hide the gun in the foyer?"

"No, it was just on the floor, so I picked it up."

"And that's when you shot them?"

The girl's eyes squinted and Donna saw her head cock to the side. "My family?"

"Yes. Tell me what happened after you picked up the gun."

The girl's eyes welled with tears. "Are you sure they're dead?"

McIntosh, Virginia
January 15, 2013
3:30 a.m.

Donna watched the interview through the viewing window. Her lieutenant stood next to her with arms crossed as he, too, watched what was taking place on the other side of the glass.

"Something's off," Donna said.

"What's that?" asked her lieutenant without taking his eyes off the interrogation room.

He was hanging so closely on every word coming through the speakers above them that Donna got the impression he didn't even know she was present.

"Something's not right," Donna said.

"A family is dead and this girl killed them, so I'd say that's an accurate statement."

"No, I mean with the girl. Look at her. She has no idea what's going on. She has no idea what Alvarez is talking about."

"You said it yourself, she's in shock. You know these kids plan these things based off whatever video game or social media is polluting their minds. Then, once they actually go through with it they want to take it back. But there are no do-overs with murder."

As Donna looked through the window of the interview room, she did not see a teenaged girl filled with remorse. She saw a confused girl who comprehended nothing about why she was being interviewed at police headquarters. She saw a girl who still hadn't fully realized that her family was dead. Donna saw something else, too, as she watched Alexandra Quinlan. It was the girl's nightshirt that started Donna's epiphany. An innocent-looking pajama top covered in blood. Why, Donna wondered, would a girl who killed her family—an event that would have taken some serious planning and contemplation—wear her pajamas to do it?

"No," Donna said, shaking her head. "We can't interview her like this. She's confused. Christ, Lieutenant, she doesn't know why she's here or what's going on around her. She hasn't even fully grasped the fact that her family is dead. We need to take a time-out, pause this situation, and think it through. Obtain proper consent, get this girl an advocate, and give her a chance."

"A chance at what? To get her story straight? Her parents are dead, so we can't get consent from them. It will be hours before DCFS gets anyone down here. We need to know as much as possible about what happened inside that house. As much as possible, as soon as possible."

"Stop the interview," Donna said.

"What?"

"Stop the interview, Lieutenant, or I will."

"We are not stopping a goddamn thing until we know why this girl killed her family. How do we know this isn't some Internet dare? How do we know other kids aren't planning the same thing tonight?" He pointed at the window. "She can tell us those things, and that's what Detective Alvarez is going to find out."

Donna took a deep breath as she watched Alexandra for another moment. She sensed the thin ice she had stumbled onto and knew pushing her lieutenant any more would be considered insubordination. She turned from the window and walked into the hallway, grabbing her cell phone and dialing as she did. She looked at her watch—3:35 a.m. She wondered if he would even answer or if he was too sound asleep to hear the phone.

"Hello?" came the groggy voice.

"Garrett!" Donna said in an urgent whisper. "It's me. I need you down at the precinct. I know it's late, but I need you right away."

McIntosh, Virginia
January 15, 2013
4:05 a.m.

Garrett Lancaster pulled his car up to the McIntosh police headquarters at just past four in the morning. He wore a Washington Wizards ball cap to tame his hair, which had been wild and uncontrollable after his wife's phone call had pulled him out of bed thirty minutes earlier. He climbed from his car and started toward the front entrance, only to see Donna bounding down the stairs and jogging toward him.

"What's wrong?" Garrett asked.

"Long story, and we don't have time for me to give you all the details. I answered a call for shots fired at a residential address. Got inside the home and found a family slaughtered."

"Jesus Christ," Garrett said, taking his wife's elbow. "You okay?"

Donna shook her head. "I'm fine. It's the girl who needs your help."

"What girl?"

He watched his wife take a deep breath, collect her thoughts, and start again.

"When I entered the house, I found two adults shot in their bed. Plus a kid—a teen boy—dead in the hallway."

"For Christ's sake."

"Just listen. I also found a girl sitting at the foot of her parents' bed with a shotgun across her lap. She's inside now being interviewed. She needs your help."

"With what?" Garrett asked. "You're not making any sense, Donna. Are you sure you're okay?"

"Listen to me, Garrett. The girl needs your help before she says something that will incriminate her. Something that she can't take back."

Donna took another breath.

"I can't figure it out right now, in the moment. Everything is swirling together, but... I don't think she did it. You need to go in there as her attorney and stop that interview."

"As her attorney?"

Garrett Lancaster was one of the top defense attorneys on the East Coast. Lancaster & Jordan was a powerhouse criminal defense firm Garrett had started two decades earlier with his partner. They had offices across the country, with the main hub located in Washington, D.C. Garrett Lancaster had a powerful reputation for defending those accused of heinous crimes. The irony of being married to a police officer was lost on neither him nor Donna. It was one of the reasons Donna had kept her maiden name. Besides that it was common for female officers to do so—it kept their private lives private, and prevented the perps they arrested from finding personal information about them online. In addition to avoiding predators out for revenge, her maiden name buffered her from Garrett Lancaster, a prominent criminal defense attorney whose job it was to keep the bad guys out of prison. Donna's job was to put them behind bars.

"Please!" Donna said. "I know I'm putting you in a bad spot, but please do this for me."

Garrett tried to think of the right thing to say. "What if you're wrong?"

"Then the truth will come out in a day or two, and you punt the case to someone else. But if I'm right, they have a seventeen-year-old girl in an interview room in the middle of the night. She just saw her family slaughtered and now they're grilling her for a confession without consent from a legal guardian. They'll keep the pressure on her until she tells them what they want to hear, and then it'll be too late."

Garrett looked at the precinct building, lighted with spot-lights shooting up the façade—a beacon of justice glowing in the middle of the night.

He cocked his head toward the entrance. "Let's go."

McIntosh, Virginia
January 15, 2013
4:15 a.m.

Garrett followed his wife into police headquarters. Donna checked him in at the front desk and Garrett obtained a visitor's badge that allowed him access into the building. Normally, defense attorneys were left to wander the halls until they found their way to wherever it was they needed to be. Inside a police precinct, defense attorneys were the equivalent of rats scurrying along the baseboards. Tonight, though, Donna led him straight to the interview room, where Garrett saw Donna's lieutenant watching through the room's window, along with three uniformed officers. Inside, he saw a detective in a suit talking with a hollow-eyed girl wearing an oversized nightshirt.

Instinct pinched the muscles of his back together, pulling his shoulders apart and inflating his chest. He was frustrated at himself for not taking the time to comb his hair or climb into a suit, having to do this now in jeans and a Wizards hat.

"Lieutenant," Garrett said in an assertive voice.

The man watching the interview turned, as did Donna's fellow officers. Garrett felt their stares. But more so, he felt Donna next to him. She deflated a bit. These officers had entered the house with her and had had her back as they'd stalked through the house looking to engage an active shooter. It was surely a traumatic and bonding experience for them all, and Garrett knew a pang of guilt had touched Donna's core for what she was doing.

"I'm Garrett Lancaster, I'm representing…"

Garrett realized he didn't even know his client's name.

"The girl," he finally said, pointing at the interview room. "I'm her attorney and I'm going to need you to stop the interview."

Lieutenant Marcus Grey looked over Garrett's shoulder and squinted his eyes at Donna. "What's going on, Koppel?"

Donna tilted her head. "Ask Garrett."

He looked back at Garrett. "What's going on, Counselor?"

"I need you to stop the interview, Marcus. I'm her attorney."

"You called your husband?" Lieutenant Grey asked Donna. "You're trying to go over my head by calling your husband?"

"I'm not going over anyone's head, sir. Something's not right. This girl deserves the same protections as anyone else."

"She shot up her goddamn family, Koppel!"

Donna took a deep breath. "She deserves to know her rights and to be protected under our constitution."

"She was read her rights!"

Garrett held up his hand. "As the girl's attorney—"

"Alexandra," Donna said, cutting her husband off. "As Alexandra's attorney."

"As Alexandra's attorney, I'm asking that this interview be stopped immediately." Garrett looked at his watch. "It's four-twenty in the morning, and this is now the second time I'm asking, Lieutenant. If you're not keeping track, believe me, I am."

Technically, Garrett knew, only his client could request the interview to be stopped. Which was why he had to get in there immediately.

"We need to find out what's going on," Grey said in a calmer voice. "The only way to do that is to speak with the shooter."

Garrett walked past Lieutenant Grey and opened the interview room door, then stepped inside. The detective looked over his shoulder, confusion on his face.

"Can I help you?"

"Yes. My name is Garrett Lancaster, Alexandra's attorney. The first thing you can do to help is stop asking my client questions and leave us alone. Please."

"Your client?" the detective said, standing from his chair.

"I understand parental consent to interview Alexandra was not obtained."

"It was not possible," the detective shot back.

"Did you go through the proper channels to find my client's next of kin, who could in emergency situations be considered her legal guardian?" Garrett waved his hand. "I'm sure you did. But then, of course, if you were unable to find any family, you would need to go through the state's department of Child Protective Services to obtain consent for a formal interview. I'm sure you did that, too, Detective, but I'm just confirming. If you did all those things before you started the interview with my client, who is under the age of eighteen, and therefore considered a minor in the state of Virginia, then you and your department are in good standing and I'll just need a moment alone with my client. But in the unlikely event that you conducted an interview on a minor without parental, guardian, or other legal consent, then you're likely in a shit-ton of trouble and have a lot more to worry about than me ending this interview."

Garrett stared at the detective. He watched as the man's eyes, which had a moment earlier been focused like laser beams on Garrett's, wandered off to the interview room's one-way window searching for his lieutenant but only seeing his own reflection.

"Give me a minute with my client?" Garrett asked in the same polite voice that he had presented the entire time.

After a second, the detective headed for the door.

"Detective," Garrett said. "Please ask your lieutenant to turn off the camera and microphone while I have a word with Alexandra. I'm pretty certain you've already conducted an illegal interrogation of my client. Recording my conversation with her would put you in a world of trouble that so far you've just flirted with."

Garrett offered a quick smile.

"Thanks."

CHAPTER 5

District Courthouse
Friday, September 27, 2013
9:12 a.m.

Even as her legs did their part to transport Alexandra to the stand on Friday morning, Garrett noticed them trembling. It was her body's way of protesting her presence in the courtroom. She likely wanted to be a million places other than sitting in a packed courtroom with television cameras aimed at her and the nation's attention hanging on her every word. But Alexandra had no choice. To win her case against the state of Virginia, her testimony was paramount. Without it, a win was unlikely. With it, Garrett believed, it was inevitable.

When Alexandra sat in the witness stand, she reached for the glass of water and trembled it to her mouth. She had turned eighteen since the night her family was killed, but the formal transition to a legal adult did nothing to stop her from looking like a scared child this morning. Garrett at once felt sorrow and confidence. He didn't want to put Alexandra through this but knew it was the only way to achieve even a sliver of justice for what had happened to her. Looking like a scared adolescent girl made his job easier and the opposing counsel's job nearly impossible.

After Alexandra was sworn in, Garrett smiled at her.

"Good morning," he said.

Alexandra nodded and adjusted her glasses, which were thick and heavy. "Hi."

"Can you please state your name for the court?"

"Alexandra Quinlan."

"Alexandra, we're going to cover some tough topics this morning. Things that will be difficult for you to talk about, and things that will be difficult for the court to hear. You and I have discussed these topics over the last few weeks, and you have indicated to me that you are prepared to offer your testimony this morning. Do you still feel that way?"

Alexandra cleared her throat. "Yes."

"Are you nervous?"

"Yes."

"Me too. I always get nervous when I'm in court, so I'm right there with you."

This was a lie, but Garrett wasn't under oath. The truth was that it had been a number of years since he'd felt any nerves in a courtroom.

Alexandra offered a subtle smile.

"If we start talking about anything you don't want to discuss, just let me know and we'll move on. Okay?" he asked.

"Okay."

Garrett paused for a moment before walking over to the witness stand. This gave the jury a moment to settle as they waited to hear from Alexandra Quinlan, a girl who they had all admitted during jury selection they'd seen in the papers and tabloids. Now, they were about to meet her in person.

"During cross-examination this week, the state of Virginia has attempted to put forth a narrative that the McIntosh Police Department did everything by the book in their handling of the Quinlan family murders in general, and Alexandra Quinlan in particular. Next week, when it's their turn to put forth their case, they'll tell us more of the same."

Garrett looked over at the defense table.

"Other than accusing the wrong person in a triple homicide, and still to this day failing to bring the actual killer to justice, perhaps that argument works. Otherwise, it's filled with a few holes."

"Objection," Bill Bradley said.

"Sustained."

"They want you to ignore a couple of early 'mistakes' they made, and to concentrate only on how well they did *after* that point. But it's not the things they did *correctly* that has brought us here to this courtroom; it's all the things they did terribly wrong."

"Your Honor," Bill Bradley said in an annoyed tone.

"Mr. Lancaster," the judge said, "we discussed this yesterday. You are not making a closing argument, you are questioning a witness. Do you have a question for Miss Quinlan?"

Garrett turned back to Alexandra.

"The McIntosh Police Department feels that they treated you correctly—by the book, as I said—starting with the journey from your home the night your family was killed. Do you agree with that argument?"

"No," Alexandra said.

"Where were you placed after you were arrested?"

"Alleghany Juvenile Detention Center."

"How long did you stay there?"

"Two months."

"After two months, what happened?"

"The charges against me were dropped and I was released."

"The charges were dropped, but for two months you were forced to fend for yourself inside a juvenile detention center for a crime you did not commit. Do I have that correct?"

"Yes."

"The defense has argued that while you were at Alleghany you were treated well. Do you agree with that?"

"No."

"But we've heard from your psychologist and your social worker, both of whom stated, under oath, that you have developed close relationships with them. Is that true?"

"Yes."

"But it wasn't the professionals you had difficulty with while inside Alleghany, was it?"

"No."

"Who did you have trouble with?"

"The other kids."

"Can you tell us about those troubles?"

"Inside Alleghany, you need to make friends to survive. Everyone is in these sort of cliques, like these groups, and you have to get in one for protection."

"Did you make friends?"

"Yes."

"And did those friends protect you?"

"When they could."

"But there were times they could not, am I right?"

"Yes."

"What were some of the things you were forced to deal with inside Alleghany?"

"Some of the other kids found leaked photos of the crime scene and taped them to the door of my room."

"Photos of your family from the night they were killed?"

"Yes."

"They hung those pictures on your door to torment you?"

"I guess I'm not sure why they did it, they just did it."

"Was the person who leaked the photos identified?"

"Yes."

"Who was it?"

"Detective Alvarez. That's what I was told."

"The detective who illegally interrogated you the night your family was killed?"

"Yes."

"I would have loved to call Detective Alvarez to the stand to question him about this but that became impossible after the detective took his own life just prior to the start of this trial. It appeared Detective Alvarez knew how badly he had mishandled your case, even if his superiors failed to admit it."

"Objection."

"Sustained. Move on, Mr. Lancaster."

"Alexandra, it doesn't matter how well the state of Virginia or the McIntosh Police Department did in the days and weeks *after* they traipsed you out of your house in handcuffs while news cameras recorded every detail. It doesn't matter how well they did *after* they publicly accused you of killing your family. It doesn't matter how well they did *after* weeks of headlines labeled you as the empty-eyed girl who slaughtered her family. It doesn't matter how well they did *after* forensic evidence proved that you were not the one who pulled the trigger that night. None of what they did *after* all that matters because the damage had already been done, hadn't it?"

Alexandra swallowed hard. "Yes."

"Let's talk about that. Let's talk about the damage the McIntosh Police Department did to you."

Garrett walked back to the podium.

"Alexandra, can you tell the court how old you are?"

"Eighteen."

"And how old were you on the night of January fifteenth?"

"Seventeen."

"You turned eighteen a week later, correct?"

"Yes. January twenty-second."

"So, that made you a senior in high school at the time this all took place?"

"Yes."

"After you were released from juvenile detention and all the charges against you were dismissed, did you go back to school for the spring semester?"

Alexandra shook her head. "No, I didn't go back."

"Why not?"

"I tried but there were too many news cameras and reporters waiting for me at school each day."

"News cameras and reporters? Waiting at your high school each morning to ask you about the night your family was killed?"

"Yes."

"Accusing you, in fact, of getting away with murder."

"Some of them, yes."

"And other students at your high school, how did they treat you?"

"I lost all my friends because... I guess it was too hard to hang around with me. Kids called me Empty Eyes."

"Empty Eyes. Where did that name come from?"

"The reporter who was there that night... the night the police walked me out of my house... she captured this image of me and in it my eyes look hollow and... empty, I guess. So she started calling me Empty Eyes during her reports."

"Lovely. Was it difficult to be labeled that way?"

"It was."

"Too difficult, in fact, for a teenaged high school student who had just lost her family to handle," Garrett said, looking at the jury. "So you stopped going to school?"

"Yes."

"But you did complete your senior year and graduate, correct?"

"Yes. I completed the spring semester through home schooling and tutoring."

"But you never went back to school?"

"No."

"You missed out on your senior year?"

"The last part of it, yes."

"So no friends. No socializing. No senior ditch day. No prom. No graduation."

"No, I didn't do any of those things."

"And college? You had applied to and been accepted to several universities, is that correct?"

"Yes. Before everything happened, I was trying to decide where to go. I was working with my parents on that."

"First semester of what should have been your freshman year of college is currently under way, but you're not enrolled at any university, is that correct?"

Alexandra nodded. "That's correct. I didn't think it would be possible to go to college with all the media and press and attention and stuff."

"Because reporters would have followed you to whichever campus you chose. Is that what you were afraid of?"

"Yes."

"In fact, the press found out which universities accepted you, made that information public, and then protests took place at those schools. From Virginia Tech, to Clemson, to Georgia. Is that correct?"

Alexandra nodded. "Yeah. Um, certain organizations at each of those schools made it known that I wasn't welcome on their campus."

Garrett looked back to the jury. "A teenaged girl loses her entire family, and because of our society's insatiable appetite for the morbid details of other people's suffering, and our constant desire for scapegoating and scandal—all of which was stoked by Alexandra being wrongly accused and publicly prosecuted—that girl wasn't allowed to properly finish high school."

He looked back to Alexandra. "So college became impossible, and your entire future will be marred by a police department's incompetence and a society's obsession with sensationalism of true crime. Do I have that right?"

"Objection," Bill Bradley said from the defense table. "Your Honor, by her own admission, Miss Quinlan completed high school. It was her personal decision not to attend college. And Mr. Lancaster is not able to predict the future. We don't know what Miss Quinlan will be doing next year, or for the rest of her life."

"Sustained," the judge said. "Mr. Lancaster, stick with present day, please."

"Of course, Your Honor. But, instead of *present* day," Garrett said, turning to look directly at Bill Bradley, "maybe we should go back to the night of January fifteenth instead."

Garrett turned back to Alexandra, his voice softer now.

"Alexandra, do you feel comfortable telling the court what happened the night your parents and brother were killed?"

"Objection," Bill Bradley said again, standing from the defense table and a bit more animated this time.

Garrett understood the man's aggression. At all costs, the state of Virginia did not want this court to hear the details Alexandra was about to provide.

"Miss Quinlan is not on trial for murder," Bradley said. "I think it would be an injustice to make her relive that night."

"An injustice?" Garrett said with more force to his words than Bill Bradley had put behind his own. "Now, *suddenly*, the state of Virginia is concerned about injustice? With all due respect, Bill, that's the biggest pile of crap that's ever been dumped in a court-room."

"Gentlemen!" the judge said, slamming his gavel to bring the courtroom to order. "Arguments come to me, not to each other. Do you understand?"

"My apologies, Your Honor," Garrett said. "I understand."

"Your objection is overruled, Mr. Bradley. Hearing Miss Quinlan's testimony about the night her family was killed is paramount to this case, and the court will allow it."

Bradley sat and Garrett made eye contact with Alexandra.

"You sure you can do this?" he asked as if he were talking just to her, but made sure the jury could hear him.

Alexandra nodded. "I am."

"Okay. Let's talk about what happened that night."

McIntosh, Virginia
January 15, 2013
12:26 a.m.

A loud noise lifted her eyelids. It sounded like something large had fallen on the hardwood floor outside her room, and Alexandra's freshly woken mind conjured an image of the grandfather clock, which had stood for the entirety of her life in the

49

corner of the second-story hallway, tipping over and splintering against the floor. But something about the noise was curious. The sound had not come and gone. It lingered. That's when her mind became fully alert and she understood what it was—the sound of a shotgun.

She knew the sound well from the mornings she spent pheasant hunting with her dad. He hadn't yet allowed her to tag along on a deer hunt, but pheasants were a Saturday morning staple. Alexandra's job had been to keep track of their dog. She used the whistle to call Zeke back if he wandered too far off in front of them, and she'd watch as he snaked through the tall reeds, listening for the crunching of the stalks to stop, indicating that Zeke had found a bird. That's when she'd yell to her dad, "On point, Dad! On point."

The wild flapping of wings would come next as Zeke flushed the pheasant from its hiding spot, and then she'd hear the sound of her father's shotgun. It was always just a single round. She'd never, in all the years pheasant hunting with her dad, heard him fire twice at the same bird. He never missed. And that was how she recognized the noise that had woken her. Out in the cornfields, her father's shotgun gave off a single blast, but then lingered. The report of the gun remained for a few seconds, as if it were a living thing, before it dissipated. Alexandra sat up in bed now as the remnants of the blast slowly faded. But then another came, and she knew something was terribly wrong.

Pushing the covers to the side, she jumped from bed and ran to her bedroom door. She placed her temple against the door frame and stared out into the hallway. Her vision was blurry without her glasses, but she dared not go back to the nightstand to retrieve them. Through the fuzziness she saw that the grandfather clock hadn't fallen to the ground, as her groggy mind had first imagined. It stood where it always had, in the corner of the hallway. For the encapsulated moment when she peeked from her bedroom, her home was calm and quiet. The spindled railing that ran the length of the second story hallway overlooked the dark foyer below, and everything seemed normal. Then she saw Raymond emerge from his room and walk down the hallway, away from Alexandra and toward her parents' bedroom. He, too, was blurry to her nearsighted eyes. And though she didn't know it then, Alexandra would later be grateful the scene she was about to witness was unfocused and distorted. When Raymond reached their parents' bedroom, he stopped and pushed the door open. A third gunshot blast reverberated through the house. The blast threw Raymond onto his back, where he lay and did not move.

Alexandra startled into action. Her knees shook as she pulled away from her door and ran to her bedroom window, pushed it open, and fumbled with the screen until it fell into the night and landed on the walkway below. She thought about jumping, but it was cold and dark and a long way down to where the screen lay on the ground. Then, for some inexplicable reason she again thought of the grandfather clock standing at the end of the hallway and just outside her bedroom door. When thinking back on that night, she had never been able to explain why the image of the clock came to her in that moment, or why she had imagined it was the clock that had fallen and made the original noise that woke her. All she knew was that she had to get to it.

She ran from the open window and into the hallway. Instinctually, she twisted the lock on the inside handle of her bedroom door before quietly closing it. It was a trick she had learned since turning seventeen—locking her bedroom door from the hallway. It was a way to fool her parents into thinking she was studying in her room when she really had snuck out to meet up with her friends.

With her bedroom door locked, Alexandra turned and ran to the place she always used to go during games of hide-and-seek when she was little. She slipped behind the grandfather clock, noticing that the hiding spot was much smaller than she remembered. The last time she'd taken refuge there was at least three years earlier and her charge toward adulthood had never been more apparent. Years earlier she had effortlessly crept behind the clock to hide from her brother. Now, she attempted to wedge herself there to save her life.

Just as she settled into the hiding spot, she heard footsteps on the hardwood floor. Alexandra did not dare peek around the edge of the clock to steal a glance down the hallway. She could see the spindles of the railing that overlooked the first-floor foyer and a sliver of hardwood that ran along it. She saw the shooter's shadow as it emerged from her parents' room, poured through the spindles of the railing, and disappeared over the edge. The shadow paused and Alexandra held her breath to stay as silent as possible. Finally, she heard footsteps again as the shooter hurried toward Alexandra's bedroom and the grandfather clock that stood just a few feet from her bedroom door. Had she not acted quickly Alexandra would be in her room now, either lying in bed or still frozen and staring through the crack between the door and the frame. She wished she'd found the courage to jump from her bedroom window. There was a row of thick bushes that might have broken her fall. But if they hadn't, her mind churned, then she would have injured herself and been unable to run away, stuck on the back walkway and staring up at the shooter as the barrel of the shotgun drifted out her open window and pointed down at her. At least here in her hiding place she had a chance. At least crammed behind the grandfather clock she might survive the night.

She heard the rattle of her bedroom door handle. Then, a cracking noise as the shooter kicked at the door. Once, and then again until the door burst open. Behind the grandfather clock, tucked as tightly as possible in the corner hallway, Alexandra squeezed her eyes closed. The pounding inside her chest caused her whole body to tremble. She didn't dare move, and she tried not to breathe as she heard first knocking, and then the squeak of her closet door opening. A moment of silence followed before she heard the loud, thundering footsteps as the shooter raced across her bedroom to the open window. The whine of the window opening fully came next, followed by more footsteps as the shooter ran out of the bedroom and down the hallway, away from Alexandra's hiding spot. The stomping continued down the stairs until she heard the front door open, and then the house grew eerily silent.

CHAPTER 6

The courtroom was silent, and Garrett allowed it to remain that way. Not just for effect this time, but to allow the gravity of what the jurors were hearing to settle in. A seventeen-year-old girl had taken refuge in an old hiding spot from her youth. The split-second decision had saved her life.

"Are you doing okay?" Garrett asked.

Alexandra nodded. "Yes."

"I think I speak for everyone in this courtroom in telling you that it takes a lot of courage to retell this story."

Garrett noticed several jurors nod in agreement.

"The shooter went to your room but couldn't find you. What happened after the shooter ran out of your bedroom?"

"He ran down the hallway, away from where I was hiding. Then down the stairs. I stayed hidden behind the clock but peeked out to look over the railing. Our upstairs hallway overlooks the front foyer. I saw the front door open and the shooter run outside."

"The shooter ran *out* of the house?"

"Yes."

"It's safe to say that the whole night is confusing for all of us in this courtroom to understand, yet in that moment you actually had a clear impression of what happened. You knew why the shooter ran out of the house, didn't you?"

"Yes. I fooled him."

"How so?"

"I opened my bedroom window because I was thinking of jumping, but I chickened out. It was too high. So I ran and hid behind the clock that's just outside my bedroom. Before I did, though, I locked my bedroom door from the hallway."

"From the hallway *outside* your room?"

"Yes. One of my friends showed me how to do it. You have to twist the handle first, then lock the door before you close it. It was a trick to make my parents think I was studying in my room when really I was out with my friends."

Garrett smiled. "A trick that saved your life. But you weren't trying to fool your parents that night, you were trying to fool the shooter."

"Yeah. I thought that if I locked the door the shooter would think I was inside and might not look for me elsewhere. When the shooter went into my room, I guess he thought I had actually jumped out the window and ran away. When I saw the shooter run out the front door, I figured he was chasing after me or at least running to the back of my house to see if I was still there."

"So at that point you were still tucked in your hiding place when the shooter ran from the house. But from that spot, you could see the front door through the upstairs railing. You noticed something after the shooter left your house, is that right?"

"Yes."

"What did you notice?"

"My dad's gun."

"Where was the gun?"

"In the foyer downstairs."

"The shooter had dropped it before he left the house, is that correct?"

"Yes."

Garrett walked back to the prosecution's table, opened the gun case that rested on the floor, and lifted the shotgun that had been used to kill Alexandra's family.

"Is this the gun?"

"Yes."

"And it belonged to your father?"

"Yes."

"You know this gun well, don't you?"

"Yes."

"And you know how to use it?"

"Yes."

"How did you learn to shoot a twelve-gauge shotgun?"

"My dad taught me when he took me pheasant hunting on Saturday mornings."

"What did you do after you noticed that the shooter had left the gun?"

"I slid out from behind the grandfather clock and ran down the stairs to retrieve the gun."

"You told me something that I found amazingly interesting, and I want you to share it with the court now. Why was it so important for you to get the gun? Some might think it more natural to run to your parents' room to check on them."

"There were only three shots," Alexandra said. "My dad's twelve-gauge shotgun holds two cartridges. I heard the first two shots—those were the ones that woke me up. Then"—Her voice cracked momentarily. Alexandra swallowed hard and righted herself—"I heard a third shot when my brother was killed. I knew the gun had been reloaded in order to shoot my brother, which meant there was still a live cartridge in the chamber."

"So you retrieved the gun for protection?"

"Yes. I grabbed the gun just in case the shooter came back."

"Knowing that there was still a single shot remaining."

"Yes."

"Smart girl," Garrett said. "After you grabbed the shotgun from the foyer, what did you do?"

"I ran up to my parents' room."

"And what did you do next?"

"I sat down on the floor in front of their bed and waited with my dad's shotgun on my lap. Just in case."

"Just in case," Garrett said, walking to the jury box while still holding the shotgun. "Just in case the shooter came back?"

"Yes."

He looked at the jury members. "The shooter never came back. But the McIntosh police showed up. I'm not sure which was worse."

"Objection!" Bill Bradley yelled.

"Withdrawn, Your Honor. I have no more questions for Alexandra."

"Mr. Bradley?" the judge asked.

Bill Bradley closed his eyes and shook his head.

PART II

The Escape

"We know where you are."

—Laverne Parker

Fall 2015

Two Years Later

CHAPTER 7

Paris, France
Tuesday, September 29, 2015
1:35 p.m.

The escape was flawless. The funds had been transferred to a blind trust. The University of Cambridge had accepted her based on stellar high school academics and never questioned why she'd taken a gap year. The chartered flight cost a fortune, but she had plenty of money since winning her defamation case and she knew it was imperative to slip out of the United States without the press knowing about it. Each detail had been meticulously planned and skillfully executed. It was everything that happened afterward that went to hell.

Shipping Alexandra Quinlan to a foreign country—alone and so soon after the traumatic events of losing her family and enduring a very public and difficult trial—may have been necessary and the only way to protect her, but it was a flawed plan from the beginning. It held too many variables and came with a complicated set of assumptions. The first was that, after a tumultuous and psychologically traumatic two years, Alexandra Quinlan would fall in line with the rest of society and go with the flow. The second was that Alex would actually *attend* college, excel in the environment of higher education, and generally adjust to the new life she had escaped to. None of those expectations held because when the dust settled, so, too, did the guilt. The guilt of surviving the night her family was killed. The guilt of hiding while she watched her brother die. The guilt of spending the immediate months after the tragedy defending herself rather than in mourning. The guilt of attempting to move on with life rather than hunting for answers to why a still-unknown intruder had entered her home on a cold January night and killed her family.

Although the move to England had worked in the sense that it allowed Alex to escape the American media, it was the concept of school and classes and study that failed. The idea of dormitory life with a roommate was so unappealing that she had never considered it. Alex fled the United States to get away from her past. She escaped to Cambridge because it was a place where no one knew her or what had happened to her. It was a place where no one would make the connection to the notorious night when she was accused of killing her family. Had she opted to live in the dormitory with a roommate rather than alone in her own apartment, it would have brought probing questions about Alex's life and her family. About her parents and brother. About what things were like "back home."

To these questions, Alex would've had to hem and haw and lie through her teeth because she would never be able to properly explain that she didn't have a home. Not since that night more than two years earlier when the figure in the long trench coat had invaded the place she once called home. After that moment, Alex had "places." First it was Alleghany, the juvenile detention center where she spent two months after she was arrested. Next was the Lancasters' home in Washington, D.C., where she secretly lived with Garrett and Donna and began gathering evidence and mounting an argument against the McIntosh Police Department and the district attorney's office. After Alex won her defamation case against the state of Virginia, which concluded with Alex being awarded a small fortune in damages, the media fervently searched for her whereabouts. When things became too overwhelming, Alex fled to the Lancasters' vacation home, which was tucked in the foothills of the Appalachian Mountains. But it was obvious by then that the reporters and true-crime fanatics would rest at nothing less than finding and questioning Empty Eyes about the heinous crimes they still, and would forever, believe she committed.

During her year in hiding, rumors frequently broke on true-crime websites that someone had spotted Empty Eyes at a particular hotel, and the freaks and geeks would flock there. News vans would roll to the hotel entrance and shoot footage of protestors holding signs and chanting their hatred toward her. Their favorite, and least inventive in Alex's opinion, was: "Alex Q, it was you! Alex Q, it was you!"

While the media and the true-crime nuts breathlessly searched for her, Garrett and Donna kept her hidden. When the pressure built to the point of explosion, they hatched the plan for Alex to head overseas. Attending an American university was out of the question. In a foreign country she would at least have a chance at anonymity. So England it was. The University of Cambridge was where Alex was supposed to study for four years. It was where she was supposed to run and hide and catch her breath. It was where a fresh start was supposed to be found.

The myth lasted one year, although the charade was still ongoing today. Donna and Garrett believed school was going swimmingly well. Alex returned to the United States and spent the summer after freshman year hiding again at the Lancasters' vacation home and lying to them about how well she was doing at school and how many friends she had made. About how Cambridge was becoming her new home, and how she couldn't wait to go back for her second year. Why Alex had been unable to tell them the truth was something she could not fully explain. She owed Garrett and Donna so much for what they'd done for her. Coming clean about school felt like a betrayal. So, at the end of summer, Alex packed her things and jumped on a plane back to England under the ruse of starting her sophomore year.

Heading back to Europe had become imperative, but Alex was going for reasons other than education. She was hunting for answers to why her family had been killed, and as she boarded the train in the Paris Gare de Lyon for the four-hour ride to Zürich, Switzerland, she was following the only lead she had come across in more than a year of searching.

CHAPTER 8

Paris, France
Tuesday, September 29, 2015
1:45 p.m.

Alex took her seat in the train's first-class cabin and spread the pages on the table in front of her. The documents had started her on this leg of her journey. They were the first real clue she had come across in a search that started more than a year ago. Alex studied the papers again, trying to understand the numbers. But no matter how hard she worked to decipher the information, she was missing a key bit of information. Alex hoped to find it in Switzerland.

"Boisson?"

Alex looked up to see a female attendant offering a menu. "Non, merci."

When the server left to attend to the next passenger, Alex rested her head back and closed her eyes. After that fateful January night when Alex was led out of her home and into the hot lights of the television news cameras, and then in the months that followed, and especially during the landmark lawsuit she brought against the state of Virginia, the public had gotten to know Alexandra Quinlan. They knew her name. They knew her face. They knew her eyes. For a full year her image had been plastered across newspapers, tabloids, and nightly newscasts. The American public was so starved for morbid details about the tragic night the Quinlan family was slaughtered that they allowed an innocent teenager to become a caricature of a pop culture obsessed with true crime. To the public, Alexandra Quinlan was not a young girl who lost her family. She was the villain in a true-crime saga, and from that saga they wanted twists and surprises and bombshell revelations. They had gotten plenty of that during the bungled investigation, and even more during the lawsuit she filed against the state of Virginia, during which all the dirty details were laid bare. The entire ordeal culminated with a final plot twist no one saw coming—Alex's disappearance from the public eye.

During the trial, and still today, the American news media were desperate to find her, and not for any good or noble reasons. The media wanted to hunt Alexandra Quinlan down and burn her at the stake. Despite a mountain of evidence proving beyond a reasonable doubt that Alex had not killed her family, and had, in fact, narrowly escaped death herself, the vultures in the true-crime community refused to believe any of it. And ever since winning a massive settlement in her defamation case against the state of Virginia, making her a millionaire many times over, the true-crime nuts were frenzied to locate her, question her, expose her lies, and make sure the rest of her life was a living hell.

As if every detail of her life had not already been laid bare for the world to see, the press wanted more. They always wanted more, and Alex had nearly given it to them. The idea of granting a prominent reporter an exclusive had been floated early on as a way to put it all to rest. But the suggestion was quickly squashed. Granting a single interview would be like chumming the water. It would attract thousands of other reporters, podcasters, and true-crime fanatics hoping for the same access. Her only option had been to up and vanish. So she did.

-

Alex opened her eyes and watched the countryside blur past as the train rumbled from France to Switzerland. She passed through small towns with houses perched in the foothills and the snow-capped Alps in the distance. Just a couple of years ago she had never been out of the United States. She had barely been out of Virginia, save for a grade school trip across the Potomac to visit Washington, D.C., and a few family vacations to Florida. And here she was now, twenty years old and sitting on a train slicing through Europe. A lot had changed in two years. She'd come a long way from that frightened teenager who'd hid behind the grandfather clock after her family had been gunned down. Today, she was no longer hiding. Today, she had become the hunter.

She made a pledge to herself to spend every waking hour searching for answers to the night her family was killed. She made this her first priority because she knew no one else was looking. Only reluctantly, and with great pressure from Garrett Lancaster and his powerful law firm, had the McIntosh police and the Alleghany County district attorney dropped the charges against her. Despite everything—the charges being dismissed, the revelations about the sloppy investigation, the glaring evidence that pointed to a stranger in her home that night, her victory in court, the judge's admonition of the McIntosh detectives and the district attorney, the multimillion-dollar judgment—still to this day many inside the McIntosh Police Department, as well as the entire district attorney's office, believed that Alex had killed her family.

The official position of the McIntosh Police Department and the district attorney's office was that the slaying of Dennis, Helen, and Raymond Quinlan was the result of a botched home invasion. The claim was that an intruder had entered the home to steal jewelry and other valuables but was startled by Mr. Quinlan. The prowler killed Dennis Quinlan, and then hastily shot his wife and son in a mad dash to escape the scene.

The theory was weak and ignored two key bits of evidence found inside the Quinlan home that pointed to something much more sinister than a burglary gone bad. First were the mysterious photos discovered in her parents' bed the night they were killed. The photos held images of three unidentified women, and Alex knew they played a role in understanding why her parents were killed. But the photos did not fit the narrative put forth by the McIntosh police so they were dismissed and never revealed to the public. The other bit of evidence was a lone fingerprint lifted from Alex's bedroom window—the window she had opened before aborting her idea of jumping two stories to safety. The fingerprint belonged to whoever was in her house that night, and painted a clear picture of a killer who was not startled by Dennis Quinlan, but who actively attempted to hunt down his daughter.

Put it all together and Alex knew relying on the authorities to find the truth would be like slipping an envelope into an abandoned mailbox and hoping it found its way to the address scrawled on it. The police were no longer looking for her family's killer because they believed they'd already found her.

Alex looked away from the window and settled her gaze on the open folder and the documents resting on the table in front of her. She read through the pages again, even though Alex had long ago committed every detail to memory. The documents had sent her back to London, and now across Europe. She would arrive in Switzerland later that night. Then, first thing in the morning she would visit the Sparhafen Bank in Zürich to find answers.

As she stared at the pages, her mind drifted back to the night she'd found them. It was the night she'd snuck into her old home on Montgomery Lane, the first time she'd stepped foot inside the house since it all had happened. The first time she had returned since taking refuge behind the grandfather clock the night her family was killed. The first, and the last. That visit, meant for a different purpose altogether, had started her on her current journey. Now, as the train rocked its way into Switzerland and her eyes skimmed over the pages, snippets of the hot August night when she made that secret trek to her old home came back to her...

Besides the occasional news van parked at random times out front, the house was left to itself—quiet and dark and eerie. Detectives and forensic teams had long since stopped invading the home. They had determined nothing more was to be found inside—all clues had been uncovered and every speck of evidence collected. More than two years after yellow crime scene tape first roped off the property, bits of it still remained. Remnants wrapped around a few tree trunks twirled in the breeze. A few strips still crisscrossed the front and back entryways. The presence of the crime scene tape was not an indication of a formal or ongoing investigation. The police, Alex knew, no longer cared about 421 Montgomery Lane. The tape remained because, as the new owner of the property, Alex had yet to hire someone to clean the place.

She had used a portion of her settlement money to purchase the house out of foreclosure. Alex hadn't purchased the home to live there. That would never be possible after the things she'd witnessed. She'd purchased it because she couldn't watch the house fall into the hands of true-crime vagrants who might turn the place into some sort of morbid museum. It was because of those delinquents that Alex felt an urgency to get inside now. She needed to collect something near and dear to her heart before the fanatics who continued to trespass onto the property eventually found their way to the attic and pillaged what was there.

Alex's worry as she tiptoed through the shadows of the yard and toward the back door was that there were true-crime junkies in the house now taking selfies in the master bedroom. She'd seen many such photos splashed around the Internet over the last few months—smiling idiots and self-proclaimed "citizen detectives" standing in front of her parents' bed snapping photos of themselves with the blood-spattered wall behind them and promising to "find justice." Such assholes, Alex thought. The dehumanizing of the event sickened her every time she saw one of those photos. How, she had always wondered, could people be so obsessed with the events of that night as to forget—or not care—that real people had died?

She twisted the handle to the back door, knowing from her previous attempts that the lock had been jimmied and broken by the lunatics who had invaded her home to have a look around like it was an abandoned museum. On earlier visits to the house, she had made it this far—to the threshold of the kitchen door—before retreating, unable to walk inside. But she was determined this time around. In the morning she was leaving for her second year at University of Cambridge and had no more time to waffle. She wouldn't return until Christmas. It was now or never.

Alex pushed open the door and listened as it squeaked into the night. She allowed no time for her mind to flash back to the night her family was killed. No time for her brain to conjure up memories of the gunshots or the fear. No time for those memories to convince her to turn around and run, run, run back to Donna and Garrett's house. Instead, she walked inside and closed the door.

The flashlight on her cell phone was all that fought against the blackness. The smell—although stale with mold and dormancy—reminded her of her old life. Through the damp odor of wood damage and the musty summer heat that had penetrated the walls, she smelled her mother and her father and her brother. Forcing herself forward, she walked through the kitchen and into the front foyer. The soft glow of the moon cast tarnished shadows of the window grids onto the floor. She paused at the spot where she remembered the shotgun lying. She looked up to the second story hallway that overlooked the foyer, and remembered staring through the spindles as she hid behind the grandfather clock. After a deep breath, she started up the steps. On each of her previous attempts, the image of the staircase had been what stopped her from entering the house because she knew that climbing the stairs would bring her to the exact location where it all had happened.

She pushed on and took the steps one at a time, closing her eyes as she came to the top. She was careful to keep the glow of her cell phone away from the master bedroom to her right. Alex had no interest in going near that room, or catching even a glimpse of the red-stained hardwood outside of it. She turned quickly at the landing and headed down the hallway toward her old bedroom, but she stopped nearly as soon as she started. In front of her, at the end of the hall, was the grandfather clock that had saved her life. It glowed eerily under the spell of her cell phone's flashlight, reflecting a splinter of light back at her that came and went, came and went, came and went. It was then that Alex realized the clock was still ticking. In this house void of electricity and life, the grandfather clock was alive and well. She walked closer until she could hear the subtle click of the clock's inner workings. The only explanation was that the vagrants who frequently trespassed had wound the clock.

She admired the clock for another second or two before raising her cell phone to the ceiling. She found a cord hanging above her head, reached up and pulled on it, unlocking the stairway to the attic. She fumbled with the sliding staircase and then pointed her cell phone into the dark hole in the ceiling before she started her ascent. Once she crested the opening and her torso was in the attic, a different smell struck her. It was another flavor of must and mold, and it brought back a whole other set of memories. This smell reminded her of Christmas. Every year, her parents lowered this door in the ceiling and, one by one, the Quinlans climbed into the attic to retrieve boxes and boxes of decorations.

Now, Alex was not after ornaments or knickknacks. On this night she was after something else. She shined her light past the decorations and into the corner of the attic. There she found boxes that she and Raymond had stashed years earlier. For as long as her brother had lived he had dreamed of being a Major League Baseball player. It was the only way Alex remembered him—in a baseball cap and dirty uniform. Alex had blocked those memories for the past year or so. It was too difficult to remember Raymond in his uniform and on the baseball diamond because those memories brought with them terrible bouts of guilt and remorse. Someday she hoped to be able to allow those images of her brother to flow freely through her mind. She missed him badly, and a deep ache came to her heart every time she pushed Raymond from her thoughts. But Raymond was the reason she had come to her old house.

From the time he was a little kid Raymond had collected baseball cards. Out of all the things Alex had left behind, for some reason she could not allow Raymond's baseball card collection to fall into the hands of groupies who would eventually discover the attic, raid everything it held, and pawn it all on the dark web as relics belonging to the Quinlan crew who was mowed down by the oldest Quinlan child.

She found the box of baseball cards in the corner and pulled it out of the shadows. It was a balancing act to lug the box down the attic stairs. When she made it, she slid the staircase back into place and pushed the attic door closed. The house fell quiet again but for the soft ticking of the grandfather clock. Before she left, Alex reached to the top of the clock where the crank was kept. She stuck it into the fitting on the side and spun it several times, raising the weights until they were as high as they could go. It wouldn't last a lifetime, but the clock would at least be ticking when Alex landed in London the following day.

It was only later that night, as she waited for the hours to pass, unable to sleep as she prepared for the flight back to England, that she discovered the box she had taken from the attic was not filled with her brother's baseball card collection, but foreign bank statements instead. They became the first clue in figuring out who had killed her family.

CHAPTER 9

Zürich, Switzerland
Wednesday, September 30, 2015
9:35 a.m.

The morning after the train deposited her in Switzerland, Alex sat in a Zürich café, sipped espresso, and watched the bank across the street. She checked her phone. She had twenty-five minutes until her appointment and used twenty of them finishing her coffee and settling her nerves. At five minutes to the hour, she gathered the papers she had spent the morning reading, organized them in a leather-bound folder, and slipped them into her rucksack before walking across the street.

Despite that she had dressed in her nicest outfit—long skirt, silk blouse, and a blazer she hadn't worn since the trial—Alex immediately felt out of place when she entered the bank. The eyes of every bank employee focused on her as she stepped into the sprawling lobby. For the past year in Cambridge, she was used to blending in and being invisible. But a twenty-year-old kid walking into this type of bank was uncommon. She was sure the typical client was middle-aged and carried an important title behind their name.

The woman behind the enormous reception counter—a block of marble that shined brightly—hesitated a moment before she asked, "Can I help you?"

"Alex Quinlan. I have an appointment with Samuel McEwen."

The woman checked the ledger with a confused expression. Surely there was some mistake, Alex could sense the woman's inner thoughts protesting. But after the woman pulled up the schedule of appointments and checked Alex's ID, she offered a hesitant smile. "Have a seat. Mr. McEwen will be right with you."

Alex sat on a stiff couch that looked like it belonged in a stuffy mansion and not in the middle of a bank. But this bank was like no other she'd seen, and she'd seen plenty over the last year as she'd met with money managers and financial advisors and attorneys who'd told her how to handle the fortune that came her way after the trial. But none of those American banks were like this one. Everything here was marble and granite that shined from the brilliant sunlight that rained down through vaulted glass from three stories above. This was a place where the wealthy stashed their treasure, and Alex guessed the couch and the granite and the marble and the dazzling sunlight were all carefully crafted to make the rich feel rich.

Her parents had not been wealthy. At least, not openly. They lived in a modest home, and Alex and her brother had attended public school. Family vacations were never more extravagant than a week in Florida. Although her parents were business owners, theirs was a two-man tax and accounting firm—Dennis and Helen Quinlan were the accountants, the managers, and the janitors. So how was it, Alex wondered since that hot night in August just a month earlier, that she had found a box in the attic stuffed with statements for an account from this Zürich bank worth $5 million? She was convinced the answer to that question would lead to her family's killer.

She waited five minutes until a young man in a suit and squarely knotted tie approached her. He couldn't have been much older than she, Alex thought as she looked him up and down.

"Ms. Quinlan?" the young man said, extending his hand. "Drew Estes. I'm Mr. McEwen's assistant. He'll be with you in a moment. If you come with me, I'll show you to his office."

After more than a year in Cambridge, Alex had become proficient at breaking through dialects and accents to understand the English underneath. But she had learned during this trip across Europe that the English dialects varied, not just from country to country, but throughout different regions of each country. Here in Switzerland, English-speaking Swiss carried heavy tones of either French or German. Drew Estes's accent was thick German with British undertones, which took Alex a moment to decipher.

"Thank you," Alex said, standing and shaking his hand.

As he held her hand, Alex noticed Drew Estes stare at her for a second too long before squinting his eyes and tilting his head.

"Have we met before?" he asked.

"No," Alex said.

"Are you sure? You look familiar."

Alex smiled. "I'm sure. This is my first time in Switzerland."

It had happened a few times in the streets of Cambridge, and once or twice on campus. Someone she met asked if they knew her from some other place or time. Not even an ocean could fully separate Alex from infamy. But as the months passed and her freshman year concluded, her notoriety faded and no one looked twice at her again. Until now. Until Drew Estes stared at Alex with a probing glare that made her skin crawl.

"How long did you say Mr. McEwen would be?" Alex finally asked.

"Oh," Drew said. "I'm sorry. I'm staring at you like I have my ass in hat. Not long. He's finishing a meeting. I'll show you to his office."

A minute later, the young man showed Alex into an elaborate office.

"Can I get you anything?" he asked from the doorway. "Coffee or water?"

"No thanks," Alex said.

"Thank you, Drew," a man said as he walked into the office. "I'm Samuel McEwen. We spoke on the phone."

Alex smiled and shook his hand, relieved to be away from the attention of Drew Estes.

"Alex Quinlan."

McEwen smiled and shook his head. "I'm sorry. I was expecting someone older."

"Nope. Just me."

"Right, then. Have a seat."

McEwen motioned to a chair in front of his desk.

"Thanks, Drew. I'll call if I need anything."

Drew Estes smiled from the doorway. Alex felt his stare linger for another moment before he left. Samuel McEwen sat behind his desk and tapped the keyboard.

"So you're interested in making a transfer of funds from an American bank into ours, is that correct?"

"Yes," Alex said.

McEwen continued to read from the screen. "I see you've already completed the paperwork. We'll have just a few more documents today. And what is the amount of the transfer?"

"One million dollars," Alex said.

McEwen looked up from his computer, paused a moment, and then nodded. Alex could sense his desire to ask how a twenty-year-old kid had gotten her hands on a million bucks. He likely suspected that she was a snot-nosed trust fund baby, and Alex wished that were the case. The media scrutiny in America, which had reached fever pitch *during* her trial against the state of Virginia, had transitioned into a buzzing fervor when the trial concluded with a verdict that awarded Alex $16 million in damages, reduced by the judge to just over eight. Other than purchasing her family's home out of foreclosure, and normal living expenses, Alex hadn't touched any of the money. Today would be the first time she'd put any of it to use. Today, she would use it for leverage.

"Very well," McEwen said. "Do you have the paperwork and information from the American institution?"

Alex pulled the folder from her backpack and handed over the information. McEwen scanned the page quickly.

"I'll need to verify this. Do you have a photo ID?"

Alex handed over her ID card.

"This will take a few minutes."

"Sure," Alex said.

Samuel McEwen left his office and disappeared for fifteen minutes. When he returned, he carried a jubilant smile. It was funny what money could do.

"Everything checks out," he said. "We should be able to make the transfer without incident and have everything wrapped up this morning."

Alex spent the next hour filling out forms and signing her name at the bottom of a dozen documents. When they finished, she was the proud new owner of a Swiss bank account at the Sparhafen Bank in Zürich, where one million US dollars now resided, transferred from a brokerage account in America.

Samuel McEwen promised to keep in touch and help Alex with any further banking needs.

"Just let me know if there is anything else I can do for you," he said.

"There is, actually," Alex said, now that she had the man's attention. Now that he took her seriously.

McEwen offered a warm smile. "Of course."

From her folder Alex removed a piece of paper.

"This is an old statement from your bank," Alex said, handing the page across the desk. "I found it in my father's belongings and wanted to know if you could give me any information about the account."

McEwen took the page and analyzed it. After a moment of study, he spoke while still scanning the information.

"This is a numbered account. No formal name is attached to it."

"Yes," Alex said. "I figured that much out. But my father's accounting firm is listed as the custodian. I'm looking for information about the account owner and why my parents' firm was listed as a curator."

"I can't offer information about private accounts, Ms. Quinlan. Perhaps you should ask your father."

"He's dead."

The bluntness caught McEwen off guard. "Oh, I'm terribly sorry."

"Here's the thing," Alex said. "Both my parents have passed. Everything they had now belongs to me, according to their will." Alex slid her parents' last will and testament across the desk.

"You'll see that I'm listed as the sole beneficiary. So when I found this bank statement in my father's belongings, I figured I'd try to get to the bottom of it. As in, does this account still exist?"

"Ms. Quinlan, I'm not able to provide information on this account without proper documentation proving what you're telling me is true. And even then, there would be many legal hoops to jump through."

"I'm just trying to figure out if the account still exists. And if it does, who opened it. I have more money I need to invest, and if you could do me this favor, I'd consider your bank for my other investments."

"I see," McEwen said. "I'm honored to serve you in any way I can." He then added, handing the pages back to her, "Unfortunately, I'm not able to help with this. There are laws that prohibit me from doing what you're asking, and I'm afraid I'd be no use to you, or any of my other clients, if I lost my license."

Alex removed a different sheet of paper from the folder and slid it across the desk. "I have another million dollars I'd be willing to move to your bank if you could help me with this. I just need a name."

"Ms. Quinlan, I'm terribly sorry. I'm not at liberty to give you information about a numbered account without proper documentation proving the account belongs to you. This will be the case no matter how much money you invest with us."

Alex stood and smiled. The old version of herself may have stewed and protested at this obstacle in her path. The new Alex would simply find another way around it. If the last two years had taught her anything, it was that sitting on the sidelines, frozen with inaction, brought nothing good to her life.

"Thank you for your time," she said before leaving.

CHAPTER 10

Zürich, Switzerland
Wednesday, September 30, 2015
11:30 a.m.

Drew Estes watched from his cubicle as the girl walked out of the bank. He had recognized her immediately. It was the eyes that gave her away. He and his girlfriend had followed the story of Alexandra Quinlan closely. The previous year they had even driven past the infamous house in America where Empty Eyes had killed her family. Holidaying in the States, Drew and his girlfriend had taken two weeks to tour New York City and Washington, D.C. They finished the trip by spending a week hiking the Appalachian Trail. True-crime fanatics, neither Drew nor his girlfriend could pass up the opportunity to see the infamous house in McIntosh, Virginia, where Alexandra Quinlan had mowed down her family.

Now, a year later, Empty Eyes herself had walked into the bank in Switzerland where Drew temped. An hour earlier, he had assisted Mr. McEwen in pulling all the forms and running the checks necessary to establish a new account for Alex Quinlan in the amount of one million US dollars. The fortune Empty Eyes had gotten away with—at least a small fraction of it—was now parked in an account in the bank where Drew Estes worked. It was almost too surreal to believe. Drew had followed the Alexandra Quinlan case forward and backward, and paid close attention to the court case when she sued the police and the state prosecutor's office. Drew knew she had gotten away with much more than a million dollars, and the world had frantically searched for her ever since. Somehow, miraculously, Drew Estes had found her.

After helping Mr. McEwen complete his morning, Drew took his lunch break. He walked outside and lit a cigarette, which hung from his lips as he swiped his cell phone.

"Hey, babe," he said when his girlfriend answered. "You'll never believe who just walked into the bank this morning."

The call lasted five minutes. By the time his cigarette burned to the filter, Drew Estes had hatched his plan.

CHAPTER 11

Zürich, Switzerland
Wednesday, September 30, 2015
9:41 p.m.

Alex sat at the corner of the bar and sipped tonic water with lime. The language barrier had made it difficult to convince the bartender to fill her glass with only ice and tonic water, without adding gin or vodka. She would turn twenty-one in a short few months, making her of legal drinking age in the States. Here in Europe, she'd been free to purchase and consume alcohol since she first stepped foot on campus. But neither alcohol nor drugs had ever appealed to her. Probably because in high school, where many kids start to dabble in such things, her time had been cut short, and the friends with whom Alex might have done the dabbling had abandoned 'her after she was sent to juvenile detention. And despite the acceleration to independence the last two years had brought, deep inside she was still the girl whose mother would kill her if she smoked a joint or considered swallowing any of the many pills she watched fellow students ingest during her first year of higher education.

There was another reason, too, that Alex steered clear of alcohol. She could see a clear path where the numbing effects of booze could take away at least some of her angst and guilt. Perhaps that path would be easier than the one she had chosen. But the easy path led only to self-pity, not to answers or enlightenment—a place she was determined to find.

She stirred her drink and thought back on her day. Her attempt to discover the name of the person behind the numbered account her parents had presided over had failed. Alex was convinced it was the key to unlocking the rest of the mysteries about that night. All the unknowns swirled through her thoughts now, with the same two rising to the surface as they always did: the photos left on her parents' bed the night they were killed, and the fingerprint discovered on her bedroom window.

Alex had learned of the photos only during her defamation case when Garrett presented them as further evidence of how badly mismanaged the investigation had been. At best, Garrett had argued, the McIntosh police had dismissed the photos as immaterial. More likely, though, the district attorney had attempted to suppress their presence because they did not fit into the narrative that Alex had been the one who killed her parents.

The pictures had always been a baffling piece of an already complex puzzle. But since discovering the foreign bank statements hidden in the attic, Alex had created a barely tangible theory that linked the photos to the lone fingerprint found on her bedroom window. Being present inside the home the night her family was killed had provided Alex with certain irrefutable truths about that night. One of them was that the shooter had entered her bedroom and pushed her window fully open. It didn't take much to recall the sound of the window squeaking as she hid behind the grandfather clock. So the lone fingerprint sequestered from the windowpane undoubtedly belonged to the shooter. Neither the McIntosh Police Department nor Garrett Lancaster, during his own quest to prove Alex's innocence, had been able to match the fingerprint to its owner. Garrett tapped his sources and had the print run through the Integrated Automated Fingerprint Identification System inside the FBI. No hits. But ever since stumbling over the bank documents in her attic, Alex had begun to form a theory that perhaps the lone fingerprint sequestered from her bedroom window belonged to the person who owned the account. And perhaps discovering the identity of this man would shed light on the women in the photos.

Her visit to Sparhafen Bank, however, had failed badly. The dead end was frustrating by itself, without considering the other problem it created. The million dollars she transferred had surely sounded alarm bells back home. Before turning over the $8 million awarded to her in the verdict, the judge had put restrictions in place. The most obstructive was that a certified financial advisor had to look after the money and offer guidance until Alex turned the arbitrary age of twenty-seven. Then, the money was hers to invest, spend, or squander as she wished. Until that point, however, every dime she touched left a trail that found its way to Garrett Lancaster's desk.

Garrett had always given Alex a wide berth, and despite him being a major part of her life, she never dealt with him directly on money matters. Instead, a financial advisor signed off on her spending. But despite this middleman arrangement, Alex was certain Garrett saw every dime she spent. It might take a little time to notice the transfer of a million dollars to a Swiss bank. It could be a day or a week. But eventually, her financial guy would see the transfer and pick up the phone to call Garrett, who would then pick up the phone to call Alex. This, unfortunately, was her life.

Alex withdrew a modest amount each month for living expenses, all of which came from interest. Garrett was adamant that Alex never touch the principle, but live only off interest the lump sum generated. As a twenty-year-old who owned nothing—other than a vacant single-family home in McIntosh, Virginia—living off interest was not difficult. Moving a million dollars to a bank in Zürich was bound to raise red flags back home.

She had a contingent plan prepared for when Garrett's phone call came. Alex had written out her response and was still committing each detail to memory. The bottom line was that the money was hers, no matter what the judge told her or however many strings were attached to it, and she could do with it what she pleased. She wanted to open a Swiss bank account, she would tell Garrett, for tax purposes. Alex knew nothing about international tax laws other than what she had quickly researched online as she'd hatched her plan. But it was enough, she hoped, to sound convincing when Garrett called. She would ramble on about her reasoning, circuitously explaining her thought process, and would even go so far as to apologize for having the gall to touch her own money. What she would not do, however, was tell Garrett the truth: that she had moved a million dollars to the bank in Zürich because she hoped doing so would get her closer to the truth about what happened to her family. That quest was hers, and hers alone.

She took another sip of tonic water, opened her phone, and scrolled through the train schedules for the following day.

–

At the other end of the bar, a couple sat in a booth. Their focus shifted from Alex to the man's phone and continued to go back and forth. Finally, Drew Estes zoomed in on the picture of Alexandra Quinlan. He smiled at his girlfriend as they continued to look from the phone to the girl at the bar.

"It's her," Drew said. "I can't believe it, but it's her."

Laverne Parker nodded. "Fucking right it's her. She ditched the glasses and cut her hair, but look at those eyes. You can't miss 'em. How much did she deposit?"

"A million US. I saw it on my boss's computer and helped create the paperwork."

"A million bucks," Verne said, her expression contemptuous as she stared across the bar. "Alexandra Quinlan, before our very eyes."

Verne smiled to reveal crooked teeth as she broke into a whispered singsong.

"We know who you are."

She placed the phone on the table. Alex's image remained on the screen.

"They gave her, like, ten mil," Verne said as she continued to stare at Alex. "Kill your family, pretend you're a scared little twat, and disappear with a fortune."

Verne went back to the singsong voice.

"You tried to disappear, but we know where you are."

CHAPTER 12

Cambridge, England
Friday, October 2, 2015
2:15 p.m.

The idea for the board came to Alex after a particularly lucid dream about the night her family was killed. Her dreams had become so vivid since escaping the circus of her old life in the United States that Alex had taken to writing down every detail she could remember about them as soon as she woke. She purchased a corkboard from a craft store—a four-foot-by-four-foot square—and hung it on the kitchen wall to collect her thoughts. Class schedules and dates of upcoming midterm exams should have been pegged to it. Photos, too, of family and friends. Instead, Alex pinned index cards around the board that contained every detail she could remember about the night her family was killed, in addition to new facts she'd uncovered in her yearlong pursuit for answers. The most recent addition to the board was a photo of the Sparhafen Bank in Zürich, next to which was one of the bank statements she'd found in the attic.

On the far left-hand side of the board was an index card with the words *Home Invasion* written across it and then X'd out by a red Sharpie. The home invasion theory, which was the current position taken by the McIntosh PD, was subterfuge. The department needed to blame the murders on someone after their lead suspect had been acquitted, so they settled on burglary gone bad. It was a lazy and uninspired theory and had been proven false a thousand times over. A home invasion for the purpose of burglary came with a motive to steal. But nothing was missing from the Quinlan home. Plus, the McIntosh PD's explanation of events did not match what Alex knew. She had been watching from her bedroom when her brother was killed, and had been hiding behind the grandfather clock when the killer entered Alex's room looking for the last remaining member of the Quinlan family. The killer had not been startled by Alex's father, as was suggested by the incompetent detectives who attempted to explain the scene. For that to be the case, her dad would have had to stumble upon the killer. That her father had been shot while lying in bed, under the covers and likely sound asleep, proved the McIntosh Police Department's official line not only impossible, but stunningly incompetent.

The middle of the board held the pictures found on her parents' bed of three women and an image of the fingerprint lifted from her bedroom window. On the far right-hand side of the board was a detailed timeline of that day. It included every detail Alex remembered from nearly every minute of that late afternoon and evening, starting with the moment she arrived home from school and proceeding to her going to bed for the night, and ultimately being woken by the gunshot. The details were painstakingly specific, including such particulars as the exact physics chapter she studied that night for homework— Newton's first law of motion, which Alex had written on an index card: *An object at rest stays at rest unless acted upon by an unbalanced force.* It was a mantra that ran through her thoughts at odd times during the past two years. The board's location in the kitchen, next to where Alex hung her jacket each day, ensured that her thoughts never drifted far from that fateful night.

-

The day after Alex returned from Zürich, she looked at the board before grabbing her coat on the way out of her apartment and headed to campus. The ruse started halfway through freshman year when Alex returned to the States to spend

Christmas break with the Lancasters. By then Alex knew that college in Europe, or anywhere else for that matter, was not for her. Yet, she couldn't bring herself to tell Donna and Garrett. The lie continued through the second semester of her freshman year and persisted over the past summer. Alex wasn't sure how long she would lie about college. Still technically enrolled, she had yet to step foot in a classroom during her second year. At some point she'd come clean to Donna and Garrett, if for no other reason than it would start an argument. Free from the reins of authority at the ripe age of eighteen, Alex now longed for someone to tell her what to do. She wanted someone to disobey. She craved an argument with someone who wanted the best for her. An argument would mean there was someone watching out for her, caring about where her decisions took her and what impact they had on her life.

This desire for affection was the only reason Alex stepped foot on campus each week. Donna and Garrett sent one letter a week, always to her university address. Perhaps this was their way of making sure Alex was at least occasionally on campus. The only reason she still had an active mailbox at the university was because the tuition had been paid in full. Alex Quinlan existed on the ledger of Cambridge University, and her account was in good standing. No one on campus would pay her any mind until the next tuition bill came due, or until midterms revealed not just failing grades, but no recorded grades at all. That impending doom was like a far-off asteroid. At first, it was nothing more than a speck in the sky too far away to cause much angst. But now, a month into her second year, Alex was walking in the shadow of that approaching asteroid. As long as she had answers to look for and clues to follow, however, she could convince herself to ignore it.

Alex strolled through campus, crossing a bridge that arched over the stream that wound through the grounds, nostalgic for what this era of her life might look like had she been able to lead a normal existence. When she reached the registrar's office, Alex walked inside and headed to a wall of mailboxes. She inserted her key and removed a small stack of envelopes, then shuffled through them looking for Donna and Garrett's letter.

"Weren't you in my criminology class last year?" the girl next to her asked.

The accent was heavy and mixed, and Alex didn't immediately recognize it. Students came to Cambridge from across all of Europe, and there were too many dialects and accents to keep track of. Alex looked up from sorting her mail. The girl had a set of keys in her hands and was preparing to open her mailbox. Alex studied the girl and tried to place the face but was certain she'd never seen her before. Although Alex had enrolled in criminology the first semester of freshman year and had occasionally attended the class, so it was entirely possible that Alex had, indeed, crossed paths with this girl.

"Uh, yeah, I think so," Alex said.

"Professor Mackity?"

Alex nodded. That might have been the name of the professor who taught the class, but she couldn't remember. "Yeah."

The girl smiled. "I thought I recognized you. I'm Laverne."

"Alex."

"Did you do okay?"

Alex paused a moment. "With what?"

"Criminology. Mackity can be a real pain in the ass. I got out with a C and was lucky to get that."

Alex had passed with a D.

"Me too. I got a C."

"Ah, cream of the crop you and I are. You know what they call C students after four years of school?"

Alex waited.

"University graduates."

Alex forced a smile. "Right."

"Hey," Laverne said, "I'm meeting some mates tonight for a drink. You want to join us?"

"Oh." Alex smiled and shook her head. "I can't tonight. I've got some, uh, studying to do."

"On a Friday night? You're a committed one, aren't you?"

Alex closed her eyes at the terrible lie she'd been caught in.

"Ah, the hell with it," Alex said. "Sure. I can grab a drink. Where and when?"

The girl smiled. "The Old Ticket Office at eight. It'll just be me and a couple girlfriends. I could swing by and we could go together. That way you're not walking into the pub with your ass in hat."

The idiom pinged some vague memory in Alex's mind. Was it a warning or just confusion? Whichever, it was too faint to make more than a ripple when it splashed into her subconscious.

"Where are you from?" Laverne asked. "I mean, America, obviously. But what part?"

Alex paused, fighting the colliding thoughts as her mind worked to figure out what had bothered her a moment before. She had always avoided talking about herself to other students.

"You all right there, mate?" Laverne asked.

"Uh, Chicago."

"Really? The blowing city, isn't it called?"

"The *windy* city."

"That's it." Laverne shrugged. "I don't have any mates from the States. You'll be my first."

Alex smiled. She hadn't had a friend for quite some time.

"Where do you live?" Laverne asked. "I'll stop over and pick you up on my way. We'll be best mates for the night."

As if Alex were helpless to stop it, her address slipped from her lips while Laverne punched it into her phone.

"About a quarter to eight?" Laverne asked.

Alex swallowed hard and forced a smile. "Sounds good."

CHAPTER 13

Cambridge, England
Friday, October 2, 2015
7:45 p.m.

There was a knock on her door, just as promised, at a quarter to eight. Throughout the afternoon Alex had gone through wild mood swings about her absurd acceptance of the mailbox girl's invitation. She was confused as to why she had so willingly offered up her address rather than just agreeing to meet at the bar. The confusion had morphed into regret. Regret had then become desperation as she'd realized that giving Laverne her address meant there was no way out of the situation. They hadn't even exchanged phone numbers, which would have allowed Alex to cancel through a text message. She was now left with two options: One, hide in her flat and refuse to answer the door. Or, two, answer the door and act like a normal college student who goes out with friends. If the night grew boring, Alex could make a quiet exit and escape back to her flat without rousing anyone's feathers. For a split second she even considered that meeting new people could be fun, and having someone to call a friend would be a good thing, not something to run from.

She walked to the door, took a deep breath, and opened it. Laverne stood in the hallway. A guy stood next to her.

"There she is!" Laverne said in a jovial voice. "Thought you stood me up there for a second."

Alex smiled and swallowed hard. "No, no. I was just getting ready. Were you knocking long? I must not have heard you."

Without invitation, Laverne walked into the flat. "No worries, mate. This is Drew. You guys have met."

It took Alex a second to place him before she remembered Samuel McEwen's assistant from her meeting at the bank. Drew was the guy who had greeted her in the lobby of the Sparhafen Bank in Zürich. Her first question was what the hell he was doing in Cambridge. Her second was why he was in her flat. Her third, and final, was how she could have been so stupid to give this girl her address.

Drew closed the door and smiled at her, twisting the dead-bolt into place and sending Alex's stomach into a free fall.

"Hi, Alexandra," Drew said, his smile stretching farther across his face. "That would be Alexandra Quinlan, of McIntosh, Virginia."

The mention of her hometown started the production of acid that burned the bottom of her esophagus and began a quick march up her sternum. Alex swallowed again to dispel the burn.

"Not Chicago, mate," Laverne said. "The *windy* city? That's the best you could come up with?"

Laverne walked deeper into the flat, looking around as if she were shopping in a department store. She picked up a figurine that sat on the table by the couch, examined it for a moment before placing it back down. In the living room, she pulled the curtains aside and looked down onto the street.

"I recognized you straight away," Drew said, still standing in front of the bolted door. "The hair threw me off at first, but then I saw your eyes. No one can miss those eyes."

"Those empty fucking eyes will give you away every time," Laverne said, turning from the front window and walking toward her.

Alex didn't move. She was frozen in place, stiff with fear so powerful she had to squeeze her thighs together to stop her bladder from emptying. In a matter of seconds she had gone from worrying about spending a night out with girls she didn't know to suddenly being locked inside her flat with two thugs, one on each side of her.

Laverne smiled, revealing terribly crooked teeth. "Empty Eyes, who disappeared into thin air. But we found you, didn't we?"

Drew walked from the door and held his phone out for Alex to see. She stared at a picture of herself. It was the image most commonly used in news stories about her, taken from one of her social media accounts that she had long ago deleted.

"Your hair is shorter and you're not wearing glasses. But it's you. I can't fucking believe it," Drew said.

Suddenly, Laverne's Swiss-German accent made sense. And so did the idiom that had given Alex pause when she spoke with this girl in the mailroom. *Ass in hat.* Drew had used the same saying at the bank.

"You deposited a million dollars in the bank in Zürich on Wednesday," Drew said. "Here's the deal. Verne and I want a cut, or we're going to out you to the whole world. You think you're safe just because you ran to England to attend university? You're gonna give us some of that money you got away with, or we're gonna post everything we know about you on every true-crime site we can find. We'll tip the media off, too. If you think the American tabloids are bad, wait 'til you see what we can do over here."

A sudden flash of light blinded her and Alex held up her hand to shield her eyes. Laverne had snapped a photo with her phone.

"Oh, shit!" Laverne said, laughing as she stared at her phone. "It looks just like the picture of her coming out of the house the night she shot her family."

Drew looked at the photo and cackled. "Holy Christ, it does. Like a fuckin' ghost come back from the dead."

Laverne looked at Alex. "I could upload this photo right now and within a day social media would blow up. The tabloids would come next, and Empty Eyes would be back in the news. Here, America, the whole fucking world."

"I think you're assuming I'm more popular than I am," Alex said.

"Not popular, mate. Infamous. And I don't *think*. I *know*. I follow this stuff, and people would go batshit to learn that Empty Eyes washed up in a little university town in England. In a day or two, paparazzi would line the sidewalk outside this flat, because I'd post your address everywhere I could."

"How much?" Alex asked.

The question seemed to stun them. Drew and Laverne glanced at each other. Alex sensed their surprise at having gotten this far so quickly. Negotiations were likely meant to happen later in the night after they'd worked her over a bit with either more threats or actual violence. Alex wasn't going to allow the night to go on longer than necessary. She was looking to end it as soon as possible, and she knew exactly how to get it done. But in order to do so, she needed to get to her bedroom. To her closet, and to the box that sat on the top shelf.

"How much?" Alex asked again.

Drew and Laverne spoke in fast German. A quick exchange that sounded like an argument.

Now it was Alex who laughed. "Amateurs," she said, stepping closer to them. "You're like a couple of freshmen at the senior prom. You two followed me all the way from Switzerland and probably had this planned for the better part of two days. Yet, now that you're here in front of me, you don't even have a number?"

Alex walked deeper into the apartment, closer to her bedroom.

"You probably didn't think you'd get this far, and now that you have you don't know what to do with yourselves. I should just call the police."

Alex pulled her cell phone from her pocket and swiped it open. Drew started toward her, but Laverne's hand moved to his shoulder.

"No," Laverne said. "Let her. Go ahead. Call the cops."

There was a long gap of silence.

"Go on." Laverne pointed at Alex's phone. "Call them. What're you going to tell them? That you agreed to have drinks with me and that I came to pick you up?"

"No, that you followed me across the continent to blackmail me."

Laverne showed her crooked teeth again. "Blackmail you for what? That's what the coppers would ask. And what would you tell them?"

There was another long, bloated stretch of silence.

"Go on," Laverne said. "Think it through. What would you tell them? You'd have to tell them the truth. You'd have to tell them who you are. And if you thought *we* could out you in a hurry, go ahead and tell the authorities who you are. Your world would blow up in a fast goddamn minute."

"A goddamn *minute*!" Drew piled on.

More silence.

Alex slipped her phone back in her pocket. "Fine. Back to my original question. How much?"

"Half a million," Laverne said.

"You're insane. I don't have that much money."

"Bull*shit*," Drew said. "You just parked a million dollars in the bank. I saw it with my own two eyes. I helped McEwen with the paperwork."

"Sure," Alex said. "And you want me to take half of it out to pay you two dimwits? As if that won't sound any alarms."

"They gave you twenty million," Laverne said. "All for crying on the witness stand and pretending you weren't the one who pulled the trigger. Half a million is nothing."

The amount of Alex's settlement had been greatly exaggerated in the press. Some got the number right—eight million. Most got it wrong, or purposely inflated it. The shadier the outlet, the more ludicrous the number. One tabloid had claimed that Alex had disappeared with a hundred million dollars. Who knew what these two psychopaths thought they could take her for. The answer was zero, but Alex hadn't told them yet.

"You either get us the money or we go straight to the press. We'll tell the world that Empty Eyes herself is enrolled at the University of Cambridge," Laverne said. "We'll dox you. We'll post your address everywhere. The press, the websites, social media. We'll do a goddamn publicity tour with what we know."

"You're not listening to me," Alex said. "I can't just withdraw half a million dollars from a bank a couple of days after I deposited it there."

"Leave the money you put into my bank alone," Drew said. "Take it from somewhere else. From wherever the rest of it is."

"And you think, what? I can get it to you tonight? You think it's under my mattress? You two are stupider than you look."

"No, not tonight," Drew said. "Tomorrow. By five o'clock or we go public with your identity."

"For someone who works in finance, you don't have much of a grasp on how banking works. I can't produce half a million dollars in twenty-four hours. And all in cash? You idiots have been watching too many caper movies."

"Oh, you're going to do it," Laverne said. "Trust me, mate. You don't want us to get mad."

Alex took a deep breath as if she were working out the possibilities. "To get my hands on that much money I need a week, at least."

Laverne and Drew glanced at each other and exchanged another barrage of German.

"We'll give you until Monday," Laverne said.

"It's Friday night, genius," Alex said. "I won't even be able to get in touch with anyone until Monday morning. I need a week if you want me to do this the right way."

"What's that mean?" Drew asked. "The right way."

"It means in a way that neither you nor I get caught. You want half a million dollars and think it's as easy as going to an ATM. It's not. And the last thing I need is you two getting stopped with a suitcase full of cash on your way back to Switzerland. Figuring out a way for you to commit the perfect crime is actually in my best interest. I need a week, and I'm not giving you half a million dollars. I'll give you two-fifty."

"Five hundred thousand," Drew said.

"Two-fifty or you can call anyone you want and post my picture everywhere. I don't really give a shit."

"Yeah you do," Laverne said, a snaggletooth protruding from her upper lip. "Or you wouldn't be negotiating. Four."

"Three," Alex countered.

"Three-fifty."

Alex paused. "Fine. But I need a week."

"We don't have a week," Laverne said. "We spent everything we had tracking you here. We need money now."

Alex rolled her eyes. "How about this. I'll give you some cash tonight to hold you over, and you give me a full week to get the rest."

"How much?"

"I've got about a thousand pounds in my bedroom. I could go to the ATM and get a little more. That should tide you over. I'll do my thing next week, and have the three-fifty by Friday."

Another glance and more short remarks in German.

"Fine, yeah," Drew said. "But we're staying here until you get it done."

"Staying at my flat?"

"Damn straight," Laverne said.

"Where do you think I'm going?"

"You disappeared once before. You could do it again. We're staying. Now go get the money for us before Drew gets angry."

Alex slowly nodded as if she were out of options. The truth was that she had plenty; she was just deciding which was best.

"Fine," she finally said. "We'll be roommates for a week."

Alex walked to her bedroom, trying hard to look defeated. She slowed her pace when all she wanted to do was run. Once in her room and out of their sight, she headed straight for the closet. It had been Garrett's idea for Alex to learn to shoot a handgun before she headed off to college. With her previous experience hunting pheasant and her proficiency with a 12-gauge, the learning curve was short. After a month of instruction and just a few hours at the range, Alex was more proficient at shooting targets with a 9-millimeter automatic than she had ever been shooting pheasants with a 12-gauge shotgun. But it wasn't learning to shoot and handle the gun that was the problem. Obtaining one in the United Kingdom was. In fact, it was impossible to do legally. But Garrett had been adamant that Alex possess a way to defend herself, and he had flexed his considerable strength to make it happen. A week after she arrived in England and settled into her Cambridge flat, a man knocked on her door. Short and stocky, with a face pocked by acne scars, the man had barely spoken the day he showed up at Alex's flat.

"If you're caught with this, you'll go to nick," was all he said before handing Alex the heavy metal box and disappearing down the stairs.

Since that day, the box had sat untouched on the top shelf of her closet. Alex had never been motivated to move the gun to a more accessible location. In her night table drawer, for instance, where it would be instantly available should she need it. The truth was that shortly after the stocky man had delivered it, the gun had rarely found its way into her thoughts after she settled into her new life in Cambridge. So perfect was her escape from the towering shadow of the American version of Alexandra Quinlan that, despite a few times on campus early freshman year when fellow students inquired about possibly knowing Alex from a previous encounter, no one had come close to recognizing her. Fear, therefore, had never been an emotion Alex had had to deal with in her new life in England. But as soon as the crooked-toothed girl walked uninvited into her flat with Drew Estes, fear had gripped her and the gun had charged into her thoughts.

She reached for the box now and noticed her hands were shaking. Alex was happy to have avoided the further precaution of locking the box, since inserting a key would be difficult with her vibrating hands. She opened the latch and lifted the lid, revealing the Smith and Wesson M&P Shield 9-millimeter. It held eight rounds, and Alex knew it was loaded—it was how the gun had arrived. Just as she lifted the gun from the felt in which it was seated, she felt a hand on her shoulder.

"Two thousand. Not a pound less," Laverne said.

Laverne's touch startled her and Alex jumped, turning quickly and discharging the gun at the same time. The blast was deafening and brought her back to the night her family was killed. Her vision shrunk to a pinhole and then disappeared entirely when the sulfurous odor of gunpowder sent her senses spinning off to the night she hid behind the grandfather clock while the same scent permeated her home.

She was unsure how long she'd been blinded, but when her vision returned Alex saw two people. The girl named Laverne lay on the floor in front of her, and Drew Estes stood in the bedroom doorway with wide eyes and an open mouth, his hands raised in surrender. Alex spied him over the barrel of the Smith and Wesson, which, during her momentary blackout, she had pointed directly at him. Both her hands were firmly on the gun, her finger over the trigger, and the tremor nowhere to be found. She adjusted her aim from the middle of Drew's chest to directly over his heart. One more correction brought her aim to just above his left shoulder. She pulled off another round that blinded her senses again and sent her back to the cold January night when her family was killed.

Although some time must have passed, Alex was unaware of it. The next thing she heard, when the ringing in her ears subsided and her vision returned, were sirens. The strange, cartoonish sirens she knew only from the movies. The two-toned sirens of the UK authorities that were so different from those embedded in her mind from a lifetime spent in the States.

Then she heard something else. Something closer. Outside the bedroom, the front door to her flat burst open, the deadbolt Drew Estes had sunk into place splintering the wood that secured it. Then she heard footsteps racing across the flat toward her bedroom.

CHAPTER 14

London, England
Saturday, October 3, 2015
10:05 a.m.

When her muscles finally released their tonic state, Alex sank into the strange bed and fell asleep. Her mind, however, kept churning. The report of the gun returned, and its lingering ring echoed in her mind. Time and space morphed during her fitful sleep and carried her to her family home in McIntosh. This time, though, Alex was the shooter. This time, as Alex hid behind the grandfather clock, the shots that rang through the house came from the gun she was firing, again and again and again. One round after another as footsteps grew louder and the trench coat shadow crept toward the grandfather clock. Then, the face of Laverne Parker peeked around the edge of the clock and smiled at Alex with those crooked teeth. Alex lifted the 9-millimeter and pulled the trigger—*bang, bang, bang.*

"Up you go."

Alex opened her eyes and Laverne Parker's face disappeared. In its place was a heavyset man whose face held acne scars shaped like deep craters.

"Come on, let's move," the man said with a thick but straight British accent.

The remnants of her dream faded and Alex sat up quickly, realizing she had been sleeping in a king-size bed in a room she did not recognize.

"It's been twelve hours," the man said. "I figured that was long enough. We've got work to do."

Alex blinked to bring him into focus. It took just a moment to place him. The stocky man standing over her was the one who had delivered the gun to her flat when she first arrived in Cambridge.

"What's happening?" Alex asked, pushing the covers to the side. She still wore the clothes she had dressed in as she prepared to go out for drinks on Friday night.

"Just a bit of excitement, mate. Like a typical American, you shot up your apartment. I got you out of there just before the coppers showed up. We're good now."

"I don't understand."

"What's not to understand, mate? I hustled you out of your flat so you didn't end up in the nick."

Flashes of the previous night came back to her. The gun. Laverne on the floor. Drew in the doorway, his silhouette visible over the barrel of the 9-millimeter. The blast from the discharge, the splintering of the door, and the heavy footsteps running toward her bedroom.

"Why?" Alex asked. "Why did you help me?"

"Because that's what I get paid to do."

The man's words barely registered. Alex's mind flashed back to the day this man showed up at her flat. "I know you. You're the one who gave me the Smith and Wesson when I got to Cambridge."

"Name's Leo."

Alex paused as she worked to figure things out. "Why were you at my apartment?"

"I told you. I get paid to keep an eye on you."

Alex raised her eyebrows. "You get paid? By whom?"

"Garrett Lancaster. He and I go back a ways. He asked me to look after you. For the past year or so, that's what I've done. I make sure you don't get into too much trouble, then I report back to him."

"You spy on me?"

"I was hired to keep you safe."

"To keep me safe? How, exactly, have you done that?"

"I haven't," Leo said. "Up until last night you hadn't been in any danger. I just kept tabs on you. Other than skipping out on university, there hasn't been much to report. But then you took your little trip to Zürich and allowed those two halfwits to follow you back to Cambridge. Last night was the first time I've had to lift a finger."

"You followed me to Switzerland? And you told Garrett about it?"

"It's what he pays me to do, mate."

"I can't believe he has you following me around."

"It's a damn good thing he does. I noticed the halfwits trailing you when you left the hotel in Zürich. I knew something was wrong when they traced you all the way back to London, and then to Cambridge. When I saw them arrive at your flat, I waited a few minutes. Just as I was about to knock on your door to see what was happening, I heard gunshots. I got you out of there before the coppers showed up."

"How? Tell me what happened. Last night is one big blank spot in my mind."

Alex tried to recall how the night had gone down but could picture only Laverne on the bedroom floor and Drew standing in the doorway with his hands raised. She remembered pulling the trigger and the deafening blast. Her mind shut down after that.

"I used to be police and I still have contacts inside," Leo said. "People I now owe several favors, I might add. I managed to make things go away for now, but that won't last forever."

"What's that mean?"

"It means this isn't America, where gunfire is a normal part of Friday nights. You should have been arrested, but I fixed things. Not permanently, but I put a bandage on things to get you out of there. I made a few calls last night to keep the heat off. For a while, at least. You'll stay here with me until we're sure things have calmed down. No one will bother you here. But you're not my issue at the moment. The other two are."

"Other two?"

"Bonnie and Clyde. The halfwits who tried to shake you down. While you were sleeping I had a nice long chat with them. They told me everything. Now I've gotta figure out what to do with them."

"They're here?"

The beefy man smiled. "I keep forgetting that you've been out for twelve hours. You missed all the fun. Come on, mate. I'll show you my handiwork."

CHAPTER 15

London, England
Saturday, October 3, 2015
10:15 a.m.

Alex followed Leo out of the bedroom and down the hallway. Her mouth was dry and she desperately needed a drink of water.

"Where are we?" Alex asked, feeling oddly at ease with the strange man named Leo.

"My place. South London."

Leo stopped in the hallway and pointed at the closed door. He twisted a handle and pushed it open, then moved to the side so Alex could look past him. In the room, Drew and Laverne were sitting on the floor, both handcuffed to a metal radiator. They looked tired and haggard. Leo pulled the door closed, leaving the image of Drew and Laverne burned in Alex's mind.

"Now I just gotta figure out what to do with them," he said.

Alex attempted to read the big man in front of her. "You can't hurt them. You know that, right?"

Leo laughed. "Says the girl who tried to put a bullet into each of them."

"Says the man who delivered the gun to my flat."

"I was just following orders. The pistol was supposed to make you feel safe. I never figured you'd actually use it. But I should've known better. There's no problem Americans can't shoot their way out of."

"I don't remember much about last night," Alex said. "I was scared out of my mind and I had no idea what those two were going to do to me. But I'm thinking clearly now. No one gets hurt or I'll call Garrett."

"Slow down. No one's getting hurt. And we need to get this situation under better control before we call Mr. Lancaster. I would've let those two go already but I wanted to speak with you first."

"About what?"

"I can pull some strings on my end, and we both know Garrett Lancaster is a powerful man. But even still, if Bonnie and Clyde decide to go to the police, you're in a world of trouble, mate."

"They tried to extort me."

"He said, she said. And you had the gun, so you'd lose that one. So, before this problem gets out of control, we need to figure things out."

The enormity of her predicament began to dawn on her. "So what's the plan?"

Leo rocked his bowling ball head back and forth. "I've got a couple ideas. But no matter what we do, those two will be unknown variables. I run my own private investigation firm now, but I used to be Special Forces before I was police. Our most unpredictable informants were useful idiots who reminded me a lot of those two. They were always a crapshoot. They had the ability to get us any information we wanted, but they were volatile at the same time."

Useful idiots.

Alex's mind was beginning to wake and fire on all cylinders after twelve hours of sleep. An idea came to her. Bonnie and Clyde, as Leo called them, were exactly what she needed.

CHAPTER 16

London, England
Monday, October 5, 2015
11:22 a.m.

The sack over Drew Estes's head was removed with a quick jerk, a door was opened, and he was pushed into the alleyway. The bright sunlight blinded his dark-adapted eyes, which had seen nothing but blackness for the last several hours. Now, he squinted against the sun as the door closed behind him. He looked around to gain his bearings. He was in an alley between two buildings somewhere in London. He walked out to the street and wandered for a while until he found his way to the train station. He hurried to the ticket counter and purchased a seat back to Zürich. The clock was ticking, the beefy man had told him, and Drew had a deadline to beat.

Two hours later, Drew Estes boarded a train to Paris, where he would transfer to another that would take him back to Switzerland. He had three days to return to London and retrieve Laverne. The beefy man had promised not to hurt her as long as Drew made it back in time, and with the information the man had asked Drew to obtain from his place of employment—the Sparhafen Bank of Zürich.

CHAPTER 17

London, England
Thursday, October 8, 2015
4:20 p.m.

"Would you like another soda?" Leo asked.

Laverne shook her head. They sat at a booth in a mostly empty pub. Leo ate pretzels from a bowl and watched a football match on the television behind the bar. He kept an eye on the front door. When the waiter delivered his pizza, Leo dug in.

"Help yourself," he said to Laverne.

"I'm not hungry."

"You should be, you've barely eaten all week."

Ten minutes later, Drew Estes walked into the pub. He hurried over to the booth and sat next to Laverne, kissed her, and took her hand.

"You made it, mate!" Leo said in a jovial voice while holding a half-eaten slice of pizza. "Bonnie wasn't so sure, but I had faith in you. How was the trip back?" he asked before taking a bite.

No answer.

"Was it as fun as your trip here last week? It wasn't quite the same, was it?"

No answer. Instead, Drew pulled three folded pages from his pocket and placed them on the table. "That's everything I could find. I printed it off my boss's computer and will probably lose my job because of it."

"Careful, mate," Leo said as he wiped his hands on a napkin. "You're going to get me emotional with a sob story like that."

Leo took the pages and placed them in the breast pocket of his sport coat. He didn't bother reading them since he was unsure what the documents were supposed to tell him. Leo didn't need to know the specifics; he was certain that Drew Estes had delivered what Alex was after. The witless man-child fluttered like a leaf as he held his girlfriend's hand. True love was always easy to exploit.

"Can we leave?" Drew asked.

"Almost," Leo said. He shoved the remainder of the pizza slice into his mouth and spoke as he chewed. He looked at Laverne and pointed to the pizza. "Sure you don't want any, love?"

Laverne shook her head, but Drew reached for a slice. Leo slapped his hand away.

"Pizza's for me and Bonnie."

"I've told him a thousand times my name's not Bonnie," Laverne said.

"No," Leo said, wiping his mouth with the napkin before balling it up and placing it on the pizza tray. "Your name is Laverne Parker. You live at Kirchstrasse twenty-seven in Zürich. You've got a sister at university and parents who live thirty minutes from you."

Leo reached back into the breast pocket of his sport coat. He produced two photos and laid them on the table. He pointed a thick finger at each person in the first photo.

"Paige, Robert, and Demi."

Leo looked up from the photos and stared at Laverne.

"Your parents and sister, yeah? So here's how this is going to work. If you say a word to anyone about Alexandra Quinlan— about her being in Cambridge, attending university, visiting the bank in Zürich, or anything about your visit to her flat the other night—I'm going to pay these folks a visit."

Leo paused to allow the moment to sink in.

"After I visit with your parents, I'm going to go see your little sister. She's in her third year at University of Fribourg, right? Lives in an apartment off campus with two other suitemates?"

Laverne stayed silent. Leo shifted his gaze to Drew and held up the second photo.

"Then I'll go see your brother. He lives in a two-flat in Wallisellen. Höhenstrasse five, isn't it? And your parents after that."

Leo returned the photos to his pocket and placed both elbows on the table so his face was inches from Drew and Laverne.

"These visits will not be pleasant. They'll be brutal and rough, and when I'm finished none of them will be the same. Do you understand?"

Both Drew and Laverne continued their silence, unable to speak.

"I'm not threatening to hurt your family if either of you say a word about Alexandra Quinlan. I'm promising. I'll hurt them badly."

Leo stood up.

"Go back to Zürich and forget all about your time in Cambridge. Do we understand each other?"

Silence.

"Gonna need an answer from each of you so I can tell my boss you understood my parting directions."

He leaned down and looked at Drew. "You understand, mate?"

"Yeah, I understand," Drew said.

Leo moved his gaze to Laverne.

"Yes," she whispered.

Leo smiled, stood up straight, and left them sitting terrified in the booth as he walked outside. For more than a year he'd watched the American girl for Garrett Lancaster. He'd delivered a gun to her doorstep a week after she'd arrived in Cambridge, and kept weekly tabs on her. Nothing too intrusive. Just enough to keep track of her and report back to his boss in the States. He'd earned a handsome stipend for his efforts and had cleared a nice payday for this final job. He was sorry to see the girl go. Keeping tabs on her had been a source of easy and steady income. But, eventually, all good things come to an end.

CHAPTER 18

Alex waited in Leo's apartment. The place was becoming claustrophobic after so many days without leaving. But Leo's instructions had been clear: Alex wasn't to leave his flat until the situation with Drew Estes and Laverne Parker was settled. Leo had left a couple hours earlier, promising that things would be over soon. It felt like an eternity before Alex heard keys rattle in the door.

She clicked off the television. "Did you get it?" Alex asked as soon as Leo walked in.

From his breast pocket Leo produced the three folded pages Drew Estes had brought back from Zürich. He handed them to Alex, who read through them. The pages contained everything she had foolishly hoped to procure from Samuel McEwen in exchange for moving a million dollars into his bank: the date the account was opened, the running balance, the transfers in and out of the account, and on the last page the name of the man who had opened the numbered account her parents had chaperoned. She wanted to sit and read and analyze every detail, open her laptop and start investigating this man and following the trail this information would lead her down.

"You can look at that later," Leo said. "Right now, it's time to go."

Alex looked up from the pages. "Right now?"

Leo checked his watch. "Right now, mate."

Alex stuffed the pages into her rucksack and pulled it over her shoulders. She followed Leo into the hallway and down a flight of stairs in the back of the building. He opened the door to the alleyway and stood to the side so Alex could walk past him.

"It's been an adventure," he said. "A boring year or so, but the last week was a blast."

"I'm glad you think so," Alex said.

She paused in the doorway.

"Thanks... for everything."

"Good luck to you, young lady. You're a survivor. That's a quality that will take you far in life."

"Will I see you again?"

Leo smiled. "Unless you need a private investigator in England, probably not, mate."

"Good-bye, Leo the Brit."

"So long, Alex the gunslinger."

Alex stood on her tiptoes and gave him a peck on the cheek before walking out of the building and into the alleyway. The door closed and Alex was alone. A Volkswagen pulled to a stop in the street to her right. After a second, its horn sounded. Alex stared at the vehicle but did not move until the back window rolled down and she saw Garrett Lancaster. Alex walked down the alleyway. She considered for an instant that this might be an extension of one of the strange dreams she had experienced over the last week since discharging the Smith and Wesson. But as she walked toward the waiting car, it was all too real. The sunlight casting shadows at perfect angles, the cracks in the concrete beneath her feet, the creases in Garrett's face as she approached the car, the deep gravel in his voice when he spoke.

"Let's go," he said. "Get in."

Alex walked around the Volkswagen, opened the door, and sat in the backseat next to him. The car drove off as soon as she closed the door.

"I don't…" Alex said, unable to find the words. "What are you doing here?"

"I've come to collect you," Garrett said.

"To *collect* me?"

"It's time to come home."

"But… school," Alex said.

She'd been telling the lie for so long it was ingrained in her. Garrett shook his head. "Maybe school was a bad idea. At least, school here was a bad idea. That's no longer an option."

"I'm being kicked out of school?"

"You're being kicked out of the country, actually. But things could have been much worse, and still could be if you don't leave immediately."

"How immediate?" Alex asked.

"You grab whatever you need from your apartment, and then we leave."

"Today?"

"Today."

"And then what?"

"Then," Garrett said, "I make you an offer."

"What kind of offer?"

"A job offer."

That day, when Alex walked out of Leo the Brit's South London flat, marked the second time in her short life that Garrett Lancaster had saved her.

PART III

The Return

"Where is Alexandra Quinlan?"

—Tracy Carr

Camp Montague

Appalachian Mountains

Eight weeks each summer. It was how her older brother had always spent the hot months of June and July. Ever since he was thirteen, she'd seen the school year end one day and her brother pack for camp the next. It was how summers had always worked. This year, however, was different. This year, she was thirteen and finally old enough to join him. Her brother would be eighteen in July, and this marked his fifth summer at Camp Montague—his last, and her first. The excitement started back in May as soon as the weather turned warm. She daydreamed about a summer filled with canoeing down the river, late-night campfires, movies on the big screen under the starry night, and a thousand other highlights she'd heard her brother speak of over the years.

She rode in the backseat and zoned out her parents' grown-up talk as they headed into the mountains. It was all she could do to contain her excitement. Her older brother sat next to her and worked hard at nonchalance—he was a fifth-year Montague veteran, after all—but she still sensed his excitement. It was surreal to imagine that she would finally get to experience the glorious eight weeks at Camp Montague.

She had no idea about the terrors that waited for her there. No idea about the predator hiding in the shadows and salivating over the influx of new arrivals. But she soon would.

The campfire began to dwindle. She had learned over the last couple of weeks that when the camp counselors stopped adding logs to the fire it meant the night was coming to an end. And when the fire died, it was time to head to her cabin and go to sleep. The older kids—the fifth-years—didn't always follow that rule. They stayed up playing cards and sometimes sneaked beer from the main cabin's refrigerator. Her brother had told her stories. Some nights the fifth-years even snuck out of their cabins to go on late-night adventures. But those things were reserved for the seasoned kids who'd spent most of their childhood summers at Camp Montague. For her, the slow dwindling of the campfire meant just the end of another great day at camp. At least, it had for the first two weeks.

Those early days had been glorious and exciting. They were everything she had dreamed Montague would be. And when the fire died each night she was happy to climb under the covers and read while her roommate slept. During that first week, she had to work through growing pains and homesickness. Her new book, Double Crossing, the first Nancy Drew and Hardy Boys Super Mystery, helped, as did the fact that her brother was a constant presence around camp. As a fifth-year, her brother was in charge of organizing activities for the first-years, and though he'd never admit to it, she knew he was keeping an eye out for her. They didn't talk much, but a subtle nod here and a smile there was all it took to ease the ache of being away from home.

But just as the homesickness began to ease, it happened. It was the night her life forever changed. The campfire had lost its luster thirty minutes earlier and the kids had begun the slow shuffle toward their cabins. Once she was back in her cabin and had brushed her teeth and changed into pajamas, she climbed into bed and pulled the covers over her head, then clicked on her flashlight to read. She heard her roommate finish in the bathroom and settle into bed. Ten minutes after the lights went out she heard the deep breathing of her sleeping roommate. She spent thirty minutes reading and was deep into the book's adventure when her cabin door opened.

She froze under the covers and listened for a moment. Then she heard heavy footsteps walking into the cabin. She slowly pulled the covers down to see Mr. Lolland, one of the camp counselors, standing over her bed. There were several camp leaders who oversaw everything that went on at Camp Montague. Mr. Lolland was in charge of the first-year squad. And now, tonight, an hour after the campfire had died to mark the end of a Montague day, he was standing next to her bed.

"I was just reading my book," she said, worried that she had broken the lights-out rule.

"Come on," he said in a whisper. "You have to come with me."

She swallowed hard. "Where?"

"Shh." He held his finger to his lips, nodding at her sleeping roommate. "You have to come now."

Still shaking off the last remnants of homesickness, she found something comforting about a grown-up interacting with her. But in the strange setting, when the rest of camp was asleep, it was terrifying, too. She wanted to pull the covers over her head and get lost again in the adventure she was reading, but Jerry Lolland would not budge. He continued to stare at her with bloodshot eyes, breathing loudly through his mouth. The standoff lasted just a few seconds before she pushed the covers to the side and stood from bed.

"Good girl," Mr. Lolland said, putting his hand on the back of her neck and leading her out of the cabin.

He quietly closed the door behind them and led her through camp. The campground, populated with over a hundred kids just an hour ago, was now desolate. Porch lights shined from each cabin. She glanced at the cabins' windows as she and Mr. Lolland walked past, but they were all dark. Far off in the distance the main lodge still had activity going on inside. She thought, for just a fleeting moment, to run there. Surely the other counselors were still awake at this time of night and planning the following day's activities. There would be grown-ups there. There would be help. Inside the main lodge would be someone other than Jerry Lolland.

As if he read her mind, Mr. Lolland twisted his hand on the back of her neck to steer her body away from the main lodge. After a few more strides, they arrived at his cabin.

"I need to show you something inside," he said.

"Inside your cabin?" she asked.

"Yes. It will just take a minute."

"Am I in trouble?"

"Not yet," Mr. Lolland said in a soft voice. "But you will be if you tell anyone about this. Tonight is our little secret."

She swallowed hard as Jerry Lolland guided her into his cabin.

Present Day

CHAPTER 19

Manhattan, New York
Sunday, January 15, 2023
8:45 p.m.

Tracy Carr put the final touches on her article, resisted the urge to read through it one more time to make additional changes, attached it to the e-mail, and hit SEND. There was always a moment of panic after e-mailing an article to her editor and knowing that it was out of her control. Knowing that her editor might read her work and think the content was worthless and the writing amateurish. This worry arose from an irrational mixture of neurosis and OCD—the curse of just about every writer she knew—but not from a lived experience. In the five years she'd worked as an investigative reporter for the New York Times, her editor had never rejected any of Tracy's articles.

Tracy carried some level of clout as a reporter, and she was sure that helped. After breaking the story about the Quinlan family murders ten years earlier when she worked as a local reporter in Virginia, Tracy rode that fame and left Channel 2 News out of Richmond for greener pastures. Recruited first by the legendary television newsmagazine host Mack Carter, Tracy was a correspondent for *American Events* for a number of years before her rise to television stardom stalled when a young journalist named Avery Mason stormed onto the scene and overshadowed anything Tracy had ever accomplished in journalism. Avery Mason went on to take over *American Events*, a gig Tracy had been in contention for, and the cutthroat environment of television news proved too daunting for her. Tracy instead took to, and flourished in, the new era of reporting: the Internet. Her stories had been so powerful, and her social media following so large, that the *New York Times* hired her to write about crime. Tracy won accolades for an investigative piece she did on the bribery of a sitting US senator that included Tracy going undercover as a small-business owner attempting to procure favorable tax breaks and building permits to get her business off the ground, all in exchange for healthy campaign donations. When the story broke, the accused senator was forced to resign in disgrace.

Writing for the *Times* was Tracy's day job. Her real passion, however, was true crime. But the gig at the newspaper lent Tracy credibility that many of her true-crime cohorts lacked. And writing for one of the leading papers in the country added to her digital platform. Her social media accounts boasted five million followers, and her self-produced videos covering true crime were must-see events when she released them. If a suburban mom was murdered or new developments came to light about a girl who'd gone missing years before, Tracy Carr was immediately on the story and offering updates to her millions of followers. The best part was that as long as she got her work done for the newspaper, her editor didn't care what Tracy did in her spare time.

Tracy closed out of her e-mail account and pulled up the video editor on her desktop to rewatch the footage that she would drop tonight. She had lured her fans with teasers for the past month as the ten-year anniversary of the Quinlan family shootings approached, and had even returned to McIntosh, Virginia, for the first time in years to capture the perfect footage. She pressed PLAY and watched the clip to see if any last-minute edits were needed.

Tracy stood in front of the two-story home. The cedar sported a fresh coat of paint, applied the previous spring. Throughout the summer, the manicured lawn glowed a lush green hue compliments of a sprinkler system that ran like clockwork. Now, in the dead of winter, a snowplowing company routinely cleared the driveway and sidewalk after each snowfall. Without any previous knowledge of the home's history, it would be impossible to know that a decade earlier it was the site of a triple homicide and had sat vacant ever since.

Tracy raised the microphone to her mouth and looked into the camera.

"I'm Tracy Carr and behind me is the infamous home where, ten years ago, the brutal killing of the Quinlan family took place. On that fateful night, Dennis, Helen, and thirteen-year-old Raymond Quinlan were shot in the middle of the night. I was the first reporter on the scene that night, breaking a story that would eventually rock not just the town of McIntosh, Virginia, but the entire country."

A faded transition took viewers back to the night of January 15, 2013, where a then thirty-two-year-old Tracy Carr interviewed the neighbor who had first called 911 to report shots fired inside the Quinlan home. The footage progressed to the front door opening and a female officer—unknown at the time, but now familiar to true-crime buffs as Donna Koppel, the officer who would eventually provide key testimony in the case of Alexandra Quinlan versus the state of Virginia—walking into the hot lights of both Tracy's television camera and the spotlights the McIntosh Police Department had erected. Officer Koppel led Alexandra Quinlan, hands cuffed behind her back and her eyes empty in a thousand-yard stare, out of the house. In the days that followed, that image of Alexandra Quinlan made its way onto every newscast in the country.

The video faded. Alexandra Quinlan's face slowly blurred as the footage transitioned back to Tracy Carr.

"Ten years have passed since I stood outside this house knowing only that shots had been fired within. At the time Alexandra Quinlan was taken into custody, I knew only what the rest of the world knew. But then I started digging. Soon, I uncovered startling details about that night. The empty eyes Alexandra offered the camera have continued to haunt those of us who seek the truth. Had a teenaged girl miraculously survived the night an armed intruder entered her home and killed the rest of her family? Or, had those empty eyes been a dead giveaway that Alexandra Quinlan had not escaped the shotgun blasts that killed her family, but had instead been the one who pulled the trigger?"

Tracy walked up the driveway of the home.

"For ten years questions have loomed. For a decade the Quinlan home has sat vacant, yet perfectly maintained. We know that the property fell briefly into foreclosure in the months after the murders but was then purchased by an anonymous trust. The house has been meticulously maintained ever since. Yet, when I look into who hired the landscaping company that maintains the grounds during summer and plows the snow in the winter, or the company hired to paint the home last year, or the company that installed the sprinkler system, I run into nothing but dead ends. Similarly, when I approach the utility companies to see who pays the electric and gas bills, I'm stonewalled.

"We know that the property came out of foreclosure soon after Alexandra Quinlan won her case against the state of Virginia, a settlement that awarded her millions of dollars. We've suspected that Alexandra is behind the anonymous purchase, and many of you armchair detectives at home have searched for proof. But protected by a small fortune and an army of attorneys, Alexandra Quinlan has not only managed to keep the trust anonymous, but to stay hidden for the better part of a decade. No one has seen or heard from Alexandra since she walked out of the courtroom the day the jury made her a very rich woman.

"There have been reported sightings from California to New York, and as far as London, England. But every one of those leads has turned up exactly nothing. Alexandra Quinlan up and vanished years ago. Despite my best efforts, and nonstop searching by many of you at home, Alexandra has managed to stay hidden ever since. On the ten-year anniversary of the shootings, my question is this..."

Tracy looked directly into the camera.

"What are you hiding, Alexandra?"

Tracy turned away from the camera, walked to the front door of the Quinlan home, and knocked on it. She waited a moment as if someone might answer, then turned back to the camera.

"As we mark the tenth anniversary of the Quinlan family killings, we continue to search for answers. We continue to search for the truth. We continue to search for Alexandra Quinlan. If she is the innocent victim she claimed to be during the trial that netted her millions, why did she go into hiding after the case was settled? Perhaps there is a simple explanation, and it is this: Instead of an innocent victim, Alexandra Quinlan is a ruthless killer who not only got away with murder, but millions on top of it."

Tracy walked off the front stoop until she was close to the camera. Her breath was a white vapor in the cold January air.

"I'm Tracy Carr, and I promise you that as the tenth anniversary of the Quinlan family murders comes and goes, I will spend every day continuing to search for answers. With your help, maybe we'll find them. With your help, maybe we'll find Empty Eyes. We know she's out there somewhere."

Tracy stopped the video. Satisfied, she uploaded it to her social media accounts. Before midnight, it had racked up three million views. Two weeks later, twenty-two million people had watched it. The world, or at least a select corner of it, was still obsessed with Alexandra Quinlan.

CHAPTER 20

Washington, D.C.
Friday, February 3, 2023
11:48 p.m.

In the ten years since the fateful night that forever changed her life, the media's breathless pursuit of Alexandra Quinlan had ebbed and flowed. At times it quieted down entirely as the lens of the mainstream media refocused on other misfortunes and tragedies. But interest never seemed to die completely, and ever since the ten-year anniversary had come and gone activity on the true-crime sites had been on the uptick. Tracy Carr was at it again; and Alexandra Quinlan sightings had started to pop up anew. So far, though, the precautions put in place years earlier after Alex returned from the debacle in Cambridge—when two crazed true-crime fanatics had followed her across Europe and attempted to extort half a million dollars from her—had been effective at protecting her anonymity.

The strongest safeguard was the name change. With the Social Security Administration, the Internal Revenue Service, the DC secretary of state's office, and everywhere else formal documentation was required, she was legally *Alex Armstrong*. It had a nice ring to it and over the years Alex had even grown comfortable with her new name, but it was just one of many firewalls erected since her return from Cambridge. The physical makeover had been just as important. Only a couple of years from her thirtieth birthday now, Alex was a long way from the baby-faced teenager most people knew as Alexandra Quinlan.

Today, she was unrecognizable from the infamous image of the wide-eyed kid who had walked from her home and into the hot lights of the news camera the night her family was killed. That image had circulated so widely around the country, and most of the world, that it had burned itself into the public's psyche. Mention Alexandra Quinlan and most people conjured that very image in their minds.

The natural evolution from adolescence—the thinning of her face as baby fat melted from her cheeks, the maturing of her body, and the youthful aging in the eyes and lips—prevented the casual observer from recognizing her today. But so too did the self-induced alterations to her body. Her once long and wavy hair was now cut into a short, spikey crop. The auburn highlights were gone, replaced by yellow blond. Her eyes were never without a dark ring of eyeliner, and the piercings were dramatic and everywhere—her nose, her eyebrow, her lip, and in arcing rivets along the cartilage of her left ear. The glasses she'd worn throughout her teens, and for the entirety of the highly watched trial that defined her persona, had been replaced by contact lenses that changed the color of her irises from dark brown to vibrant blue. She wore black lipstick one day and bright orange the next, the wild spectrum of colors chosen each morning based on her mood. The oxymoronic plan of standing out was what helped her blend in. Together, it had all been enough for Alex to live a quiet existence in the DC area without being recognized or harassed.

Of course, taking a job as a legal investigator for Lancaster & Jordan was another important move. Working for Garrett Lancaster's law firm allowed gainful employment without having to go through a formal background check. The job came when Alex was at the end of her rope, had nowhere to go, and was on the brink of twisting her life into an unrecoverable tailspin. Garrett's offer of employment was her last shot at finding normalcy and balance in a life that had been teetering on the edge two years after her family was killed. Had Alex not found purpose at Lancaster & Jordan, she would likely never have found it at all.

During her introductory years at the firm, just after her return from Cambridge, Alex had worked under the tutelage of Buck Jordan, the firm's lead investigator and the brother of Lancaster & Jordan's cofounder and senior partner. Hired at the firm's incorporation, Buck possessed the longest tenure of any employee. He'd been chasing leads for Lancaster & Jordan for over two decades. A third of his life had been spent following suspects, taking recon pictures, logging hours on stakeouts, and completing his fair share of opposition research. Buck Jordan had forgotten more about the law than the snot-nosed rookies who joined the firm straight out of law school would ever learn. And everything Buck knew, he taught Alex. She had become his protégée. Years earlier, Buck Jordan had been instrumental in providing opposition research when Garrett Lancaster went after the McIntosh Police Department and the Alleghany County DA's office during Alex's defamation case. Alex was happy to be under his tutelage. The education was hands-on and still ongoing today, which was why Buck had accompanied her on that night's stakeout.

Alex sat behind the wheel of her SUV, which was parked in front of a meter she had fed for hours, and focused the lens of her Nikon COOLPIX P1000 on the front entrance of the high-rise building across the street. Her right leg was starting to go numb as midnight approached. But the waiting didn't bother her, the aggravation of her sciatic nerve was ignored, and Alex considered the formal transition from today to tomorrow as simply the beginning of the night. Twenty-eight years old and powered by rebellion, regret, and Red Bull, it took more than a boringly long stakeout to discourage her.

Her subject came into view through the lens of the Nikon as the man exited the building. Buck sat in the passenger seat and looked up from his phone when Alex began snapping photos.

"We found our man," Buck said. "Are you getting clear shots of his face?"

"No," Alex said. "Just his shoes."

"Always the smart-ass."

Once her subject was out of range, Alex handed the camera to Buck. Her stakeout had officially ended. Now it was time to get to work.

Garrett had put her on the Byron Zell case to get information, and she had no intention of letting him down.

CHAPTER 21

Washington, D.C.
Friday, February 3, 2023
11:56 p.m.

One of the many responsibilities of the firm's investigators was to look into potential clients to determine whether they were innocent of the crimes they were accused of or as guilty as sin. It was common practice in criminal defense to never ask clients about their guilt or innocence. If an attorney had to ask, it meant they had doubts. And if they had doubts, they could not mount a viable defense. But at Lancaster & Jordan, the question was unnecessary. Every client was innocent until proven guilty, and the firm had a score of investigators to verify it.

Byron Zell's former employer had accused him of embezzling company funds, and Mr. Zell had approached Lancaster & Jordan seeking legal representation after he was terminated and brought up on charges. An executive vice president with nearly two decades of loyalty to his company, Zell vehemently denied the allegations during his initial consultation with Garrett Lancaster. Alex had been tasked with looking into Mr. Zell. The case was technically hers, and hers alone, but as was common with mentor and protégée she and Buck routinely worked cases together. Eight years in, Alex no longer needed the supervision, she just preferred the company.

Her goal was to dig deep enough into Byron Zell's life to determine—not unequivocally, but damn close—whether he was an innocent man fighting for his livelihood or as guilty as sin. The process by which Alex went about this task fell into the hazy moral area of legal investigation, the specifics of which were left up to the imagination of each investigator. Alex Armstrong had an active imagination.

Alex believed that Zell's finances were the best place to start her dive into the man's life. Zell had already turned over financial documents to Lancaster & Jordan, and Alex had spent the past week picking through the man's bank accounts, investments, and assets. So far, everything Byron Zell presented to Lancaster & Jordan had been on the up-and-up. But Alex hadn't expected to find anything nefarious in the documents Zell had willingly provided to the firm. If the man was hiding something, it would be on his personal computer, and Alex was about to have a look.

As soon as Zell disappeared around the corner of the building, Alex pulled her ball cap low over her eyes.

"Did you practice on the lock?" Buck asked.

"Yes."

"How long?"

"All of last night."

"No, how long to pick it?"

"Under two minutes."

Buck nodded. "You'd best hurry."

Alex opened the door and hustled across the street. Vetting clients was instrumental to winning cases, and no laws could be broken in the process. Garrett had been explicit about this with Alex during her formal interview with the firm. The firm needed to know the truth about potential clients, but that truth had to be obtained legally. Garrett had lectured her about this *once*. He explained the firm's rules and the ramifications of obtaining information illegally during her intake interview, a meeting that included both Jacqueline Jordan— Garrett's partner and the other founding member of the firm— and Buck Jordan. Garrett told her this to get it on the record, and then never mentioned it again. Instead, he unleashed Alex at the ripe age of twenty-one to learn the tricks of the trade from the legendary Buck Jordan, a man who had broken more laws in the pursuit of justice than any of the clients Lancaster & Jordan represented.

Over the years, Garrett had never asked about the methods Alex used to gather the information she provided. In the early days of her employment, Alex had assumed Garrett's silence was a sign of his trust. Years later, after witnessing firsthand the behind-the-scene shenanigans of her fellow investigators, she knew better. Garrett didn't ask because he didn't want to know.

Alex's situation at Lancaster & Jordan was complicated. Alex held some indefinable need to impress Garrett, and it forced her to perform a delicate balancing act that plagued no other investigator at the firm. She was willing to bend rules and laws but would never put Garrett in jeopardy. Their relationship was complex and had originated the moment Garrett had barged into the interrogation room the night her family was killed.

She had been just seventeen years old when Garrett and Donna Lancaster entered her life. With her parents gone, no other family to take her in, and the only home she'd ever known roped off with crime scene tape, she had nowhere to go. Garrett and Donna convinced a judge to grant them temporary (and anonymous) custody. Because her ordeal had started when Alex was a minor, and was still ongoing when Alex turned eighteen, the terms of her release from juvenile detention included stipulations on guidance and supervision. Alex agreed to stay with the Lancasters when they offered to take her in. Her court case against the state of Virginia commenced a few months later, rushed to trial by the egregious nature of what had taken place and by the legal might of Garrett Lancaster's law firm. Throughout the trial, no one in the media had uncovered that Alex was staying with the lawyer who represented her. And this many years later, none had sniffed out that she was working for that same man who had saved her life.

As Alex hurried across the street now, she knew the building would not be easy to access, but it was far from impossible. She just needed to stick to the plan. She'd done a run-through the day before and was confident she'd have smooth sailing tonight. At least getting as far as Zell's apartment door. There, she'd need to rely on skills learned during her apprenticeship with Buck Jordan if she hoped to get farther. She passed the front entrance and turned the corner into the parking garage. She used a card key stolen the previous day to gain access, then snuck through the aisles of cars until she came to the service elevator, where she punched in the four-digit code (also stolen) that allowed access. Alex assumed her movements were being recorded by the security cameras that hung from every corner of the garage. She was confident that the ball cap, sunglasses, and extra-large Columbia raincoat would camouflage her size and gender. She was confident, too, that the security cameras on the thirty-eighth floor had been disabled.

Since the police and the press had incinerated her old life—and every friendship from high school—her only friends today came from the seventy-one days she'd spent in juvenile detention. It was a kinship made up of a group of unlikely allies forced to fight for each other inside Alleghany once the lights went out and the true delinquents roamed the floors. Those relationships had lasted and included a short list of people who were more than willing to take odd jobs from Alex when she needed something shady. For tonight's mission she'd paid one of her juvie friends a thousand dollars to spray paint over the security cameras on the thirty-eighth floor, where Byron Zell's apartment was located. If he came through for her, and she knew he would, he'd be sneaking off the thirty-eighth floor right about now.

After pulling open the accordion doors to the elevator, she took a quick look at the parking garage to confirm she was alone, then climbed inside. A minute later she exited on the sixth floor, as high as this particular elevator rose. She'd mapped out her route the day before—first with a copy of the building's blueprints, which she'd downloaded from the county's website, and then with a practice walk-through—and now she easily snaked her way through the maze of utility rooms. Approaching midnight, the janitorial crew was sparse and Alex met no opposition as she darted from room to room. She finally pushed through a door and emerged into the main hallway. A standard passenger elevator was just around the corner. She pressed the call button and waited only a few seconds for the doors to open. Inside, she hit the button for the thirty-eighth floor and kept her head down, using the brim of the ball cap to shield her face from the elevator's security camera. Less than ten minutes after watching Byron Zell leave the building, Alex was standing in front of the man's apartment door.

On her recon visit Alex had dressed as a custodian and blended in with the scores of people hired to clean and maintain the building. During a sweep of the thirty-eighth floor, Alex had snapped a photo of Byron Zell's apartment door and spent the rest of the night inspecting the lock to see what she was up against. Now she pulled a leather case from her back pocket. The lock-picking tools, originally gifted to her by Buck for her one-year anniversary with the firm, had served her well over the years. This many years later, the small leather folder felt familiar and comfortable in her hands.

She pulled the tension wrench from the set and chose the proper-sized pick, determined during her research the previous night; inserted the wrench into the core of the door's lock; twisted it slightly to the left; and kept steady pressure on it. Then she inserted the pick above the wrench and went to work on the puzzle inside. Picking a lock was just that—a puzzle. Instead of scattered jigsaw pieces, the riddle of a lock was figuring out the binding order of the locking pins and how much pressure was needed to set them. Attempting this on a lock never worked on before was called a blind pick, and Alex had a great deal of experience with it.

This particular deadbolt had five pin stacks. She closed her eyes and moved the pick to each stack, feeling for the one with the most resistance. Once she found it, the second stack in this case, she bent the pick upward to set the top driver until she heard it click into place. She went back to the first stack and started again, this time finding the new resistance on the fourth pin. She set it in place with a gentle flick of her wrist. Repeating the process for each of the five pins, it took just over three minutes until she had each of them set in place. She turned the tension wrench, grabbed the handle of Byron Zell's apartment door, and pressed her thumb down on the latch. The door opened like magic.

Inside, she placed her tools back in the leather wallet and slipped them into her pocket. The apartment was dark and she took a moment to allow her eyes to adjust. Then, she slipped her hands into a pair of latex gloves as she crept through the apartment. She was after one thing, and one thing only: Byron Zell's financial records. Using a small flashlight to guide her, Alex found the man's office, sat behind the desk, and fired up the computer. The screen came to life and lit the room in an eerie blue glow. Her first bit of luck was that Mr. Zell had not password protected his computer. Scrolling through his files, she was in Zell's financial documents folder a few minutes later. There was no time to read them, but that had never been the plan. Copying the files was too risky, as she might leave behind a digital fingerprint in the process. Alex's plan was much simpler, and left only Byron Zell as an accomplice.

Alex quickly logged into the man's e-mail account, which was password synced. Composing a new message, Alex attached each financial document to the e-mail, addressed it to Garrett Lancaster of Lancaster & Jordan, and titled the e-mail *Private Documents for Your Review*. In the body of the e-mail, Alex typed a single sentence:

Mr. Lancaster, attached are the documents you requested.
—Byron Zell

Alex sent the e-mail and then logged off the computer just as her phone buzzed.

"Yeah," she whispered when she raised the phone to her ear.

"He's back," Buck said. "You've gotta move."

"Back, meaning?"

"He just walked into the lobby. He's probably in the elevator by now."

"Shit, Buck! You *just* saw him? He appeared out of thin air?"

"Yell at me later. But right now, get the hell out of there, Alex!"

Alex ended the call, slid the phone into her pocket, and put the computer to sleep. She set the chair back into place and hurried through the apartment. She checked to make sure the lock engaged after the door clicked behind her, then wiped the handle with a cloth and hustled toward the elevator. As she was about to press the call button, the elevator sounded, indicating an arrival from the lobby. She turned and sprinted down the hall, pushing through the stairwell door just as Byron Zell appeared in the hallway. Alex prevented the door from fully closing and stared through the crevice between the door and the frame. She watched Zell walk down the hall away from where she hid in the stairwell, insert his key into the lock, and enter his apartment. Once he was inside, she allowed the stairwell door to close before scampering down the steps to the floor below. There, she walked into the hallway and caught the elevator on the way down to the sixth floor. She wound her way back through the custodian rooms, took the service elevator down to the parking garage, and was out on the main street a moment later. She opened the door to her SUV, climbed behind the wheel, and looked at Buck.

"You did that on purpose, didn't you?"

"What are you talking about?"

"You waited until Zell was in the lobby before you called me."

"Of course not," Buck said in a faux tone meant to convey his shock at the accusation. "I got distracted, that's all."

"Bullshit. Buck Jordan does not get distracted on stakeouts."

Buck only smiled in return. Alex shook her head and started the engine before putting the SUV in gear.

"I could have used an extra minute," she said. "I nearly ran into him on the elevator."

"How'd you do otherwise?"

Alex nodded. "I got everything we needed."

"Then I'd say it was a successful night timed just right."

CHAPTER 22

Manhattan, New York
Friday, March 3, 2023
9:20 a.m.

Laura McAllister was as nervous as hell as she sat on the set of *Wake Up America*, the number one morning program in the country. She could hardly believe she was sitting across from Dante Campbell, the queen of morning television. Earlier in the morning when Laura had arrived at NBC Studios, the show runner had set her up in the green room. Before long, Dante Campbell had walked through the door to introduce herself and welcome Laura to the set. Now, the lights were blinding and her skin was hot. Her armpits were sticky and her blouse clung to her back. Her mouth was cotton dry and she thought about reaching for the glass of water the producers had set on a table next to her, but she worried the glass would slip from her clammy hands. Instead, she stared at the television camera just like she was coached to do and tried to breathe easy, hoping that when she spoke her voice wouldn't flutter and her words wouldn't catch in her throat.

The producer yelled last-second instructions and Laura heard a countdown begin. Then, suddenly the set was silent but for Dante Campbell's voice.

"Journalism is a popular major on American campuses," Dante Campbell said to the camera in her perfect, practiced pitch. "More than fifteen thousand students graduate each year from four-year programs with hopes of entering the world of journalism. When communication majors are included in the total, the number is even larger. I, myself, was once a journalism major, and I'm sitting here today because of the path I chose in college. But the face of journalism is changing. Social media is allowing a wider variety of voices to be heard, and some journalists are breaking stories in ways not possible just a few years ago. Podcasts, substacks, and other nontraditional outlets are allowing journalists to tell their stories and reach their audience in new and unique ways.

"Laura McAllister is a perfect example. Laura is a senior at McCormack University, a small liberal arts school tucked in the heart of Washington, D.C. Only fifteen hundred students attend McCormack University, which is why Laura's story is so impressive. As a freshman, Laura spearheaded a small university radio program called *The Scoop*, which was originally meant to be a casual show about gossip and pop culture that a few of her friends might listen to. Today, Laura is a senior and *The Scoop* is something much more than a university radio program. Laura has managed to grow her tiny show into something heard around the country, and we're very happy to have her with us this morning."

Dante took her gaze from the camera and looked at her guest.

"Laura, welcome to the show."

"Thank you. It's great to be here."

The words came out clearly and without a stutter.

"You've become the epitome of making a small voice heard, and heard loudly. *The Scoop* broadcasts from a tiny studio on the campus of a tiny university. You and McCormack University were kind enough to allow our crew into the studio last week to take some footage. But despite the small size of your microphone, a lot of people are listening to what you have to say."

"I've been really lucky to have such support from the school, and for some of the stories I've covered to be so widely distributed."

"And that's what I wanted to talk with you about this morning: the distribution of news and information today as compared to years ago, and the way social media is changing journalism. Decades ago, most people got their news from the evening newscast or the local paper. Cable news grew that medium in the nineteen nineties. The advent of the Internet yet again changed the landscape of news. And now social media is repaving the information highway."

Dante Campbell glanced down to the index card on her lap.

"During your sophomore year, you produced a show high-lighting the ways colleges and universities can make campus life, and the college experience as a whole, safer for female students. You secured interviews with a wide range of experts who not only pointed out inherent dangers on college campuses, but offered ideas on how to fix them. Through word of mouth, that episode spread from McCormack University to other campuses. I heard about it and linked to it on my own social media accounts. Now today, many universities, including McCor-mack, have adopted all or part of the Safe Haven Project you called for. One major strategy of Safe Haven is university-hired and background-tested drivers to shuttle students from off-campus sites safely back to dormitories—an idea that has been adopted by colleges around the country. It's a remarkable accomplishment when you consider that your episode, just based on the bandwidth of the studio, was meant to reach the fifteen hundred students who attend McCormack University, but went on to reach nearly every campus in the country."

"Yeah," Laura said. "I'm still blown away by how big that episode became and how widely adopted the Safe Haven Project has been. I'm really proud of that episode, and grateful that so many administrators were able to hear it. Not just *hear* it, but listen to the content and take action. And I wanted to pass on my gratitude to you for linking to my story and introducing your followers to *The Scoop*."

Dante smiled. "Of course. It was an important and powerful story. You're a senior now at McCormack University. Where do you see yourself after graduation, and what role do you see social media playing in your career?"

"After graduation I see myself pursuing some form of investigative reporting. Where that will be, and in what form, I'm not sure yet. As far as social media goes, I think there are lots of pitfalls, for sure. Especially for younger kids, and girls, in particular. But I also believe, if used correctly, a lot of good can come from those platforms. I was perfectly happy broadcasting my little campus radio show to anyone at McCormack University who wanted to listen. But I'm thrilled to have found a larger audience, and I understand that with a larger following comes more responsibility to report not just interesting stories, but accurate ones."

"And that's a pivot for you. You've described yourself as a gossip girl. I think the term you used was 'Pop-goss' to describe popular gossip that you oftentimes cover on your show."

"I'm a pop-culture addict, and I don't think that will ever change. A big part of my audience loves the show's take on pop culture, and I don't see that changing. But yes, once my platform started growing and more people started listening to the in-depth stories I was covering, I did have to pivot. But it was natural for me. I never wanted to be an entertainment reporter. I always planned to cover more hard-hitting topics. The campus safety issue was just the first of, hopefully, many more."

"Which is a great segue to my next question. What can we expect from you and *The Scoop* during your final semester at McCormack U?"

"One good thing about being a student journalist, rather than a *real* one, is that I can pick and choose what I report on, and I do it without deadlines. I have a few things planned for *The Scoop* before I graduate."

"Any hints?"

Laura smiled. "I guess you'll have to tune in to see."

"Spoken like a true journalist. Great to have you on the show, Laura. Keep up the good work. And I can't wait to see what blockbuster story you cover next."

Later that morning, Laura McAllister's social media accounts topped one million followers. She was, indeed, becoming a force to be reckoned with.

CHAPTER 23

Washington, D.C.
Saturday, March 4, 2023
11:58 p.m.

It was late on a Saturday night when the girl found herself alone in a tucked-away room of the fraternity house. Not alone—she was with a guy—but away from her friends she'd come to the fraternity party with. She remembered a dark stairwell and shuffling feet and the guy laughing and urging her on. She remembered a hand under her arm, assisting her up the stairs because her legs were weak and her balance was off. She hadn't had much to drink, but she had a low tolerance to begin with so it was possible, she tried to convince herself, that she had overindulged. She usually stuck to hard teas and seltzers because they tasted good and were no stronger than beer. Tonight, though, at the fraternity party, she had accepted a red Solo cup filled with punch served from a giant vat behind the bar. Now, her thoughts were cloudy and the room was spinning. The face of the guy who brought her here was blurred and wavy. His voice was garbled like he was talking underwater.

He lifted her arm by putting gentle pressure on her elbow, raising to her mouth the hand that held the Solo cup. He told her to drink up. Despite her reluctance to drink more punch, she obliged. She couldn't remember the guy's name now. She and her friends had decided at the last minute to go to the after-hours fraternity party, and the guy she was with now had found her near the dance floor. He'd flirted with her for a while and before long she was talking to him in the corner while her friends mingled. Now, somehow, inexplicably, she was alone with him despite that she couldn't remember exactly how she had gotten there.

She felt him kiss her neck. The stubble on his chin startled her. She forced herself to laugh despite feeling terrified, and tried to lift her hand to push him away. The muscles of her arms, however, were too weak to fend him off. She tried again, with the same result, and felt like she was in a dream she couldn't wake from. She swallowed hard as the guy continued to kiss her neck, then her lips. He thrust his tongue into her mouth and all she wanted to do was get away from him. Then she felt him press her shoulders backward. She tried to resist as he pushed her onto the couch.

–

She woke on the floor, the matted carpet clawing at her cheek. When she opened her eyes she was stunned by photophobia and a headache that emanated from behind her eyes and ached deep into her brain. The first thing she noticed, as the light sensitivity dulled, was that she was not wearing pants. Disoriented and mortified, she sat up and covered herself with her hands. Her bra was still on, but her tank top was pulled up over her breasts. Her jeans were in a heap next to her, and her underwear was wrapped around her left ankle.

She reached down quickly to pull them up, fighting a second wave of aching in her head before noticing the stabbing pain between her legs. Adrenaline allowed her to ignore the discomfort while she scrambled for her jeans and pulled them on. She looked around and tried to figure out where she was. Snippets of memory came back to her from the previous night. The party. The fraternity house. Her friends on the dance floor, drinking and having fun. But then her memory ended. It didn't fade out or have segments missing; it was gone entirely. She couldn't remember a thing after the dance floor. Not about her friends, or about how she ended up here—on the floor next to a couch in, what looked like, a room inside the fraternity house.

Getting to her feet was difficult due to both the headache and the pain between her legs. Something was wrong, and she feared the worst. She looked for her shoes but abandoned the search to attend to the urgency she felt to get out of the house. She walked to the door and opened it to find a hallway that led to a staircase. She took the stairs gingerly, placing one hand on the railing and the other over her abdomen as she descended. When she opened the door at the bottom of the landing, brilliant morning sunlight assaulted her eyes with a searing agony that pierced through her head. Her ears rang. Outside, she gained her bearings, realizing she had exited the fraternity house into the back parking lot. Her apartment was two blocks away, and she carefully made her way there. When she reached the parking lot of her apartment complex, she fumbled her car keys out of the pocket of her jeans, held the key fob over her head, and pressed the button several times until she heard the chirping horn of her car. Squinting against the sunlight, she stumbled to her vehicle, opened the door, and fell into the driver's seat.

Ten minutes later she walked into the emergency room and approached the reception desk. She was happy to see a woman behind the counter. She suddenly and inexplicably worried less about her disheveled appearance—wild hair, smeared makeup, and no shoes—than if a man had greeted her.

"Hi," the woman said with concern. "How can we help you, sweetie?"

"I'm a student at McCormack University…" The girl swallowed hard as tears filled her eyes and ran down her cheeks. "I think I was raped last night."

CHAPTER 24

Washington, D.C.
Monday, March 6, 2023
9:10 a.m.

Larry Chadwick had been anointed. Although not beckoned by God Himself, the Honorable Lawrence P. Chadwick of the US Court of Appeals for the District of Columbia had been summoned by the president of the United States, and that was damn close. Rumors came and went over the years about Larry's name being added to the short list of potential nominees for the Supreme Court whenever the next vacancy came around, but Larry had seen too many of his colleagues place too much hope on such unlikely odds. So much, in fact, that when they were passed over for the appointment, the regret derailed their careers. Larry's objective had never wavered: Do the job, do it well, and do it honestly. And when honesty was not possible—and there were many instances when it was not—cover your tracks well enough so that whatever oversight committee decided to take a look would find nothing.

As he ascended up through the courts, Larry had been aware that the eyes of the country's elite and powerful were watching his every move, evaluating his character, and charting his rulings in some unseen database that weighed the pros and cons of his opinions, positions, and politics. He played the part and acted unconcerned with those keeping score. He stuck to his plan, believing that someday, perhaps, his name would come up. That day had finally arrived.

Larry had been short-listed to fill the most recent Supreme Court vacancy, which opened when Jonathan Miller died the previous month. Justice Miller's death was not a surprise. Eighty-eight years old and obese, the man had battled diabetes his entire adult life. Not even a pancreatic cancer diagnosis could entice the man to step down. A stubborn old-school southerner, he battled through two years of chemotherapy without missing a day of work before he died in his sleep.

Justice Miller's ailing health had long been a political talking point, and the new administration had come into office with a list of potential nominees to replace him. Twelve nominees made up the list, but most were just for show. The candidates were diversified and distinguished and offered hope to just about every voting demographic. When the list was boiled down, however, only a couple of nominees rose to the top. Lawrence P. Chadwick was one of them.

Larry cleared his schedule for the afternoon and now stood outside his DC office wearing a crisp charcoal suit and navy tie. The black SUV with tinted windows pulled to the curb and Annette Packard, the FBI special agent assigned to scouring through his life, climbed from the passenger seat.

"Larry," Annette said as she walked toward him with an outstretched hand. "Good to see you again."

Larry shook the woman's hand. "You too, Annette."

They shared the fakest of fake relationships. They pretended to like each other, when in fact they each had a vested interest in seeing the other fail. Annette Packard was the gatekeeper to his spot on the Supreme Court. Her job was to pick through Larry's life and find any and all transgressions that might make him a poor choice as the president's nominee. Larry's job was to make sure she found nothing.

"I'll brief you on the way over," Annette said, opening the back door of the government SUV for Larry to climb in.

Larry took his spot next to a serious-looking man in a buy-one-get-one Brooks Brothers suit. The driver in the front seat appeared to be wearing an identical suit.

"Sir," the man said with a slight head nod as Larry settled in.

Larry offered an awkward smile as the SUV pulled from the curb. Annette turned so she could speak to Larry over the front seat.

"The president is in a meeting with the foreign intelligence committee. He's due to finish at ten-ten. He's set aside thirty minutes to speak with you."

This would be Larry's third meeting with the president. Third, and final, if the rumors were true. If all went well during the next month, the next time he met with the leader of the free world after today would be during a public meet-and-greet in the Rose Garden in front of the entire press crew. It would be then that the country would know for certain that Lawrence P. Chadwick was the president's choice to fill the vacancy on the Supreme Court.

For the past three months Larry had met with members of the Secret Service and FBI, Annette Packard being the point person and overseeing the process. She poked around Larry's past—formally termed the debriefing and vetting process—looking for red flags that could hurt his chances of making it through the grueling nomination process. More than that, Annette looked for things that would prove embarrassing for the president. This vetting process was a forensic examination of a candidate's life, and Larry had learned through his own research that Annette Packard excelled at it. She'd vetted senators, congressmen and congresswomen, vice presidential candidates, and governors. Larry Chadwick was her first Supreme Court vet.

Starting with his high school days, Annette Packard had methodically picked her way through Larry's life, sniffing at anything she found suspicious and turning over any rocks she believed might be hiding secrets. Annette did this from his teenage years to present day. She was searching, Larry knew, for transgressions, embarrassing gaffes, stupid mistakes, cover-ups, crimes, or anything unsavory that might cast him, and therefore the president, in a bad light during the confirmation hearings.

"Trust me," Annette had told Larry during an initial meeting. "If you did it, we'll find it."

They could look, but Larry was confident they would find nothing. Early on he'd set his life on the correct trajectory. The son of a navy commander turned prominent businessman, Larry grew up sailing in Connecticut and attending private school. The worst thing he'd done in high school was break Renee Beckham's heart when he'd dumped her for a cheerleader. But even this minor transgression, Larry believed, had been atoned. He married Renee five years later when he was a first-year law student. That their marriage had survived twenty-five years and produced three children was evidence that Renee had forgiven him. The extracurriculars since then were well buried, and Larry was confident Annette Packard would not dig deep enough to find them.

If Larry's high school experience had been benign, his college days had been anemic. At Yale he'd never fallen under the myth of secret societies, had rejected the lure of fraternity life, and had spent most of his time in the library. His three years of law school at Duke had been crowded with books, work, and internships. Larry Chadwick had simply never found time to get into trouble.

So, Annette Packard and her team of FBI agents and the Secret Service goons who were picking through his life could look all they wanted. There was nothing to find. At least, nothing they would find easily.

CHAPTER 25

Washington, D.C.
Monday, March 6, 2023
8:36 p.m.

Her condo sat on the top floor of a five-story building that overlooked the Potomac. Never a city girl until her time in Cambridge, which by no stretch of the imagination could be considered a big city but was still a stark contrast to tiny McIntosh, Virginia, Alex could no longer imagine herself in a small town. She had grown up in a quiet suburban neighborhood where the closest city was a two-hour drive, but today the hustle and bustle of city life had grown on her. Perhaps the appeal was the dual sensation of feeling invisible while never being alone.

Despite that Donna and Garrett's second home—where Alex had escaped to during her trial and where she stayed after her failed attempt at college—was hidden in the foothills of the Appalachian Mountains, Alex constantly feared being recognized when she was there. In the months following her return from Cambridge, Alex sensed that she stood out in the small town, with its empty streets and laid-back establishments. The relentless worry of being recognized as the empty-eyed girl who had once been accused of killing her family was yet another scar that slashed through her disfigured psyche, this one delivered by Drew Estes and Laverne Parker. Enough years had passed now, however, for the uneasiness to fade. She purchased her Georgetown condo when she was twenty-three and now felt like just another face in the crowd. No one gave her a second glance, and she felt at home on the crowded streets of Washington, D.C.

Some would count this as progress and maturity—a young woman making her way in the world. Others would count it as overcoming a difficult past that included a horrendous trauma, and making the most of a terrible situation. But Alex knew the truth. Her ability to cope with her past came from neatly organizing her life into three categories. Her *anonymous* self, Alex Armstrong, the spiked-hair rebel who moved invisibly through the world, worked as an investigator for Lancaster & Jordan, and lived a mostly normal existence. Her *old* self, Alexandra Quinlan, who the world knew only as the empty-eyed girl whose family had been killed. And her *true* self—some combination of those other personas, but with some additional ingredient mixed in. Although not easily defined, that ingredient kept Alex hungry for answers to what had happened to her family, and confident that no matter how much time passed she would eventually find the truth.

The circle of people who knew each of her personalities was small. It included Donna and Garrett Lancaster, as well as a handful of attorneys at Lancaster & Jordan who had worked her case. Then there were her friends from juvie, who knew just about everything since they met Alex inside Alleghany. And finally, there was her psychiatrist, who had, over the years of weekly sessions, pulled every detail of Alex's past out of her subconscious. Dr. Moralis likely knew Alex better than she knew herself.

Although she was hesitant at first, the weekly sessions allowed Alex to understand what made up her DNA. Years of therapy had provided Alex with the tools needed to understand that her decade-long journey had been skewed from the beginning. There were others, she knew, who suffered similar loss or endured comparable tragedy. But they had likely gone through the grieving process in a more structured and traditional manner. Alex's journey had been wrong-footed from the start. She had been granted no time to properly mourn the loss of her family, or even process their deaths. She'd gone from the trauma of that night to a ruthless juvenile detention center where the time needed to grieve was instead spent trying to survive and fend off the truly vile kids she was locked up with. After Donna and Garrett had secured her release, the safeguards put in place to avoid the media had overshadowed the work Alex needed to do to process what had happened that fateful night. Then came the defamation case against the state of Virginia. The first time Alex spoke about the night her family was killed had been on the witness stand with a packed courtroom staring at her while television cameras recorded her every word. Her journey had, indeed, been skewed, and her therapist continued to point out that correcting her trajectory through life was more important than arriving at some imagined utopia in the end.

So it was not unreasonable, or even unexpected, that ten years after her family was killed Alex's sleeping hours continued to transport her back to the moment the first gunshot woke her. Over the years the dreams had become vivid to the point of lucidity. On rare nights, Alex became fully conscious while dreaming, aware that what was happening was taking place within a dream state. She grew courageous during those lucid dreams and would sneak from behind the grandfather clock and slowly creep toward her parents' bedroom. But reality and fiction would collide then—two worlds that overlapped but could never fully merge—and stop her at the foot of her parents' door frame. Occasionally she would try to fool her mind during those dreams, telling herself that she planned only to walk to her parents' doorway and listen. Instead, though, she'd burst through the door hoping to see what her mind could only imagine. Hoping to see her brother standing in their parents' bedroom, alive and waiting for her to save him. Hoping, too, to see the person holding the shotgun. To finally put a face to the figure she knew only as the shadow she'd seen from behind the grandfather clock. But as soon as she charged through the doorway in her dreams, she'd wake with a startle.

It was after one of those dreams, in her small Cambridge flat, that she started the construction of her board. When she woke, she wrote down every detail she could remember on a note card and pegged it to her board. Young and motivated people, Alex had read in a self-help book, created similar collections called vision boards. Those collages contained people's life goals and things they hoped to accomplish in their careers. Those boards included promotions and cars and houses. Alex's board contained evidence. Her board contained everything she had ever remembered—imagined or real—about the night her family was killed. It contained every bit of evidence that had ever been collected or assigned to the case. What started as a bulletin board that hung on the kitchen wall of her Cambridge flat had grown years later to a six-foot-by-eight-foot standing easel that took up a good portion of her dining room.

Although Alex had Drew Estes and Laverne Parker to blame for the constant habit of looking over her shoulder, they also were responsible for providing the biggest clue on her board. Years earlier, with help from Leo the Brit, Drew Estes was incentivized to provide the name of the man who had opened the numbered bank account her parents had presided over, the statements to which Alex found hidden in an abandoned box in her attic. That man was Roland Glazer. Over the years, Alex had meticulously researched the man to the point of obsession. The research wasn't difficult. Roland Glazer had been all over the news. An American businessman convicted of sex trafficking of teenage girls, Glazer died in jail while awaiting trial in 2012, a couple of months before Alex's family was killed.

Connected to the who's who of the business, entertainment, political, and tech worlds, the news articles Alex had read—many of which were now pinned to her board—revealed that Roland Glazer owned an island off the coast of Miami, where he routinely held parties for the rich and famous. It was on this island, and at those parties, where teenage girls were passed around to the wealthy businessmen, celebrities, and tech moguls who attended. As the feds moved in and rumors of sex-trafficking charges leaked, three of those women went missing. The women were longtime employees of Glazer's and resided on his private island. It was suspected that the women might have been able to provide key details about who had attended the clandestine parties, and specifics about the girls Glazer shuttled to and from the island. Speculation was high that Glazer had something to do with their disappearance. Images of the three women were included in the new articles and posted on websites. It was then, while researching Roland Glazer, that Alex had made the most substantial discovery in her quest to find answers to why her family was killed. The three women who had been linked to Glazer were the same women in the photos found on her parents' bed the night they were killed.

The exposés and news articles Alex had read suggested that Roland Glazer had been a ticking time bomb that would have blown to bits some major careers and uncovered a clandestine underworld had his story gone mainstream and his case made it to trial. Instead, Glazer hanged himself in his jail cell the night before his trial was to start. What on earth her parents had to do with this man was the biggest unknown Alex had come across in her years of searching for the truth.

A red thumbtack pinned Roland Glazer's photo to the middle of the board. Surrounding Glazer's image and the photos of the women found on her parents' bed were dozens of index cards and news articles. An image of the lone fingerprint sequestered from her bedroom window occupied its own section on the right side of the board, as big a mystery today as it was from the start. As Alex examined the board, she was unsure if she was any closer to finding the truth now than she had been when she created her board years earlier. Her lack of progress was an internal dialogue Alex constantly worked to mute.

Perhaps her shrink was correct. It's not the destination, but the journey.

CHAPTER 26

Washington, D.C.
Monday, March 6, 2023
8:36 p.m.

The freestanding easel that was her evidence board resided in the area of her condo where a dining table and chairs should be and was visible to Alex every day. When she had company, which was infrequent, she pulled an accordion-style room divider in front of the board to hide it from view.

Her doorbell rang and pulled Alex's attention away from the board. She walked to the intercom by the front door and pressed the button.

"Hello?"

"Hey, Alex, it's me," Garrett said. "Can I come up? I've got to talk to you about some office business."

"Sure." Alex pressed the button to unlock the building's front door.

She walked back to the board and pulled the accordion divider in front of it. The elevator chimed just as Alex opened her front door. Garrett emerged at the end of the hallway a moment later.

"Want a beer or something," Alex asked after Garrett walked into her condo.

"Sure," Garrett said.

Alex retrieved a bottle of Sam Adams from the fridge and handed it to him.

"So what's the house call about? Something that couldn't wait until morning?"

"It probably could have," Garrett said, taking a sip of the beer. "But I didn't want to have this conversation at the office."

Garrett walked over to the window and looked out at the Potomac.

"I had an interesting development with the Byron Zell case."

Alex swallowed hard and did her best to sound indifferent. "Oh yeah? I'm still working on that case. He's been a hard nut to crack. I couldn't find much online. The financial records he handed over looked clean. That's as far as I've gotten."

Garrett was still facing the window, and he didn't immediately respond, leaving her words to hang in the air like a stale odor.

"So what's going on?" Alex finally asked.

"Byron Zell sent me an e-mail. It contained all his financial records."

"Really? He already provided them, I thought. Isn't that what you gave me to dig through?"

"Yeah," Garrett said, turning from the window. "Which was why I was surprised when he sent the documents a second time."

"Yeah, that's… weird." Alex paused. "Did they match what he already gave us?"

"Word for word."

"Ah, well, I guess you have your answer then. Byron Zell sounds legit. Unless you… what? Don't think the files he sent are authentic?"

"No, they're the real deal," Garrett said, walking from the window and into the kitchen, where Alex stood. "But a different problem surfaced with the e-mail. There was something else in the documents Byron Zell sent me."

"Something else?" This time Alex's tone was sincere. She had only attached financial documents to the e-mail, so the "something else" was news to her.

"One of the files contained some disturbing child pornography."

"What?"

"Awful stuff," Garrett said, ignoring Alex's surprise. "So I found myself in a difficult spot. I'm legally required to keep the financial documents confidential since they pertain directly to my client and the case he's hired me for. Even if something nefarious had been in them, attorney-client privilege would prevent me from reporting it. But the child pornography was something else. I had no choice but to alert the police. Had I not, I could be considered liable in the crime. The authorities are looking into the situation now. I'm sure they'll have a team of forensic computer pros go over every detail of Zell's computer."

"Shit," Alex said to herself.

"Good," Garrett said. "You see my concern, so we can stop the little dance we're doing. I need to ask a question and I need you to tell me the truth. No bullshit."

Alex nodded.

"Is there any way—*any* way, Alex—the e-mail that came from Zell's computer can be linked back to Lancaster & Jordan?"

Alex knew enough not to blurt out her answer. She knew that Garrett was asking a question that needed careful contemplation, so she gave it. She replayed in her mind the night she'd broken into Zell's apartment. She went through every detail, step-by-step, and could think of no mistakes she made.

"No," she finally answered.

"Are you sure?"

"Yes."

Alex knew that Garrett had placed a great deal of trust in her over the years since hiring her as a legal investigator. She walked a fine line between trying to impress him with the information she uncovered for the firm and being careful never to put him in harm's way.

"I promise," Alex said. "There's no way any of it can come back to us. It's why the documents came to you in an e-mail from him. It's untraceable except back to Zell."

She watched Garrett nod his head and take a sip of beer.

"And I didn't know anything about the child porn stuff. I was just making sure the financials he provided to the firm matched his private files."

Garrett nodded again. "Okay. Are you hungry? I'll take you to dinner."

Alex forced a smile. "Starving," she said before walking into her bedroom to change. That was how she and Garrett operated. There was never a lot of back-and-forth. Information was exchanged, they both believed the other was telling the truth, the discussion was settled, and they moved on.

Alex emerged from her bedroom a few minutes later to find Garrett standing in front of her board. He had moved the accordion divider to the side and now analyzed the photos and notes and newspaper articles pinned to the board.

Alex cleared her throat. "Are you ready?"

Garrett didn't move from the board. He spoke with his back to her. "I thought you'd given up on this."

"Yeah, well, I figured out that I couldn't. So I got back into it."

Garrett finally turned around. "You okay?"

"I'm fine."

A long pause followed.

"It's not good for you, Alex. To keep everything so fresh in your mind. It's unhealthy—isn't that what the psychiatrist tells you?"

Garrett knew about Alex's therapy sessions. The psychiatric therapy was not court ordered, but was highly recommended by the judge who'd awarded Alex the $8 million verdict. Part of the compensation awarded was earmarked for therapy, and she was encouraged to participate in it.

"Dr. Moralis and I don't agree on everything."

"Sometimes it's good to let go of the past," Garrett said. "Not everything. Not the good stuff. But some of it."

"Well, the bad stuff is just part of me. I've tried to let it go, but that doesn't work for me. Looking, not necessarily finding anything, but *looking*... it makes me feel like I'm not forgetting about them. And since I don't want to forget about them, I'll never stop looking."

There was another long pause.

"Are we going to dinner?" Alex asked.

Garrett nodded. "Yeah. Pizza?"

CHAPTER 27

Washington, D.C.
Monday, April 10, 2023
7:48 p.m.

At fifty-six years old, Annette Packard maintained her athletic build through a combination of Pilates and swimming. Pilates was new to middle age; swimming was in her blood. As a teenager she had dreams of, and a legitimate shot at, swimming for the US Olympic team. But a labrum tear stole half a second from her 400-meter butterfly, and with that fraction went her swimming career. Despite an early retirement from competitive swimming, and like many who grew up in the sport, she never left the water. It helped that the J. Edgar Hoover Building housed an Olympic-sized pool. Home to FBI headquarters, the Hoover building was dubbed the ugliest building in Washington, and the pool paid homage to the building's moniker. Located on Underground Level 2, the aquatics center was a dilapidated mess of missing tiles and badly patched concrete. The voluminous space was without windows or natural light and was shadowed by poorly functioning overhead fluorescents in perpetual need of replacement. But when Annette was working late, as she was this night, the pool's twenty-four-hour access came in handy. She was a member at a private health club in the suburbs, but the pool hours ended at 7:00 p.m. and her current project rarely allowed her freedom at that time of night.

She walked from the showers in the staging area between the women's locker room and the pool, happy to see only one of the six lanes occupied. An older gentleman was kicking his way through the water in some hybrid of breaststroke and doggy paddle. His name was Len Palmer, an eighty-year-old retired special agent who was recovering from hip replacement. Annette knew the man's life story from their conversation the week before when the pool was full and she was forced to share a lane with him. Tonight, she headed to the opposite side from where Len splashed.

Annette Packard had worked for the FBI for twenty-five years. Breaking in as a field agent, she quickly deduced that toting a gun and chasing bad guys was not her calling. After a year she was transferred to surveillance, and two years later she was tasked with doing preliminary research on a district attorney with political aspirations for the governor's mansion. It was on that task force that Annette, as a thirty-four-year-old disillusioned FBI agent, had found her calling. Sometimes, she learned, talents were discovered without cultivating them, and goals reached without pursuing them—or even knowing they existed.

Thrown onto a task force in her midthirties, Annette Packard cultivated a knack for probing into people's personal affairs. Over the years, she proved damn good at it. *Ruthless* might better describe her ability to pry the lid off one's life and root for worrisome tidbits. For the past many years, when a prominent political figure went through the vetting process, it was Annette Packard who got the call to do the digging. The bureau still required her to carry a firearm at all times, but instead of chasing bad guys, she sniffed out the secrets politicians tried to bury and hide.

She tucked a few remaining strands of hair underneath her swimming cap and jumped into the pool. With her arms wrapped around her chest, she speared feetfirst to the bottom. The cold water was like an embrace from an old friend. Many complained about the pool's frigid temperature, but Annette preferred it on the icier side. The cool water prevented her from overheating and jolted her mind into a sharp state of concentration. She flexed her knees when her feet hit the bottom, then pushed upward, releasing air from her lungs until she broke the surface. Positioning herself against the wall, she took a deep breath and pushed hard off the crumbling tile, kicking underwater for half the length of the pool before starting into a freestyle stroke.

After three laps she found her rhythm and kept a steady pace for thirty minutes, barely noticing her increasing heart rate. This many decades in the water, it took a lot to gas her. She had to push herself if she wanted a cardiovascular workout, which at times she did. Mostly, though, she preferred a slow and steady fat burn. It kept the weight off, and her muscles toned. It also helped keep her thoughts organized—something her position inside the Federal Bureau of Investigation demanded.

After forty minutes, she decided to burn her remaining energy on a hundred-meter sprint. She flipped at the wall and dug long strokes into the water, kicking what energy she had left into the wake behind her. As she approached the final turn, she felt a presence above the water—someone was standing at the edge of the pool watching her. She aborted her flip halfway through her underwater turn and broke the surface, then peeled her goggles off and rested them on her forehead.

"James," she said to her assistant, and the number two agent involved with the vetting of Lawrence Chadwick. "What's up?"

"We've got a situation," James said.

They were three months into the Chadwick vet and had hit no significant potholes, a comforting yet worrisome situation. Annette's occupation bred suspicion, not confidence, the longer she went without finding dirt on the subject she was vetting. Annette *always* found dirt, and when she didn't it usually meant they were hiding it.

"What kind of situation?" Annette asked in a heavy breath of exertion.

"A bad one. We need you upstairs right away."

"How bad?" Annette wiped the chlorine water from her eyes. "A course correction or engine failure?"

Over the years, Annette's team had taken to describing problems that arose during their vets in terms of traveling the ocean on a cruise line. Course corrections were common and manageable. They meant something minor had come up and they needed to pivot and regroup to get around it. An engine failure came up less frequently but could usually be handled if caught early enough.

"Uh, I'd classify this more of an iceberg in our direct path."

"Shit," Annette said, peeling her swim cap off her head. "How big?"

"Titanic big."

CHAPTER 28

Washington, D.C.
Thursday, April 13, 2023
10:32 p.m.

Laura McAllister sat alone in the small recording studio on the campus of McCormack University, pulled the headphones off her ears, and pushed the microphone away from her. Besides the glimmer of her laptop and the few lights glowing on the dashboard of the control panel, the studio was dark. She took a deep breath to calm her nerves now that she had finished the recording, but still her hand shook when she pulled the USB flash drive from her computer. The memory stick contained the final edits of the episode she had been working on for the past month. Now, with her voice-over completed and testimonials polished, the episode was nearly ready to drop. Last month, when she appeared on *Wake Up America*, Dante Campbell had asked her what she would be working on next. At the time, Laura had no idea. A month later, she believed she had a story that would send shock waves throughout the university.

Stored on the flash stick was a wide-ranging episode that covered her monthlong investigation into allegations of rape at McCormack University, and the blatant cover-up by faculty and administrators who hoped they could bury the story deep in the ground, where it would die and decay before anyone knew it existed. The episode was the most far-reaching and legitimate piece of investigative reporting she'd done. It contained interviews with students who knew the facts, faculty who were brave enough to talk, scientists who explained how date-rape drugs work, and psychiatrists who clarified why rape victims don't always or immediately come forward to tell their stories. The episode named the offenders and confirmed the accusations with timelines and photos. Laura had even gone quasi-undercover to a fraternity party to prove that its members were spiking drinks with gamma hydroxybutyrate, a date-rape drug commonly referred to as Liquid G.

Laura McAllister was about to prove again that small outlets like her little university radio show could break huge stories. Her ex-posé was poised to make a huge splash. It not only tackled campus rape at McCormack University, date-rape drugs, and university cover-ups, but also poignantly examined the debate about consent and dove deeply into the choices students make about sex.

The episode was sure to have the university and those in charge scrambling. It had the power to ruin lives and end careers, which was why Laura was starting to have reservations about airing it. The story was so volatile that Laura worried about the fallout it would cause. She'd done her homework, confirmed every accusation, and collected proof of each bomb-shell she would drop, yet some part of her psyche questioned whether she should go through with it. For one of the accused, in particular, things would go haywire in a way Laura knew she could not predict. She imagined having to testify in front of Congress about the legitimacy of her findings, and she worried about the powerful people who would do anything to thwart the story and discredit her as nothing more than a college kid with dreams of being the next Jodi Kantor, Megan Twohey, or Ronan Farrow. She wondered whether the scrutiny would be worth it.

Then she thought of the victims. The girls whose stories she would tell had already had their lives ruined, and somehow Laura had become their voice. Laura had become the only one who would shine light on their tragedy because the people in charge wanted the story to go away. Laura and her little radio show had become the only avenue to get their stories out, and she felt obligated to use her platform to help. If the lives of those who perpetrated the crimes and then tried to cover them up were destroyed in the process, so be it. And if powerful people came after her and tried to smear her reputation, she would push back. She had Dante Campbell's information stored on her phone and an offer from one of the most powerful and well-known journalists in the country to help if Laura ever needed advice.

Her cell phone buzzed and pulled Laura from her thoughts. When she looked at the caller ID, she saw Duncan Chadwick's name. His father had been all over the news lately as the president's likely nominee to fill the Supreme Court vacancy. As Laura stared at her phone, two things dawned on her. The first was that, despite her efforts at secrecy, her story had leaked. The second was that she was now in a race against time.

CHAPTER 29

Washington, D.C.
Friday, April 14, 2023
6:45 p.m.

Annette Packard sat in the back of the SUV and read through her notes. During her career, she'd overseen the vetting of dozens of judges, scores of senators, and countless congressional candidates. Nearly a third of America's sitting governors had had their lives picked apart by Annette Packard before starting their campaigns and making their runs. Smooth sailing was never expected when rooting through the private affairs of political hopefuls. Yet, until recently, Annette had found exactly that in the last three months of picking through Larry Chadwick's life—clear skies and calm winds. The man was a choirboy. It had been a refreshing change, but now the other shoe had dropped. It usually did. This time, it was Chadwick's son who threatened to derail the process.

As the SUV pulled up to the Chadwick residence Annette contemplated that up until this latest development the worst she'd found during her forensic review of the judge's life and career were a couple of favors called in to get his delinquent son out of trouble. They were nothing most parents wouldn't have done if they had the power and influence to do it. At least, that was how she and her team had presented the information to the president. There was no denying that Larry Chadwick could be accused of abusing his position to bail his son out of trouble, but in the grand scheme of things the transgressions were minor. The biggest had been Larry skirting his son around a DUI charge when Duncan Chadwick was seventeen. Sketchy, but not bad enough to sink Larry's nomination. At most, the incident would lead to a few uncomfortable questions and accusations of privilege from particularly nasty senators out for blood. And this would happen only if the events were discovered. The DUI, in particular, had been so well concealed that Annette and her team had barely managed to uncover it, and she had the power of the entire Justice Department behind her.

In the event that an eager senator *was* able to unearth the DUI and other minor incidents, Larry could handle the questions. They would coach him on how to respond. Going after a nominee's kid was dangerous. If the tactic got classified as a cheap assault on the candidate's child, it would backfire. Bottom line, attacking Larry Chadwick for his son's nonviolent offenses would be an unwise approach by the opposition. Going after Larry Chadwick for his son's role in a series of rapes on McCormack University's campus, however, would not only be fair game, but lethal to Larry's chances.

When the driver pulled to the curb, Annette climbed out of the SUV and headed toward the Chadwicks' brownstone. Dark thunderstorms were forming on the horizon, threatening to ruin months of blue skies and clear sailing.

CHAPTER 30

The FBI's presence in his chambers no longer surprised him. It was when they showed up unannounced at his home that Larry Chadwick became uncomfortable. Annette Packard and her team had taken a wrecking ball to his past, knocking down everything that was questionable and picking through the rubble for suspicious or nefarious remains. He resigned himself to the fact that in order to be handed a lifetime appointment on the highest court in the country his life was going to be dismantled ahead of time to make sure there was nothing rotting behind the walls. The demolition, however, never seemed to end.

As Larry pulled up to his DC brownstone, he saw the black government-issued SUV parked out front, hazards blinking and an agent behind the wheel. House calls always meant a "development" had come up, on which Annette needed Larry's immediate attention. They were nearing the end of the vetting period. Larry had been through his life's history with Annette on a number of occasions and could think of nothing more he could offer about himself. In recent weeks, Annette had moved away from his academic years and had started concentrating on his adult life and career. But his finances were in order with no blemishes of bribes or corruption. Larry was confident in his professional choices throughout his career. He'd offered the right opinions and decisions from the bench, and they were all grounded in logical legal analysis. His hires and appointees had been diverse and without controversy. Everything to this point had been deemed squeaky clean. So he wondered what new development had brought the FBI to his home at seven in the evening.

Larry pushed through his front door, hung his coat in the closet, and walked into the kitchen to find Annette Packard sitting at the table across from his wife.

"Annette," Larry said. "I didn't expect to see you tonight."

"Sorry to barge in unannounced," Annette said. "Something's come up."

She wore dark slacks and a blazer and looked professional as always. The woman was the very definition of no nonsense.

Larry walked over and gave his wife a kiss. "Hey, babe, everything okay?"

"Yes," Renee Chadwick said. "Annette and I were just catching up until you got home. She has something she needs to discuss with both of us."

"Okay," Larry said in a casual tone. "I'm having a drink. Can I get you something?"

"No," Annette said. "I'm fine, thank you."

"Glass of wine?" Larry asked his wife.

"Maybe in a moment. I'm anxious to hear what Annette has to tell us."

Larry walked to the kitchen bar and scooped ice into a glass tumbler. "What's so urgent? This couldn't wait until morning?"

"I'm afraid not," Annette said. "We have a problem, Larry."

There was a soft pain somewhere in his gut, fear that perhaps one of his affairs had been uncovered. "What now? My taxes are clean. Didn't you just finish with them?"

"Yes. Taxes are fine. I'm afraid this has to do with your son."

"Duncan?" Larry turned from the bar, holding his scotch. "It was a DUI, Annette. And the bloodwork was equivocal. They dismissed it more out of a lack of evidence than any influence I was able to apply."

"It's not the DUI."

Larry saw that Annette's expression was straight-faced and stoic.

"What is it?" Larry asked.

"Have you ever heard of a McCormack University radio program called *The Scoop*?"

Larry sat down next to Renee. "No. Should I?"

"It's produced by a student named Laura McAllister. The show is broadcast from the school of journalism's recording studio on campus and is quite popular. It sounds like the whole university tunes in to listen each week. The girl has gained national notoriety for scooping breaking stories and was recently featured on *Wake Up America* with Dante Campbell."

"Okay," Larry said.

"What started out as a little university program has turned into a pop-culture sensation. Laura McAllister is being dubbed the female version of Joe Rogan. He's a popular podcaster who appeals to a young audience."

"I know who he is."

"For a senior in college, Laura McAllister has been able to attract legitimate A-list guests on her show, and no topic is off limits. Through social media, more than a million people— mostly college students across the country—listen to her show each week when she uploads the episodes to her social accounts. Her show's growing exponentially."

"Okay," Larry said again. "And this affects me how?"

Annette folded her hands and placed them on the table. "We have sources telling us that this student journalist is looking into allegations of rape on McCormack University's campus and is preparing to air a show spilling all the details."

Larry exhaled an exhausted breath. "Do I want to ask?"

"Probably not, but you need to know. Laura McAllister is preparing to make allegations against the Delta Chi fraternity— your son's fraternity—claiming that members were involved with spiking drinks at fraternity-run parties with the drug gamma hydroxybutyrate, referred to as Liquid G. It's a tasteless, odorless drug commonly used as a date-rape chemical. There're accusations from a number of girls, but one of them— a girl named Kristi Penny— claims she was raped earlier in the semester at the Delta Chi fraternity and has filed a formal police report."

"For Christ's sake," Larry said. He took a large gulp of scotch. "Why haven't I heard anything about this from the school?"

"They're investigating it internally, from what my sources tell me. You haven't heard about it because the university is desperate to keep a lid on the crisis. McCormack has a significant endowment and strong financial support from alumni. The university is positioned nicely as an elite academic institution that rivals the Ivy Leagues. A rape scandal would be bad for business, devastating to the university's image, and would close the spigot of alumni donations. It would put the president of the university and the dean in a difficult situation, one from which it's unlikely either would survive. Not to mention that a rape scandal would hinder recruitment. These cases of sexual assault have been ongoing for some time, my sources tell me. The university has been working hard to keep the stories quiet, but now that the latest victim has filed a formal police report, keeping a lid on things for much longer won't be possible. And if Laura McAllister airs her show, depending on what, exactly, she has uncovered, the scandal will be all over the news."

"Is Duncan involved?" Renee asked.

"That's what we need to find out. But even if Duncan wasn't involved, it might not matter as far as your nomination is concerned. The scandal alone might be enough to tank you."

"Goddammit!" Larry said.

"Before we overreact," Annette said, "We need to talk to Duncan. Everything we've heard so far is second sourced. We may be able to get out in front of this if we know the specifics.

If Duncan can provide us with insider details. If he wasn't involved, then we can make a statement before the story drops that will hopefully defuse things."

"What kind of statement?" Larry asked.

"You, Renee, and Duncan make a public statement via press conference, denouncing any wrongdoing by the fraternity and speaking out definitively against sexual assault. You make a strong statement about consent. Of course, Duncan will have to speak as well, and will have to distance himself from the fraternity. You don't have any daughters, so that's going to work against you because you won't be able to mention how empathetic you are to the victims. People will call you out on it if you try. Anyway, there's an avenue around this. It's narrow, treacherous, and needs to be navigated very carefully. But it exists. The first thing we need to do is talk with Duncan."

Larry nodded. He finished his scotch in one giant gulp. "What did you say this girl's name was? The student journalist?"

"Laura McAllister. Why, do you know her?"

Larry shook his head. "No, just trying to get my brain around this thing."

CHAPTER 31

Washington, D.C.
Monday, April 17, 2023
12:20 p.m.

Situated along the banks of the Potomac River, McCormack University was gorgeous, prestigious, and a stone's throw from the Chadwicks' brownstone. That Duncan Chadwick had ended up at a school so close to home was no accident. Larry knew the dangers of unleashing his delinquent son at a faraway college where Larry's ability to bail him out of trouble would be limited. Larry had insisted on Duncan staying on the East Coast in order to keep his political influence available. Washington, D.C. was even better. Now, his son needed Larry's far-reaching political powers more than ever. But this time he wasn't fighting to keep a DUI off a minor's record. This time Larry was fighting for both Duncan's future and his own.

The outdoor press conference was standing-room only. Fifty folding chairs had been set up in front of the podium that stood outside the arched gates of McCormack University. Every seat was full, and overflow press stood in a ballooning crown behind them. News cameras waited at the ready, and at exactly 12:20 in the afternoon Larry ushered Renee and Duncan to the podium. Both he and Duncan had dressed in charcoal suits with blue ties, offering a not-so-subtle message that Duncan was the spitting image of his father, a well-respected public servant.

Larry took his position behind the podium and adjusted the microphone as he allowed the news cameras to zero in on him and his perfect family.

"Good afternoon," he said. "It has been brought to my attention that something terrible has taken place at McCormack University, where my son, Duncan, is enrolled. A girl, whose name I will not mention in an effort to honor her privacy, has been raped. The information I have tells me that this incident happened not only on the McCormack University campus, but at the fraternity where Duncan is currently a member. First and foremost, my thoughts and prayers go out to this young woman."

Larry paused and looked down at his notes. Camera shutters clicked in rapid succession from the gallery.

"This news was a shock to Renee and me, and it was a stunning revelation to Duncan. As a united front, we want to speak out against any and all forms of sexual assault. Renee and I have had long and sometimes awkward discussions with Duncan about consent and about what constitutes assault. We are proud of the values we've instilled in our son, and Duncan is eager to speak about this incident today."

Larry looked over.

"Son?"

Duncan nodded and replaced his father at the podium. The camera shutters clicked with a new intensity when Larry Chadwick's son stood behind the microphone. He swallowed hard and cleared his throat before speaking, an audible quiver to his voice.

"Like my dad said, I was shocked to hear that a classmate had been raped. And even more surprised to learn that the rape took place at my fraternity. Details are still coming out, but I'm here with my parents today to say that I believe the victim, who, like my dad said, we won't name because she wants to remain anonymous. But I believe her, and I stand by her. I also want to say that despite the strong friendships I've made through the Delta Chi fraternity, effective immediately I will be revoking my membership and working in any capacity possible to help the victim find justice. Thank you."

Duncan stepped back from the podium as reporters began to shout questions. Larry resumed his spot and held up his hands to quiet the crowd.

"Judge Chadwick!" an aggressive reporter shouted. "Will this affect your nomination to the Supreme Court?"

"We won't be taking questions this afternoon," Larry said. "However, before we close this press conference I want to make a pledge to the victim and her parents that I will do everything in my power to help bring her attacker to justice. I encourage the victim and her family to reach out to me if they feel that I can be of help in any way. I'd also like to mention that immediately following this press conference, Duncan will be speaking with the police to help the authorities in any way possible."

"Judge Chadwick, are you still the president's nominee for the Supreme Court vacancy?"

"Thank you for your time this afternoon," Larry said. "God bless. And God bless the victim of this horrific crime."

Reporters continued to shout questions as Larry gathered his family and solemnly walked from the podium and climbed into a waiting town car.

CHAPTER 32

Washington, D.C.
Friday, April 21, 2023
11:35 p.m.

All hell had broken loose.

Her story had leaked. Laura knew that the longer she invest-igated and the more people she spoke with certain details about her story would begin to circulate through campus. She had always figured she'd be able to stay ahead of the gossip, but somehow her story had leaked. Not just a few teasers, but nearly every detail of her episode was floating around McCormack University in some form. Duncan Chadwick's phone call had tipped her off; the Chadwicks' press conference had confirmed it. Laura hadn't answered Duncan's call and had kept a low profile for the past week to avoid running into him or other members of the Delta Chi fraternity.

The press conference had sent shock waves through campus and was all anyone was talking about. It had come out of nowhere, and Laura knew it was explicitly timed to preempt her episode and take the bite out of her story. The press conference had accelerated things in a way Laura had not anticipated, and now she had a decision to make: drop her episode and reveal everything she had discovered over the last month, or sit back and allow the police to uncover it all on their own. But the university had known about the rape for weeks and had done nothing about it. She worried that the authorities would follow the same path of victim blaming until the story went away, keeping the university's reputation unsullied. Although nervous about the position the episode would put her in—at the center of a massive controversy involving a prominent political figure and his son—Laura had no choice but to go forward with it.

She twirled the memory stick between her fingers as she sat in the School of Journalism's recording studio. Laura had completed her interviews, finished the investigative legwork, polished her voice-over work, and stored the completed episode on both the thumb drive and as a downloaded file on her phone. Of course, the entire episode was also stored on the recording studio's computer hard drive, but airing the episode from the studio was no longer an option. Things had changed dramatically since she sat in the studio a week earlier. Back then she believed she had time to decide when and how to drop the episode. But now that her story had leaked, the names of those involved had started to spread through campus, and the Chadwicks were on the offensive. Word had trickled down to her that the university was considering shutting her show down. Laura needed to act, and to act now.

Her plan was bold. She would bypass using McCormack University's bandwidth and broadcasting platform, which had always been Laura's first method of distributing her stories before uploading them to her social media accounts. Instead, she'd go solo on this one and just post the episode online to her million-plus followers. Then, she'd go into hiding for a few days. Maybe she'd hole up in a hotel and see how things unfolded. She thought about going home but didn't want to bring attention to her parents in case the press or the police—or the federal government, for Christ's sake—came looking for her.

"Holy shit," she whispered into the darkened studio, trying to understand how this story had gotten so big.

She slipped the thumb drive into her backpack and zipped it closed. After pulling the straps over her shoulders, she locked the recording studio and headed across campus. She had some serious thinking to do and even considered reaching out to Dante Campbell in the morning to discuss the story and ask for Dante's help getting the word out. But she knew that might take too long because Dante and NBC would need to comb through every detail of her story to confirm the accuracy of it. Laura had already done the combing, though, and knew her story was accurate.

As she exited campus, she cut through Horace Grove, a wooded area that skirted the campus. It was a shortcut that shaved five minutes off the commute to her apartment and was frequented by students at just about every hour of the day and night. Although on this night, it was strangely abandoned. She secured her AirPods and clicked on the download of her episode to listen to it one last time. If she found no errors, the decision was made. She'd drop it tonight and let the pieces fall where they may. The intro to *The Scoop* chimed through the earbuds as she started off along the path through the woods.

It was the last time anyone would see Laura McAllister alive.

PART IV

A Missing Persons Case

"I'm on a deadline."

—Annette Packard

Camp Montague

Appalachian Mountains

They waited until late to go out. The campfire had ended more than an hour ago, and they had passed the time playing Texas Hold'em in his cabin until they were sure the camp was sound asleep and the counselors were no longer on their nightly prowl to catch kids out past curfew. After five summers at Montague, he and his friends knew their way around. His first time at camp was the summer after eighth grade, when he was thirteen—the earliest Montague allowed kids to register. Now he had just finished his senior year in high school and would soon be off to college. This was his last summer at Montague. The finality of things allowed him, and the rest of the fifth-years, to take more chances. There could be no real penalty for breaking the rules. The normal course of action each summer was for the counselors to add up each camper's merits, subtract any strikes, and then adjust their ranking for the following summer. Since neither he nor his friends were coming back to Camp Montague, this was the first summer that earning merits and accumulating strikes was meaningless. All the fifth-years were aware of the loophole, and it explained why each summer this select group of campers ran by their own rules.

He opened his cabin door and took a cautious look around. When he saw that the camp was quiet, he nodded, and the group of four hurried out of the cabin and disappeared into the woods, clicking on flashlights to find the path. After fifteen minutes, the sound of the falls made its way faintly through the trees, and they picked up their pace. When they made it to the clearing, the moonlight reflected off the waterfall and colored the pond a tranquil shade of silver.

"Hey," came a whisper from the other side of the pond.

He smiled and waved when he saw the girls. He and his friends hustled over. There were eight of them: four guys and four girls. One of them had snuck a case of beer from camp. They preferred fruity seltzers but took whatever they managed to steal from the main lodge. Tonight it was Budweiser, which went down badly. No one complained. They were a bunch of eighteen-year-olds on their last summer excursion to Montague, a place that had defined their adolescent experience. None saw each other outside of camp each summer. They lived in different towns and different states. But this summer they ruled Montague and would wring every ounce of adventure out of their last summer here.

After they'd all had a couple of beers, the guys threw their shirts onto the rocks and dove into the pond. The girls stripped off their cutoff shorts to reveal bathing suits underneath and followed the guys. Together they swam toward the falls and for twenty minutes braved the water that poured down from the mountain. When it was time to head back, they entered the woods and found the trail. When they got back to camp and split off in different directions, they tried to stay in the shadows.

He cut around the east side of camp and was about to step out of the woods when he heard one of the camp counselors' cabin doors squeak open. He took a quick step behind a tree, made sure he was bathed in darkness, and watched. He saw Mr. Lolland—one of Montague's lead counselors—walk from his cabin. With him was a girl. Mr. Lolland had his hand on her neck as if he were consoling her.

He slunk through the woods and followed them through camp, using the foliage as cover as he watched Mr. Lolland lead the girl back to her cabin and usher her inside. A moment later, he saw Jerry Lolland head back to his own cabin. A sickening feeling came over him. He knew what had happened. During his first summer at Montague, he, too, had been one of Mr. Lolland's victims.

The campfire was dying. He stayed hidden in the spot he had staked out after dinner—a small clearing in the woods behind the trunk of a sturdy oak. The location provided a perfect view of Mr. Lolland's cabin. Off in the distance he saw the campsite begin to thin as his fellow campers concluded the night with the Montague Pledge and headed to their cabins. It was forty minutes later, after cabin lights blinked off, that he saw Mr. Lolland's door open.

He pressed himself against the trunk of the oak and waited until Mr. Lolland was a good way into camp before he crept from the shadow of the oak and started his silent march through the forest as he followed. He watched through the foliage as Mr. Lolland passed through the area of camp reserved for second-year campers. Stepping through a stream, he crept closer to the edge of the forest to get a better view as Mr. Lolland entered the area where first-year recruits were housed and approached a cabin.

A minute later, Mr. Lolland emerged from the cabin with a girl by his side. He retraced his steps as he followed them through camp, eventually returning to the small clearing behind the sturdy oak. It was there that his life changed. It was there that he watched Jerry Lolland lead the girl into his cabin. It was there that he hesitated. He should have done so many things. He should have run from the woods and stopped Mr. Lolland from taking the girl into his cabin. He should have run to the main lodge and found the other counselors and told them what was happening. But to do that would mean to admit that the same thing had happened to him, and the shame he harbored from his time in Jerry Lolland's cabin was greater than the guilt he felt for allowing it to happen to someone else.

He didn't stop Mr. Lolland that night. But as he stood in the dark shadows of the forest, he came up with a plan to make sure Jerry Lolland never hurt anyone again.

CHAPTER 33

Washington, D.C.
Saturday, April 22, 2023
11:45 p.m.

Byron Zell sat at his desk and tapped away at his new computer—a small MacBook he had purchased to replace his desktop after authorities confiscated it. In just a few short weeks his life had gone to hell. In addition to the financial crimes his company had accused him of, he now had the bigger issue of several felony counts of possession of child pornography to deal with. Garrett Lancaster had cut all ties with him, and although Byron couldn't yet prove it, he was certain someone had either been in his apartment or, more likely, hacked into his computer. It was the only explanation for how his private financial documents, in which he kept his stash of pornography from the dark web, had been sent to Lancaster & Jordan.

He'd reached out to three different criminal defense firms until he finally found a taker. But the firm was a far cry from the powerhouse that was Lancaster & Jordan. Still, his best approach was to attack the method by which the authorities had obtained his personal information, which was through a fraudulent e-mail sent to Garrett Lancaster. Byron possessed a receipt from the convenience store where he had purchased two Red Bulls and a bag of chips. On the receipt was the date and time of the purchase, which coincided with the time the e-mail was sent. Byron's new attorney was in the process of pulling surveillance footage from the convenience store to prove

Byron's whereabouts. If Byron could prove that he was away from his apartment and his computer at the time the e-mail was sent, then the evidence—two gigs' worth of child pornography from the dark web—would not be admissible and the charges against him would be dropped.

It should be enough, but even then there would be fallout. He'd likely still have to register as a sex offender and would never hold a meaningful job again. And once this latest disaster was behind him, Byron would begin anew his fight against embezzlement charges. It was, he dwelled as he pecked away at his new laptop, a shit life he was leading.

He tried not to dwell on what would happen if his attorney could not get the child pornography charges dismissed. If convicted of the financial crimes he was accused of, they would send him to a country club prison for a few months. He had friends who'd done time in such establishments and made it through unscathed. But his infatuation with children was another story. That carried a harsher penalty, and going to a real prison would be a death sentence, especially if the caged animals learned why he was there.

Still, with all the dread and worry on his mind, he felt a familiar urge bubble up inside of him as he sat in front of his computer. It was an urge he had never been able to quell. A few minutes on the dark web wouldn't hurt anyone. This time, he would resist the temptation to download the images that particularly aroused him. He tapped the keyboard and turned on the private browsing feature so that his search history would not be logged. Then, he went through a series of webpages and logins. This seldom-explored corner of the Internet was a familiar place, somewhere he visited to break free from social norms that constrained his life and his urges. He planned to spend just a few minutes there that night. Half hour, at most. In this shadowed corner of the Internet there was no judgment or shame. He was allowed to like what he liked. And no matter what *that* might be, it could be found there at the darkened edge of humanity. For Byron Zell, his vice was children.

He spent a little longer than intended browsing the sites. He convinced himself that if he somehow managed to escape the shit-storm he was in, tonight would be his last time on the dark web. That final perusing of underage children would be a way to get it out of his system, once and for all. Some part of his psyche believed it. Deeper down, though, he knew it was a lie. He suffered an addiction that could never be cured.

After an hour, he closed his computer, turned off the desk lamp, and left his office. The lights of the city were visible through the living room windows of the high-rise apartment. The night was clear, and the moon a waxing crescent that lighted the hardwood floor just enough for Byron to navigate to the kitchen, where he opened the refrigerator and reached for the milk carton.

The glow from the open refrigerator cast his shadow across the kitchen island. Out of the corner of his eye he caught the image of another shadow that did not belong to him. Byron turned and the carton of milk fell from his hand when he saw the figure in black standing on the other side of the kitchen, the barrel of a gun reflecting the light from the refrigerator.

Instinctively, he raised his hands. "I have money."

The figure in black held up photos of child pornography. Byron tried to protest, to deny it, but the words caught in his throat and he was unable to breathe. Two suppressed hisses came from the gun in rapid succession. The noise registered, but that was all. He waited for the pain but it did not come. He was aware of his surroundings one moment, and dead the next.

Byron Zell fell in a heap to the kitchen floor. He did not fall forward and was not propelled backward by the bullets that entered his body—one to the face, the other to the chest; he simply collapsed. His knees buckled and his legs folded underneath him like a blowup toy that had been deflated.

The shooter walked over to the heap, threw the photos of child pornography onto his dead body, and then hurried out of the apartment.

CHAPTER 34

Manhattan, NY
Tuesday, April 25, 2023
8:02 a.m.

Tracy Carr's body dripped water as she climbed from the shower and grabbed the towel off the rack. She dried off before bending forward and capturing her soaking hair in the towel and spinning both on top of her head. She walked into the bedroom, clicked on the television and let the morning news play in the background as she pulled on underwear and a bra.

Her phone vibrated from the night table and Tracy saw that it was her editor calling. She swiped the phone to activate the call.

"Hey, Gary," she said.

"Are you watching the news?"

Tracy turned her attention to the television, where a CNN anchor was speaking while a red news alert banner blinked at the bottom of the screen—a ploy that had long ago lost its shock value. A lost dog was breaking news to most twenty-four-hour cable programs.

"I just stepped out of the shower," Tracy said. "What's going on?"

"Remember Larry Chadwick's news conference from last week?"

"How could I forget? It was basically a campaign commercial to show how caring he and his son were toward victims of sexual assault. Political theater."

"Yeah, well, that news conference is starting to look less like theater and more like an attempt to deflect guilt. A McCormack University girl named Laura McAllister is missing. Word on the street is that she was the student journalist who was looking into the rape Larry Chadwick and his son referenced during their news conference. Details are scarce but I'm sure there's a bigger story there. I want you on it."

Tracy read the glowing banner at the bottom of CNN's broadcast: COLLEGE STUDENT MISSING IN WASHINGTON, DC.

"When?"

"Now. As soon as possible. Get down to DC and see what you can uncover. I want an opening article for tomorrow's edition. As much as you can get. Then, more details as you uncover them. You'll be on the story until we see how this thing ends, and if it's in any way connected to Larry Chadwick."

"I'm on it. I'll call you when I'm down there."

Tracy ended the call. She watched the rest of the CNN segment. A missing college student on the heels of a bizarrely timed press conference from the president's likely choice to fill the Supreme Court vacancy. Could there be a connection there? Tracy planned to find out, and she couldn't have asked for a better story to fall from the sky. It was a potential blockbuster. Hard facts were still unknown, which meant speculation would be wild—perfect for drawing in viewers to her social channels. It meant that the truth was still waiting to be found, and her ravenous audience would eat up any tidbit of information she was able to turn up. Tracy was a master manipulator of society's sad but real affliction: a gluttonous appetite for the gory details of true crime. It was how Tracy made her living. Add a quasi celebrity—as Lawrence Chadwick had become over the last month as he was courted by the president—to the disappearance of a young, attractive college girl, and Tracy Carr had ratings gold in front of her.

In addition to her gig as a crime reporter for the *New York Times*, Tracy Carr ran a successful YouTube channel that covered true crime. She sported six million subscribers and the channel was fully monetized, earning her six figures from ad revenue alone. She employed three people to run the channel: Her old college roommate organized the advertising and optimized the channel's placement on YouTube and around the Internet. A production editor collected the raw footage Tracy recorded and truncated it down to short, watchable videos. And then there was Jimmy, her cameraman. Shoots were typically structured and scheduled, but the quickly developing story she had just been assigned required fast action. She picked up the phone.

"Jimmy," Tracy said. "Something's come up. I need you to pack a bag, and all your equipment. We're heading to DC."

"When?" Jimmy asked.

"Right now. A college girl's gone missing. But that's just the beginning of it. I'll pick you up in an hour."

CHAPTER 35

Washington, D.C.
Tuesday, April 25, 2023
9:15 a.m.

The offices of Lancaster & Jordan were located on the tenth floor of the One Franklin Square building in Washington, D.C. The conference room was prepped for this morning's meeting. Garrett had cleared his schedule, as had Jacqueline Jordan, the other founding partner of the firm. Jacqueline would, in fact, be lead counsel should Lancaster & Jordan take Matthew Claymore on as a client.

Garrett and Jacqueline stood when Matthew and his parents entered the large conference room, which was dominated by a long mahogany table that shined with morning sunlight spilling through the windows that overlooked Franklin Park. The dome of the Capitol Building was in the far distance.

"Matthew," Garrett said as he extended a hand. "Garrett Lancaster, nice to meet you. This is my partner, Jacqueline Jordan."

"These are my parents," Matthew said. "Patrick and Sheila." Handshakes were exchanged.

"Thanks for taking the meeting so quickly," Patrick Claymore said.

Garrett and Jacqueline's research told them that Patrick and Sheila Claymore owned a string of grocery stores on the East Coast and were obnoxiously wealthy. Their son, Matthew, was a business major at McCormack University. The school had been in the news the past week after Larry Chadwick's press conference. When the Claymores requested a meeting to inquire about Lancaster & Jordan representing Matthew in a potential missing persons case involving a McCormack University student, Garrett and Jacqueline quickly set up a meet and greet.

"Of course," Jacqueline said. "Have a seat. I hope we can help. Coffee, before we get started?"

The Claymores declined.

Matthew sat at the head of the conference table, since he would be doing most of the talking. His parents sat to his left with Garrett and Jacqueline to his right. Jacqueline opened a leather folder and turned a few pages on a yellow legal pad.

"Matthew," she said, "your parents gave us some preliminary information over the phone, but Garrett and I will need you to get us fully up to date."

"Okay," Matthew started. "I'm a senior at McCormack University. Over the weekend, my girlfriend... I don't know, she stopped returning my texts and went quiet on social media. She's done that before when she gets busy with her show."

"Her show?" Jacqueline asked.

"Yeah, she's a journalism student with, um, like a really popular campus radio program."

"Popular is being modest," Patrick Claymore said. "Laura's radio show, a podcast, really, is listened to by hundreds of thousands of people each week—based on downloads."

Jacqueline scribbled some notes. "What's your girlfriend's name?"

"Laura McAllister."

Jacqueline nodded as she continued to write on her legal pad. "Go on."

"*The Scoop* started out as a radio program Laura did each week from the broadcasting studio on campus. At first it was just, like, pop culture and gossip. Laura did this segment called *Camp-sip*—as in campus gossip, where she found the wildest stories from colleges around the country and talked about them. Anything from student-professor hookups to a formal gone wrong. During my freshman year everyone started listening each Thursday night. It was, like, a McCormack U thing, and Laura's show became really popular.

"Then, sophomore year she did a more serious show about how college campuses can feel, and can actually *be*, unsafe for female students. She interviewed girls from all over the country, not just McCormack, and the consensus was that girls felt most frightened and vulnerable when they were walking alone off campus. So Laura came up with solutions on how to fix it, which was for the university to hire private drivers to shuttle students to and from campus on nights and weekends. She called the program 'Uber U.' And it caught on. Not only did McCormack adopt the Uber U program, but so did colleges across the country. Laura was invited onto *Wake Up America* and interviewed by Dante Campbell. Ever since then, the popularity of Laura's show has skyrocketed. She has over a million followers on her social media platforms."

Matthew shook his head to get back on track.

"Anyway, over the last few weeks Laura told me she had been investigating a story about rape on campus."

"McCormack University's campus?" Jacqueline asked.

"Yes. I don't know all the details because Laura was real quiet about it. She didn't want the story to leak. But then, last week the campus blew up after the Chadwicks' press conference. It was totally about the story Laura was getting ready to tell. Then, like I said, Laura stopped returning my calls and texts over the weekend, and went silent on social media. Her parents called me on Sunday to ask if I'd heard from her. I told them I hadn't and Laura's parents reported her missing on Sunday. Then, yesterday two police officers showed up at my apartment to ask a bunch of questions."

"About Laura?" Jacqueline asked.

"Yeah, about Laura and about whether we'd had a fight recently and about a bunch of other stuff."

"Did you answer their questions?"

"Yeah, but after a while I started getting scared so I told them I wanted to call my parents."

Mr. Claymore leaned forward onto the conference table. "The police asked Matthew if he would come down to the precinct office to answer more questions during a formal interview, and to provide DNA samples. I instructed him to do no such thing until we obtained legal counsel. I pray Laura is safe and this turns out to be a big scare or misunderstanding. But I've heard enough horror stories to know that if something has happened to this poor girl, then the first person the authorities are going to look at is her boyfriend."

Jacqueline nodded. "Have you had any contact with the police since they questioned you yesterday?"

"No," Matthew said. "A detective left a voicemail this morning asking me to call him back."

"But you haven't?"

"No."

"Okay," Jacqueline said. "And as far as you know, no one has yet heard from Laura?"

"No." Matthew shrugged. "I've texted her a bunch of times and I talked with her friends. No one's heard from her and no one's seen her."

Jacqueline tapped her pen on the legal pad as she thought.

"First things first. Do not speak to the police without Garrett or me being present. If they come to your apartment, tell them you want to call your attorney and then get in touch with me immediately. I'll give you my cell number. In the meantime, one of our investigators will be in touch with you to more thoroughly go over the details of your relationship with Laura, as well as some other information we're going to need. Then, and only then, I'll arrange a formal interview with the police. But we'll do it under our rules. And I'll be present with you when it happens."

Parting handshakes were exchanged, and just like that Lancaster & Jordan had a new, high-profile case on their hands.

CHAPTER 36

Washington, D.C.
Tuesday, April 25, 2023
10:00 a.m.

At a formative age Alex recognized the dangers alcohol posed and made the decision to never touch the stuff. Had she lived a normal adolescence, it might have been different. She might have experimented with alcohol during her high school days, as most kids do, and come out unscathed. But in the wake of a tragedy suffered when she was young and impressionable that had her bouncing between continents, running from the press, and being cornered by psychopaths attempting to extort her, Alex knew that the lure of alcohol came with pitfalls. Now, twenty-eight years old and far into the next phase of life, she was at a point where perhaps alcohol could be enjoyed as a social tool rather than a crutch. But she wasn't very social and her occupation never placed her in situations where communal existence was necessary—save for a yearly Lancaster & Jordan Christmas party that she usually skipped. And so, at some point between breaking free from the angst of her teen years and reaching her late twenties, the window of opportunity had closed and she no longer found curiosity in what alcohol might do for her or to her. Coffee, however, was another story.

Her latest fascination was vacuum siphoning, a dual-chamber device that allowed vapor pressure to force hot water to mix with the coffee grounds. Alex had experimented with the timing and found that six and a half minutes produced the smoothest blend. She tasted her morning's brew now and, satisfied, took her mug to the couch and pulled up her laptop. She started each morning the same way. Coffee and news followed by an hour working at her evidence board before heading into the office. After thirty minutes of scanning world news headlines, she narrowed her interests to the DC area and came to a story that stopped her cold. It was in the *Washington Times*.

Local Businessman Shot in Home Invasion

Byron Zell, the former chief financial officer for Schuster Industries, was found dead in his DC apartment early Monday morning. Police have offered few details about the homicide other than that Zell died from gunshot wounds and was found by a family member.

Zell was involved in a lawsuit with Schuster Industries over alleged embezzlement of company funds. But Zell's legal problems did not end there. He had also recently been charged with possession of child pornography, and that case was still under investigation at the time of his death.

No other information has been released. This is a developing story.

Alex swiped her screen and began searching for other articles when her phone rang. It was Garrett.

"Hello?"

"I need you at the office right away. We have a developing situation."

"What's up?"

"I have a folder at the office that covers the details and will bring you up to date. New client, a missing persons case, and a possible connection to the mess going on with Larry Chadwick and McCormack University. Don't know all the details yet. We want you on the case but need to be fast on this. The potential for media coverage is high, and before long McCormack University will be teeming with nosey reporters. We want to know what we're dealing with before we get too deep. Jacqueline's taking the lead and she'll brief you at the office."

"I'll be there in thirty minutes."

"See you then."

"Hey, Garrett? Did you see the news about Byron Zell?"

"I did."

"What do you make of it?"

"We'll talk about Byron Zell later. Somewhere in the back of my mind I'm worried about your little adventure now that his apartment is a crime scene. But I'm trying to run a law firm, and we have bigger worries at the moment. I'm sure the police will want to speak with me about Byron Zell and the child pornography angle. I don't plan to mention that you were the investigator assigned to his case unless I'm pressed. Please help me help you, Alex. Stay away from the Byron Zell story."

A pause fell onto the conversation.

"Alex?"

"Yeah."

"You understand what I'm telling you?"

"Yeah. Got it."

"See you in thirty?"

"Yeah," Alex said, staring at the Byron Zell article. "See you soon."

She ended the call and ran once more through her stealth break-in to the man's apartment. By the time she finished her coffee, Alex had almost convinced herself that she had left nothing behind that would point to her presence, even if a crime scene unit dusted every surface.

CHAPTER 37

Washington, D.C.
Wednesday, April 26, 2023
10:32 a.m.

The following day, Alex pulled her car into the parking lot of an apartment complex located just outside the campus of McCormack University. The front of the three-story building sported sets of zigzagging stairs offering access to each level. Alex stood from her car, climbed the stairs to the second level, and knocked on apartment number 211. A moment later, a young man answered the door.

"Matthew Claymore?"

"Yeah?"

"Alex Armstrong. I work for Lancaster and Jordan. Jacqueline Jordan asked that I work with you on a few things before you and Jacqueline meet with the police later this week."

"Yeah, come on in," Matthew said.

Alex walked into the small, college-esque apartment, which was made up of two bedrooms, a living area, and a kitchen. She set the folder she was carrying onto the kitchen table and sat down.

"You want something to drink?" Matthew asked. "Coffee's still hot."

Alex glanced at the coffeemaker, a standard Mr. Coffee drip brewer whose glass pot was stained a filthy brown.

"I'm good, thanks."

Matthew sat across from her.

"A girl named Laura McAllister is missing," Alex said. "The police want to know if you're involved."

Matthew nodded. "Yeah."

"You and Laura were dating?"

"Yeah."

"First things first. Did you have anything to do with Laura's disappearance?"

"No."

"We're going to be diving into some specific details about the weekend. If you're lying it's going to hinder Lancaster and Jordan's ability to defend you."

"I'm not lying."

"Okay," Alex said. "My job is to prove it."

"How do you do that?"

"Lots of ways. The first thing we have to do is produce a rock-solid alibi, and then confirm that alibi with proof."

Alex opened the brief Jacqueline Jordan had given her. It contained the details of "The Matthew Claymore Case," as it was now referred to at the offices of Lancaster & Jordan.

"First, you're going to tell me about Laura. Here's what I know," Alex said. "Laura McAllister was reported missing by her parents on Sunday afternoon. According to our sources, the last time anyone saw her was Friday evening. That person was Laura's roommate, who told police that Laura was on her way to the university's recording studio to finish a project she'd been working on. No one's seen her since. Does this match what you know?"

Matthew nodded. "Yeah."

"Did Laura have enemies? Is it reasonable to think that something has happened to her, or is it more likely she up and left for some reason?"

Matthew bobbed his head back and forth. "I mean, I guess either is possible. Laura was getting ready to drop an episode for her show, and there was a lot of controversy around it. Did Ms. Jordan tell you about it?"

"*The Scoop*. Yes, it's in the brief."

Alex knew all about Laura McAllister, her radio program, and her social medial platform that boasted over a million followers. Jacqueline had briefed her on the situation and Alex had spent an hour poring through the details of the preliminary file her boss had put together.

"Okay," Matthew continued. "So even though Laura was trying to keep a lid on the rape story she was working on, rumors started going around campus. And then, you know, after the press conference by Duncan Chadwick's dad, things have been really crazy around school for the last week or so."

"Crazy how?"

"Crazy with rumors about what Laura was about to reveal. Rumors about who the girls were who were raped and which fraternity members were involved. People were freaking out. Also, Laura told me that the school was putting pressure on her."

"The school?" Alex asked.

"McCormack University is... well, the school is prestigious. It's sort of the alternative to the Ivy Leagues, and it attracts students whose parents are wealthy and powerful. Laura, from what little she told me about her investigation, had confirmed that a fraternity had used a date-rape drug at one of their parties. There's a police record filed by one of the girls who was raped. Laura's story was not only going to highlight this one incidence of sexual abuse, but point to past issues that the university had swept under the rug. Laura said McCormack was more interested in maintaining its pristine reputation and keeping its alumni happy and proud so the steady stream of donations continued to pour in each year. The school has an endowment that rivals Harvard's, and Laura was going to accuse McCormack of taking any and all measures to protect it, including keeping a story about rape on its campus quiet."

Alex jotted a few notes.

"So back to your original question," Matthew said. "Laura both had made some enemies, and had good reason to go off somewhere and hide until all the rumors settled down."

"Who were the guys Laura was going to name?" Alex asked. "What are their names?"

Matthew shook his head. "She never told me. Like I said, she was pretty secretive about the story she was working on."

"Then how did it leak so badly?"

"No idea. People knew Laura was poking around the rape story, but there were only a few rumors circulating until Duncan Chadwick's press conference. Then, everything just blew up."

"How close was Laura to finishing her story?"

"Close. I think she was actually done with it, just had to do some voice-over work at the recording studio."

"Why hadn't she dropped the episode? If she was finished with it, why didn't she air it on Thursday night? Isn't that when *The Scoop* airs?"

"It is, but Laura was hesitant to drop the story. The university told Laura, through a written letter, that any recording work she did inside the university's studio belonged to them and could not be disseminated without their approval."

Alex took more notes.

"Okay. Let's move on to you and Laura. When was the last time you saw her?"

"Friday morning. She stayed at my apartment Thursday night and left early Friday for a class."

"Which class?" Alex asked. "We're going to get into specifics and I need every detail."

"It was, uh, media law and ethics, I think. Yeah," Matthew said, nodding his head, "that was her early morning class on Mondays, Wednesdays, and Fridays."

"Good. Details will help."

"Help with what?"

"Your credibility. The longer Laura stays missing, the more suspicion you're going to come under. We need every detail of your weekend mapped out. What time did she leave on Friday?"

"It was a nine o'clock class, so, like—"

"Not *like*, Matthew. What time did Laura leave your apartment, exactly?"

"Eight-twenty. She wanted to go back to her place to shower before class."

"And you didn't see her again?"

"No, haven't seen her since then."

"Did you communicate with her after she left your apartment on Friday morning? Phone call or text? Anything on social media?"

"No."

"When did the police first come to see you about Laura?"

"Monday afternoon. Like—I mean, at… it was just after one o'clock in the afternoon."

"Okay. We have two bookends at the moment: you were in your apartment at eight-twenty Friday morning, and the police came to your apartment at one o'clock Monday afternoon. You and I are going to sit here and account for every hour in between. And you're not just going to *tell* me where you were, we're going to *prove* it."

"Every hour?"

"Yes."

"How are we going to prove every step I took over an entire weekend?"

"Lots of ways. You're going to walk me through your weekend and tell me every detail from every hour that you can remember. I've got a laundry list of questions that will help jog your memory. Then, independently, I'm going to confirm what you tell me. And, Matthew, if you lie to me, I'll figure it out because I'm going to talk with every person you can remember seeing, from friends to classmates to professors. I'm going to go through your phone and highlight every call you made, every text you sent, and every social media footprint you made. I'll pull cell tower logs to confirm the pings your phone registered and track your movement, and I'll confirm everything using your cell phone's GPS locator to map out every step you took. I'll pull surveillance video from every establishment you were at and match them to receipts. Credit cards, debit cards, and digital payment transactions will confirm your whereabouts."

"Holy shit."

Alex pouted her lower lip. "It's hard to navigate through this world without leaving a trail. And I'm going to use this complete invasion of our privacy to prove you had nothing to do with Laura McAllister going missing. So, are you ready to prove to me that the last time you saw Laura was Friday morning, or would you like to amend that statement before we start?"

"No amending. The last time I saw her was Friday morning. Let's start."

CHAPTER 38

Washington, D.C.
Friday, April 28, 2023
8:15 a.m.

The den was located on the ninth floor of the One Franklin Square building, a floor below the main offices of Lancaster & Jordan. The den was reserved for the investigators, the paralegals, and the new law grads who spent ten hours a day with their noses buried in law books or pressed against computer monitors scrolling through thousands of archived records doing research for the real attorneys upstairs. The partners at Lancaster & Jordan dictated protocol on the tenth floor, but the investigators ran things on the ninth. The perimeter of the den held modest offices that paled in comparison to the massive corner units upstairs, but they still had four walls and a door and carried clout. The longest tenured investigators claimed them, and with eight years under her belt, Alex was one of them.

She sat at her desk while the laser printer chugged away. She'd had a busy and productive two days since she sat down with Matthew Claymore. Now she was printing her efforts for her meeting with Jacqueline Jordan. Alex had worked enough cases for Jacqueline to know exactly what the woman wanted and exactly how she wanted it. And she knew that her research on this particular case needed to be perfect. It often looked like Jacqueline had a family bias when assigning investigators to the cases she handled, most of the time appointing her brother to the high-profile ones. But the real reason Jacqueline appointed Buck to important cases was because Buck was the best investigator Lancaster & Jordan employed—a point Alex would never argue. But the fact that Jacqueline had selected Alex for the Matthew Claymore case—one that had the potential to become newsworthy—was testimony to the fact that even though Buck Jordan held the top spot among the firm's investigators, Alex was a close second.

She heard a knock on her door and looked up to see Buck poking his head into her office.

"Hey, kiddo," Buck said. "Here before nine. Must mean you're working a case for the boss lady."

Alex smiled. "Gotta work Jacqueline's hours when you're on one of her cases."

"Just playing dumb. We all know you snagged the Claymore case. Good for you. Anything juicy?"

Buck's smile pushed his drooping jowls upward, causing his eyes to squint nearly closed. Almost sixty, Buck Jordan wore the years of his profession on his face. Long, chain-smoking stakeouts and alcohol-fueled all-nighters had taken their toll. Alex knew Buck well and over the years had even tried to tame his drinking with subtle encouragements aimed at pointing out that functioning alcoholics are still alcoholics.

"Working on it," Alex said.

"Let me know if you need anything."

"Thanks, Buck."

When the printer finally quieted down, Alex gathered her research, ran the pages through a hole-punch machine, bound everything in an L&J binder, and headed up to the tenth floor. She walked to the corner office, held up the binder for Jacqueline's assistant to see—an unspoken password that meant the boss was waiting for something important—and received a nod to proceed. Alex knocked on Jacqueline's door at the same time she opened it.

"Hey, Jacqueline, I've got the early research on Matthew Claymore."

Emblematic of a big-city attorney, Jacqueline Jordan always dressed impeccably. That morning she wore smart business attire made up of a white silk blouse under a gray blazer that matched her knee-length skirt. The woman looked perpetually fresh and sharp. Notorious around the firm for being the first attorney in her office, usually arriving before 7:00 a.m., she rarely left before 7:00 p.m. And there was no fluff baked into the woman's schedule. She was the founding partner of one of the biggest criminal defense firms on the East Coast and her services were in high demand. Married to a prominent anesthesiologist, Jacqueline Jordan was half of a powerful DC couple, and, Alex knew from conversations with Garrett, the woman had money to burn. She worked long hours not for any need of monetary gain, but because it was in her blood.

She was somewhere in her fifties, the only evidence of midlife being the cheaters that balanced at the end of her nose when she worked. Unlike her older brother, whose dogged career in the back alleys of legal investigation had creased Buck's face with deep furrows, Jacqueline Jordan was wrinkle-free—the result, Alex assumed, of monthly Botox sessions. Jacqueline looked up from the brief she was reading and peered at Alex over her glasses.

"And? How do we look?"

"First pass, the kid looks clean," Alex said, taking a seat in one of the chairs in front of Jacqueline's desk. Alex handed over the binder that held her work.

"I can definitively place him with Laura McAllister Friday morning at his apartment, confirmed by Matthew's room-mate, who saw Laura leave, and by his cell phone's GPS. Two professors confirm seeing Laura in their classrooms Friday morning and afternoon, so we have proof Laura was alive and well after the last time Matthew saw her. Laura was last seen by her roommate Friday evening, reportedly on her way to the school of journalism's recording studio. No one's seen her since. She was reported missing Sunday afternoon by her parents, and police knocked on Matthew's door at one-twelve Monday afternoon, confirmed by a police report I obtained.

"I was able to create a detailed timeline of Matthew's movements from the time Laura left his apartment Friday morning to when police spoke with him Monday afternoon, all confirmed with credit card usage, ATM camera, social media posts, cell phone pings, and the GPS tracker on his phone. Everything. It's pretty tight other than Matthew's sleeping hours, which technically cannot be vouched for. An eager prosecutor or rogue detective could use those hours of anonymity to claim that they were when Matthew was on the prowl."

"Any way around those hours when Matthew was asleep?"

"Not really. I spoke with his roommate and he confirms that he *believes* Matthew was asleep in his room. No eyewitness proof, though. Unfortunately, those are blank hours in Matthew's timeline that we can't account for."

"How about a Fitbit or smart watch?"

Alex shook her head. "Already asked. He doesn't wear one. His cell phone puts him at his apartment during those hours, but it could be argued that he left his phone at his apartment to do his dirty work."

"Okay, we'll have to deal with the dead hours later, if the subject comes up. Any red flags?"

"He was dating Laura, so he'll be an immediate suspect no matter what we do. And he was a member of the Delta Chi fraternity, which was the house Laura McAllister was about to accuse of using date-rape drugs to spike drinks at their parties. I don't have a lot of information on that angle yet, but I'm working on it."

"Okay," Jacqueline said as she paged through Alex's work. "So far, I'd say the good outweighs the bad. What's your take on the kid? Personally."

"I believe him. I've worked with liars before. Matthew Claymore is not lying. He's scared to death, but he's not lying."

Jacqueline nodded. "Here's the plan, then. I need ammunition in case Laura McAllister doesn't turn up, or, God forbid, something's happened to her. We need to bulletproof Matthew from accusations the police might levy against him. That will require us to not only make sure he's as innocent as he claims, but to also come up with alternate theories as to what might have happened to Laura McAllister. We need to know details. The who, how, and why. You know the routine."

"I'm already working on it," Alex said. "The obvious question is whether Laura McAllister's disappearance had anything to do with the rape story she was about to break."

"Exactly. I need you to find out everything you can about this girl and the story she was working on. Who was involved, who was going to be named, who might want to keep her story from reaching the mainstream. We need to make sure Matthew was not part of Laura's story, but we also need the names of those who were. I pray this girl materializes soon and we never have to use any of it, but she's been missing for nearly a week and we need to prepare for the worst-case scenario. This timeline of Matthew's movements is a good start, but we'll need more if this turns ugly."

"Understood," Alex said as she stood up. "I'll have a better picture by next week."

"Thanks, Alex. I'm glad you're on this case with me."

Alex nodded. She left the building and headed back to McCormack University to continue her investigation into what might have happened to Laura McAllister. This time, it would include some nontraditional methods of information gathering.

CHAPTER 39

Washington, D.C.
Friday, April 28, 2023
9:00 a.m.

"He's worried," Annette Packard said.

Sitting in the booth across from her, Larry Chadwick twirled his coffee mug as steam spiraled upward. She had pulled him from his chambers fifteen minutes earlier to speak in private.

"What else does he want me to do? Duncan has upended his life over this. He's cooperating with the police. There's nothing linking him to this girl other than his fraternity, which he has publicly denounced and resigned from."

"It looks bad, Larry, and the president is worried that his opponents in the Senate will use this crisis to their advantage. If he nominates you and you don't get the votes, it makes him look weak going into an election year."

"We have the votes," Larry said. "Isn't that what the internal polling says?"

"*Said.* That polling was from two weeks ago, before this story broke. We're running the numbers again, and many votes that were solidly in favor of you are now undecided."

"A rebellious college girl hoping to be the next Bob Woodward runs off for a couple of days and we're supposed to act like it's the crime of the century. Worse, we're supposed to play to our opponents and constantly deny that my son is involved. Just mentioning Duncan and this girl's name in the same sentence begins to tie him to her. You understand this, don't you, Annette? Please tell me you understand how a smear campaign works."

"I understand, Larry. And it appears to be working."

"Duncan had nothing to do with that girl going missing, end of story."

"I'm afraid that's just the beginning of the story."

Larry took a deep breath. "I thought kids were off limits in politics."

"Not in a missing persons investigation."

"One that has nothing to do with my son. The closest association to this girl is that my son attends the same college? That's what the other side is running on?"

"They're running on more than that, Larry. Although he no longer is, Duncan *was* a member of a fraternity that has now come under great scrutiny for allegedly using a date-rape drug to spike drinks at their parties."

"Whether that's true or not—and we don't know it's true; at the moment it's nothing more than a rumor—Duncan wasn't involved."

"Whether you believe this is a smear campaign or a legitimate story involving your son, I hope you see the problem either way."

He stirred his coffee without answering. He finally looked up at her.

"Are you recommending that he pass on nominating me?"

"No. Not yet, anyway. You're the president's first choice. He wants you, and right now he wants *only* you. My job is to make sure that if he nominates you, you'll make it through the confirmation hearing. If you don't, it's not just bad for him, it's bad for me. I'm batting a thousand, Larry. Every person I've vetted and vouched for has made it to the Promised Land. If I clear you to the president, and this mess ends up tanking your confirmation, my career will be at stake as much as the president's. I might not have the free world to run, but I've got bills and a mortgage to pay."

"This is such a goddamn mess," Larry said. "My life's work is spiraling down the drain."

It shouldn't have surprised Annette that Larry Chadwick's political ambitions blinded him to the fact that a girl was missing. Or that he considered the potential derailment of his Supreme Court nomination more a tragedy than the disappearance of a twenty-two-year-old college student. He was, after all, a politician.

"Will you please tell the president to give this thing some time? Ask him to wait just another week. Allow the police to at least start an investigation before we dump my nomination."

Annette thought for a moment before slowly nodding.

"Okay. I'll ask him for a week," she said.

A week gave her time to find answers to questions the president would surely want answered. It gave Annette time to figure out if she should tell her boss to confidently back Larry Chadwick, or cut his losses and avoid a political tsunami.

CHAPTER 40

Washington, D.C.
Friday, April 28, 2023
1:35 p.m.

On Friday afternoon, a few hours after she left Jacqueline Jordan's office, Alex sat in the back booth of a diner in Georgetown. She stirred her coffee, a filtered brew served from a round glass pot that had likely held several previous brews that day. Her first sip proved as awful as she anticipated. She had to suffer only a few more sips before Matthew Claymore walked through the front door. He took a seat in the booth across from her.

"How'd your meeting with the police go?" Alex asked.

Matthew's first formal meeting with the police had taken place earlier that morning.

"Fine, I guess. Ms. Jordan did a lot of the talking and she had… I guess you gave her all the work we did together, because every time one of the detectives asked me about where I'd been over the weekend, she offered proof. Thanks for doing all that for me."

"That's what you pay us for. But in case something *has* happened to Laura, we're going to need a lot more than a timeline."

"Like what?"

"I need to know more about the story Laura was working on. The longer Laura stays missing, the more the police are going to look for answers. And the more they look, the more likely it is they'll find what they're looking for, whether it exists or not."

"What's that mean?"

"Just trust me. I've been doing this for a long time, and I've had my own unpleasant experience with a police investigation. You're already on their radar. You're ahead of the game because you've secured good—really good—legal representation. But the police have a theory of what happened to Laura, and it's safe to say you're part of that theory. We can't sit back and wait for them to create a narrative. We need to go on the offense by offering our own theory of what might have happened to Laura."

"Even though I told them, and *showed* them, where I was all weekend?"

"It doesn't matter, Matthew. That's what I'm trying to tell you. It doesn't matter that you're innocent. There are blank hours in your weekend. The hours when you were sleeping. And since you were alone during those hours, the police and the detectives will use them to fit their narrative. They'll say you spent that time—those hours when no one can account for your movements—abducting Laura and hiding her body."

"Jesus! We don't even know if anything's happened to her."

"I'm just explaining how the police and detectives work. My job is to keep you in front of the storm that may be coming. In order to do that, I need your help."

A waitress approached and splashed coffee into Alex's mug.

"Can I get you anything, hon?"

"A Coke, please," Matthew said.

After the waitress left, Matthew looked at Alex. "My parents told me to do whatever Ms. Jordan said, so I will. I'll give you whatever you need. If I can."

"Good. Let's start with a few questions. Were you and Laura exclusive?"

"Like, were we seeing other people?"

"Yes."

"No. We were pretty serious."

"How long had you been together?"

"Since the middle of junior year. Almost a year and a half."

"Do you know anyone who might have been interested in Laura romantically?"

"Not that I can think of."

"Did Laura have an ex-boyfriend?"

"Probably, but she never mentioned anyone. She never had a boyfriend at school during her freshman or sophomore years. So, maybe from high school."

The waitress delivered Matthew's soda.

"You two going to order any food?"

"No thanks," Alex said.

The waitress placed the bill on the table.

"Refills are free, just flag me down," she said before hustling off to the next table.

"Okay," Alex said. "Tell me about the story Laura was working on."

Matthew shrugged. "I don't know a lot about it. Laura was really private about it. All she told me was that she had been tipped off about a rape that had happened on campus. After she started looking into things, she came to me to let me know that the rape had happened at my fraternity house. Or, you know, *allegedly* happened."

"Did you know about it?"

"No. I mean, there were rumors but that was it."

"What sort of rumors?"

"That maybe some of the guys had gotten Liquid G and had spiked the punch."

"Who? What were their names?"

"I don't know. It was just a rumor. I wasn't part of it, so I didn't know if it was true or not. But then, like, a couple weeks ago, we heard that a girl had gone to the police and filed a report that she'd been raped at the fraternity house. We were all freaked out. We figured the police would come around and start asking questions, or the dean would call us in, or the fraternity charter would get shut down. But nothing happened. That's why I figured it wasn't true."

"What did Laura tell you?"

"Nothing. Like I said, she was worried that her story would leak before she dropped it, so she was careful not to tell me anything."

"Were you worried about Laura's story?"

"I don't know, I guess. I didn't know what was true and what was made up. I didn't want any of my friends to get in trouble, especially if none of it was true. And, you know, just to be totally honest with you, Laura and I got into a fight about it the night before she… you know, before she disappeared."

"What kind of fight?"

"Just an argument. I wanted to know what kind of proof she had and she didn't want to tell me anything about it. She was stressed because so many rumors were flying around campus about her story. I was stressed because it had to do with my fraternity. So it just all blew up into a big argument."

"Did you tell the police about this argument?"

"No. They never asked. And Ms. Jordan told me not to offer any details unless I was asked about them."

Alex paused long enough to manage a sip of coffee.

"How did Laura get onto the story in the first place? How did she hear about it?"

"Through her tip line. She set up an e-mail account last year when *The Scoop* started getting popular. People would e-mail her all sorts of crazy stories and Laura would check out the interesting ones, and then start investigating them to see if they were legit."

"Who tipped her off about the rape on McCormack University campus?"

Matthew shook his head. "I don't know."

Alex managed a final swallow of coffee. "Okay. I'm going to do some investigating. I might have questions. If I call, answer your phone. Got it?"

"Yeah. Do you need help? I can help."

The last thing Alex needed was an unstable accomplice aiding and abetting her as she bent or broke laws in her effort to protect him.

"Just keep your phone on," she said as she stood from the booth. "I'll call if I need anything."

CHAPTER 41

Washington, D.C.
Friday, April 28, 2023
2:45 p.m.

Alex sat in her car and stared at the apartment complex. Her research had told her that Laura McAllister lived in unit 7, and that her roommate was named Liz Chamberlain, a fellow senior who was taking fifteen credits this semester and should be about to leave for her 3:00 p.m. poli sci class. Alex waited and watched. At 2:48 p.m. the door to unit 7 opened and Liz Chamberlain appeared. The girl locked the door behind her and walked off in the direction of McCormack University's campus. Alex took one last look around the parking lot, saw no one, and exited her car. She pulled out her leather-bound lock pick set as she approached Laura's apartment door. The lock proved to be a less complicated mechanism than Byron Zell's a few weeks before, and Alex was inside in less than sixty seconds.

She closed the door behind her and slipped her hands into latex gloves. The college apartment had a floor plan similar to that of Matthew Claymore's place: kitchen, common living area, and two bedrooms. Alex headed to the first bedroom, saw a photo of Laura McAllister and her parents on the desk, and entered the room. Laura's bed was made and organized. The desk was fastidiously organized, and a quick glance into the closet revealed a wardrobe perfectly hung on matching hangers. The shelves above the hanging clothes held department store-folded jeans, leggings, and sweatshirts. There was nothing out of place to suggest anything nefarious had occurred in this room, or that Laura had been in any rush to leave.

Alex knew that detectives either had already been, or would soon be, in this room looking for evidence. She would be careful to leave no signs of her presence. She held a deep-seated mistrust of detectives; the contempt was rooted in the mismanaged investigation of her family's murder and was watered often by memories of her time at Alleghany Juvenile Detention Center. Every case she worked for Lancaster & Jordan was done so with the memory of her illegal interrogation fresh on her mind, and all the dishonest tactics that had been used to try to paint her as a killer. In a heart-to-heart with Garrett years earlier, Alex promised to use her abilities as an investigator to prevent what had happened to her from happening to anyone else. Currently, that "anyone" was Matthew Claymore, and she felt no remorse for the strategies she employed to protect him. That included breaking into a missing girl's apartment and rooting through her things.

Alex sat at the desk and shook the mouse that rested on the Apple pad. Laura's iMac came to life and a screensaver of spring flowers greeted her. She clicked the e-mail icon on the top right of the home screen. The computer was password synched and took Alex directly to Laura McAllister's inbox. She chose the e-mail titled "The Scoop Tip Line" and began scrolling through the messages. Alex spent fifteen minutes reading subject lines for anything that caught her eye. Finally, one did. It carried a date from March 13, more than a month ago, and the subject line read: "Rape at McCormack U." Alex opened it. There was a conversation thread consisting of two e-mails. Alex scrolled to the beginning.

Dear Laura,

I'm writing to tell you about my recent experience on campus. Have you heard of gamma hydroxybutyrate? It's called Liquid G, and it's being

used so girls can be raped. On this campus. I have proof.
　　—Ashley Holms

Farther down the thread, Alex read Laura's response.

Ashley, you've piqued my interest. Let's talk.
　　—Laura

Alex logged out of the e-mail and put the computer to sleep. She made sure nothing was out of place, and then left the apartment in search of Ashley Holms.

CHAPTER 42

Washington, D.C.
Friday, April 28, 2023
3:30 p.m.

During her eight-year career as an investigator for Lancaster & Jordan, Alex had been tasked with tracking down a number of unsavory souls, including random gangbangers on the streets of Washington, D.C. with nothing more than a first name. Finding Ashley Holms, who lived on the campus of McCormack University, took thirty minutes. There was only one sophomore dorm, Wakington Hall, which housed 156 second-year students. A confident lie to the kid behind the dorm's front desk, explaining that Alex was there to surprise her cousin, Ashley, but didn't know her dorm room number, was all it took for Alex to be knocking on number 455.

"Ashley?" Alex asked when the door opened.

"Yeah?"

Alex recognized the confusion on Ashley Holms' face. Students from affluent families made up the enrollment at McCormack University, and Alex was certain there were rules banning tattoos and rogue piercings. That Alex's right arm was covered with ink, the remnants of another tattoo crept up her neck and peeked from under her collar, and a nose ring pierced her left nostril was likely enough to get her thrown off campus. It was at least enough for Ashley Holms to give her a second glance. The spiked blond hair and today's shade of lipstick—bright magenta—likely added to the girl's confusion as to why this foreign creature was knocking on her door.

"I'm Alex Armstrong. I'm doing some legal work involving some things going on at McCormack U. Do you have a minute to talk?"

"Um, I guess," Ashley said. "Is this about Laura McAllister?"

"Peripherally. Can I come in?"

Ashley pushed through the doorway, stepped into the hallway, and closed the door behind her.

"Can we just talk out here?" she asked.

"Sure, that's fine."

"Who did you say you work for?"

"A law firm. Lancaster and Jordan."

It was a vague answer and the girl seemed to accept it. Even if she wanted to ask more questions, Alex didn't give her a chance.

"When was the last time you saw Laura McAllister?"

"Last week. The police already asked me about it."

"Do you remember the day, exactly?"

"Thursday. We were working on something for *The Scoop*. That's her show. She does a radio show for the student body."

"Yes, that's what I want to talk with you about. I'm trying to figure out how serious Laura's story was."

"How did you get my name?" Ashley asked.

From her discussions with Matthew, Alex knew the vibe on campus since the Chadwicks' press conference included a sense of foreboding. And since news of Laura's disappearance had trickled into the headlines, McCormack University had been populated with reporters and media. Alex would have to be honest about what she needed if she hoped to get this girl's cooperation.

"My firm is representing Matthew Claymore. Do you know him?"

"Yeah, he's Laura's boyfriend."

"In the work I'm doing for Matthew, I started looking into the details of Laura's story. I know you were the one who tipped Laura off, and I need to know if Matthew was part of the story Laura was working on. If he had any involvement in the allegations of rape on McCormack's campus."

"Matthew? No, his name never even came up."

A sense of relief flashed through her and tingled her fingertips. Alex had worked on cases before where the innocence of her client was less certain. It was always easier to fully commit to a case when she was confident she was working for an innocent person's freedom.

"When you saw Laura last week, where was it?"

"At the recording studio."

"For something with her story?"

"Yes. I was finishing the interview Laura was doing with me. She needed a few clarifications and then she said she was going to do some voice-over edits."

"What was your role in Laura's story? You tipped her off about what might have been going on at the Delta Chi fraternity. How much did you know?"

"A lot."

"Do you know who was involved?"

"I know one of them, yes."

"Who?"

Ashley paused. Alex could tell that the girl was having trouble determining how much to reveal.

"Listen, Ashley, I know I'm just some strange woman who knocked on your door. But trust me when I tell you that even though my firm is representing Matthew Claymore, I have Laura's best interest in mind. I need to know as much as I can about Laura's story. Anything that helps me figure out what happened to Laura will also help me make sure Matthew doesn't get falsely accused of something he had no part of."

There was another gap of silence.

"I need your help here, Ashley."

"I told Laura everything I knew. She did the rest of the work to confirm it."

"Tell me what you told Laura."

Ashley swallowed and looked up toward the ceiling, then finally back at Alex.

"A girl was raped a month or so ago. She's a friend of mine and she doesn't want her name mentioned. It happened when we were at the Delta Chi house. I heard she had gone off with a guy, and I figured, you know, they were hooking up. I wasn't worried or anything, it didn't even faze me. But the next day she told me what happened. She blacked out and couldn't remember anything. When she woke up at the fraternity house the next morning, she knew... she knew that she'd been raped. She went to the hospital and when her blood work came back, it showed she had Liquid G in her system."

"Did the police find the guy who raped her?"

"No. They didn't even look. They said that because my friend had drugs and alcohol in her system, and because she had no actual memory of the rape, they couldn't do anything about it."

"Does she know who the guy was?"

Ashley shook her head. "That's the thing. All she can remember from that night is bits and pieces. That's what Liquid G does. It's a date-rape drug that makes you unable to defend yourself, and then it, like, erases your memory. But..."

"But what?"

"But we know... my friends and I know who the guy was. We have pictures of them from earlier in the night. We were all together at the party and we took a bunch of selfies. She was with the same guy in all the pictures, and another one of our friends saw them head upstairs late at night."

"Who was it? Who was the guy?"

Ashley ran her hands through her hair. "I don't know if I should say any more. This is why Laura was so worried. So many rumors were starting to spread and she wanted to get her story out before it was too late."

"It might already be too late, Ashley. Listen, no one knows what's happened to Laura, but the police have decided that Matthew Claymore is involved."

229

"Matthew? I told you, he had nothing to do with Laura's story."

"Help me make that case. The police have Matthew in their sights, and I've been hired to help him. Tell me who raped your friend and I promise to get that information to the police and make them act on it."

Ashley paused for another moment. "It was Duncan Chadwick. That's why he and his father held that press conference, because Duncan knew Laura was about to link him to the rape."

Alex's fingertips tingled again, as if a jolt of electricity had coursed through her body. Jacqueline Jordan had sent her to find alternative theories as to what might have happened to Laura McAllister. At the moment, Duncan Chadwick was one of them.

"Was Laura finished with the story?"

"Yeah. She was just wrapping things up and sort of polishing my interview, but she was worried that the school would shut her down. It was... The rape allegations cast a wide net and a lot of people were implicated in it, not just Duncan Chadwick and his fraternity. The school was trying to keep the story quiet. Because Laura recorded everything at the recording studio, and because the recording studio is owned and operated by the university, Laura said the school technically controls anything that's recorded there. That's why she was thinking about just dropping her episode to her social media accounts, and bypassing the studio."

"So she must have had the episode stored somewhere?"

"Yeah. On a thumb drive. I don't know how it all worked, I just put on the headphones and spoke into the microphone. Laura did the rest. But I saw her plug a thumb drive into her computer when we finished recording. Laura said that everything that gets recorded at the studio also gets stored on a hard drive and technically belongs to the university."

"A hard drive at the recording studio?" Alex asked.

"Yeah. But it's locked. I walked past it the other day. No one's allowed in there for now. We used to be able to use our school IDs to unlock the door, but when I tried, my ID didn't work."

"Too bad," Alex said. "I guess that's a dead end. Thanks, though. You've been a big help."

Alex turned and headed down the hallway before Ashley Holms could respond or ask any questions. She pushed through the front doors of the dormitory and headed across campus.

CHAPTER 43

Washington, D.C.
Friday, April 28, 2023
4:05 p.m.

Alex hurried across the campus of McCormack University, heading toward the school of journalism. She noticed two news vans parked outside the main entrance, with crews pulling cords and preparing to shoot live reports for the evening news. Larry Chadwick's press conference the week before had summoned the DC press to McCormack University, but Laura McAllister's disappearance had opened the floodgates to the national media. McCormack University and the surrounding area were teeming with reporters, and it was sure to get worse the longer the girl was missing.

As Alex walked and watched the action, the crews and reporters and vans and cameras all brought back images from that fateful night a decade earlier when Donna had led her out of her home into the hot lights of similar news crews. A bitter taste of bile crept into her throat. The only thing that could be deemed juicier to the press than a young girl gone missing would be uncovering that a woman formerly accused of killing her family was looking into the case.

Alex had a sudden urge to get as far away from the cameras and news crews as possible. While she looked toward the commotion outside the gates of McCormack University, where reporters scrambled for the best location to deliver their reports, she collided with someone on the sidewalk.

"Oh God, I'm sorry," Alex said, gaining her bearings and realizing she had walked into a woman who was holding a microphone and delivering her own report. The cameraman lowered his camera from his shoulder and waved a hand in disgust.

"Cut," he said. "Gonna have to do that all over."

Alex looked at the cameraman. The fact that the reporter would have to reshoot the segment meant, at least, that they weren't live on the air. Alex looked back to the reporter.

"I'm really—"

She tried to finish her apology but the words caught in her throat. It felt as if her trachea had narrowed, and no matter how hard she tried to speak, no words would come. It took only a moment for Alex to understand why her body was shutting down: she was staring at Tracy Carr, the reporter who had stuck the microphone in her face ten years earlier when Alex walked out of her house the night her family was killed.

She was standing face-to-face with the reporter who had stalked her for a decade, and who had earned a substantial following by offering anniversary updates on the whereabouts of Alexandra Quinlan. This was the woman, Alex knew, who had coined the nickname "Empty Eyes." And here she was, staring straight at her.

"Sorry," Alex finally managed. "I wasn't paying attention."

Alex averted her gaze, breaking eye contact for fear that, despite the years since their last encounter and Alex's physical transformation, Tracy Carr had recognized her. Alex offered no time for the woman to piece things together, quickly walking away with the sinking realization that the entire encounter, however brief, had been captured by the news camera. And if Tracy Carr suspected who had ruined her report, the woman had the digital evidence to review and confirm it. As Alex hurried away, she snuck a glance over her shoulder as she was about to turn the corner of the journalism building. Tracy Carr continued to watch her and they locked eyes for just a moment before Alex disappeared behind the bricks.

Alex spent time wandering the halls of McCormack University's school of journalism looking for the recording studio and trying to calm her nerves. As her heart raced and her head swam with dizziness, she spotted a restroom and pushed through the door. After staggering to the sink, she splashed cold water on her face. When she looked up and into the mirror, for an instance she saw Alexandra Quinlan staring back. That teenaged girl still existed in her mind, but to actually see her in the mirror was something new and startling. The image of Alex Armstrong—with the spiked blond hair, piercings, tattoos, and wild shades of lipstick—had for years supplanted the image of her old self. To the point, at least, that when she looked into a mirror she never thought of the girl she used to be. Until now. Until moments after she'd come face-to-face with the reporter who had shattered her life.

Alex blinked a few times until Alexandra Quinlan disappeared. She realized, though, that no matter how easily her mind displaced the old image of herself, it would take something much greater to prevent Tracy Carr from piecing things together. To a casual observer with no, or little, memory of Alexandra Quinlan, glancing at Alex today was nothing more than looking at a stranger. But to the woman who had obsessed over Empty Eyes for a decade, staring into Alex's eyes was sure to trigger recognition.

She spent another few minutes calming her nerves and finally exited the washroom to wander the empty halls until she found the recording studio. It was located on the second floor of the Westcott School of Journalism building, and just as Ashley Holms promised, the door was locked when Alex tried the handle. A window was etched in the wall and the recording studio was dark inside. Alex waited in the hallway to gauge the level of foot traffic. After five minutes, no students or faculty materialized. Alex removed her pick set and made fast work of the studio's door lock, despite her hands still carrying a slight tremor from her run-in with Tracy Carr.

Inside, she contemplated whether she should turn on the lights or work in the dark but decided that being spotted in the studio with the lights off would be more suspicious than sitting at the dashboard with the studio fully lighted. Overhead fluorescents brought the studio to life, and Alex immediately recognized the space from her previous night's viewing of Laura McAllister's appearance on *Wake Up America*. It was hard to believe stories produced in such a small studio reached so many listeners. Ten minutes after she clicked on the lights, she had still not seen anyone walk past the studio. She went to work at the recording studio's computer, taking a few minutes to bypass rudimentary firewalls until she was into the hard drive's saved documents. The files were titled by students' names and ID numbers. Alex scrolled until she located Laura McAllister's last saved document, which was dated April 21—the previous Friday, which represented the last time anyone had seen or heard from her. The document was an MPEG-4 audio file.

Alex took a quick look through the window. The hallway was quiet and still. She removed a thumb drive from her rucksack, inserted it in the USB drive, and copied the file. The large file took fifteen minutes to transfer. Alex spent the time sitting at the studio's table acting casual for anyone who passed by the window. No one did. When the transfer was complete, she removed the thumb drive, locked the recording studio on her way out, and was overly cautious when she exited the building. Seeing no reporters or news crews, she headed home to listen to Laura McAllister's episode.

CHAPTER 44

Washington, D.C.
Saturday, April 29, 2023
7:15 a.m.

Early Saturday morning, just over a week since Laura McAllister had last been seen, and while the campus was still asleep, Professor Martin Crosby finished lecture notes for the upcoming week, answered a few e-mails, and then changed in the faculty washroom. He emerged in running shorts and gym shoes. It had been his New Year's resolution to get into shape, and four months of his ritual of putting in an hour of work each Saturday morning before tackling a three-mile run had prevented him from losing the gains he'd made during the week. He'd managed to lose fifteen pounds since the New Year and had kept it off. He had even started to enjoy running. He exited the Reiner Faculty Building into the quad, set the timer on his watch, and took off across campus.

Thirty minutes later he was breathing heavily as he finished his third mile jogging along the forested path that cut through Horace Grove. He was feeling good and decided to push himself for an extra mile. It turned out to be a bad idea. As he rounded a turn halfway through his fourth mile, he felt a tweak in his hamstring and slowed his pace. A small clearing was just up ahead and he limped gingerly into it and bent over to stretch. Touching his hands to the ground, he noticed something shine through the leaves in the forested area next to the running path. A closer look revealed a silver ring with a green gem that appeared to be perched on top of leaves. He leaned farther and attempted to pinch the ring out of the leaves. His first attempt failed when his fingers slipped free from the stone—emerald or peridot. In preparation for a second attempt, he brushed the leaves away before noticing that the ring was still set on a finger, the hand covered by leaves.

He stumbled backward until his perspective was able to take in the fact that the hand, bleach white and overstuffed, led to a wrist and a forearm. He struggled to pull his phone from his pocket.

—

An hour later police cruisers blocked the running path, their lights blinking. The coroner's van had backed into the clearing and was parked at an angle with the back doors open. Yellow crime scene tape roped off the area while a crime scene photographer snapped photos of the body. A detective stood waiting in the background. The coroner waited next to her. After everything was documented, the detective approached the body and got her first look. The victim was covered in leaves, as if her killer had haphazardly attempted to hide her body. The skin on the girl's face was bone white and contrasted stiffly with the dark strands of hair that lay across her cheek.

"Female victim," the detective said to the coroner, crouching next to the body and brushing the dead girl's hair to the side. "Ligature wounds to the neck."

The coroner crouched as well. He touched the dead girl's neck with his gloved hands.

"Looks like it was done with a thin length of rope, maybe three-eighths of an inch," he said. "I'll take measurements when I get the body back to the morgue. I'll likely recover fibers to help identify what type of rope was used."

The detective brushed the leaves off the rest of the girl's body. "Shit," she said when she saw that the victim was naked from the waist down. "She was probably raped."

"Have to assume," the coroner said. "But we'll know for sure once I start my exam. We're gonna need the parents to come down to make an ID."

Neither the detective nor the coroner mentioned the victim's name. They didn't have to. It was obvious to both that they were looking at Laura McAllister.

CHAPTER 45

Washington, D.C.
Saturday, April 29, 2023
9:20 a.m.

Alex had pushed for a coffeehouse but had been overruled. And since she was requesting the meeting and sniffing for details, she had no room to negotiate on the location. After her visit to the school of journalism's recording studio, Alex had spent the previous evening listening to, and taking copious notes on, Laura McAllister's explosive episode. She'd come across a lot of information and still had more work to do. But despite the demands of the Matthew Claymore case, she had been unable to get Byron Zell out of her mind since reading about his death. She was worried, and despite Garrett's warning to stay away from the situation, Alex couldn't help herself.

Benjamin's Tavern was a cop bar hidden in the basement level of a building in Truxton Circle and frequented by law enforcement of all kinds, from beat cops to campus security, transit cops to detectives, and everything in between. To accommodate the schedules of Washington, D.C.'s finest, Benjamin's kept odd hours. Like an airport bar that served stiff drinks to jet-lagged customers at 8:00 a.m., Benjamin's saw a steady stream of customers all through the night and into the morning hours as tired cops finished their shifts and looked for a place to unwind.

Hank Donovan was a fifty-something divorced detective who drank too much. The drinking aside, though, he was a useful source of information. Alex had a working relationship with Hank that, over the years, had produced a lot of give-and-take. As a Washington, D.C. detective, Hank Donovan had access to information that was occasionally useful to Alex, depending on which Lancaster & Jordan case she was working. And Alex—as an off-the-books investigator who had worked in the underbelly of legal investigation for nearly a decade and was still close to a dozen or so shady friends from Alleghany, many of whom had graduated from juvenile offenses to more sophist-icated forms of crime—had her fair share of street connections that were sometimes useful to Hank's investigations.

Alex had met Hank years ago through Buck Jordan, and since both men walked a fine line of functioning alcoholics, Alex was not surprised to see Buck and Hank bellied up to the bar when she walked into Benjamin's. It looked like they'd been there for quite some time. Newton's first law popped into Alex's thoughts when she looked at the two men: An object at rest stays at rest unless acted upon by an unbalanced force. The law of inertia had been forever imprinted on her psyche ever since she'd studied for a physics test on the night her family was killed. From time to time, and out of the blue, Newton's laws became applicably apparent. This morning, she knew it would take quite an unbalanced force to move these two from the bar.

"Boys," Alex said when she walked over. "Am I late?"

Buck looked at her with bloodshot eyes glassed over from too much bourbon.

"Not at all," he said. "Hank and I were catching up. We haven't seen each other for a while."

"Good to see you, Hank," Alex said.

The detective lifted his glass to her. "Alex, it's been a while."

"What can I get you?" the bartender asked.

Alex looked around the somewhat crowded bar, amazed that so many people were drinking at this time of morning.

"You don't by chance serve slow-poured Americanos, do you?"

The bartender shook her head and smiled. "Just beer and liquor. Twenty-four-seven."

"I'll have a water, thanks."

"I'll have another Jameson." Hank pushed his glass to the end of the bar. "You on the wagon again, Alex?"

"Was never off, Hank. And it's not even nine-thirty in the morning."

"I just finished an overnight."

"Maybe a diner for breakfast and coffee might have been a better idea."

"I'd be up the rest of the day if I started drinking coffee at the end of my shift. I need a couple of Jamesons to put me to sleep and get me ready for tonight."

"Fair enough, just answer a few questions for us before you doze off."

"Fire away."

"Byron Zell," Buck said. "Tell us what you know."

"Not much," Hank said.

"But more than nothing," Alex said, "which is what we know."

"Why are you two so curious about a pedo who got knocked off?"

Alex was curious for a number of reasons, not the least of which was that she had recently been inside the man's apartment. An apartment that was now a crime scene, every inch of which was being dusted for prints and combed for fibers. She'd been careful during her rogue operation, but only to a point. Her barometer had been outwitting a wealthy businessman who would want to figure out how someone had gotten into his computer to send an errant e-mail. The bar she had set was low and hadn't included outsmarting CSI teams or fingerprint experts or forensic scientists. Her worry, ever since reading the news about Byron Zell, was that she had sloppily left a print behind. Although Alex Armstrong would not show up in any database, Alexandra Quinlan would. Somewhere in the dusty corners of the national fingerprint database were the prints Alex had provided as a seventeen-year-old girl when she was arrested for the murder of her family. What a field day the press would have if Alexandra Quinlan's fingerprints were found in the apartment of a man who was shot dead. Good Lord, the mess that would cause.

"Byron Zell was a client at Lancaster and Jordan," Alex said. "Buck and I had briefly been assigned to his case."

"Lancaster and Jordan was repping him on the pedo charges?"

"Hell no!" Buck said with a force that accentuated the slur to his words. "We don't defend perverts."

Alex looked at Buck. She was fashionably late for the 9:00 a.m. meeting but was sure Buck had been there long earlier than that. Hank Donovan had an excuse for drinking so early in the morning: he'd just finished a night shift. Buck had no such pretext.

"We don't take clients like that," Alex said. "As Buck so eloquently stated."

"Perverts," Buck said again.

"He gets it, Buck. Lancaster and Jordan doesn't represent pedophiles." Alex put her hand on Buck's shoulder and lowered her voice. "You okay?"

Buck nodded and went back to his bourbon. Over the years Alex had grown accustomed to the dark valleys Buck Jordan occasionally descended into. Certain subjects seemed to pull him into an abyss of anger and depression. The episodes were always fueled by alcohol. She knew that Buck was concerned about her having been in Byron Zell's apartment, and that he was currently teetering on the edge of a meltdown because he considered Alex his responsibility—at least as far as her work at Lancaster & Jordan was concerned.

Alex looked back at Hank.

"Zell came looking for representation against embezzlement charges. I was looking into his finances."

"A kiddie predator *and* a thief. Lancaster and Jordan is attracting quite the clientele these days."

"We didn't know about the pedo stuff when we agreed to rep him, Hank. And we cut ties as soon as we learned about it."

"Immediately," Buck added.

"If you look closely," Alex said, "you'll see that it was Garrett Lancaster who originally brought the child pornography to the police."

"Really? How'd that come about?"

"Uh," Alex said, lifting her glass and taking a sip of water. She and Buck stole a glance at each other. "Zell accidentally sent the dirty pictures to Garrett Lancaster."

"Accidentally?"

"The pictures were included in a batch of financial documents he sent to Lancaster and Jordan. Apparently, the guy hid his porn in the financial files on his computer."

"And Lancaster turned him in?"

"Garrett turned over the illegal files to the police. That's all I know about it."

"So we've got a thief, a child predator, and an idiot."

"Well," Alex said, "for what it's worth, it looks like he wasn't embezzling funds from his company."

"Gee, let's throw the guy a parade."

"Tell us what you know about the homicide, Hank," Buck said.

"There's not much to tell. Our guys got called to the scene by one of Zell's relatives—a niece, I think. She'd been unable to get a hold of him for a couple of days, so she convinced the super to let her into Zell's apartment to check on him. Found him dead in the kitchen. Two gunshot wounds. One to the face, one to the chest. Uniforms arrived, roped the place off. Crime scene folks documented everything, then my guys got there."

"And?"

"And what, Buck? You want a blow-by-blow?"

"Just an overview," Buck said. "We need to know what you found in the guy's apartment."

"ME said the guy died quickly. The shot to the face was first and would have killed him by itself, but the second through the heart made sure of it. Gun was a forty-caliber Smith and Wesson. Forensic guys are looking to trace it, but no hits yet. That's about it so far."

Buck looked at Alex and nodded before taking a sip of whiskey.

"Oh, there *was* something interesting. The CSI guys found kiddie porn around the guy, so we're tracking that for now. Trying to ID the kids in the pictures to see if maybe it was an angry parent of one of the kids."

Alex looked at Hank, her eyelids squinted and her head tilted in a curious posture. "There were pictures around the body?" she asked.

Hank nodded. "Initial angle is that whoever pulled the trigger placed the photos around the body as sort of an explanation for the killing. The photos were printed from Zell's computer. The forensic guys found the images on his hard drive. The geeks are looking now. New computer, incidentally. His old one had been confiscated, so it looks like he was at it again."

Alex's heart began to pound as beads of sweat sprouted on her forehead. She thought about her evidence board, on which she had fruitlessly worked over the years, pinning any fringe detail to the board, believing that someday the details would make sense and lead to her family's killer. It had been years, though, since she'd found anything meaningful. Years since she'd made her last inch of progress. But now, ten years after her family had been killed, she'd stumbled across Byron Zell, whose murder looked vaguely similar to her parents'. There were thousands of shooting homicides each year in the United States, so Alex couldn't count that as a similarity. But the photos definitely were. Her family's killer had also placed photos around her parents' bodies—photos of three women thought to be victims of sexual abuse and trafficking.

"You okay?" Hank asked. "You're white as a ghost."

"Christ, kid," Buck said. "Don't faint on me. Have a sip of your water." Now it was Buck who lowered his voice. "You got nothing to worry about. If they were going to find anything to link you to that apartment, they'd have found it by now."

Alex closed her eyes and worked to regain her composure. Her presence inside Byron Zell's apartment was the farthest thing from her mind.

"You two want to tell me what's going on?" Hank asked.

Alex shook her head. "Any luck tracking the kids in the photos?"

"No, and there won't be. Most of those kids are in the system and untraceable. The sex-trafficking world is sad, but it's where ninety-nine percent of that stuff comes from. It won't lead anywhere, but my guys'll chase it anyway. They'll put a search through the Center for Missing and Exploited Children, but they won't get any hits."

Hank continued his suspicious inspection of Alex's reaction before taking a sip of whiskey.

"So that's about all I've got for you guys. The apartment was clean. No useful prints. A bunch of Zell's and a few strays, but none that matched anyone in our database."

Buck looked over and winked at her. Alex should have sunk her shoulders a bit, relieved to hear that she hadn't left any prints behind, but the tension stayed in her body. The photos left by Byron Zell's body had hit too close to home.

"You're freaking me out, kid," Hank said. "You sure you don't want a real drink? Something with some punch behind it?"

Alex blinked, pulling herself back from the hypothetical that ran through her mind—the idea that Byron Zell's crime scene was chillingly similar to her family's.

"She's just freaked out by the situation," Buck said. "We were investigating this guy, and now he's dead. A dead pedophile is not a bad thing, it's just the connection to Lancaster and Jordan that had us curious. Keep us updated if something comes up or you get any leads, will you? I know Garrett Lancaster will be interested, too."

"You bet," Hank said. "Now don't either of you forget to pick up the phone next time I call asking for a favor."

"Will do," Buck said.

Alex nodded and offered a weak smile as Buck dropped money onto the bar.

"I'm going to get Alex home. Thanks for the information, Hank."

Alex turned to leave, her mind pulling her back to the night her family was killed. It was a place she had managed well over the last ten years, allowing the memories into her consciousness only when she wanted them there. But as Buck walked her out of the bar she was deluged with uncontrolled thoughts and images from that night, and a wild notion that she was closer to the truth than she understood.

CHAPTER 46

Washington, D.C.
Saturday, April 29, 2023
9:50 a.m.

Annette Packard sat at the end of the bar at Benjamin's Tavern. Although she no longer frequented the place, she knew it existed. The place was not just for cops. Benjamin's was popular with field agents, and Annette had years ago been a regular at the tavern. It had been her attempt to fit in before she realized that chasing bad guys for the FBI was not her calling, and that she was better suited digging through politicians' lives, although at times the two felt like one and the same.

She waited a couple of minutes after she saw the woman leave before she raised her hand and spoke.

"Hank Donovan?"

She saw her old friend turn his head at the sound of his name. She slid off her stool and walked over, offering a huge smile as if the encounter were due to chance and not dumb luck that the woman Annette had been following since the previous morning had ended up sitting at a bar next to an old cop friend of hers.

"Annette? Get out of here!" Hank said, standing to embrace her in a bear hug. "What are you doing here? I thought you were off to greener pastures."

"No, I've been back in DC for a few years. I just travel all the time, so it feels like I'm never here."

Annette and Hank had been Washington, D.C. beat cops a lifetime ago.

"What have you been up to all these years?" Annette asked. "You're in a suit and tie. Don't tell me they made you detective."

Hank smiled. "Head of homicide."

"Wow, Hank. Well done."

"Thanks. And you? You're still with the bureau?"

"Twenty years this June."

"A lifer, huh?"

Annette smiled. "Feels that way."

"They still have you doing surveillance work?"

"Sort of. They've got me vetting politicians, if you can believe that."

"I can," Hank said. "I've actually heard that you're doing a great job and that your services are in high demand."

"They keep me busy and keep paying me, so I must be doing something right."

Hank looked at his watch. "They don't have you working third shift, do they?"

"No," Annette said. "I was meeting a contact. He chose the place, I obliged."

Hank tapped his watch, and Annette recognized the embarrassment on his face. "They've got me on overnights, so my day is winding down. That's the only reason I'm drinking whiskey at this hour."

"I get it, Hank. I know the hours can be brutal. Hey, just out of curiosity, who was the woman you were just talking with?"

Hank pointed at the empty stool next to him, Alex's empty glass still resting on a square coaster on the bar. "Oh, that was a legal investigator I sometimes work with. We help each other on cases when we can. Her name's Alex Armstrong. Works for Lancaster and Jordan, a big firm here in DC. We were just exchanging information on a case. And I'm divorced, by the way, in case you're worried you caught me in an illicit affair."

"You've gotten paranoid in your old age."

"Probably so." Hank smiled again. "Annette Packard. Man, it's been years. I know it's early, so I won't ask if I can buy you a drink, but you want to grab breakfast?"

"I wish I could, Hank, but I'm in the middle of a case right now and I'm up to my neck. Can I take a rain check?"

"Of course. Thanks for flagging me down. It was good seeing you."

"You too, Hank."

Hank checked his watch again. "I'd better hit the road myself. But let me grab your number so I can hold you to that rain check."

They exchanged contact information and both turned to leave, Annette allowing Hank to walk in front of her. In one quick motion she reached to the bar and retrieved Alex Armstrong's empty glass, then slipped it into her bag before anyone noticed. If she was going to tap the woman for information about Larry Chadwick and his son, Annette needed to run a background check on the woman to make sure there were no red flags—typical protocol before enlisting someone as a source in one of her vets.

CHAPTER 47

Alex's mind was spinning as she entered her condo. The idea that Byron Zell's killer had dropped photos of child pornography around his body had conjured up the images of her parents' bedroom in McIntosh. Although Garrett had never shared the crime scene photos with Alex—despite that he had access to them when he was fighting for her freedom in the weeks after she was arrested—Alex had still managed to see them. They were leaked by the McIntosh Police Department in a misguided attempt to win favor with the public, as if seeing the horror that took place inside her parents' bedroom would prove to the public at large that Alex was a killer.

She'd first seen the photos when a group of kids at Alleghany printed them off the Internet and pinned them to the walls of Alex's room while she was in a group therapy session. The images continued to show up throughout her time in juvenile detention—in her room, in the bathroom stall, in the recreational area, in envelopes stuffed into her mailbox. Alex had no choice then. She was forced by the vile kids who made up the population at Alleghany to look at the images from the night her family was killed. It was after her release that viewing them became voluntary.

She had dedicated hours and hours of therapy to organizing and compartmentalizing those images and the thoughts they brought with them, trying to work out what made sense and what was a figment of her imagination. There was a period of time during the dark days when Alex had even allowed herself to believe what everyone around her—from the detectives who interrogated her, to the reporters who wrote about her, to the true-crime fanatics who stalked her—was suggesting: that she had pulled the trigger that night, and that her mind had somehow erased it from memory and replaced the truth with a fantasy of her escaping the night by hiding behind the grand-father clock in the hallway. Alex had traveled so far down that rabbit hole that some distant part of her mind still considered it a possibility.

Although she had not been able to bring herself to fully admit her failure the fact that she had searched for a decade without finding an alternate theory added to the smoke-filled corner of her mind where that hazy theory resided. But now she had something. Now she had a link to another homicide. It wasn't much—the photos left around Byron Zell's body—but it was more than she'd had the day before. It was the first clue she'd come across since returning from Cambridge years ago. And it was just enough to push the door to that hazy part of her mind closed a little farther.

Alex had always known that the pictures of the girls left on her parents' bed were the key to figuring out the truth about that night. The pictures were of three women who had worked for Roland Glazer, the business tycoon who had been arrested on child sex trafficking charges and who had hung himself in his jail cell the night before his trial was to start. The knowledge that whoever killed Byron Zell had also dropped photos by his body had Alex's mind churning in a redundant loop from which she could not escape. Could the slaughter of her family be linked in some way to Byron Zell?

She hurried to the dining room, where she pushed the accordion divider to the side and stood in front of her evidence board. She looked at the photos of the three women who were still missing to this day. It was widely suspected, Alex had learned from her deep dive into the Roland Glazer case, that Glazer had killed the women in order to protect his secrets. Alex moved her gaze from the women to the photos of her parents. Then she stared at the photo of the Sparhafen Bank in Zürich and the statement for the numbered account she found hidden in her attic. An account that had been opened by Roland Glazer. There was a connection there that she still couldn't understand.

Alex turned from her board and ran to the kitchen. She grabbed the *Washington Times* article that covered Byron Zell's death. Foregoing scissors, she tore the article from the newspaper, pinned it to her board, and allowed her gaze to jump from her parents to Roland Glazer to the bank account statement to the three women and, finally, to Byron Zell. She stared for twenty minutes, searching for understanding that would not come. Only when her doorbell rang did Alex finally give up.

She turned from the board and walked to the kitchen, where she activated the intercom.

"Hello?"

"Alex, it's Jacqueline. We have a problem."

Alex was used to Garrett making house calls. Their relationship was such that it was not unusual for Garrett to stop by unannounced. Sometimes it was work related, but oftentimes it was with Donna and for no other purpose than a visit. For Jacqueline Jordan to make an appearance meant something was happening in the Matthew Claymore case. Alex buzzed her up and waited with her door open until the elevator arrived. When it did, Jacqueline emerged.

"Sorry to barge in on a Saturday," Jacqueline said as she exited the elevator and walked up the hallway.

"No worries," Alex said. "What's going on?"

"They found Laura McAllister's body early this morning."

"Oh, God. That's awful."

Jacqueline walked into Alex's apartment.

"I'm only getting early details. Her body was found by a professor on a running trail near campus. My source at the police department said early indications are that she was raped and strangled."

Alex put her hands to her face but didn't speak.

"Matthew Claymore's parents just called me. The police took Matthew in for questioning."

"On what grounds?"

"Detectives discovered a backpack near Laura's body that they've linked to Matthew."

"Linked how?"

"They're saying it's his backpack."

Alex swallowed hard. "Now what?"

"If it's true, and early indications say it is, then the backpack ties Matthew to the scene and we've got a major problem."

"Jacqueline, I don't believe it. I spent a lot of time with Matthew this past week. He's not a killer."

"Matthew provided DNA samples when we had our interview yesterday, so we'll know soon enough."

"Was there DNA on Laura's body?"

"My source didn't know, but he said it was a messy crime scene. If Matthew's DNA is absent from the scene, that should take the suspicion off of him—backpack or not. If his DNA shows up on her body, then we'll have some decisions to make. But the backpack found at the scene is my first priority. I'm on my way to the precinct to meet with him now, but before I do I wanted to see if you turned up anything since yesterday morning."

"Yes, a lot," Alex said, pointing to the couch. "I know just about everything about Laura's story. Sit down and I'll tell you. Can I get you something to drink?"

Jacqueline sat on the couch. "Ice water, please."

Alex headed to the kitchen and prepared a glass of ice water. She handed it to Jacqueline as she sat across from her boss. As she did, Alex became awkwardly aware that her evidence board was in full view. She'd forgotten to pull the accordion divider closed, and now the standing corkboard easel, littered with photos of her parents, newspaper articles, and Post-it Notes, was on display for Jacqueline to see.

Alex stood and pulled the divider closed.

"Sorry, just a pet project of mine," Alex said.

"I saw a photo of your parents," Jacqueline said.

Alex smiled. "I'm sure Garrett's mentioned it to you."

Despite the crisis unfolding with Lancaster & Jordan's newest client, Alex saw Jacqueline's eyes take on a softer demeanor. Although Jacqueline had played only a supporting role years ago during Alex's defamation case against the state of Virginia, she had been Garrett's right hand in his fight to convince a judge to drop the charges against Alex and spring her from Alleghany. Alex's past, and the case Garrett and Jacqueline had won for her, was a never-mentioned event at Lancaster & Jordan but would remain a time in history when all three had become inextricably linked to one another.

Jacqueline shook her head. "He hasn't."

Garrett's silence about her board was more proof that he was the most honorable man Alex knew. If there were anyone Garrett would share the details of Alex's lifelong obsession with, it was Jacqueline.

"It's just… this thing I do," Alex said. "Whenever I find new details about my family's case, I pin them to the board." Alex shrugged. "I know it sounds stupid."

Jacqueline squinted her eyes. "Not at all. And don't let anyone tell you it is. If it's important to you, it's important. Period."

Alex smiled. "Thanks, Jacqueline."

Jacqueline pointed to where Alex's board was now hidden by the divider. "I don't mean to pry, but did I see Byron Zell's photo?"

Alex shook her head. "You did. But I don't know, it's just this strange thing I found."

"Want to tell me about it?"

Alex smiled. "Not really."

Jacqueline returned the smile. "Let's get to work?"

"Yes."

Alex took a deep breath.

"Okay, so Laura McAllister's story was going to cover alleged rapes committed by members of the Delta Chi fraternity. Although only one incidence of sexual assault was reported to the police, Laura had uncovered several other victims who were willing to speak about their ordeal. Nowhere in Laura's story was Matthew Claymore mentioned. But what you'll be most interested in is that Laura uncovered strong evidence that the girl who filed the police report believed that Duncan Chadwick raped her."

"Larry Chadwick's son?"

"Yes. That's why they created such a spectacle with the press conference that essentially broke the scandal."

"Rather than allowing Laura to drop her story, they tried to defuse things by getting out in front of it."

"Exactly. And it goes without saying that Judge Chadwick had a lot to lose if a story about rape that involves his son went mainstream. So we have an angle there, and that's what you told me to find. We have someone with motive to keep Laura's story quiet."

"Accusing a sitting judge about to be nominated to the Supreme Court is risky."

"Not Judge Chadwick, but his son."

"Take me through your theory," Jacqueline said.

"My information comes from getting my hands on Laura's story. I listened to the episode she was going to drop. Here's what I know. A girl was raped at a Delta Chi party after she drank punch spiked with the date-rape drug dubbed Liquid G. She took all the correct measures—went to the hospital, had a rape kit performed on her, and filed a police report. There's proof that she was at the fraternity party that night with

Duncan Chadwick: a friend of hers has photos of the two of them together. Laura McAllister got tipped off about the rape through an e-mail and started investigating. She found witnesses who said they saw Duncan and the girl together that night. The friend, a girl named Ashley Holms, went to another Delta Chi party two weeks after the rape and got a drink from the bar, which she smuggled out of the party. She and Laura had it tested to confirm that Liquid G was present. Laura started to compile all of this evidence for her story, including the ways the university was working to keep the details quiet. But then bits of the story started to leak. Duncan heard that he was about to be named in the scandal. The following day the Chadwicks held a press conference where Duncan Chadwick played the role of a concerned and outraged classmate, rescinded his Delta Chi membership, and promised to work with the police in any way possible."

Jacqueline nodded her head. "Damn fine investigative work, Alex. Well done." Jacqueline stood. "Can you put all the details together in a brief for me, with names of sources?"

"I'll get right on it."

"I'm heading to see Matthew now. He knows enough not to say a word until I'm there. And if they don't have something more substantial than a backpack, they're not going to be able to keep him detained."

"I've got a source inside the Washington, D.C. detective bureau. I can reach out to see how credible the backpack angle is."

"Perfect. Do that," Jacqueline said. "And I'll keep you posted if I learn anything new on my end. Police are being tight-lipped at the moment, but they'll have no choice but to tell me everything if they hope to keep Matthew in custody. We'll talk soon."

With a wave of her hand Jacqueline was through the door and gone. Alex stood alone in her condo. Along with the silence came a sense of hopelessness. Despite the pressing matters of the

Matthew Claymore case, Alex walked into the dining room, pulled the divider to the side, and stood in front of her board. Jacqueline's words were kind, but Alex had seen the sorrow in her boss's eyes when Jacqueline realized that, ten years after the murder of her family, Alex was still looking for answers that would likely never come.

Her efforts felt suddenly futile, and Alex wondered how long she could go before she admitted to herself that she'd reached a dead end years ago. And that no matter how skilled a legal investigator she was, her talents fell far short of being able to discover any trail that might lead to her family's killer.

CHAPTER 48

Claustrophobia descended over Alex's condo after her meeting with Jacqueline, so she headed to a coffee shop on the corner, The Perfect Cup. She wouldn't agree that their Americanos were perfect, but the coffeehouse was the best she'd found in the area. Syrupy drinks only peripherally related to coffee were written in marshmallow letters on a chalkboard on the wall behind the bar. Alex ordered a slow-poured Americano, found a seat at a tall table for two, and pulled out her phone. She started writing a text to Hank Donovan. It had been a couple of hours since she'd left the detective bellied-up to the bar at Benjamin's, and one of two things had likely happened since then: Hank had continued to order drinks and was still at the bar and drunk as a skunk or he was asleep at home. Both situations meant she was unlikely to hear from him anytime soon. And the fact that Laura McAllister's body had been discovered early that morning meant Hank would be oblivious to the details. His shift had ended by then, and he'd count himself lucky that the call had gone to another detective. Still, Hank was her only contact inside the Washington PD, and even if he wasn't working the Laura McAllister case, he'd have access to it. It was at least worth a text message to find out.

She pressed SEND just as someone sat down across from her. Alex looked up from her phone.

"Hi," the woman said.

Alex spoke with a wrinkled brow. "Can I help you?"

"Maybe. My name's Annette Packard. I work for the FBI."

Alex watched the woman reach into her blazer and remove her identification. When she did, Alex noticed the shoulder strap, holster, and gun tucked under her left armpit. The woman laid her credentials on the table.

"I think you and I are after the same thing. At least, that's what I've surmised after watching you run all over campus yesterday."

Alex squinted her eyes. "The FBI?"

"Sorry," Annette said. "That always comes off as intimidating when I say it without context. I work for a surveillance branch of the FBI, and my latest client is Lawrence P. Chadwick, Duncan Chadwick's father."

Alex chose her words carefully. "Why is the FBI interested in Lawrence Chadwick?"

"Not interested so much as forced to be curious. When someone runs for public office or, say, is about to be tapped for a lifetime appointment on the Supreme Court, they have to undergo security clearance-type background checks. That's what I do."

Alex lifted her chin, staring at the bulge under the woman's left arm. "And you need a gun to do that?"

"Definitely not," Annette said, pulling her blazer closed to conceal the holster and the gun it held. "I hate this thing, but the bureau requires agents to carry firearms at all times, so I'm stuck with it. And I should clarify what I mean when I say background checks. I vet politicians to make sure they don't have skeletons hiding in their closets, and I've been involved with the Chadwick family for a number of weeks now. I'm sure you've heard that Larry Chadwick's name has been floated as the president's next Supreme Court nominee. I've been tasked with making sure the judge has no secrets to hide. Everything was checking out splendidly. In fact, I was about to put my seal of approval on him. I was this close to reporting back to the president that Larry Chadwick and his family were clean as a whistle. But then I started hearing rumors about Larry's son, Duncan, and his fraternity's involvement in rape on McCormack University's campus. A story like that could be damaging if it was credibly linked to the judge. And if the rumors are true that Duncan Chadwick was directly involved in sexual assault… well, that would be a game changer. So, I started my due diligence. Rolled up my sleeves and started looking for answers. Just as I started digging, Laura McAllister disappeared. You can imagine the position that put me in, especially because my boss needs to name a nominee soon. There's a lot of pressure to get the confirmation process started and over with before next year's election cycle heats up. So, I've got a big mess on my hands."

Alex raised her eyebrows. "The mess is bigger than you think," she said. "Laura McAllister's body was found early this morning. Someone strangled her and dumped her in the woods."

Annette sat back in her chair. "Well, shit. That definitely complicates things."

Alex heard genuine surprise in the woman's voice.

"So why are you talking to me?" Alex asked.

Annette paused before she spoke.

"I saw you break into Laura McAllister's apartment," Annette finally said. "You made impressive work of that lock."

Alex's breath caught in her throat, preventing her from responding even if she had been clever enough to think of something to say.

Annette shook her head. "Don't worry, my arresting-bad-guys days ended decades ago when I left the police department. I chase information these days, not criminals. And the information I have tells me that you're an investigator for a law firm named Lancaster and Jordan, and that you're poking around McCormack University because your firm represents Matthew

Claymore, who was dating Laura McAllister. Matthew is likely a person of interest—boyfriends of missing, and now dead, girls usually are."

"So you want something from me? Is that what this is?"

"Yes. I need to know what you've found out about Laura McAllister's story and whether Duncan Chadwick was involved in any way."

"And what? I either help you or you turn me in for breaking into Laura's apartment? This is like a little extortion plot?"

"No. I think you're misunderstanding why I brought up the fact that you broke into a dead girl's apartment to get information. I don't look down on it, I admire it. I wish I could break the rules when I'm digging for information, but I have the federal government constantly breathing down my neck. I have to keep my snooping strictly by the book. I can't be as brazen as you. I'm forced to be more subtle. Let me give you an example. After I saw you go to Laura McAllister's apartment, I figured you were working an angle on a case that's tied directly to my vetting of Larry Chadwick. So I followed you. I was at Benjamin's Tavern when you met with Hank Donovan, who happens to be an old colleague of mine from back in the day. He told me you were an investigator for a big firm. It was then that I knew I might need to know what you know, and that I might be able to use you as a source. You see, there's a loophole there. I, *personally*, can't break any laws to obtain information, but I can source that information to others who are more liberated in their information-gathering skills. If you agree to help me, you'd become a source of information. And when I recruit a source for information, I need to dot my i's and cross my t's to make sure I'm not getting in bed with a felon, or an otherwise unsavory soul, who could later be deemed unreliable. So I took your glass off the bar and ran the prints."

Alex sat back in her seat and folded her hands on the table. It was a poor attempt to hide her angst, and she was sure Annette Packard knew she had Alex sweating.

"To my surprise, those prints came back not belonging to Alex Armstrong of Lancaster and Jordan, but to a woman named Alexandra Quinlan. There's not much out there in the Ethernet about Alex Armstrong, but man, type the name 'Alexandra Quinlan' into a search engine and your computer damn near blows up."

Alex calmly reached into her purse and removed a tube of bright orange lipstick. She applied it to her lips and puckered when she was finished. It was all she could do to stop her hands from shaking.

"I don't mean to intimidate you," Annette said.

"Really? You ambush me at a coffee shop, place an FBI badge on the table, make sure I see that you're carrying a gun, and then tell me that you secretly ran my prints. I think that's the very definition of intimidation."

"I'm just showing you how I operate. And I thought I could use the information I discovered about you to gain your trust. I don't care who you were, I only care what you know. You've been poking around McCormack University for a few days, and I'm interested in what you've learned. I have a vested interest to learn if Duncan Chadwick was part of the story Laura McAllister was going to tell. My job depends on me getting this right. I've got my crew on it, but it might take a while for them to get me the details. Details that you, with your ability to take liberties with how you investigate, might already have. So I'm here to make an offer."

Alex returned the lipstick to her purse. She looked at Annette and nodded.

"I'm listening."

"I have the entire Justice Department at my fingertips. If you help me with this case and tell me what you've uncovered about the story Laura McAllister was working on, consider me in your debt. If you ever need help with a case—maybe you need something that will impress your boss at that big firm you work for—I'll use my credentials and my connections to get it done. A straight quid pro quo. You help me now, and I'll help you later when you need it. No questions asked."

"And the details about Laura McAllister's story? If I give them to you, what would you do with them?"

"My only goal is to determine if anything about Laura McAllister and the story she was working on will be detrimental to Larry Chadwick's chances of getting through a senate confirmation hearing."

Alex paused. She felt that the pendulum of the conversation had finally swung back to give her some leverage. She nodded.

"It will," Alex said.

Annette cocked her head. "Ah, progress. Care to elaborate?"

"Not yet. I need to do my own background check. And I'm not sure what I can share with you until I speak with my boss at Lancaster and Jordan."

"Sounds fair to me."

Annette pushed a business card across the table.

"Call me when you're ready to talk. And as a courtesy, if you decide you have something to tell me about Larry Chadwick's son, the sooner the better for me. I'm on a deadline."

The woman was up and out of the café before Alex had a chance to catch her breath or respond. Alex looked down at the card: ANNETTE PACKARD, SPECIAL AGENT, FEDERAL BUREAU OF INVESTIGATION.

CHAPTER 49

Tracy Carr sat cross-legged on the bed of her hotel with her laptop in front of her. Comfortably in work mode with head-phones covering her ears, a pen between her teeth, and hair pulled up in a bun, she was balancing both of her gigs. On a hard deadline to deliver a thousand-word article meant to bring *New York Times* readers up to date on the latest developments in the Laura McAllister case, she was also putting out content for her social channels to satiate the appetite of the true-crime fanatics who followed her. Many of her followers had never picked up a newspaper in their lives and acquired their news (or gossip) from videos dropped on social media.

Tracy had done two shoots over the last two days. The Laura McAllister case was turning into a true bonanza of a story and was gaining national attention due to the tangential connection to Lawrence Chadwick, whose potential nomination to fill the SCO-TUS vacancy appeared to be unraveling at lightning speed. The fact that Chadwick's son had been floated as poten-tially being connected to Laura McAllister was true crime that could not be ignored. Now that the girl had turned up dead, the story was exploding across the Internet.

Still, despite the demand of her social channels and her deadline for the *Times*—her article was due to her editor in two hours and was only half written—Tracy could not shake the encounter she'd had on Friday. In the middle of her report, a woman had stumbled into the shoot and collided with her. This, alone, was not unusual. For a beat reporter, dealing with an inept public was part of the job. But the interruption was not what had her mind churning; it was the woman herself. Tracy refreshed the footage on her computer and rewatched the incident unfold. On the screen, she saw herself delivering her report, and then, from the right side of the screen, the woman with short blond hair appeared. She was looking to her left, to where other reporters were recording their shoots, and never saw that Tracy was in front of her until they collided.

Tracy slowed the footage as the woman walked into the frame. She paused the video at the moment just after the collision, when the woman turned in confusion and looked directly into the camera. Tracy studied the woman. Short blond hair spiked with product. Piercings in her left ear, eyebrows, nose, and lower lip. Tracy zoomed in on the still image, concentrating only on the woman's eyes. They were bright blue, but artificially so, probably made that way by colored contact lenses. Tracy knew those eyes as brown, and when she got past the distractions it dawned on her.

"Holy shit," she whispered to herself. She lifted the laptop off the bed and brought it close to her face. "It's Empty Eyes in the flesh."

CHAPTER 50

Washington, D.C.
Monday, May 1, 2023
1:55 p.m.

"Turn on your television," Alex heard Jacqueline say as soon as Alex answered her phone.

"What happened?"

"Just turn on one of the local stations."

Alex and Jacqueline had been working nonstop since Matthew Claymore was brought in for questioning on Saturday morning. As promised, Jacqueline had yielded enough power to avert a formal arrest until DNA testing came back. A backpack alone, she argued, was not proof of murder. The police had promised an expedited forensic lab run and gave Matthew strict orders not to leave the District of Columbia, or even his parents' house.

"Are you watching?" Jacqueline asked through the phone.

Alex picked up the remote and clicked the television on. The local NBC station had a breaking news alert with a headline that read: ARREST MADE IN THE LAURA MCALLISTER MURDER INVESTIGATION.

Alex turned up the volume and watched as the news anchor inside the studio handed things over to a female reporter standing outside the gates of McCormack University.

"We are outside McCormack University, where there has been a break in the Laura McAllister investigation, the student journalist whose body was found early Saturday morning.

Laura's boyfriend, Matthew Claymore, was questioned on Saturday morning for several hours before being released. Now, just moments ago, police have arrested a different man. The Washington, D.C. police chief made a statement indicating that the arrest came after DNA evidence tied the suspect to the murder scene."

The report cut to footage of a man—white, middle-aged, with greasy hair, thick glasses, and a salt-and-pepper scruff—being led from his double-wide trailer. He wore a dirty T-shirt and his hands were cuffed behind his back as police led him to a squad car and deposited him in the backseat.

"The man has been identified as Reece Rankin, a forty-eight-year-old Maryland auto mechanic. Police apprehended Rankin at the mobile home park where he lives. Again, police have indicated that DNA evidence has linked Rankin to the crime scene but are saying no more at this time other than they are confident they have their man. We hope to learn more during a scheduled news conference later this afternoon."

The footage cut back to the studio anchor and Alex muted the television.

"Who is he?" Alex asked.

"Just a random," Jacqueline said. "I don't know more than what I just watched with you. Matthew's parents called me when they heard. No word from the police. No apology, no statement that Matthew had been wrongly accused. So goddamn typical. I'm heading to see him now."

"Okay," Alex said in a hesitant tone. "Are you buying it?"

"Buying what?"

"That a random auto mechanic from Maryland wound up at McCormack University and just happened to rape and strangle a student journalist who was about to drop an explosive story about the university and the Greek system it supports?"

The silence from the other end of the line was evidence that Jacqueline, too, doubted the sudden conclusion to the Laura McAllister saga.

"I agree that this development is surprising, but evidence doesn't lie, Alex. Reece Rankin's DNA was all over the scene. But Reece Rankin is not my concern at the moment. Matthew is. And until he's fully out of the woods on this case, and no longer on the police department's radar, he remains our main priority."

Now it was Alex's turn to pause.

"Matthew Claymore is our client and our only concern," Jacqueline said.

"I got it," Alex finally said. "I hope this nightmare is over for Matthew."

"Me too," Jacqueline said. "I'll touch base when I know more."

The call ended and Alex continued to watch the muted television, knowing that either Matthew Claymore had just gotten extremely lucky, or something wasn't quite adding up.

CHAPTER 51

Washington, D.C.
Monday, May 15, 2023
10:00 a.m.

Two weeks had passed since Reece Rankin, the random drifter from a Maryland trailer park, was arrested and charged with the murder of Laura McAllister. Although there had been no motive for the crime other than a deranged man stalking a college student while she walked a forested trail near campus, the evidence of his guilt was overwhelming. The man had left his DNA all over Laura McAllister's body—it included epithelial cells from where the rope he used to strangle her had frayed away the skin on his hands, pubic hair, and sperm. In addition, fibers recovered from Laura's hair matched a rug that lined the trunk of Rankin's Toyota, and footprints sequestered near Laura's body were an identical match to the man's work boots. It was a certainty beyond a reasonable doubt that this man had strangled and raped Laura McAllister for a reason that appeared to be no more complicated than lust, a lack of self-control, and a complete disregard for life.

The press coverage had calmed down since the arrest of Reece Rankin. Of course, there was a breathless, yet brief, dive into the man's background—who he was, where he worked, what his neighbors thought of him—but the interest in Reece Rankin was fleeting, and the media were now on to other sensational stories. The press would circle back to Laura McAllister for brief updates when Reece Rankin appeared in court and when he was sentenced. They would flash photographs of the pretty girl on newscasts and in tabloids. But the media and the public would soon forget about Laura McAllister. A missing girl was more interesting than a dead girl. And a dead girl was interesting only as long as her killer was on the loose. It was the sad reality of American society. Gory crimes captured the public's interest, especially if they involved young, attractive women. But that curiosity lasted only as long as there was mystery surrounding the gore and the girl. Once the pieces were laid out and the puzzle was assembled, the public's thirst was quenched. Until, that was, another girl went missing or another family was mowed down in the middle of the night. Then society morphed into a thirsty nomad wandering the desert and denied of water for days. The public would gulp insatiably from any trickle that dripped from the media spigot. True crime had become pop culture—an ugly, circuitous guilty pleasure to which most people were so accustomed as to not even be embarrassed by it.

Despite the open-and-shut case surrounding Laura McAllister, no one had been able to explain how Matthew Claymore's backpack ended up at the crime scene. It was an unknown that kept Lancaster & Jordan active on the case and interested in any new developments as they pertained to their client. During follow-up questions, which took place under the watchful eye of Jacqueline Jordan, Matthew had explained to detectives that he'd lost his backpack a week earlier. He surmised under questioning that perhaps Laura had taken it accidentally the morning she'd left his apartment—the last time he saw her. The police were less than satisfied with the explanation, but with no other forensic evidence tying Matthew to the crime, they had no choice but to drop him as a suspect.

Alex's work on the case was finished, and she had already been assigned to another. Matthew Claymore was in her rearview mirror, but the case had brought her to an interesting crossroads. During her investigation she had managed to get her hands on Laura McAllister's unaired episode chronicling rape accusations at McCormack University, and that information produced an opportunity.

She walked into The Perfect Cup, ordered two slow-poured Americanos, and took a seat at the same table where Annette Packard of the Federal Bureau of Investigation had ambushed her a couple of weeks before. Today, however, it was Alex who arranged the meeting and would be doing the negotiating. She was halfway through her Americano when Annette walked in and sat across from her.

"Thanks for calling," Annette said. "I was glad you reached out."

"I got you a coffee."

Annette wrapped her hand around the cup. "Thank you."

"I've thought about your offer."

"And?"

"And, I think we might be able to help each other."

"I'm listening."

"I've managed to get my hands on Laura McAllister's unaired story. Just because Laura was killed doesn't mean her story is dead. It's alive and well, and I'm in the strange position of being the only person with access to it. Well, that's not true. I made a copy of it from a hard drive in McCormack University's recording studio, so the university has the story as well. But the administration at McCormack will bury Laura's story and hope for it to quickly decay. I feel like I owe it to this girl I've never met to make sure that doesn't happen. And trust me, you're going to want to know the details of Laura's story before it goes live. It'll have a direct impact on Larry Chadwick."

"Duncan Chadwick was involved?"

Alex nodded. "Laura had proof—well, she wasn't a detective, so 'proof' might be overstating it—but she had damning veri-fication that Duncan Chadwick was the one who purchased a date-rape drug called Liquid G, spiked the drinks at his fraternity party, and raped the girl who filed the police report.

Laura did a lot of legwork. Her story is big and towering, and its shadow covers many people, including school brass that did their best to keep the story quiet. But as Laura's story pertains to you, Larry Chadwick's son is not only going to come off terribly, but will likely be questioned in regard to the claims made in Laura's story, and possibly charged with rape. If they can trace the purchase of the gamma hydroxybutyrate back to Duncan—and Laura managed to track down the dealer who sold it to him—things will be even worse for him."

Annette stayed quiet for a moment and Alex saw that she was considering her options.

"If Laura's story comes out," Annette finally said, "and Duncan is attached to the scandal, it would sink his father's chances of being confirmed to the Supreme Court. If I were made privy to this information before it made it to the mainstream media, I'd have no choice but to advise the president against nominating Larry Chadwick."

"Come on, Special Agent Packard. You'd be a hero if you sniffed out this story before it made it to the mainstream. You'd be credited with helping the president avoid a potentially embarrassing nomination that would sully his reputation and give his adversaries ammunition leading into the election next year. I can see the political hit-job commercials now. How can the American public trust a president who put his faith in Larry Chadwick, a judge whose morals are so skewed that he raised a son to be a rapist?"

Alex watched Annette carefully and knew that she had planted a realistic scenario.

"I'll need proof," Annette said. "About Duncan and the date-rape drug and his connection to the girl who was raped. I can't just go to the president with accusations."

"Laura's story has proof. Or, like I said, strong confirmations."

"How strong?"

"Strong enough that once Laura's story is out there, the authorities will get involved. The girl already filed a police report. After Laura's story goes mainstream, Duncan will be named as her rapist. The police will investigate, and I'm certain that with the other information Laura uncovered Duncan will be charged. There's a rape kit, and they'll take a sample of Duncan's DNA to see if it's a match."

"And the proof, what Laura uncovered, you'll give me?"

"Yes. I created a series of briefs for my boss at Lancaster and Jordan. I can give you those, as well as let you listen to the episode Laura was about to drop before I make it public. Even in the extraordinary event that the Chadwick family can flex its political muscle to dodge this bullet and avoid Duncan being arrested or charged, his name will forever be tied to Laura McAllister and to rape at McCormack University."

Annette nodded. "Okay. You don't need to sell it any more than you have. I need this information, and I need it soon. So I guess we've reached the quid pro quo part of this conversation. What are you asking in exchange?"

Alex took a deep breath. "You ran my prints, which means you know my history. That's what I need help with."

"Your history? Meaning what happened when you were a teenager?"

"Meaning what happened to my family."

Alex had spent the last few days organizing this deal in her mind. The truth was that the search for her family's killer had reached a dead end years ago when Garrett rescued her from Cambridge and brought her home. Since then—since her discovery of mysterious bank statements hidden in her attic, her trip to the Sparhafen Bank in Zurich, and her discovery of a link between her parents and a sex-trafficking businessman named Roland Glazer—Alex had made no real progress in the search for her parents' killer. But the vague similarity between her parents' crime scene and Byron Zell's—in which photos of victims were left by the killer—had stirred the embers that still smoldered inside her. The rousing had been enough to reignite the desire to continue her search.

Alex knew this bold attempt was likely her last hurrah. She understood that stirring those last remaining ashes might finally extinguish them for good. But she also knew that with someone like Annette Packard holding the fire iron and poking those dying coals, they might finally combust in a way Alex could never manage on her own.

"Alex," Annette said. "I told you before. I ran your prints because I planned to tap you as a source and needed to make sure you had no priors or other red flags that would make you unreliable."

"Being accused of killing my family might make me unreliable in the eyes of some."

"You're legally Alex Armstrong now. Your past doesn't matter to me."

"Either way, you won't be getting Laura's story from me. Technically, you will be, but you'll be able to plausibly claim it came from a reliable source."

"I don't follow you."

"I'll give you the details once I have everything squared away. Before I do, though, I want to know if you'll help me."

"Help you with what, exactly?"

"Figuring out who killed my family."

Alex saw the apprehension in her eyes.

"How can *I* help with that?"

"You told me that you have the entire justice system at your fingertips."

"I have access and liberties pertaining to my specialty. Your family, and what happened to them, that's not what I specialize in."

"No. You specialize in digging and investigating and uncovering the truth. You find the right people who can get you what you need. Just like I do for my job. But I've used every bit of skill I've ever learned and every instinct I've developed to try to understand why my family was killed. I've made no progress. I need help. And you're the only person who's come along in the last decade who might actually be able to provide that help."

"Listen, Alex, I looked into your background and I remember your family's case. I think what happened to you was terrible. I'd love to tell you I can help, but I don't know what I'd be getting into or what I'd be agreeing to do. I need the information you have about Duncan Chadwick, and I need it badly. But I don't want to take that information and promise you something in return that I can't deliver."

Alex reached across the table, took Annette's Americano, and dumped it, along with her own, into the trash can next to the table.

"The coffee here is terrible," Alex said. "Come back to my place. I'll brew you some real coffee and I'll also show you exactly what you're getting into."

CHAPTER 52

Back in her condo, Alex stood next to Annette Packard and pulled the accordion divider to the side, revealing her evidence board and the decade-long journey she'd been on. Alex looked at Annette, who stayed silent as she scanned the board.

"What is this?" Annette asked.

"This is everything I've ever learned about the night my family was killed. Everything I remember about that night. Everything I've ever dreamed about that night. Every piece of evidence I've ever come across on my own or from the formal police investigation."

Annette continued to scan the board.

"Over the years," Alex said, "I've become too close to it. I'm too far into the details to be able to see a pattern, if there is one to see. I need fresh eyes to look at what I've found. I need someone to look at this board with a new perspective and without my preconceived ideas and biases about that night."

Annette squinted her eyes and raised her chin toward the board. "Is that Roland Glazer?"

"It is," Alex said. "And he's just one of the many strange pieces in this impossible puzzle."

Annette walked slowly toward the board. Alex saw that she had gotten the woman's attention.

"How about that coffee you promised," Annette said without taking her eyes off the board.

Alex nodded. "I'll get right on it."

An hour later they each sipped a second vacuum-siphoned Americano while they sat on the couch, the evidence board in front of them.

"So," Alex said. "Can you help me?"

"Me, *personally*?" Annette said. "No. Like I said, this"—she pointed at Alex's evidence board—"is not what I do. It intrigues me, but that's not the type of investigating I do. However"— Annette looked at Alex—"I know someone who can help."

"Who?"

"An old FBI friend of mine named Lane Phillips. He's a forensic psychologist who used to be one of the bureau's top profilers. He retired a number of years ago and now runs a corporation that tracks, if you can believe it, serial killers. And this"—Annette pointed to the board again—"is *exactly* what he does. I can call him and see if he's interested in helping."

Annette took a sip of coffee.

"So the deal is this: if I can convince one of the FBI's best criminal profilers to take a look at your family's case, you'll share everything Laura McAllister uncovered about Duncan Chadwick before you go public with her story?"

"Yes," Alex said. "That's the deal."

Annette stood up. "Okay. I'll make a call and get back to you."

Annette walked toward the front door. Alex opened it for her and Annette walked into the hallway and then turned.

"Just curious about something," Annette said. "You said the information won't come directly from you, but from a credible source. Care to explain that?"

"Not yet, but I know someone who might be interested in telling Laura's story on a bigger stage than I could ever provide on my own. Details to come."

It was another part of her plan that would either work to perfection or backfire horribly.

CHAPTER 53

Washington, D.C.
Monday, May 15, 2023
8:30 p.m.

Annette Packard poured a Maker's Mark and sat down on her couch. Her Columbia Heights apartment was small but comfortable, and her living room window had a partial view of the city lights and a feel of the Potomac far off in the distance. In her midfifties now, she had wondered for the last few years about her earning power should she creep from under the comfortable, but thin, blanket the US government provided. In three years she could retire from the FBI in good standing, with a nice pension, years of energy in front of her, and options.

She'd had offers over the years. Many had been attractive. The money alone had always made her listen. She earned $72,000 as a special agent in the FBI. Her role as lead scavenger into the lives of any high-profile political candidate had moved her up the ranks and padded her with power and influence but had done little to help her bottom line. The US government and all its subsidiaries, the Federal Bureau of Investigation included, was notorious for hanging awards and titles around the necks of the hardest working employees without rewarding them monetarily. The promise of a lifelong pension, however, was the reward for a job well done and a career hard worked. Before she turned sixty, Annette would be earning $70,000 a year for simply getting out of bed. And the gravy train would continue for the rest of her life, regardless of whether she took on employment elsewhere.

Some of the lucrative offers she'd gotten over the years had come from large corporations that tried to entice Annette Packard and her unique snooping abilities for their private security detail and cyber crimes divisions. Her skill set could be put to good use in corporate America or Wall Street, not only in the hiring of CEOs and other powerhouse executives, but also with opposition research into rival companies and potentially nefarious dealings that ran rampant through the business, financial, and tech industries.

The most interesting offer, however, had come from Lane Phillips, a former bureau colleague who had, indeed, bucked the system to go off on his own. The wild success Lane found in the private sector was the envy of every agent who dreamed of capitalizing on their skills and knowledge to turn their government experience into a lucrative payday. In his heyday Lane Phillips was the FBI's leading forensic psychologist and criminal profiler. Today's young guns learned the tricks of the trade from Lane's PhD dissertation, a lengthy thesis that forensically dissected the mind of a killer and was appropriately titled "Some Choose Darkness." It was read so widely through the Behavioral Science Unit inside the FBI that the bureau turned Lane's dissertation into the main training manual and blueprint to help young psychiatrists and psychologists understand the thought process of serial killers.

Lane later turned his exploits into the minds of killers, which was based on his personal interviews of over one hundred serial killers, into a best-selling true-crime memoir. The book sold millions of copies. He followed his best-selling book with a deep and unique dive into studying current and still active serial killers. Lane did this by meticulously analyzing, cataloguing, and archiving grouped murders in the United States. Using his fierce and unrelenting mind, he developed a computer program and progressive algorithm to do this analysis for him. He turned the idea into a private company called the Murder Account-ability Project, or MAP, as it was called in the industry. The algorithm proved so proficient at recognizing patterns between previously unrelated homicides that Lane Phillips had been credited with the identification and arrest of dozens of serial killers—formally defined as individuals responsible for the death of three or more victims.

Dr. Phillips's program became so successful that his services, and the Artificial Intelligence computer algorithm, had been licensed by hundreds of police departments and detective bureaus around the country, as well as implemented into the FBI's own database of the criminal offense divisions. Lane's best-selling book had made him comfortably wealthy. The licensing of his computer program that tracked and identified similar-ities between otherwise unlinked homicides had made him a millionaire many times over.

Lane's offer for Annette to come work for him and the Murder Accountability Project had been most enticing. She'd have the chance, Lane had told her, to put her snooping skills to better use than discovering that a businessman who decided to run for public office during a midlife crisis had cheated on his taxes and was currently keeping a mistress half his age. Her work at MAP would have real-world impact, Lane had tried to convince her, and he needed her skills badly. But still, leaving the bureau early would disrupt her pension, so Annette had politely declined Lane's offer. She did, however, agree to reconsider things when she turned fifty-seven and was free to retire from the FBI in good standing.

She kept in regular touch with the profiling savant and picked up her phone now to call him.

"You've decided to come work for me," she heard Lane say in the way of a greeting.

"Not yet," Annette said. "I have to secure my pension first, remember?"

"I'll pay you multiple times what the government is paying you."

"I'm going to hold you to that promise."

"Please do," Lane said. "But if you're not calling about a job, what's up?"

"Maybe nothing. But I think I've got an interesting case… Well, it's not even a case, really, or anything I'm formally working on. But it *is* right up your alley and I need your mind on it."

"Do tell."

"You remember the Quinlan family shooting from years ago?"

"No. Tell me about them."

"A mother, father, and their teenage son were killed in the middle of the night. Mowed down with a shotgun. Gory crime scene, press went wild with it. The seventeen-year-old daughter was found holding the shotgun and the police pinned her for the murders until the investigation fell apart. Some real bad detective work and an overly aggressive DA botched the hell out of the case. This was in McIntosh, Virginia."

"Sure, I remember that now. The press called the girl Empty Eyes. What was her name?"

"Alexandra Quinlan."

"That's it. Then she sued the police department."

"The state of Virginia, actually. Big defamation case that ended with a huge verdict that awarded the girl millions."

"Yeah, yeah. I remember now. What's going on?"

"Long story short, this current thing I'm working on— vetting a big-name judge—crossed my path with hers."

"With Alexandra Quinlan?"

"Yeah, but she doesn't go by that name anymore. You don't need the details, and I'm not at liberty to give them. What I was hoping for was that you'd take a look at the Quinlan family shooting, along with some other leads the girl's come across over the years, to see if you can pick up on anything useful."

"Useful how?"

"The murders are still unsolved. They were pinned on the girl, and when that theory blew up, the case went cold. I suspect no one looked too closely at the case after the debacle with Alexandra Quinlan. But the thing is, she never stopped looking herself."

"The Quinlan girl?"

"Yes. Ten years later, she's still hard at work trying to figure out who killed her family. She's the only one looking, and it's just as much of an injustice today that no one is helping her as it was a decade ago when she was falsely accused. She could use your help, Lane, and I have a feeling you'll be interested in some of the details she's managed to turn up."

"You're starting to excite me," Lane said. "You think there's a serial killing connection to the Quinlan family?"

"I have no idea. That's your specialty. But only Dr. Lane Phillips could get away with admitting they were excited at the prospect of a serial killer. Look, it's not my area of expertise, but judging by some of the research Alex has done and some of the names she's managed to peripherally link to her parents, I think it's worth your time to take a look. She's collected all her research and put together a board of the highlights. I took a picture of it, and I want to send it to you. It'll be enough to get you started. If you find anything interesting, I'm sure I can get my hands on all her other research."

"Send it," Lane said. "I'll take a look and get back to you."

"Thanks, Lane."

"How, exactly, did you get pulled into this?"

"The girl can help me with a time-sensitive case I'm working on. We agreed to swap favors. It would be a huge help if you came through for me on this."

"Happy to take a look. I'll consider it pro bono work," Lane said. "But if I turn up anything, you come work for me."

"If you're able to figure this out, I'll put in my two weeks that very day."

"Careful what you promise," Lane said.

PART V

Revelations

"This killer has been at it for much longer than ten years."

—Lane Phillips

Camp Montague

Appalachian Mountains

The day after he hid behind Jerry Lolland's cabin and concocted his plan was the start of Trek Week, the time each summer when the entire camp made a three-day, fifty-mile, round-trip journey down the Muscogee River. Each night, the kids of Montague set up camp next to the riverbank with the supplies they brought with them. Counselors were present but the fifth-years were in charge. They were responsible for assigning the campers to canoes, for leading them all downriver, for setting up camp each night, and for providing dinner. It was a coming of age for those who had been with Camp Montague the longest, and a chance for the fifth-years to show off their years of experience.

Only two counselors accompanied the campers on the three-day trek, and they were very much in the background. Their presence was nearly undetectable, for the purpose of the expedition was to build unity among the kids and allow leaders to rise to the top. He and the other fifth-years had spent the previous week making plans, and now they were executing the departure from camp. They had all the students assigned to groups and everyone was in their canoes—three to a boat, for a total of thirty canoes. He made sure she was in his group.

It was just after 3:00 p.m. on Monday by the time they made it to the first base camp. It was an hour later before everyone had their canoes secured on dry land, their tents assembled, and a campfire roaring. Barbecue grills were present at each of the base camps and the fifth-years got busy lighting the charcoal and preparing dinner. By 8:00 p.m. everyone was fed and they started their nightly ritual around the campfire just as if they were back at the main camp. He took a seat next to her and smiled.

"How're you doing?"

It was the first time they'd spoken all summer.

"Good," she said.

"Blisters?"

She looked at her hands. "Yeah, a couple small ones."

"We have gloves. I'll give you some in the morning. And some balm. You should put it on tonight before bed."

"Thanks."

"Hey," he said, looking into the fire. "I, uh, saw you last night."

She looked at him.

"I saw you with Mr. Lolland. I saw him take you to his cabin."

She directed her gaze back to the fire.

"Did he touch you?"

No answer.

"It's okay," he said. "You can tell me."

She shook her head. "He told me not to tell anyone or he would hurt me."

"That's not true. He's not going to hurt you anymore."

He looked at her, tried to make eye contact.

"Do you believe me?" he asked her. "That he's not going to hurt you anymore?"

"You can't tell Mr. McGuire."

"We're not going to tell Mr. McGuire," he said. "We're not going to tell anyone."

Three days later, Camp Montague was back to normal—post Trek Week normal. It took all of Thursday for the campers to pull the canoes from the river and store them in the giant hangar that stored all things Montague. Life vests, helmets, paddles, and tents were cleaned, dried, and stowed for next year's trek. The clean-up took two days, but by midafternoon on Friday the camp looked back to its usual self, and there was some rare downtime at Camp Montague where no activities were planned and the kids had an open afternoon and evening.

They went about the afternoon without drawing attention to themselves. They had spent the second and third night of Trek Week plotting and brainstorming until they'd come up with the perfect plan. At 3:00 p.m. they met behind the crafts shed—a long log cabin where wood-crafting projects took place.

"Everything we need should be in the back supply closet," he said.

"What do we need?" she asked.

"Probably just a pair of pliers, but I'll grab a few other tools just in case."

The supply closet was an organized maze of tools. Hammers and screwdrivers hung in organized rows from pegboard. Several red Craftsman tool cabinets lined the back wall, their drawers filled with screws and nails. They went to the wall and grabbed a pair of slip joint pliers, a hammer, and a flathead screwdriver.

"This oughta do it." He looked at her. "Okay. Stay away from your cabin. I'll meet you in the clearing at ten."

She nodded.

CHAPTER 54

Washington, D.C.
Tuesday, May 30, 2023
10:45 a.m.

Jacqueline Jordan placed her shoulder bag on the conveyor belt and watched as it made its way through the X-ray machine. A security guard stared at a monitor on the other side of the metal detector and inspected the bag's contents, looking for weapons and contraband. Jacqueline had been through the process before. It was the same at nearly every prison she visited, and she'd visited the Central Detention Facility in DC many times during her years at Lancaster & Jordan.

She passed through the metal detector without incident, and stretched her arms out to her sides for the guard to run a wand up and down her body.

"Thank you, ma'am," the young prison guard said with a smile.

Jacqueline collected her bag, hung it over her shoulder, and followed another guard through a set of locked doors until she was shown into the visitor section of the prison. She had requested, and was granted, a private room for that morning's meeting. After all, she had claimed that it was the first meeting with her new client. They would need as much privacy as possible.

The guard opened the door to the meeting room and showed her inside. She took a seat in one of the two chairs and unpacked her folder from her bag, placing it on the table in front of her. Ten minutes later, an inmate wearing an orange jumpsuit was shown into the room. Jacqueline recognized the confusion on his face as he stared at her—she was a complete stranger to him. The guard clipped the man's handcuffed wrists to an eyebolt at the edge of the table.

"You've got thirty minutes," the guard said. "If you need something sooner, press the buzzer."

"Thank you," Jacqueline said and smiled as the guard left them alone.

"Who are you?" Reece Rankin asked.

"I'm your attorney," Jacqueline lied.

"You ain't the lady I met with before."

"She was a public defender, assigned to you by the court."

"That's 'cause I ain't got no money for a real lawyer. You a real lawyer?"

"I am."

Rankin smiled, displaying badly decayed and yellow teeth. "How you think I'm gonna pay you if I don't got no money?"

"My firm takes a limited number of pro bono cases. That means we work on your behalf but don't ask for compensation in return. So don't worry about money, just concentrate on answering a few questions for me. Afterward, I'll let you know if I can help you."

"Pro bono?"

"That's right," Jacqueline said. "Would you be willing to answer a few questions for me?"

Rankin nodded, and Jacqueline was content knowing she had scaled her first obstacle. Like Alex, she too was suspicious of the Reece Rankin development. It would be something much greater than coincidence that a random pervert from Maryland happened to rape and kill a girl who was about to unleash an explosive story that would rock the lives of more than a few powerful people.

"The police claim that you've confessed to killing Laura McAllister. Is that true?"

"Yeah, I signed the papers even. But that was only 'cause they said they believed me when I told them somebody paid me to kill her. They said if I signed a confession, it would help them with the rest of the investigation and I'd do less time."

"But you *did* kill her?"

"Just said as much."

"But it wasn't your idea?"

"Shit no. Didn't even know who the bitch was."

Jacqueline paused at the man's crassness but decided to ignore it and moved on. She needed to keep him on track.

"So why did you do it? Why did you kill Laura?"

"'Cause they gave me a bunch of money and promised I'd get more after I did it."

"Someone paid you money to kill Laura McAllister?"

"You got some kinda hearin' problem, lady? Why you keep repeatin' what I say?"

"You told this to the police? That someone paid you?"

"Yeah. They said if I copped to killin' the girl, I'd get off easier 'cause I was paid."

"Did they ask who paid you?"

"Nah, we didn't get into that yet. They said I had to sign the papers first, the confession, then we'd get into the details. But I signed those papers a long time ago and ain't never seen a cop since. Figured maybe that's why you showed up out the blue."

"Do you know the name of the man who paid you to kill Laura McAllister?"

"Nah. I just saw a bunch of cash and they told me what they needed. I didn't ask no questions."

"*They?* There was more than one man?"

"Yeah. A kid did mosta the talkin', but there was another guy with him. He never talked, though. He just sort of stayed in the background."

Jacqueline opened her folder and removed a photograph of Matthew Claymore. She slid it across the table.

"Is this the kid you spoke with?"

The man looked at the photo for a moment and shook his head. "Nope. That ain't him."

Jacqueline retrieved another photo. This one was of Duncan Chadwick. She slid it in front of the man and waited.

"Yep," the man said, nodding his head and smiling with his yellowed teeth. "That's him. Real arrogant sumbitch."

"You're sure?"

"Sure as shit."

Jacqueline slowly pulled the photo of Duncan Chadwick away and replaced it in her folder, along with the photo of Matthew Claymore, then slipped the folder back into her bag.

"The other person," Jacqueline said, "was it someone his age? Another student?"

"No. Older guy. Sorta got the impression the older guy was actually in charge, but the kid was doin' all the talkin'."

Jacqueline pulled out her phone and logged onto her search engine. She scrolled for a few minutes until she found a good photo, zoomed in on it, and held her phone out for Reece Rankin to see.

"Is this the other man who paid you to kill Laura McAllister?"

The man squinted his eyes and smiled. "That's him, no doubt about it."

Jacqueline pulled her phone away and looked at the image of Larry Chadwick for only a moment before closing the browser and placing the phone in her bag.

"They were the ones that gave me that backpack, too," Rankin said. "I was supposed to leave it by the girl's body 'cause it would throw the cops off. That's what they said."

Jacqueline offered a smile. "Yeah, but you left more than the backpack. You left your DNA all over Laura McAllister's body. Skin cells, pubic hair… your fucking semen. So, you see, dumping an innocent kid's backpack *after* the fact wasn't really going to fool anyone."

Jacqueline stood and walked toward the door.

"So you gonna help me now that I told you all that?"

Jacqueline turned before pressing the buzzer.

"Maybe," she said. "One more thing, though. These men who paid you to kill Laura McAllister, did they tell you to rape her, too?"

"Yeah," he said with a shrug. "Supposed to look like a crime of passion. That's what the kid said. I didn't wanna do it but, you know... money talks. I'm just bein' honest with you. If you're gonna be my attorney, I gotta be honest, right?"

"Right," Jacqueline said as she pressed the buzzer.

"You gonna help me now? Be my attorney?"

The door opened and a guard waited for Jacqueline to exit the room. Before she did, she turned back to Reece Rankin.

"You need a priest a hell of a lot more than you need a lawyer."

CHAPTER 55

Washington, D.C.
Tuesday, May 30, 2023
12:30 p.m.

Annette Packard pulled through terminal traffic at Washington's Dulles airport, spotted Lane Phillips, and pulled to the curb. Lane placed his small suitcase in the backseat and climbed into the passenger's seat.

"Thanks for the ride, Special Agent Packard."

"Lane, good to see you," Annette said as she checked her side mirror and pulled back into traffic. "I didn't expect you to make a trip from Chicago just for my request."

"I didn't. I'm giving a presentation tomorrow for the new recruits at the BSU. I figured we could hook up and have dinner while I'm in town. I found a few interesting angles with the Quinlan girl's case. Were you able to reach her to see if she's available?"

"I was. She was a little gun shy. The press coverage about her case has died down over the years, but it's not completely without life. She's still careful with her identity and who she allows in her inner circle."

"How did you get in?"

"I didn't, really. She's helping me and I'm helping her—that's the extent of our relationship. But, yes, Alex agreed to meet you tonight. She didn't want to do it at a restaurant, so we're meeting at my place. Does that work?"

"Sure thing," Lane said. "I'll get my research together at the hotel, take a quick shower. Then, I'll see you tonight. What time?"

"Eight."

CHAPTER 56

Washington, D.C.
Tuesday, May 30, 2023
7:45 p.m.

She found Annette Packard's building in the Columbia Heights neighborhood, worked hard to control her nerves, then climbed the steps to the building's front door. She took one last deep breath and pressed the doorbell.

"You made it," Annette said when she opened the door. "Come on in."

Alex followed her into the kitchen, where Annette had dinner in the oven—a rack of lamb that filled the house with a savory scent.

"Can I get you a drink? Beer or wine?" Annette asked.

"I'll have a water, if you have one."

Annette grabbed a bottle of Pellegrino from the fridge.

"So, tell me who this guy is again," Alex said.

"Dr. Lane Phillips. He was once, and is still today, considered the FBI's most famed profiler. His PhD dissertation was centered on understanding why killers kill, and proved his innate ability to climb into a killer's mind in ways no one else can."

"But how is a profiler going to help me with my family's murder?"

"I'm not sure. I only knew that alone I could not, so I reached out to Lane. He's not only an accomplished criminal profiler, he's the creator of the Murder Accountability Project, a program used by countless police departments and homicide units across the country that helps solve cold-case homicides. Basically, Lane and his company analyze random homicides to see if and how they are linked to one another. I showed him the photo of your evidence board and he became quite interested. Then, with your permission, I sent him the details of the things you've discovered over the years."

A week earlier, Alex had turned over the details of her decade-long journey into understanding the night her family was killed. She'd given Annette everything she'd ever learned about that night in the hopes that a forensic psychologist named Lane Phillips could somehow make sense of it all.

"After looking at all your work," Annette said, "Lane believes he's found a pattern. He wanted to talk, so here we are."

Alex felt a sudden pulsing in her rib cage and tried to control her emotions.

"He came from Chicago just to tell me about this pattern?"

"He has business in DC, so the timing worked out."

The doorbell rang.

"There he is," Annette said.

Alex closed her eyes and took a deep breath as Annette headed for the front door. Her anxiety came not from the thought of listening to what Lane Phillips had to say, but from the idea that his insights might actually lead to answers. She'd searched so long for a resolution to her family's murder that looking became her identity. Answers were a mythical thing too far down the proverbial road she'd been traveling to worry about. Her personality had been built from the hunt. But here she was, potentially arriving at the faraway place where her work and research collided with answers.

"Lane," Annette said. "This is Alex Armstrong. Alex, this is Dr. Lane Phillips."

Alex worked herself away from her fear and smiled. "Dr. Phillips, thanks for coming all the way from Chicago."

The man was not what she expected. In her mind Alex had conjured the image of an academic-looking older man with white hair and glasses and a resigned personality cultivated from a lifelong exposure to the most ruthless killers society had known. But instead Lane Phillips was a vibrant-looking fifty-something-year-old man with a full head of bushy hair who could pass for someone much younger. He wore jeans and a light gray sports jacket over a button-down shirt and smiled pleasantly when he looked at her—affected not at all, it appeared, by his lifelong obsession with killers.

"Call me Lane, please. Only my students use such formalities."

"Dinner will be ready in about thirty minutes," Annette said. "Let's sit at the kitchen table to talk. Lane, something to drink?"

"Sure. You have beer?"

"I have a variety."

"Something light. The hazy stuff gets to my stomach."

A minute later they all sat around the dining table. In front of Lane was a leather-bound folder. He opened it and removed three packets.

"I'll just jump right in, if that's all right," he said.

Alex nodded.

"And excuse me ahead of time. I understand how emotional and traumatic discussing the details about your family's case can be, even this many years later. So I apologize in advance for my directness. It's an affliction that I move from cordial conversation directly into clinical diagnosis mode."

"Understood," Alex said. "Did you... find anything?"

"I think so. There're always gaps in these hypotheses so I can't be sure. But the more eyes that look at my findings, the more likely it is someone will see what I cannot."

Lane handed both Alex and Annette a packet, each several pages thick and held by a paper clip.

"I took the work and research from your board, plus everything you provided to Annette, and extrapolated from there. Very good work, by the way. You have an eye for detail."

Alex nodded. "Thanks."

"Here's what I know. Your family was killed on January fifteenth of twenty-thirteen. Your diligent research proved that there were no connections to similar killings that involved other families, specifically not in the vicinity of the East Coast of the United States. But in order to shed light on your family's killer, we have to figure out if that unknown killer has killed before or after. Of course, it's my confirmation bias to assume we're dealing with a serial killer.

"Now, if your family's case was a random act of violence, or the work of a one-and-done killer, then the likelihood that I'll be able to help you is not good. My expertise is in identifying similarities between random homicides and determining if there is a link that ties them together. When I sat down with your information, my goal was to determine if your family's murder was part of a series of murders committed by the same person."

"And did you?" Alex asked.

"Maybe." Lane pointed at the packet. "It's all in there, so let's go through it. Chasing a few of the leads you were able to come across, specifically that your parents were associated with a man named Roland Glazer, was the key."

"I followed that lead for a long time," Alex said, "but gave up on the Glazer angle. I could never make sense of it."

"That's because *alone* it makes very little sense," Lane said. "Together with many other factors, it brings a complicated puzzle together. Or at least leads us to more pieces."

Lane held up his copy of the packet, turned a page, and began to read.

"Roland Glazer hanged himself in jail the night before his trial. But he was, as your diligent work showed, tied to your parents' accounting firm. This is where my algorithm took an interesting turn. And remember, the AI attached to my computer program is not perfect. It picks up links that we might otherwise miss. Oftentimes, those links don't necessarily lead anywhere. But in this case, what the algorithm picked up was a connection to your law firm."

Alex looked up from the packet. "My... law firm?"

"Yes. Your parents had a connection to Lancaster and Jordan. After charges of sexual assault and sex trafficking were levied against Roland Glazer, shocking the celebrities, businessmen, and royalty who associated with him, many of his associates looked for legal representation. Your parents, as accountants who handled some of Glazer's finances, did the same."

"My parents..." Alex said, "were clients of Lancaster and Jordan?"

"Yes. My research showed that in twenty-twelve, Dennis and Helen Quinlan entered into a contract for legal representation with Lancaster and Jordan and paid a retainer fee of fifteen thousand dollars. From what I could tell, the relationship amounted to simple legal advice as no charges were ever filed against your parents, and no formal legal representation was required. A common occurrence, as I'm sure you're aware. What's interesting, though, is that Mr. Glazer, too, had entered into a legal agreement with your firm. My algorithm picked it up as a *hit*, which means only that the AI software found a way to connect your parents and Glazer—other than that Glazer was a client of your parents' accounting firm—the commonality being that they both were associated with Lancaster and Jordan, if just briefly."

Alex returned her gaze to the page, reading and rereading the connection Dr. Phillips had uncovered between her parents and Glazer, struggling to understand what it meant.

"Again, this connection to Lancaster and Jordan may mean nothing," Lane said. "My algorithm simply identifies links between homicides. My analysts take over from there to see if those links lead anywhere further. Because Annette just asked me recently to look into this case, my analysts haven't had the time to complete their research. But here's what we've found so far."

Lane turned a page in the packet.

"Since twenty-thirteen, I was able to identify four clients of Lancaster and Jordan who were victims of homicide, all on the East Coast."

Alex felt the room spin as a wave of light-headedness came over her. She looked up briefly but neither Lane nor Annette noticed her struggle. Lane was reading from his packet and Annette was following along, hooked on every word. Alex took a deep breath and tuned back in to Lane's findings.

"In twenty-sixteen, a man named Karl Clément died by gunshot wound after a home invasion. Police never had any leads and the case is still unsolved today. In January of that year, Clément was a college counselor at a local high school and was charged with sexually assaulting one of his students. He sought legal counsel from Lancaster and Jordan. In twenty-seventeen, a man named Robert Klein was arrested for aggravated assault and molestation of his neighbor's twelve-year-old daughter. He, too, sought legal representation from Lancaster and Jordan. He was killed in his home six months later."

Lane looked up from his packet.

"Any guesses how Klein was killed?"

"Gunshot wound," Annette said. "During a suspected home invasion."

"Bingo. Police chalked it up to a burglary gone bad."

Lane turned the page.

"Okay, stick with me. Two more. In twenty-nineteen, a guy named Nathan Coleman was arrested for soliciting sex from a minor. He sought representation by Lancaster and Jordan, but charges were dropped due to a technicality. Two months later he was found dead in his living room. Official line? Shot and killed during a home invasion."

Lane turned the page of his packet.

"Finally, we have a guy named Byron Zell."

The sound of Byron Zell's name caused Alex's stomach to sink and her forehead to bead with sweat.

"Wait a minute," Annette said. "I've heard that name."

"So has Alex," Lane said. "Byron Zell was on her evidence board."

Alex's vision blurred as she thought back to her meeting with Hank Donovan, the detective who had given her the details about Zell's crime scene: pictures of Zell's victims had been left around his body. Alex had drawn a faint connection to her parents' crime scene but had run out of real estate from there. But now, the FBI's most renowned criminal profiler had also connected the murder of her parents to Byron Zell, but through a different link: they were all clients of Lancaster & Jordan.

Lane looked at Annette. "The name probably rings a bell because the homicide happened right here in DC about a month ago. It took a sophisticated computer algorithm constantly updated with new artificial intelligence technology for me to arrive where Alex got all on her own."

"Sexual assault," Alex managed to say.

"What's that?" Annette asked.

"All the cases have to do with sexual assault."

"Exactly," Lane said. "Sexual assault against *minors*, more specifically."

The dizziness consumed her for a moment and Alex rocked in her chair before gripping the table to right herself.

"You okay?" Annette asked.

Alex regained her bearings, swallowed hard, and then looked at Annette. "They had photos around them."

"They had what?" Annette asked.

Alex's mouth was cotton dry and she gulped from her water bottle before continuing.

"My parents. Whoever killed them dropped photos of Roland Glazer's victims near their bodies. Three young women who worked for Glazer. They disappeared shortly after Glazer was indicted on sex-trafficking charges. Many believe Glazer killed them to keep them quiet about what was going on at his private island. Whoever killed Byron Zell did the same thing— deposited photos of his victims around his body."

Annette slowly turned her head to look at Lane. "Any idea if these other victims you've identified had photos left by their bodies?"

Lane nodded. "All of them." He held up the packet. "So what we have is a cluster of victims who were all tied in some way to the sexual assault of minors. All were clients of Lancaster and Jordan. And all were killed by gunshot, and with the same calling card attached: photos of their victims left behind."

Lane turned a page in his packet.

"This brings us to the point in the conversation where we transition from computer algorithm to human analytics. Or, my specialty—criminal profiling. I've created a detailed profile of what this killer may look like."

Alex and Annette quickly turned the pages of their packets to follow along.

"The algorithm found a common connection to four homicides. But remember, that was a search starting *after* your family was killed in twenty-thirteen. So we have five homicide cases starting in twenty-thirteen if we include your family."

"That's either a bizarre coincidence," Annette said, "or it's very dangerous to seek legal advice from Lancaster and Jordan."

Alex stayed quiet. Her mind was racing too quickly to organize her thoughts into coherent questions.

"There is no coincidence," Lane said. "Only the illusion of coincidence. And to get to the bottom of that illusion, I constructed a profile of the type of person who might be behind a string of homicides like the ones the algorithm picked up on."

Lane paused to take a sip of beer.

"Let's start with age and gender. Considering that we're talking about someone who committed the Quinlan family murders in twenty-thirteen, the killer would be well into his thirties. But considering the sophistication of the crimes, I suspect the killer is older. Midforties to midfifties."

"Sophistication?" Annette asked.

"All the homicides occurred at the victims' homes. In order for that to be possible, the killer had to gain access to the home, kill the victim, and flee. That takes cunning, patience, and planning. This is not some kid running around shooting people."

Lane went back to his packet.

"So we've got someone who's forty-five to fifty-five, cunning and intelligent, and likely holds a job of some importance. White collar much more likely than blue collar. And, most importantly, this person has a vendetta against those who commit crimes of sexual predation against minors. But it's not just a vendetta, it's a *personal* vendetta. In all likelihood, the killer was sexually assaulted as a child."

"And he's now taking revenge for his own sexual abuse on predators today," Annette said.

"Correct."

"So we've got a middle-aged guy who was abused as a kid who is now finding sexual predators and killing them," Annette said. "Those predators have bottlenecked as clients at Lancaster and Jordan."

She looked briefly at Alex before turning back to Lane.

"You think it's someone at Lancaster and Jordan? Is that the idea?"

"Maybe," Lane said. "But so far we've only concentrated on homicides *since* twenty-thirteen. To paint a complete picture of this killer, I looked at the years *before* Alex's family was killed and came across an interesting incident that occurred in nineteen eighty-one at a summer camp in the Appalachian Mountains."

"A summer camp?" Alex asked.

"Yes. Camp Montague. What I found indicates that this killer has been at it for much longer than ten years."

PART VI

The Profile of a Killer

"An object at rest."

—Alex Armstrong

Camp Montague

Appalachian Mountains

They hid in the darkness of the clearing behind Jerry Lolland's cabin. Cicadas buzzed in rhythmic tones and blended into the night. Neither talked while they huddled close to the trunk of the large oak and tried to ignore the mosquitos. Eleven o'clock approached and Camp Montague finally settled for the night as the cabins, one by one, went dark. Mr. Lolland's cabin stayed brightly lighted, however, and soon his screen door squeaked open. They watched from the darkness as he stood on the front porch and surveyed the camp, surely, they thought, deciding if it was safe to embark on his stalking. Would it be her cabin he went to tonight? She hoped so, but she knew there were others he preyed on. She knew this because Jerry had used a Polaroid camera to take photos of her while she was in various stages of undress. The click-shin sound the camera made when he pointed it at her and snapped the photos, as well as the sound of the film ejecting from the camera, sickened her when she thought of it.

"Ah, good girl," Jerry had said the first time he'd photographed her. "Look how pretty you are."

She'd barely been able to look at that first photo he showed her. She'd seen herself naked in the bathroom mirror, but that image existed only in her own mind, and it disappeared once she left the bathroom. The photo Mr. Lolland held had made her feel embarrassed and ashamed, knowing that it would never vanish like her reflection. When Mr. Lolland opened his dresser drawer to deposit the photograph inside, she'd seen the photos of his other victims. There were too many to count during her quick glance into the drawer—maybe ten, maybe fifteen. The kids in the photos were also naked, like her. She remembered them now as she hid in the woods and knew that tonight was not just retribution for what Mr. Lolland had done to her; it was reprisal for all his victims—past, present, and future.

They watched him walk from the front porch. He headed toward the middle of camp, to where her cabin stood. He would be surprised to find her bed empty, and they were counting on his anger to distract him when he came back. They hurried from the clearing and ran to the side of the cabin. Every counselor's cabin was fitted with a natural gas source to fuel the barbecue grills that stood outside the screened porches. They scurried to the grill and crouched down.

"Watch him," he said as he took the tools from his pocket.

She moved to the edge of the cabin and peered off into the distance, squinting her eyes as she watched Mr. Lolland disappear into the darkness of Camp Montague. They figured they had five minutes. But that was if he simply turned around and came back once he found her cabin empty. They were counting on Mr. Lolland taking an extra few minutes to look for her, checking the outhouse and then the main lodge.

She returned to the grill and took her spot next to him.

"He's gone," she said.

She watched him reach behind the barbecue grill until he found the gas line that ran from the cabin. He used the pliers they'd taken from the utility closet to twist the bolt that secured the gas line to the grill. It took a few seconds of forced effort until the bolt broke free, and then it turned easily. He spun the fitting until the line fell free from the grill, then stood and pulled the slack out of the line until it was stretched to its full length. It was just long enough to reach the window.

"It's locked," she said when she tried to open the window that led to Mr. Lolland's bedroom. "I'll go in and unlock it."

"What if he comes back?"

"It won't take me long," she said, taking a hard swallow before speaking again. "I've been in there before."

In a mad dash she skirted past him and cut around the corner, then scrambled up the front steps of the cabin—stairs she climbed for the first time weeks ago with Mr. Lolland's firm grip on the back of her neck. The screen door squeaked now as she opened it and slid inside. She ran to the lone bedroom and tried to ignore the images and memories that littered her mind when she stepped foot inside the room—Jerry Lolland with his shirt off, exposing his bloated, hairy belly; the way his callused hands felt when he touched her; the sound of the Polaroid camera spitting out photos of her. She crossed the room quickly and twisted open the window lock. It had taken less than thirty seconds. She was back outside and around the corner of the cabin before they saw Mr. Lolland in the distance, walking back to his cabin.

"Hurry!" she said, placing her hand to the glass and pushing upward until the window was cracked open.

He handed her the gas line and she snuck it over the sill and into the cabin before closing the window again just as they heard Mr. Lolland climb the steps of the front porch. It was too dangerous to run back to the clearing, so they instead crouched below the window and tried to make themselves as small as possible.

The bedroom light clicked on and the glow fell onto the ground in front of them and spilled into the forest. They waited, barely breathing, for thirty minutes until the bedroom light went out. They waited thirty more before they contemplated moving. And thirty more after that until they were certain he was asleep.

He nodded at her and she reached to the red valve at the base of the cabin's outer wall. She twisted the lever until it was parallel with the line, allowing gas to flow into Jerry Lolland's cabin. They waited another moment and then crept away from the cabin and headed back into camp. She was too scared to sleep in her cabin for fear that Jerry would somehow escape their trap and come for her. Plus, she still had work to do, and for this last part of the plan she needed no accomplice.

While the rest of the camp slept, she settled into one of the chairs that encircled the fire pit. Orange embers glowed from the night's fire, and she forced herself to stare at the smoldering coals to stay awake. The hours passed, but did so slowly, as if each minute were a perversion of time, made up of some value greater than sixty seconds. When, finally, a hazy and far-off glow came to the horizon, she crept back into the forest and made her way to the clearing. Mr. Lolland's cabin was quiet and calm and dark. Slowly, she emerged from the forest and approached the back of the cabin, then crouched below the window before lifting herself to peer over the windowsill. It was dark inside but for the glow of the alarm clock on the night table, which offered just enough light to see Mr. Lolland lying in bed. He was lifeless and still, but to simply kill Jerry Lolland was not good enough. The world needed to know his sins and judge him accordingly.

She hurried around to the front of the cabin and silently climbed the three steps of the front porch. The screen door screeched, putting the fear of death in her that if Mr. Lolland was still alive he'd be waiting for her. After a moment of silence, though, she knew he was dead. She slipped inside the cabin and tiptoed down the hallway. The odor of gas was strong and permeated from the bedroom. When she pushed open the bedroom door, she saw him lying on his back with one arm hanging over the edge of the mattress. The sheets covered him from the waist down, and the early glow of dawn spilled through the window to illuminate his hairy stomach, causing her own to roil with nausea. Still, she forced herself to stare at the man's torso, which she did for a full minute to make sure he wasn't breathing.

When she was certain, she went to his dresser and opened the top drawer. There she found the photos of herself and his other victims. Their faces blurred together and she could hardly bring herself to look at the photos as she grabbed them from the drawer, feeling as ashamed for Jerry's other victims as she did for herself. But one face in the photos stood out from the others. She lifted the photo close to her eyes, urging the breaking dawn to prove her wrong. But there was no mistaking her brother. He was younger in the photo, and she realized it was probably taken when he, too, was a first-year recruit at Camp Montague. He'd never told her.

She took the photo of her brother and slipped it in her pocket. His secret would stay safe with her. The same way she would never discuss with another soul what Jerry Lolland had done to her, she would never force her brother to do so either. She would protect his secret as long as he wanted to keep it. But Jerry's other victims would not stay anonymous. There was no other way. She walked to the bed, stood over Jerry Lolland's lifeless body, and placed the photos, one by one, across his chest and around his face. The man deserved to die, but she would not allow death to hide his sins.

When she finished, she stared at the man who had abused her. A feeling of satisfaction came over her. It filled her with a sense of peace and worth, knowing the anguish she had endured at the hands of this predator now held purpose. She needed to go through the pain of this man's abuse because she was meant to stop Jerry Lolland from hurting others. Her pain was fuel she used to punish him for what he did to her, to the others in the photos, and to her brother. Jerry Lolland would start her on a lifelong quest to root out those who abused others and deliver justice to them that a moral society could not.

Two hours later, just after 7:00 a.m., she was asleep in bed when she heard them. The sound dragged not just her, but all the residents, from bed. Along with other confused kids, she wandered out of her cabin and congregated by the campfire area as Camp Montague came to life in the most unusual of ways that morning. Not through whistles from the counselors or Mr. McGuire's voice over the loudspeaker, as they were accustomed to waking each morning, but instead by an ambulance siren.

CHAPTER 57

Washington, D.C.
Tuesday, May 30, 2023
9:32 p.m.

"Camp Montague was a summer camp for thirteen- to eighteen-year-olds," Lane said. "It shut down in nineteen eighty-one after one of the counselors killed himself."

"And the place has something to do with my family being killed?" Alex asked.

"Maybe. What happened at Camp Montague adds to the profile I've built of this killer, and allows me to connect the past to the present."

Alex glanced quickly at Annette, then looked back down at the packet as Lane continued.

"A counselor at Camp Montague named Jerry Lolland died in the middle of the summer in nineteen eighty-one. They found him in his cabin. The autopsy report I managed to get my hands on lists the cause of death as asphyxiation due to carbon monoxide poisoning."

"He killed himself?" Annette said.

"That's the official line."

"How does the suicide of a camp counselor in nineteen eighty-one have anything to do with my family?" Alex asked.

"Well, that's the kicker. This happened forty-plus years ago, so I had trouble tracking down anyone who was directly involved in the case. After I found the connection, I mostly relied on public records. But I *was* able to tap my sources and get hold of one of the detectives who handled the case, a guy named Martin Crew. He's in his late seventies now and has been retired for years. Still, he remembered the case like it was yesterday."

"What was so memorable?" Alex asked.

"The fact that Jerry Lolland was a pedophile."

Annette squinted her eyes. "How could a pedophile get a job as a camp counselor?"

"No one knew the guy was a predator until they found him dead in his cabin. And only then because they found pictures of his victims spread out around his body."

The packet fell from Alex's hands.

"I know," Lane said. "It's shocking. If my profile is correct, whoever killed your family also killed Jerry Lolland. And that means the killer was one of Jerry Lolland's victims."

"Do you have the names?" Alex asked.

"Of Lolland's victims? No, they were sealed and not made public back then. I haven't had the time to dig deep enough to find them on my own."

Alex stood up. Her hands were trembling when she ran them through her hair. "Do you have contact information for the detective you spoke with?"

Lane turned to the last page in his packet and held it up for Alex to see. He pointed to the name and phone number of the detective who ran the Jerry Lolland investigation.

"I figured you'd ask for it."

CHAPTER 58

She left Annette's house in Columbia Heights and drove straight to Lancaster & Jordan. The parking lot was empty that late at night. Even the diehards who lived in the den had given up by 9 p.m. Her phone was pressed to her ear as she rode the elevator to the ninth floor, hurried through the den, and entered her office, clicking on the lights as she went.

"Hold on," Alex said into the phone. "I'm not there yet."

On her way to the office she had called Kyle Lynburg, an old Alleghany friend whose savant-like computer skills had likely saved him from a life of violent crimes. He landed in Alleghany for armed robbery: at age sixteen he held up a 7-Eleven. Inside Alleghany, Alex had told him how very stupid it was to use a gun to get what he wanted. She was particularly touchy about that subject, and her words had resonated with Kyle Lynburg. After his release, he never picked up a gun again. Instead, he honed his computer skills and put them to good use. These days he made a living by farming his savant-like talents out to those who needed high-tech computer hacking. Alex was happy to have him on speed dial.

She told him what she needed him to do: scale the firewall that protected confidential and archived files at Lancaster & Jordan. The firm's attorney-client privilege agreement called for inactive or retired files to be archived and sealed. Those files were accessible only by the attorney who handled the case. Active cases were not as protected. Many employees, including Alex, could use their password to gain access to those files. But once a case was concluded, the files were stashed in a digital vault, accessible only by the attorney who worked the case.

At her desk, she set Lane Phillips's packet next to her keyboard and shook the mouse to bring her monitor to life.

"Okay," Alex said, putting her phone on speaker. "I'm at my computer."

"Enter your password," Kyle said, "to get me into Lancaster & Jordan's motherboard. I'll do the rest from there."

Alex typed her password and clicked ENTER.

"I'm in."

"Okay," Kyle said. "I'm taking control of your computer."

Alex heard a violent flurry of keystrokes as Kyle went to work. Her computer screen turned black and a series of nonsensical code appeared in white font. For ten minutes the screen continued to fill and refill with gibberish until the monitor went completely dark for an instant before blinking back to life.

"In," Kyle said. "Your IT guy almost knows what he's doing. I had to back-end gerrymander a couple of firewalls, and I left a few digital footprints in the process. If a good IT geek looks, they'll see that we hacked it. I still have time to turn around and erase everything, but only if we decide not to go any farther."

"Not gonna happen," Alex said. "I can get into the files now?"

"Yeah. Use 'morsecode4' whenever a file is password protected and you should be granted access. That password disappears in twelve hours and will then be useless. Until then, you've got free reign of any file you're interested in."

"Thanks, Kyle. I'll call you back if I run into any dead ends."

"You won't. Wanna tell me why you're hacking into your own computer system?"

"Not really."

"Bill's in the mail," he said.

"It took you all of ten minutes."

"Gotta eat, girl," he said before the line went dead.

Alex concentrated on her computer and started pulling up archived files that held two decades' worth of Lancaster & Jordan clients. She scrolled through until she found the year 2012. Listed alphabetically were all the clients Lancaster & Jordan represented that year. Alex scrolled to the Qs and found her parents' names: Dennis and Helen Quinlan. Tears pooled on her lower lids as she stared at her parents' names and tried to make sense of it all. She entered the temporary password and checked her parents' file.

She wiped her eyes and grabbed Dr. Phillips's research packet. She took fifteen more minutes to confirm that every name of every victim in the packet was also listed in the Lancaster & Jordan archives: Karl Clément, Robert Klein, and Nathan Coleman. She didn't need to confirm Byron Zell. She printed a single page from each file—the client profile page—and laid them on her desk. She needed to see them all together in one space rather than toggling back and forth through the files. Printed at the bottom of each page was the name of the Lancaster & Jordan attorney who handled the case: Jacqueline Jordan.

Alex shook her head, trying to determine if what she was thinking was possible. She scooped up the files and placed them to the side of her desk before going back to her computer. She closed out of the Lancaster & Jordan database and pulled up the Internet. She typed *Camp Montague* into the search engine, and then narrowed her hunt by adding the camp counselor's name. When she typed *Camp Montague and Jerry Lolland* into the search engine, she found several news articles chronicling the suicide death and the scandal that ensued.

"Alex?" someone said, startling her.

When she looked up, Jacqueline Jordan was standing in the doorway of her office.

CHAPTER 59

Washington, D.C.
Tuesday, May 30, 2023
11:05 p.m.

Jacqueline Jordan pulled into the parking lot of Lancaster & Jordan and saw a lone car parked there. It was normal to see sporadic vehicles sitting in the dark, but even the hardest working scrubs packed things up by 10:00 p.m. Jacqueline rode the elevator to the tenth floor and looked around the office. Other than the emergency lights that glowed twenty-four hours a day, the place was dark and quiet.

She took a stroll through the hallways, eventually passing Garrett's corner office and then making her way to her own. She spent a few minutes writing up what she'd learned from her jailhouse visit to Reece Rankin. The police were mostly satisfied that they had their man, but Matthew Claymore's backpack was still an explosive piece of evidence that might require defusing in the future, especially if Rankin's argument that he was a hired thug came to light and gained traction. But it was unlikely anyone serious would listen to Rankin's story. Still, she needed to be prepared in case it became something from which she needed to protect Matthew.

Jacqueline finished her brief and shut off the office light. In the elevator she pressed the button for the ninth floor instead of the lobby, then walked out into the den, as it was called by the associates, paralegals, and investigators who spent their time there. One office glowed with light and stood out against the otherwise dark space. She headed toward it.

"Alex," she said. "What are you doing here so late?"

Jacqueline noted Alex's fear, a look in her eyes like the girl were staring at a demon.

"Sorry, I didn't mean to startle you."

"No, you didn't." Alex said, standing quickly and gathering the papers that were strewn around her desk. "I'm just… I didn't know anyone was here."

"Are you sure you're okay?"

"Yeah, yeah. I was just trying to get some work done. I'm finished now."

Jacqueline watched Alex fumble with the papers until she gathered them all in a haphazard bundle.

"What are you doing here so late?" Alex asked.

Jacqueline narrowed her eyes as she watched Alex's frantic behavior.

"I was working on the Matthew Claymore case," Jacqueline said.

"Really? I thought that was finished."

"It is, mostly. I'm just tying up some loose ends."

"Anything interesting, or something you need my help on?"

"No," she said. "Matthew's in the clear now. Just making sure nothing can come back and hurt him if Reece Rankin decides to recant his confession."

Alex nodded. "Well, let me know if you need anything."

Jacqueline moved to the side when Alex skirted past her and into the hallway. She sensed Alex willing her to follow. When Jacqueline didn't, Alex forced the issue by reaching past her to close the office door.

"I was just on my way out," Alex said. "Are you coming or going? Going, probably, at this time of night."

Jacqueline took a moment before she answered, highlighting Alex's rapid speech and nervous demeanor.

"Going," Jacqueline finally said.

"I'll head down with you."

A few minutes later they both walked out the front doors of Lancaster & Jordan and on to their respective vehicles. Jacqueline started her car and looked in the rearview mirror. Alex's headlights came on, and Jacqueline watched her drive out of the parking lot. Jacqueline waited a minute and then turned her engine off and exited her car. She was through the lobby and in the elevator a minute later.

When the doors opened on the ninth floor, Jacqueline stepped into the den and headed straight for Alex's office. She clicked on the lights and stepped behind Alex's desk. The surface had been cluttered with papers when Jacqueline had surprised her a few minutes earlier, but now the desk was empty. She sat down and shook the mouse. Alex's monitor blinked on and Jacqueline began to analyze the screen. It took just a moment to recognize that she was looking at the archived records of Lancaster & Jordan—an alphabetical list of clients arranged according to year.

Jacqueline clicked on the menu at the top of the screen to see the last few searches that had been made, each name appearing in a dropdown menu:

Nathan Coleman, 2019

Robert Klein, 2017

Karl Clément, 2016

Dennis and Helen Quinlan, 2012

Jacqueline breathed calmly as she stared at the names. She thought back to Alex's jittery behavior a few moments earlier. Finally, she dragged the mouse to the corner of the screen and closed the window that held Lancaster & Jordan's archived files. When she did, she was met by an image that took her back to her past. Like a portal through time, the image of Camp Montague transported her across the years and turned her briefly into the thirteen-year-old girl she was during her first and only summer at Camp Montague. On Alex's computer screen was a *Washington Post* article about a camp counselor named Jerry Lolland who had killed himself in the summer of 1981.

It took ten long years, but now Jacqueline knew that her visit to the Quinlan home in McIntosh, Virginia, had finally caught up with her.

CHAPTER 60

Wytheville, Virginia
Wednesday, May 31, 2023
7:32 p.m.

The GPS estimated the drive to Wytheville, Virginia, would take five hours. Alex took her time, drove in the middle lane, and allowed her mind to roam. She'd snuck out of the office early and was on the highway and the open road by 2:30 p.m. She should have been frantic. She should have driven like a lunatic. She should have been desperate to get to Wytheville, Virginia, where the detective who worked the Jerry Lolland case lived. Detective Martin Crew had agreed to meet Alex and discuss everything he remembered about the Camp Montague case from 1981. With potential answers waiting, Alex should have been filled with urgency and anxiousness. Instead, she drove the limit and allowed other cars to zip around her.

Ten years of torment and searching was coming to an end. Alex had dreamt of this moment. During her sleeping hours she had often imagined a similar scene where the mystery of her family's death was on the other side of the proverbial door she'd encounter during her dreams. All she needed to do was open that door for the answers to spill forth. But during those dreams something had always stopped her. The door had no handle or was bolted with the only lock she'd ever found that she could not pick. But now, here she was, driving to meet a detective who might hold the key to that door. She should be speeding. She should be restless. Instead, Alex was filled with sorrow for what she feared she might find.

Wytheville was situated in the foothills of the Appalachian Mountains, had a population of eight thousand, and a hotel résumé to match. Alex pulled into town at just past 7:30 p.m. Detective Crew had agreed to meet on short notice but could not do so until eight o'clock. Alex knew she wouldn't be able to make the hours-long drive back to DC after her meeting, so she found a motel on the edge of town, paid for a single night, and pulled her car to the front of room 109. She exited the car, then keyed the door and entered. Small but clean, the room offered a full bed, nightstand, and dresser with a television. She set her overnight bag on the bed, brushed her teeth, and applied a dark shade of lipstick to match her mood. She locked the door on the way out and drove into town. The Sly Fox, whose name was displayed in red neon along with glowing Budweiser and Pabst Blue Ribbon signs, was located on a corner in the middle of the main drag.

Inside, Alex saw an older man sitting at the bar and, since the establishment was otherwise empty, deduced that he must be Martin Crew. Country music played from unseen speakers and a television behind the bar showed a baseball game. She walked up to the man.

"Detective Crew?"

"Alex Armstrong?" the man asked, offering a sideways glance at Alex's piercings and tattoos.

Alex nodded. "Yeah, thanks for meeting on such short notice."

"When I heard you were willing to drive all the way from DC to talk, I knew it was something urgent."

"The drive wasn't bad, about five hours."

"It's not the length of the drive that's got me curious, it's the fact that you're the second person in two weeks who's tracked me down about a pedophile camp counselor who killed himself forty-plus years ago. It was a prickly case back then, and I was never satisfied with its conclusion. The fact that it's somehow resurrecting itself this many years later has my attention. I'm as curious to know why you're interested in this case as you are to hear what I have to say."

"Let's talk."

Alex took the stool next to the detective.

"What are you drinking?" Detective Crew asked.

"Soda and lime."

The detective waved down the bartender.

"So," Crew said. "Is your inquiry related to Dr. Lane Phillips contacting me a week or so back?"

"It is," Alex said. "Well, technically, *his* inquiry was related to mine. Either way, I'm hoping you might be able to provide the answers I'm looking for."

"Fire away. I hope to get some myself."

"I'm a legal investigator for a big firm up in DC. There've been some interesting developments with a few of the firm's clients, brought to my attention by Dr. Phillips."

"What sort of developments, how interesting, and what's it got to do with Jerry Lolland?"

"Maybe nothing, but that's what I'm here to figure out. A few of the firm's clients have died under suspicious circumstances, and Dr. Phillips managed to link the deaths, possibly, back to Jerry Lolland's suicide. Can you tell me what you remember about the case?"

"Now I'm more curious than ever. The Lolland case was a while ago, but after I got a call from Dr. Phillips, I headed back into the Wythe County Sheriff's Office. I worked there for twenty years before I did detective work for the state, so I still had some people I could reach out to."

"You were a detective for the state of Virginia?"

"Yes, that's how I got involved with the Jerry Lolland case."

"Was it typical to call in state investigators for a suicide?"

"No, not at all. We got called in because of the kiddie porn that was found around Lolland's body."

"Right, can you tell me about that?"

"Camp Montague was a prestigious summer camp in the area, just about ten miles from Wytheville. People sent their kids there from all over the state and even farther. It was an eight-week summer camp that taught teenagers independence and helped them make the transition into college. You know, typical camp mantra. At least, that's how the place was billed. Montague shut down after Jerry Lolland's suicide and the scandal that followed. Lolland was one of the longtime counselors. He basically ran the place and was in charge of recruitment, too. If a parent was interested in sending their kid to Montague, they met with Jerry Lolland to hear the camp's pitch, all that Montague had to offer, and how safe their children would be. It was chilling to learn that this man preyed on the very children he recruited."

"Tell me how you found out about Jerry Lolland and his abuse against children."

"It was the summer of nineteen eighty-one. I got a call to investigate a death out at Camp Montague. It was a suspected suicide but with a twist. A bunch of photos had been found around the body—photos of naked children, all identified as kids enrolled at Camp Montague. The kids were first-year recruits, all of them between thirteen and fourteen years old. The photos were taken on an old Polaroid camera—state of the art back then—the kind that spits out a photo as soon as you take it. Pretty disturbing stuff. I spoke to the kids identified in the photos and they all told similar stories: Jerry Lolland came to their cabin late at night and lured them back to his own cabin."

"Lured them how?"

"Told them he needed to speak with them privately about something urgent, and that they'd get in trouble if they didn't go with him. Remember, these kids were young and impressionable, and were likely scared and homesick the first time they went away to summer camp."

"Truly vile," Alex said.

"Yes, a predator in the true sense of the word. At any rate, Lolland got the kids back to his cabin and sexually abused them. Part of his routine was to take photos of them."

"The photos might be the link to the case I'm working. They were found around Lolland's body? As in, he was looking at the photos when he killed himself?"

Detective Crew took a sip of his drink. "The working theory at the time was this: Lolland succumbed to his guilt and shame, piped the barbecue gas line into his room, sealed up the windows, and laid in his bed to die. Pulled out all the photos of his victims over the years, and laid them out as his confession, of sorts."

"But now you believe something else happened?"

"I've *always* believed something else happened. I just couldn't prove it. Could never even *pursue* it due to the sensitive nature of the case."

"You don't think Lolland killed himself?"

"No, I don't. But the problem with detective work is that what you think and what you can prove are different things." Crew lifted his drink. "It's the reason so many detectives are raging alcoholics."

Alex smiled. "I thought that was a cliché saved for bad television."

"Maybe it is. I guess I can only speak for myself."

Detective Crew finished his drink and flagged down the bartender.

"If Jerry Lolland didn't gas himself, then how did he die?"

"Oh, the gas killed him, that's not up for debate. I saw the gas line with my own two eyes. He died from asphyxiation due to carbon monoxide poisoning. But it's not the *cause* of death that I'm questioning, it's the manner. Suicide was listed on the autopsy as the formal manner of death. I've always believed it was homicide."

The detective's drink arrived and he took a sip.

"The problem was that I could never prove who killed him, even though I was damn sure I knew who it was."

Alex swallowed hard. She remembered Lane Phillips's guess from the day before: *If my profile is correct, whoever killed your family also killed Jerry Lolland. And that means the killer was one of Jerry Lolland's victims.*

CHAPTER 61

Wytheville, Virginia
Wednesday, May 31, 2023
7:35 p.m.

Jacqueline Jordan had kept close tabs on Alex since finding her at the office late the previous night. In a rare moment of panic and irrational thought, she'd even driven to the girl's Georgetown condo with the thought of ringing the bell and allowing Alex to invite her inside, where Jacqueline would have finally tied up the loose end that had been unraveling for ten long years. But that impulsive moment passed, and Jacqueline opened her mind to other, better options to solve the problem of Alex Armstrong.

When Alex left Lancaster & Jordan that afternoon, Jacqueline had followed. When Alex pulled onto the highway out of DC, Jacqueline stayed at a safe distance as she trailed Alex through the mountains. It didn't take long to understand where the girl was headed. Of course she was going to Wytheville. Of course she was tracking down everything she could about Jerry Lolland and Camp Montague. Buck had turned the girl into a fierce investigator, and Alex had uncovered enough clues that Jacqueline knew it was only a matter of time before she arrived at the truth. As she drove, Jacqueline considered the irony that things would finally end at the same place they had started.

After hours of driving, Alex slowed as she entered the town of Wytheville and turned into the parking lot of the Shady Side Motel. Jacqueline continued ahead but doubled back to spot Alex's car parked in front of room 109. She pulled to the shoulder and waited, tapping the steering wheel and contemplating her next move. The slow-building anxiety began to overwhelm her as Jacqueline remembered the night she'd gone to Alex's condo to discuss the Matthew Claymore case. It was then that she had seen Alex's evidence board. Now, as Jacqueline sat in her car on the side of the road outside a cheap motel, her mind flashed with images from Alex's board: Roland Glazer, Dennis and Helen Quinlan, Byron Zell. During her brief inspection of the curious evidence board, Jacqueline had also seen the photo of a lone fingerprint. She knew the print was hers, left the night she'd entered the Quinlan home and touched Alex's window after her latex glove had split.

Ever since that day at Alex's condo, Jacqueline had started to put in place a plan to take care of the girl. Things had been drastically accelerated since the previous night, and Jacqueline knew her current thoughts were clouded by panic and fear. The idea that this girl would expose the truth was more than Jacqueline could tolerate. The idea that Alex would shine light on it all—starting with the abuse Jacqueline had endured in the dark cabin at Camp Montague where Jerry Lolland had forever changed the course of her life—was too much to rationally sort out. Jacqueline's secret would be revealed for the world to see, and there was only one way to prevent it.

Her nervous tapping on the steering wheel turned to pounding, and in a tantrum-like outburst she pressed her foot to the accelerator and spun gravel as she turned into the motel parking lot. She parked two doors down from Alex's car, grabbed her bag of supplies from the passenger seat, and burst out of the car. She walked straight to room 109, her breathing erratic and her pulse pounding in her ears. If the door was unlocked, she'd simply walk into the room and get it over with. If not, she'd knock and push her way in when Alex answered. Neither were perfect solutions, but Jacqueline had an overwhelming need to quell her anxiety. She needed to quiet the voices that were telling her it was now or never to put this threat to rest.

She'd taken only a couple of steps toward room 109 when the door opened. It startled her, and before her body understood the commands from her brain, she turned away and walked in the opposite direction. She heard a beep from a car being unlocked by a key fob, and then the opening and closing of a door. When she finally looked over her shoulder, she saw Alex driving out of the parking lot.

Jacqueline hurried back to her car and followed Alex into town, where she watched her park on the street and then walk into a bar called the Sly Fox. She was tempted to go inside to see what Alex was doing there, but it was another impulsive thought that Jacqueline quickly pushed aside. In a small town like this, walking into a corner bar was like announcing your name over a loudspeaker. People took notice, and the last thing Jacqueline needed was anyone noticing her that night.

She was happy that her rash decision to force her way into Alex's motel room had been derailed. Jacqueline breathed deeply as she sat in her car and tried to calm herself. She had a plan and needed to stick to it. She knew where Alex was staying, and a stealth approach would be the best way to handle things. It was poetic, really. Alexandra Quinlan would end her life ten years after the tragedy that had befallen her family, in a cheap motel in the middle of nowhere.

CHAPTER 62

Wytheville, Virginia
Wednesday, May 31, 2023
8:30 p.m.

"Was it one of his victims?" Alex asked. "Who you believe killed Jerry Lolland?"

Detective Crew took another sip of whiskey and nodded. "It was."

"How did you come to that conclusion? And if you were so certain, why was it so hard to prove?"

"You have to understand what I was up against. I got called to the scene of a suspected suicide, not a homicide. So the first people there were not cops, but the evidence eradication unit."

Alex squinted her eyes. "Who?"

"That's what we call the EMTs and fire department. Their job is to save lives, not preserve crime scenes. By the time I got called to the scene, camp counselors, EMTs, and an entire fire department had all traipsed through Lolland's cabin. So there wasn't a lot of good evidence we could pull from the scene. It was just too contaminated. But still, I managed to find enough to make me suspicious."

"Like what?"

"Fingerprints. If the theory was correct that Lolland had killed himself, his prints should've been on the gas valve on the side of the cabin since he'd have been the last person to touch it. But of course, after the camp's director, a guy named Allen McGuire, found Lolland unresponsive in bed, he also smelled gas, found the gas line wedged at the windowsill, and ran outside to shut off the supply. McGuire's prints were on the gas valve, but he had a rock-solid alibi. If there were other prints on the valve, including Jerry Lolland's, they were destroyed when McGuire touched it. The bedroom window, however, that was another story."

"The window?"

"Yes. The techs pulled a clear, full palm and five-fingerprint impression off the window of Jerry Lolland's cabin."

Alex's mind flashed back to her evidence board and the lone, unidentified print that had been found on her bedroom window.

"Were you able to ID the print?" she asked.

"We ran it through the database but got no hits, and I knew we wouldn't. The palm print was small and clearly made by a kid. When we didn't get any hits, we asked the parents of the victims—the kids in the photos—if we could take their kids' prints. There were fourteen kids in the photos, and they all agreed to be printed."

"And? One of them matched the window?"

"Yeah," Crew said, taking another sip of whiskey. "The problem was that since Lolland used his cabin to abuse the kids, it was without question that the kids in the photos had been in Lolland's cabin. Hell, the pictures were taken when the kids were in the cabin. So we found several prints in various parts of the cabin belonging to the kids, and that angle quickly became a dead end. In fact, I was ordered by my superiors not to even consider that one of the kids had killed Lolland by snaking the gas line into his cabin while he slept."

"But you suspected it?"

"I did."

"Why?" Alex asked. "Because of the palm print on the window?"

"It wasn't the print itself that made me suspicious. It was the location of the print."

"Because… what, it was on the window, right? On the glass?"

"Yes. But it was on the *outside*, as if someone had opened the window while standing outside the cabin."

"Oh shit."

"Exactly," Crew said. "Someone opened Lolland's window from the outside and snaked the gas line into his bedroom. But here's the kicker. If Lolland had succumbed to his guilt and placed the photos around himself as a confession before killing himself, you'd expect the photos to be covered with *his* fingerprints."

"They weren't?"

"No. The Polaroid photos around Lolland's body were covered with someone else's prints. And the prints from the window matched prints lifted from each of the photos around Lolland's body."

Detective Crew reached into the breast pocket of his sport coat and removed a slip of paper. He placed it on the bar.

"This is a list of Jerry Lolland's victims—all the kids who were in the photos, plus a few more who came forward after the story broke."

"He didn't take pictures of all his victims?"

"Apparently not."

Alex pulled the sheet of paper in front of her.

"You won't find those names in any public records," Crew said, "because the victims were kept anonymous."

Alex scanned the list of names. Anxiety flooded her system when she saw the name toward the bottom of the list. She looked up.

"Whose fingerprints were on the photos and the window?"

Crew reached over and pointed at the list. Alex followed his finger down the page until it stopped at a name.

Jacqueline Jordan.

CHAPTER 63

Wytheville, Virginia
Wednesday, May 31, 2023
9:30 p.m.

Alex unlocked the door to her motel room and walked into room 109. It was late and she was exhausted after her meeting with Detective Crew, but still she considered driving back to DC. With her mind racing as it was, sleep would be difficult and the nighttime hours might better be spent on Highway 81 with an open road in front of her and nothing but her thoughts to keep her company as she figured out what, exactly, her next move would be. She needed to talk with Garrett, at least. Maybe the police. But what would she tell them? How could she articulately explain that ten years of searching for her family's killer had somehow led her to Jacqueline Jordan's doorstep—the very woman who had helped clear Alex's name years earlier. The very woman who had played a pivotal role in her defamation case against the state of Virginia. The very woman who had employed her for the last eight years.

The sight of the bed, though, changed her mind. The adrenaline rush was fading and she felt suddenly overwhelmed with grief and uncertainty. She took a quick shower before climbing under the covers. Her mind continued to flash back to Jacqueline's name scrawled on the list of Jerry Lolland's victims. Could this path she'd been following for ten years really have led to this place? Was it even conceivable that Jacqueline had killed her family? The compassionate side of her brain told her no, it was not possible. But the rational side, the side that had learned to follow the evidence wherever it led, told her that her research had been impeccable and that evidence doesn't lie.

To be sure, though, a thought came to her. A foolproof way to arrive at the truth. Every attorney in DC was required to provide fingerprints to the state bar association in order to be licensed. All Alex had to do was gain access to Jacqueline's fingerprints—a simple task that would take no more than a few phone calls and a couple of favors. Then, she'd have Jacqueline's prints matched against the lone print found on the bedroom window of her childhood home. Alex would enlist Donna's help for this. Despite Donna's exile from the McIntosh Police Department in the wake of Alex's trial, Alex was sure Donna still had contacts there.

Settled on a plan of action, she spent an hour in bed staring at the ceiling before her thoughts quieted enough for her to drift off to sleep. Despite that it was a shallow and fitful sleep; she never heard the motel door opening.

CHAPTER 64

Jacqueline's face materialized in her dream. It faded in and out. Alex ran for the grandfather clock and squeezed behind it, but Jacqueline's face peeked around the corner.

"Now don't give me a hard time," Alex heard Jacqueline say. "This will only be difficult if you make it difficult."

Alex forced her eyes shut, put her fingers to her ears so she wouldn't have to listen to Jacqueline's voice. Then she felt something touch her elbow. It was Jacqueline pulling her left arm away from her ear and straightening it out. Alex opened her eyes and realized that she was no longer hiding behind the grandfather clock, but instead lying in bed. Scanning the room, she could not understand where the dream had taken her. When she felt the sharp prick on the inside of her left forearm, her eyes snapped into focus. Jacqueline was standing over her and inserting a needle into her arm. As she watched Jacqueline depress the plunger of the syringe, a thought came to Alex that perhaps this was not one of her lucid dreams.

She reached up with her right hand to touch Jacqueline's face. Her hand nearly made it to its destination but her arm fell across her chest before getting there, as though the limb had been deflated. She tried again to lift her arm but nothing happened.

"You can fight it all you want," she heard Jacqueline say. "You can resist until you're exhausted, or you can accept that no matter how hard you try, you won't be able to move a muscle. The extraocular muscles that control your eye movement will be least affected, so you'll still be able to look at me."

Filled with panic, Alex tried to sit up but quickly realized her efforts were useless. She tried to convince herself that she was in the midst of dream paralysis, a phenomenon where one's mind wakes before the body, and despite a herculean effort, movement is impossible until the nervous system and the motor system decide to link up. But Alex knew this was not the case. The fictional world she was in a few minutes earlier had morphed into reality. She was not merely looking at an image of Jacqueline Jordan, she was staring at the woman herself. And Jacqueline had just injected her with a chemical that made her feel as though her veins were filled with lead.

CHAPTER 65

The drug was called succinylcholine. Administered intravenously, it brought on paralysis in seconds. Intramuscularly, it worked just as well but took slightly longer to take effect. Depending on dosing, the paralysis could last hours. Jacqueline had obtained the drug in preparation for that night's plans. She'd found the succinylcholine in the surgical bag that her husband lugged to and from the hospital and had packed it in her things when she went to Alex's the night before, with the impulsive thought of killing her at her condo, but then had abandoned that idea. Killing the girl in her home would bring more problems than it would solve. Jacqueline decided the best way for Alex to die was to make it look like she killed herself. It was poetic that Alex's suicide would happen so close to Camp Montague, where Jacqueline's quest for justice had started so many years ago with the staging of a different suicide.

"Jac... queline," she heard Alex sputter.

"No talking," Jacqueline said. "Soon your vocal cords will stop functioning anyway. I'll talk, you listen."

Jacqueline pulled a chair to the side of the bed and sat down.

"You've been looking for answers, and tonight I'm going to give them to you."

"I already... know," Alex said in a strained voice, as if speaking through a savagely sore throat. "The... pictures. Jerry... Lolland. Just like all the others. Just... like my parents."

338

"Yeah," Jacqueline said, nodding her head. "When I saw your board a few weeks ago, I knew it was only a matter of time before you'd figure it out. Then last night, I found you in your office. When you looked at me it was like you were looking at a ghost. I doubled back and saw your work. You pulled the files of Clément and Klein and Coleman. You went back into the archives and found your parents' file. You saw that I was the attorney who represented them. And when I saw that you had searched the Internet looking for stories about Jerry Lolland, I knew the end had arrived."

"Why?" Alex wheezed.

"Your parents? Because they aided and abetted Roland Glazer, a sexual predator just like Jerry Lolland. Your parents helped him hide his money, which meant they helped him perpetrate his crimes against children. After I killed Jerry Lolland all those years ago, I promised myself I'd never let another predator's sins go unpunished."

"But... why... Raymond?"

"Yes, I know that has tormented you most over the years. Unfortunately, your brother was collateral damage. My heart still aches for that child. He was in the wrong place at the wrong time. But his death was for the greater good. And your death will be the same. I know it's difficult to hear. But it's finally time to stop babying you. Everyone looks out for little, frail Alex. Everyone treats you with kid gloves and makes sure your life is perfect. I only wish I had received a fraction of that concern from those who were supposed to be watching out for me when I was being abused as a child."

CHAPTER 66

Wytheville, Virginia
Wednesday, May 31, 2023
11:45 p.m.

Alex blinked her eyes. She couldn't turn her neck to face Jacqueline, but she moved her eyes as far to her left as possible and was able to see that Jacqueline was sitting in a chair next to the bed.

"I thought about doing this last night," Jacqueline said. "I went to your condo to get it over with, but decided it was too risky. When you left the office this afternoon and headed out of DC and south on eighty-one, it dawned on me where you might be headed. Of course, the investigator Buck turned you into had you looking for answers. And you believed those answers could be found by digging into Jerry Lolland's death at Camp Montague. This works out much better. A lonely girl takes her own life at a lonely motel in the middle of nowhere. A troubled girl succumbing to a troubled life."

Alex kept her eyes on Jacqueline, or as far as her gaze could reach. Her legs and arms felt too heavy to even attempt to move, so she started with the fingers on her left hand, which were tucked down by her thigh. She hoped Jacqueline didn't notice. It was too dangerous to test the fingers on her right hand, since the paralysis had caused her right arm to fall across her chest, and her hand and fingers were in clear sight.

She squeezed with all her energy and felt her left index finger poke into her thigh. After a few more attempts, she realized that physical effort was less important than mental concentration. She closed her eyes and tried again. When she fully concentrated on the fingers of her left hand, she found that she was able to move them. She was certain, in fact, that she could open and close her hand but stopped short of proving it to herself for fear that Jacqueline would notice the movement and empty another syringe into her arm.

Alex kept her eyes closed and continued to test her theory that concentration would allow her to break the drug-induced paralysis. She focused on her right foot this time and wiggled her toes. It was much easier than the fight she had put up to initially move her fingers.

"He talked me out of it anyway," she heard Jacqueline say. "Your mentor for so many years."

Alex opened her eyes and saw that Jacqueline was now pacing the room.

"He told me that doing this at your condo last night was a terrible idea. In fact, he thinks this is a terrible idea in general. But he doesn't know what I know. He hasn't seen your board. He doesn't know how close you are to figuring it out."

Alex tried the toes on her left foot next, with the same result.

"He was so proud that he took you under his wing. So proud of his little prize that he could never understand what I've always known."

Jacqueline continued to pace back and forth. Alex attempted to move her head from left to right. This took more effort, but with focused concentration she managed. She felt as if she were on the verge of waking from a dream and that at any moment her strength and mobility would return.

"But I knew this day was coming," Jacqueline continued. "I've always known it was inevitable. I've always known that in order to keep purging the world of predators, we'd have to tie up the only loose end we'd ever left behind."

Alex was about to test the strength in her right arm, which lay across her chest, but Jacqueline materialized above her, looking down with a despondent expression on her face.

"You're such a loyal follower, aren't you? It was always your greatest weakness."

She saw Jacqueline offer a sad smile as she turned a small glass vile upside down, stuck the syringe's needle through the rubber stopper, and withdrew a cloudy white chemical until the chamber was full.

Then she heard a crash as the motel room door burst open. "FBI! Put your hands in the air!"

CHAPTER 67

Wytheville, Virginia
Wednesday, May 31, 2023
11:55 p.m.

Alex tried to move her head to the right and was surprised when the muscles of her neck responded. Annette Packard was standing in the doorway, crouched in a shooter's stance with both hands on a gun aimed at Jacqueline. In the confusion of the moment, the thought crossed Alex's mind that Annette looked out of place. Alex had only known her as the sophisticated and well-dressed woman who probed into politicians' lives, not as a true FBI agent trained in firearms. Perhaps this bias was what confused Alex and made her think something was off. But another moment of clarity told Alex that Annette was not in an FBI flak jacket or windbreaker. She was wearing a stylish outfit of tapered slacks, a white blouse, and high heels. And there were no other agents with her. No backup. No sirens. Just Annette and the gun she'd complained about having to carry at all times.

"Put your hands up!" Annette yelled.

"Annette," Alex said in a raspy voice that startled her.

The sudden burst of adrenaline was overtaking the effects of the paralytic drug.

"Alex," Annette said. "Come over here."

"She can't," Jacqueline said.

"Alex. Come. Over. Here."

Alex heard Annette enunciate each word slowly, never taking her eyes off Jacqueline as she stayed balanced in her stance.

"I can't," Alex said, feeling the strength returning to her vocal cords. "She injected me with something."

"Succinylcholine," Jacqueline said. "Injected into her arm, it paralyzes her muscles. Injected into her heart, it'll kill her in seconds."

There was a brief standoff where none of them moved: Alex lay in bed, Annette was frozen in her shooter's stance, and Jacqueline was like a statue, holding the full syringe in her hand like a dagger.

"Drop the syringe," Annette said.

Still no one moved.

"Drop it or I'll shoot you."

The stalemate ended when Jacqueline brought the syringe up over her shoulder and then down in a stabbing motion toward Alex's chest. The blast of the discharging gun echoed off the walls of the motel room, and the sulfurous odor transported Alex's mind back to the night her family was killed. The night her home smelled like Fourth of July fireworks. She was helpless to stop the images from flooding her system, even as she watched Annette plow into the room, dive across the bed, and ram headfirst into Jacqueline.

CHAPTER 68

Wytheville, Virginia
Wednesday, May 31, 2023
11:57 p.m.

For a moment, her mind placed her behind the grandfather clock again, peering around the edge and watching Raymond take one step after another toward their parents' bedroom.

"Stop," she tried to whisper.

When her brother continued his trek down the hallway, she spoke louder.

"Stop."

Her brother continued on.

"Raymond! Stop!"

Alex screamed the words, reaching deep into her core to make them as loud as possible. The effort snapped her mind into a different dimension of consciousness. Suddenly, Raymond was no longer wearing his pajamas or walking toward their parents' bedroom. Instead, he was dressed in his baseball uniform and standing at home plate, holding a bat high over his right shoulder, waiting for the next pitch. Alex was seated in a lawn chair watching the game like she'd done a thousand times during her childhood. She had worked hard over the years to avoid memories like these. Picturing her little brother as a living, vibrant person brought too much pain and guilt for not doing more for him that night. For years Alex had fought back the guilt of allowing Raymond to walk to their parents' bedroom that night, rather than running from her own bedroom to stop him. One of the tools she used to beat back the guilt was to avoid thinking of Raymond entirely. But now, somehow, she wanted to think of him. Needed to remember the animated thirteen-year-old she knew him as.

The pitch came and Alex watched Raymond swing the bat. She heard the echoing clink ring out into the afternoon as he smashed the ball into left field. The ball shot between the outfielders and bounced all the way to the fence.

Raymond raced around first base and headed to second.

"Go, Raymond!" Alex cheered.

Her brother cut around second and headed to third just as the center fielder picked up the ball and threw it to the cutoff man.

Alex saw Raymond fly around third base and head for home.

"Go, Raymond!" Alex yelled again as she jumped from her lawn chair and ran to the fence to get a better view.

The cutoff man fired the ball to the catcher, who was crouched over home plate. Alex watched as Raymond scrambled down the third-base line and dove headfirst across home plate just as the ball arrived and the catcher swiped a tag. Then there was silence. The raucously cheering crowd, the umpire and players all went quiet. A plume of dust mushroomed around home plate from Raymond's headfirst slide, and Alex squinted her eyes to see the conclusion of the play. To see if Raymond was safe or out. But when the dust settled, there was no one there. Raymond had vanished. As had the crowd, and the baseball diamond, and the park.

Alex opened her eyes and was back in the motel room. The burst of adrenaline from cheering for Raymond had brought her body into an upright sitting position. To her left, Annette and Jacqueline were against the wall engaged in a fierce battle, both women flailing and struggling for a dominant position. Alex noticed that Annette's gun had landed near the bathroom door, and it appeared both of them were attempting to stop the other from retrieving it.

Alex heard a piercing scream come from Jacqueline as the woman stumbled toward the bed, bringing Annette with her. Like a Greco-Roman wrestler, Jacqueline lifted Annette off the ground as she fell backward and rolled over the bed, so that when they hit the floor on the other side of the bed Jacqueline was on top. The move was violent, and the crashing of their bodies shook the bed like an earthquake. Both women began struggling again. Alex saw that the battle was now focused on Jacqueline's right arm and the syringe still gripped tightly in her hand.

Alex watched as Jacqueline secured a dominant position straddling Annette. She wanted to help, but despite the adrenaline flooding her system she was still fighting to move. A strange but clairvoyant thought entered her mind, and for a moment she believed again that she was dreaming since the image of the page from her physics textbook—the one she had studied from the night her family was killed—came clearly into focus. Newton's first law played in a loop through her thoughts.

An object at rest stays at rest unless acted upon by an unbalanced force.

From her sitting position, Alex threw herself backward, causing the mattress to propel her in the process. She twisted her body to the left when the momentum of the box spring sprang her off the bed. She landed on the floor and rolled toward the bathroom door. She made it far enough so that the gun was within reach. Her muscles were working again, if only in a jerky and uncontrolled fashion. She got to her hands and knees and crawled the rest of the way to the gun, gripped the handle in her palm, and fell to her side. She scooted to the wall, turned, and used her legs to bring herself into a sitting position. With her back pressed against the wall, Alex had a clear view over the top of the bed. She saw Jacqueline free her wrist from Annette's grasp and, in a blurry swift motion, bring the needle down.

The mattress blocked her view. Alex didn't see where the needle penetrated, only heard Annette's scream and knew it had connected. Then, silence but for Jacqueline's heavy breathing. Alex lifted the gun and steadied it. It felt like an anvil in her hands. She saw Jacqueline's hunched back first, then her head as Jacqueline sat up. Alex considered firing, but her arms were swaying too much for her to believe she'd be accurate.

Jacqueline stood up, staring down at Annette, who was paralyzed at best, and dead at worst. It took a moment before Jacqueline turned to see that the bed was empty. Another moment longer before her gaze settled on Alex and the gun that was pointed at her chest.

Alex took a calming breath, focused her mind like a laser, allowing the image of Raymond standing outside their parents' bedroom to fade from her thoughts long enough for her to concentrate. First on her shoulders, then her arms, her hands, and finally her right index finger. Then, she squeezed the trigger.

PART VII

Full Circle

"There's no way I can stay."

—Alex Armstrong

CHAPTER 69

Washington, D.C.
Saturday, June 10, 2023
3:32 p.m.

Jacqueline Jordan had been pronounced dead by EMTs when they arrived at room 109 of the Shady Side Motel. Alex and Annette were taken to the hospital and released the next morning after the succinylcholine had been flushed from their systems with copious amounts of saline delivered through an IV drip. They were no worse for wear, and Annette's only injury was a dislocated shoulder suffered when Jacqueline Jordan had crashed down on top of her during their violent struggle.

Both Alex and Annette had been questioned by police. They each offered a similar story. They were working together—Alex on a case for Lancaster & Jordan, Annette on a vet for the federal government—when they learned that their respective cases overlapped, with the common denominator being Duncan Chadwick. They were chasing a lead that brought them to Wytheville. Annette went to Alex's motel room for a scheduled meeting, and all hell broke loose when she found Jacqueline Jordan standing over Alex's paralyzed body. The story had plenty of holes, but it held enough water to get them by. Annette's standing at the FBI, and her direct ties to the White House, prevented many follow-up questions that might have otherwise been asked.

As promised, one week after their harrowing experience, Alex met Annette to turn over everything she had managed to discover about Laura McAllister's story: her notes, her briefs, and a copy of Laura's episode. They met at The Perfect Cup and drank Americanos as they talked.

"This hardly seems like a fair trade," Alex said. "I'm giving you information in exchange for you saving my life."

"No," Annette said. "You're giving me information in exchange for information, just like we agreed to."

Annette's right arm was secured by a sling that immobilized her injured shoulder.

"And the whole saving my life thing?"

Annette smiled. "I could argue that it was the other way around."

Alex took a sip of coffee, reflecting on that night. "I guess we helped each other, but you instigated it."

"*That*," Annette said, "I'll take credit for."

"I was pretty out of it when you showed up, but were you wearing high heels when you busted through the motel room door?"

"Standard issue," Annette said with a laugh. "I knew the information Lane turned up was pretty devastating to you, so I planned to keep an eye on you. See if you needed anything. I ended up following you out of town, and that's when I saw Jacqueline Jordan follow you to the motel. I wasn't planning on getting into a gun fight."

Alex shrugged as she turned over her research, pushing a large accordion file folder across the table. "I owe you more than this, so if there's ever a way I can repay you, let me know."

Annette took the information. "I'd say we're even. If you ever decide to come back to DC, look me up. We'll have a coffee."

"Will do."

Annette reached over and took Alex's hand.

"Thanks, Alex. You're going to be okay."

Alex nodded. "I know."

An hour later, Alex knocked on Garrett and Donna's door. As a united front, and surrogate parents, they answered the door together.

"Hi, sweetie," Donna said.

Alex smiled. "Hi. Did it come back?"

"It did," Donna said. "Come on in."

Before she'd fallen asleep in the motel room ten days earlier, Alex had devised a plan to obtain Jacqueline's fingerprints from the District of Columbia Bar Association and test them against the print found on her bedroom window the night her family was killed. After her night at the Shady Side Motel, the fingerprint confirmation was a formality but would provide full closure on an event that had defined her life. After searching so long for the truth, Alex needed to be sure.

Although police were still attempting to piece together a motive for why a prominent attorney had attempted to kill one of her investigators, no answers had yet been found and Alex wasn't offering any clues. There were two reasons Alex had decided to keep the details about Jacqueline Jordan's role in her family's death to herself. The first was selfish: the last thing Alex wanted was to resurrect the story of her family's murder and put it back in the headlines. Telling the authorities what she knew about Jacqueline Jordan would do exactly that. Alex had narrowly escaped the media scrutiny a decade ago. She was sure she would not survive the tabloids and true-crime nuts a second time. The other reason was selfless, and it had to do with her love for Garrett and Donna Lancaster. Revealing the sensational details that Jacqueline Jordan—the attorney who played a crucial role in getting the original charges against Alex dismissed, and who helped win Alexandra Quinlan's defamation case against the state of Virginia—was, in fact, the one who had mowed down the Quinlan family was a story so powerful that it would undoubtedly sink Lancaster & Jordan, ruin Garrett's career, and send him and Donna into exile. Alex had spent too many years there to deliver the same sentence to the people she loved most on the planet.

Instead, her closure would come privately. Donna still had contacts inside the McIntosh Police Department, and Alex had asked her to tap those resources and obtain the lone print from her bedroom window that was stored in evidence. Alex had asked Annette Packard for a final favor, and Annette worked with Donna to have the print analyzed against Jacqueline's. It had taken a week, but now, as they all sat in the kitchen nook, Donna now pushed a single piece of paper across the table so that it was in front of Alex. She stared at Donna for a moment, building up courage until she finally looked down at the page.

Jacqueline Jordan's print was a match to the one lifted from Alex's bedroom window. Alex inhaled sharply, even though she was all but certain what she'd find. Still, finally arriving at the truth after so many years took her breath away. Tears welled in her eyes and Garrett was immediately next to her. He put his arm around her as Alex turned her head into his chest.

"I'm so sorry," Garrett whispered.

Donna reached over and took Alex's hand—completing the unlikely family they had become.

"We need to decide," Donna said, "what we're going to do with this information."

"Nothing," Alex said, lifting her head from Garrett's chest. "We're not going to do anything with it."

"But, Alex—" Donna started.

"No," Alex said, cutting her off. "This should be my decision. You need to allow me to make it. I can't go through it all again. I can't go through my family's image on every grocery store tabloid. I can't go through the press hovering outside my door. Plus, this time you'd both have it as bad as me."

"We don't care about what this would do to us or my firm," Garrett said.

"But I do. And this is what I want. I want this to stay among the three of us. I don't want anyone else to know."

"What about Annette Packard and the FBI?" Garrett asked.

Alex shook her head. "Annette was doing me a favor. She worked with an ex-FBI profiler who is a friend of hers. She didn't go through any formal channels, and she won't say a word."

Garrett and Donna looked at each other, and Alex saw the silent confirmation between them.

"You're sure?" Donna asked.

"I'm sure."

Garrett pulled her close one more time. "Any chance we can stop you from leaving?"

Alex placed her head against his chest again and closed her eyes.

"There's no way I can stay."

CHAPTER 70

McIntosh, Virginia
Monday, June 12, 2023
10:04 a.m.

She pulled up to her old house on Montgomery Lane and parked in the driveway. The in-ground sprinklers were running and the lawn was a gorgeous shade of green—freshly mowed the day before, with the edges trimmed and corners at sharp ninety-degree angles. The hedges were pruned and the azaleas sparkled with morning sunlight and dripped as they bathed in the sprinkler's mist.

Alex climbed from her car and looked around the neighborhood. It was her first time back in McIntosh in some time. The house had been on a good run with no hiccups in the last two years that required her presence. A few minor things had come up but were easily handled by the maintenance crew Alex had hired to look after the property. The hot water heater had needed a new pilot light, a woodpecker had drilled a hole in the cedar siding, and a slab of concrete on the walkway to the front door had sunk and needed to be raised.

A wave of nostalgia crashed over her as she looked at her childhood home. The good memories from the first eighteen years of her life had, over time, outshined the darkness of a single night when the home had turned into something else. Despite the time it took to happen, her mind had managed to juggle things back into the proper order. She could once again look at the house and bask in all the joyous memories it held.

Alex wasn't sure how the transformation had taken place. It was likely the result of some combination of therapy, time, and the closure she had finally found. However it came to be, she was happy to finally stand in front of her childhood home without fear. For years she had meticulously kept it maintained and cared for, but now she was ready to let it go. Not, however, before she took care of one last thing.

She keyed the front door and stepped into her past. She remembered back to the hot summer night when she snuck into the home just before leaving for Cambridge. It was the night she came to retrieve Raymond's baseball card collection but found the bank statements instead that started her down a years-long journey. She remembered the dank odor the home held that night—the sticky summer air having penetrated the walls to fill the home with a bitter smell of vacancy and neglect. Today, on this bright, sunny morning, the home was immaculate and airy, carrying the scent of lemon wax from hardwood floors that shined with sunlight.

She walked through the first floor and took in the empty rooms. The freshly painted walls were bright and welcoming, the newly finished floors smooth and glossy. The kitchen was straight out of an HGTV series, with quartz countertops, a butler's pantry, and a decorative hood over the oven. The contractor had done a great job, and the home would make some family very happy.

Finished with her inspection of the first floor, Alex walked back into the foyer and started up the stairs. She did so without hesitation or fear. Enough time had passed now and those memories, although never eradicated, could be well controlled and kept at bay. At the top of the stairs, she turned and walked down the hallway to her old bedroom. Empty now and with hardwood in lieu of carpet, the room looked smaller than she remembered. She had the same sensation when she walked into Raymond's room.

Finally, she emerged into the hallway and walked to the edge of her parents' bedroom. The door was open and she walked inside. Here, too, the walls were freshly painted and the carpet was replaced with immaculate hardwood to match the rest of the home. Alex smiled. The house was perfect.

There was a knock on the front door and Alex headed down the stairs.

"Hi. Alex?" the woman said when Alex opened the door.

"Yes."

"Tammy Werth."

"Hi, Tammy," Alex said to the Realtor. "Come on in."

Tammy looked around the home and smiled. "The outside is gorgeous and so well maintained. And the interior is just as immaculate. I don't think the house will be difficult to sell."

"Really?" Alex asked.

"Not in today's market, and in this sort of condition. It's move-in ready. I'll just take some photos and measurements for the website."

"Sounds good," Alex said. "Do your thing and let me know if you need anything else."

Tammy smiled and got to work. A few minutes later, Alex saw the moving van back into the driveway and two strapping young men emerge. She opened the front door and waved them in.

"Hi," one of the guys said. "We're here from On-the-Go Movers." The guy looked around. "Not much to move, I see."

"Just one item," Alex said. "It's upstairs."

Alex led the two movers upstairs and pointed to the end of the hallway where the grandfather clock stood.

"That's it?" the guy asked.

"That's it."

"And it's going to our packaging and shipping facility?"

"Yes," Alex said. "I provided them with the address where it's to be shipped."

The two men removed straps that were wrapped around their shoulders before they approached the grandfather clock. A few minutes later, Alex smiled as she watched the men load the clock into the back of the truck. She imagined what it would look like in her new flat in London. She'd seen photos of the place online and had already decided where the clock would go.

"Just need your signature," one of the guys said after he closed the back of the truck.

Alex scribbled on the page and handed the clipboard back. The men climbed into the cab, and Alex watched the moving truck pull away.

"All set," the Realtor said, walking out the front door with her camera strapped around her neck. "I'll have my crew stake the FOR SALE sign in the front lawn later today, and I'll formally list the house on our website tonight. I'll let you know if we get any interest."

"Thanks," Alex said.

"I'm betting we have an offer before the end of the week, but I'll keep you posted."

Alex stood in the driveway as the Realtor pulled away. She took in the normal sounds of the neighborhood—birds chirping and a lawn mower buzzing from a few houses away— as she sat on the front porch and waited. Fifteen minutes later, a car pulled into the driveway. Alex stood up and watched the car closely.

Eventually, Tracy Carr, the reporter who had been the first on the scene the fateful night her family was killed, climbed out of the car and stared at her from the driveway.

"Funny meeting you here," Alex said in an attempt to break the ice.

"You knew I recognized you that day at my shoot," Tracy said as she closed the door and walked up the front path to where Alex stood.

"I did."

"You look a lot different," Tracy said. "But your eyes gave you away."

"I figured," Alex said.

The two women stared at each other for a moment.

"You called me. Now what?"

Alex retrieved her lipstick from her pocket, a sharp orange hue, and coated her lips before she smiled. "Now I make you an offer."

CHAPTER 71

London, England
Saturday, July 1, 2023
1:05 p.m.

Two weeks after the for sale sign was staked in the front yard of her childhood home, Alex arrived in London. Years earlier she had come as Alexandra Quinlan, on the run and in hiding. This time she came as Alex Armstrong, running from nothing and hiding from no one, determined to make the fresh start she had failed at the first time.

When she analyzed her life, she determined that there was nowhere else she could go. Remaining in DC and continuing her work at Lancaster & Jordan felt neither feasible nor appropriate. She had, over the years, developed a unique set of investigative skills, and she knew London was the best place to put them to use. Donna and Garrett understood but made her promise to keep in touch. Alex had agreed, but the unwritten contract was not necessary. Garrett and Donna Lancaster had been woven into the fabric of her life, and Alex could no more exist without them as she could without air.

Her London flat was of a modest size and price. Alex had no reason to purchase something larger, even though she could afford to do so. She wanted to make as small a splash as possible when she landed in her new town and started her new job. When the doorbell rang on Saturday afternoon, Alex smiled. She had trouble controlling her excitement and couldn't quite explain why she was so happy to finally see the man who rang her bell. Perhaps it was because he had made the new chapter in her life possible. And despite that she'd spent less than a week with him, for some reason he'd taken up a meaningful place in her heart over the years. Not romantically. He was twice her age. And not as a father figure—Garrett Lancaster would always hold that spot in her life. But the man who rang her doorbell occupied some special place in her life Alex could not define.

She walked to the door and opened it.

"Leo the Brit," Alex said with a smile.

"Alex the gunslinger," Leo said in his thick British accent, holding up his hands as if under arrest. "You're not gonna fill me with holes, are ya?"

Alex smiled. "You're never going to let me live that down are you?"

"Unlikely, mate."

"Come on in."

The last time Alex had seen Leo was when she'd kissed him lightly on the cheek years ago after he'd saved her from Laverne Parker and Drew Estes. It was then that Alex had learned that Garrett Lancaster had hired Leo to look after her. Despite the years that had passed since they'd last seen each other, Alex considered Leo a friend. Eight years of texting and FaceTiming had allowed them to form a close bond. Leo was an enigmatic but endearing presence in her life.

Back when Leo was hired to look after Alex, he was starting his private investigative practice in London. For all intents and purposes, Alex had been his first case and Garrett Lancaster his first client. Leo had spent a year and a half following Alex around Europe and keeping tabs on her. When the gravy train ran out and Alex hopped on a plane back to the States, Leo was forced to look for other paying clients. He'd found them, and now ran a successful PI firm. When Alex texted him to let him know her investigative skills were for sale, Leo jumped at the opportunity. Things were getting busy and he needed some help. To date, he hadn't been able to find a competent partner. Alex promised she was the answer.

"So you probably want to know how much I'm gonna pay you and what I'm gonna ask you to do."

"No," Alex said. "We can discuss all that later. I'm sure you'll pay me fairly, and I'm more than confident that I'll exceed your expectations with anything you ask me to investigate."

Leo squinted his eyes. "If you didn't ask me over to talk about the job, then what am I doing here on a Saturday?"

"I was going to butter you up with a beer first, but let's leave the beer for when we're done."

"Done with what?"

"Come on," Alex said, heading toward the door. "I need a hand with something."

A delivery truck was parked on the street outside her flat. A man sat on the back fender with the sliding door open.

"Are you going to be able to handle this?" the truck driver asked Alex as he gave her a clipboard.

"I am now."

Alex signed for the delivery and handed the clipboard back to the driver. Leo the Brit looked into the back of the truck, where a tall item was bubble wrapped and waiting.

"I need you to help me carry this upstairs," Alex said.

"What is it?" Leo asked. "And how much does it weigh?"

"A grandfather clock. And a lot."

Leo looked from the formidable obstacle waiting in the truck to Alex. "I'm deducting the cost of my services from your first paycheck."

Alex smiled. "Sounds fair and reasonable."

–

Later that night, Alex sat in her new flat. It was late, the television was off, and the only sound came from the grandfather clock standing in the corner of the room. Alex had wound the clock to bring its weights as high as they could go. Now she listened to the clock tick as the pendulum swung. For most of her childhood the clock had been an unnoticed thing in the second-floor hallway outside her bedroom. Alex had passed by it a thousand times, paying no mind to its beauty. Then it became something else the night her family was killed—something grand and protective.

With nothing but the ticking clock keeping her company, Alex reached for the day's copy of the *New York Times*. Tracy Carr had finished her article about Laura McAllister and the story of rape at McCormack University that the girl was about to break before she was killed. It included the names of those who were incriminated in her episode. The article thoroughly covered Duncan Chadwick's role in obtaining the date-rape drug used to spike drinks at his fraternity. An investigation was sure to follow, and even before the article was published, Larry Chadwick had voluntarily removed himself from the running of nominees to fill the Supreme Court vacancy. The story was explosive and Tracy did a great job honoring Laura McAllister in the article.

Alex sat back after she finished reading. There were sure to be hangers-on. There were sure to be true-crime fanatics who would never stop looking for Alexandra Quinlan. But without a prominent reporter leading the way, those fanatics would soon burn out. Alex's offer to Tracy Carr had involved tipping the reporter off to a potential blockbuster story involving Larry Chadwick's son and Laura McAllister. In exchange for the information Alex would hand over, Tracy Carr had agreed to stop her pursuit of Alexandra Quinlan. No more yearly updates. No more lurid videos. No more travel to McIntosh to shoot footage in front of her family's home.

She put the newspaper to the side. It had been an arduous journey, but she had finally arrived at that fork in the road of life that marked her fresh start. She leaned back into the cushion of the couch, closed her eyes, and listened to the swinging pendulum of the grandfather clock as it clicked. Back and forth. Back and forth.

CHAPTER 72

The Appalachian Mountains
Saturday, October 14, 2023
9:52 p.m.

He drove the SUV through the winding roads of the Appalachian Mountains. Although far from city surveillance cameras, he avoided gas stations and rest areas where his image might be recorded and had taken the precaution of swapping out his plates for ones lifted from a Maryland junkyard. As he drove, the rock face climbed vertically next to the guardrails, boxing him in as the road sliced through a canyon with mountains on either side. Other parts of the drive were wide open with nothing but undulating mountains in the distance. When he saw smoke spiraling from the chimneys of tucked-away homes, he knew he was getting close.

Had Larry Chadwick been appointed to the Supreme Court, the night's mission would have been exponentially more difficult. The nine Supreme Court justices were closely shielded by government agencies. Inside the confines of the District of Columbia, the Supreme Court Police protected the justices day and night. Outside of DC, the US Marshals Service provided security detail. Thankfully, Judge Chadwick had been passed over for the Supreme Court. Technically, he stepped down and voluntarily removed himself from consideration. Either way, as a federal judge and not a Supreme Court justice, security detail for Larry Chadwick came only by request, not by commission. On test runs to the judge's vacation home, he'd seen no such detail. Tucked away in the foothills of the Appalachians, the judge likely felt isolated and safe. The town of Heathrow was small and quiet. It consisted of a single road with two stoplights and mom-and-pop shops and restaurants lining each side of the street. Residents were cordial and made up of wealthy East Coasters who cherished their privacy.

He made the final turn and accelerated down the road that ran behind the judge's vacation home. The judge's usual schedule involved Chadwick and his wife leaving DC in the midafternoon on a Friday and returning to the city Sunday evening, in time for dinner and a glass of wine before the judge read briefs in preparation for his Monday morning docket. It was one of America's great ironies, he thought now as he slowed his vehicle, that the man who had hired Reece Rankin to rape and kill Laura McAllister had been given the power to preside over the justice of a nation.

Jacqueline could have gone to the police with what she'd learned from her visit with Reece Rankin. She could have told the authorities about Rankin's confession and that he had raped and killed Laura McAllister after being hired by Larry and Duncan Chadwick. But to do so would have placed the Chadwicks in the protective hands of the American justice system, where it was unlikely a proper sentence would have been handed down. Chadwick and his son deserved more than America's system of justice could provide.

He pulled to the side of the road and turned into a wooded area. He edged his car far enough into the foliage so that it was out of sight from passing vehicles, then got out and trudged through the forest for three-quarters of a mile until the narrow path ended at the back of Larry Chadwick's vacation home.

He was early. Lights still brightened the home's windows, and he settled down in a clearing to wait for the Chadwicks to retire for the night. He removed the Smith & Wesson from his waistband and placed it on the ground next to him. He took a moment to listen to the calmness of the wilderness around the property. The closest neighbor was more than a mile away. A loon cooed from a far-off location on the lake. The sound reminded him of his youth, when he spent his summers away at camp. The clearing in which he sat brought him back to the night they had killed Jerry Lolland.

It was at Camp Montague that his life's journey had begun. It was at Camp Montague that he had first taken matters into his own hands. It was there, after enduring a summer of abuse and then witnessing that same abuse befall Jacqueline, that he had decided some people were not worthy of the soft justice America delivered—a comfortable existence in prison where predators enjoyed three daily meals and the joys of enter-tainment that included books and television and more. No, some perpetrators were deserving of more than a pampered life behind bars. Those who committed the most heinous acts of violence—sexual assault on children—and those who assist them deserved a justice this country could not provide.

As he sat in the clearing at the edge of the Chadwicks' prop-erty, he remembered Jerry Lolland. He remembered staring at the man's body as paramedics wheeled him out of the cabin, a white sheet covering him from head to toe, confirming how well their plan had worked. Jerry Lolland had been their first kill. Jerry Lolland had been the first time he and Jacqueline had teamed up to stop a predator. Others followed through the years, but he still remembered Jerry Lolland most vividly.

He remembered them all to varying degrees because he learned something new from each of them. Most had gone as planned and had been perfectly executed. One, however, still haunted him. One had produced collateral damage that had, in the end, been their downfall. Now, he would have to continue their work alone.

As he sat in the woods behind Larry Chadwick's home and waited for the house lights to dim, he remembered that night.

The town of McIntosh was small and tight-knit. Killing Dennis and Helen Quinlan would have consequences, but he had been unable to talk Jacqueline out of it. There was irony there—that he had started their vigilante duo decades earlier at Camp Montague, but that Jacqueline had been the catalyst that kept it going all these years. That night's mission was something she would not be denied, despite his protests about the potential pitfalls.

He pulled the car into the industrial lot that butted up against the quiet neighborhood where Dennis and Helen Quinlan lived. In addition to being clients, the Quinlans were, after great scrutiny of their tax records and financial documents, the accountants who had helped Roland Glazer perpetrate his sex-trafficking ring. The Quinlans were the financial wizards who had helped Glazer hide his money. They were the ones who had issued the checks and initiated the money transfers that allowed Glazer the freedom to travel to his secluded island where young women were delivered on a weekly basis. Others were involved—politicians and businessmen and royalty—but none of those players were touchable. The Quinlans, however, were accessible and had had their fingerprints on Glazer's dirty dealings for years. The excuse they offered when they approached Lancaster & Jordan—that they didn't know where Glazer's money originated from, or where it went after they finished protecting it—was fragile at best, an outright lie more likely. The explanation may have been true at first, perhaps. But it was unfathomable that their ignorance persisted longer than a fleeting moment. Their guilt was evidenced by the fact that after Roland Glazer came under federal indictment, the Quinlans ran to Lancaster & Jordan for protection against prosecution.

He turned off the headlights and drifted to a stop as the wheels crunched over gravel.

"In and out," he said to Jacqueline.

A quick nod of her head was all he got in return. Then, she opened the door and disappeared into the forest. With the headlights off, he kept the engine running. They had clocked the mission three different times and had a top and bottom for how long it should take her to trek through the woods, sneak across the back lawn, retrieve Dennis Quinlan's shotgun from the garage, enter through the back door, climb the stairs, take care of Dennis and Helen Quinlan, exit the home, race back through the woods, and make their escape.

He watched the clock as he waited. The bottom time limit came and went. He began sweating when the upper limit approached and grew restless when it passed. Something had gone wrong, and he thought for a fleeting moment about heading into the woods to see what had happened. But that was a poor decision that would put both of them at risk. The other option was worse: abort the mission and leave without her.

He could do neither, so he waited. And waited longer, until, finally, he saw a figure in the woods. Jacqueline was running in a frantic way he had never seen before. Something had gone wrong. He shifted the car into reverse, and as soon as she clambered into the passenger seat, he hit the gas pedal and spun gravel as he swung the car into a wild backward U-turn. After shifting into drive, he ripped out of the industrial park. Once on the main road and with some distance between them and the Quinlans' home, he turned on the headlights and reduced his speed to the legal limit.

He looked over at her and saw that she'd placed her gloved hands over her face. The index finger on her right hand protruded through the glove where the latex had split.

"Your glove is broken," he said.

She took her palms from her face and inspected her right hand.

"You might've left a print behind," he said.

She shook her head and closed her eyes. "That's only the beginning of our problems."

He pulled to the curb outside her house and they listened to the scanner for a few minutes as reports of shots fired came through. During the ride she had offered him a summary of the events that took place inside the Quinlan home, transfixed the whole time she spoke on her right hand and her bare index finger.

"Did you touch anything?" he asked.

He watched as Jacqueline did a run-through in her mind. "The window," she said. "I opened the window in the kid's bedroom to look outside. And the front door handle, but that might have been with my other hand."

He watched as she continued to stare at the bare finger that stood out from the others.

"What should we do?" she asked.

"We can't do anything at the moment. Go inside. Try to sleep. I want to get off the road."

There was silence as she sat unmoving in the passenger seat.

"Did the girl see you?" he asked.

"I don't know. I don't think so. The bedroom window was open and she was gone." She paused before looking at him. "The boy... he saw me. I had no choice."

He nodded. "I know. Go inside. We'll talk tomorrow. Burn the clothes. Boots, gloves, everything. Do it tonight."

Without responding, she opened the door and climbed out of the car. She said nothing more as she walked to her front door and disappeared inside. He put the car in gear and drove home. When his garage door opened, he pulled inside and sat in the dark for a few minutes, running through the night and wanting to ask what, exactly, had transpired inside the Quinlan home. Jacqueline was too shaken to tell him all of it. Only that she had, after killing Dennis and Helen Quinlan, also killed their thirteen-year-old son when the boy opened the Quinlans' bedroom door and startled her. She hadn't shared details about how it had transpired. She was too shaken to get more out of her, other than that the daughter had escaped and was now an unknown.

After a few minutes in the dark, he stepped out of the car and entered his home. He kept the lights out and climbed into bed. He tossed and turned for an hour, unable to sleep. In all their years, nothing like this had happened before. They were careful and meticulous. Only the guilty were punished, never the innocent. He and Jacqueline were the ones fighting for the innocent. They were the ones exacting justice on the truly vile members of society, justice the American system could not properly provide. They had always been protectors of the innocent. Until tonight.

It was 3:10 a.m. when he checked the bedside clock. Finally, after much consternation, his eyelids sagged and he drifted off to sleep. Twenty-five minutes later the phone rang and jarred him from a shallow, restless slumber. When he lifted his cell phone to check the ID, a sinking feeling came to his stomach.

"Hello?" he said in a groggy voice.

"Garrett!" Donna said in an urgent whisper. "It's me. I need you down at the precinct. I know it's late, but I need you right away."

Garrett Lancaster asked no questions. His willingness to rush to police headquarters and help his wife in the middle of the night would come off as heroic—the act of a devoted husband eager to do anything to help his wife. In reality, his lack of curiosity about why his wife was summoning him to police headquarters came from knowing that a triple homicide had occurred in their small town. That his life was about to collide with that of Alexandra Quinlan's was impossible to predict. And that some part of his heart would forever bleed for the girl would only be realized later.

He climbed from bed, thought briefly about taking a shower and changing into a suit and tie but opted instead to simply slip on jeans, pull a Washington Wizards ball cap over his unkempt hair, and head out the door.

ACKNOWLEDGEMENTS

My sincere gratitude goes to the following people:

All the folks at Kensington Publishing who champion my books each year and do so much work behind the scenes to help make my novels successful. Especially John Scognamiglio, who helps me get my stories straight; and Vida Engstrand, whose clever marketing helps them get noticed.

Amy and Mary, for being the first to read, first to critique, and first to encourage.

Detective Ray Peters, for helping me get my facts in order about crime scenes and interrogations.

Michael Chmelar, attorney and friend, for generously donating your time to read an early draft and help me stumble my way through the opening courtroom scene. I'm sure I didn't execute exactly how you drew it up, but your suggestions helped me make it real enough.

Eric Bessonny, M.D., for answering my questions about succinylcholine, and getting strangely excited about the possibilities of conscious paralysis. I certainly used my literary license to make the drug work for my story, but you helped me keep it inside the lines.

Donna Kopkash, for your generous donation to One Million Monarchs—a magnificent charity that addresses the public health issue of childhood bereavement, and offers support to kids who have lost a parent or sibling. Your kind gift came with the added bonus of having a character in my book named after you.

And finally, all the readers—whether you've just discovered my novels, or have veraciously read every one—thanks for making my dream come true.

Do you love crime fiction and are always on the lookout for brilliant authors?

Canelo Crime is home to some of the most exciting novels around. Thousands of readers are already enjoying our compulsive stories. Are you ready to find your new favourite writer?

Find out more and sign up to our newsletter at canelocrime.com